Julie Miller is an award-winning *USA TODAY* bestselling author of breathtaking romantic suspense—with a National Readers' Choice Award and a Daphne du Maurier Award, among other prizes. She has also earned an *RT Book Reviews* Career Achievement Award. For a complete list of her books, monthly newsletter and more, go to juliemiller.org.

USA TODAY BESTSELLING AUTHOR

JULIE MILLER

Kansas City Secrets
&
Kansas City Confessions

HHARLEQUIN® INTRIGUE CLASSICS

ISBN-13: 978-1-335-15997-7

Kansas City Secrets & Kansas City Confessions

Copyright © 2018 by Harlequin Books S.A.

The publisher acknowledges the copyright holder of the individual works as follows:

Kansas City Secrets
Copyright © 2015 by Julie Miller

Kansas City Confessions
Copyright © 2015 by Julie Miller

Recycling programs for this product may not exist in your area.

This edition published by arrangement with Harlequin Books S.A.

For questions and comments about the quality of this book, please contact us at CustomerService@Harlequin.com.

® and ™ are trademarks of Harlequin Enterprises Limited or its corporate affiliates. Trademarks indicated with ® are registered in the United States Patent and Trademark Office, the Canadian Intellectual Property Office and in other countries.

HARLEQUIN®
www.Harlequin.com

Printed in U.S.A.

CONTENTS

KANSAS CITY SECRETS

For my mom. It was challenging to write this book among unforeseen events that demanded my attention. But I wouldn't have traded your wonderful visit and recovery time for anything. I'm glad you're feeling better. I love you.

CHAPTER ONE

"Why did you kill that woman, Stephen?" Rosemary March asked, looking across the scarred-up table at her younger brother. "And don't tell me it was to rob her for drug money. I know that isn't who you are."

Rosemary studied the twenty-eight-year-old man she'd done her best to raise after a small plane crash several years earlier had left them orphans. She tried to pretend there weren't a dozen pairs of eyes on her, watching through the observation windows around them. It was easier than pretending the Missouri State Penitentiary's tiny visitation room with its locked steel doors wasn't making her claustrophobic.

But it was impossible to ignore the clinking of the chains and cuffs that bound Stephen March's wrists and ankles together. "You ask me that every time you come to see me, Rosemary."

"Because I'm not satisfied with the answers you've given me." She ran her fingers beneath the collar of her floral-print blouse, telling herself it was the heat of the Missouri summer, and not any discomfiting leer from another prisoner or the unsettling mystery of why her brother would kill a woman he didn't know, that made beads of perspiration gather against her skin. "I hate seeing you in here."

"You need to let it go. This is where I deserve to be. Trust me, sis. I was never going to amount to much on the outside."

"That's not true. With your artistic talent you could have—"

"But I didn't." He drummed his scarred fingers together at the edge of the table. For as long as she'd known him, he'd been hyper like that—always moving, always full of energy. Their father had gotten him into running cross-country and track; their mother had put a drawing pencil in his hand. Ultimately, though, neither outlet could compete with the meth addiction that had sent his life spiraling out of control. "Losing Mom and Dad was no excuse for me going off the deep end and not helping out. Especially when your fiancé…" The drumming stopped abruptly. "Just know, I was really there for you when you needed me."

"Needed you for what? If you had anything to do with Richard's murder, please tell me. You know I'll forgive you. We never used to keep secrets like this from each other. Please help me understand."

"I kept you safe. That's the one thing I got right, the one thing I'm proud of. Even the Colonel would have finally been proud of me," he added, referring to their father.

"Dad loved you," Rosemary insisted.

"Maybe. But he wasn't real thrilled having a drug addict for a son, was he? But I took action. The way he would have." His gaze darted around the room, as if checking for eavesdroppers, before his light brown eyes focused on her and he dropped his voice to a whisper. "For the last time, I killed that lady reporter to protect you."

Understanding far more about tragedy and violence and not being able to protect herself and her loved ones more than she'd ever wanted to, Rosemary brushed aside the escaping wisps of her copper-red hair and leaned forward, pressing the argument. "Dad wouldn't have wanted you to commit murder. I didn't even know that woman. That's what doesn't make any sense. What kind of threat was she to me?"

Stephen groaned at her repeated demands for a straightforward explanation. He slumped back in his chair and nodded toward the family's current attorney standing outside the window behind her. "Why did you bring him?"

Fine. She'd let him change the topic. Although it was good to see Stephen clean and sober, he looked exhausted. Her younger brother had aged considerably in the months since he'd pleaded guilty to second-degree murder and been incarcerated, and she didn't want to add to his stress. She glanced over her shoulder to the brown-haired man in the suit and tie and returned his smile before facing her brother again. "Howard insisted on coming with me. He didn't want me driving back to Kansas City at night by myself. It was a kind offer."

The drumming started again. "He reminds me too much of his brother. Are you sure he's treating you right?"

She flinched at the remembered shock of Richard

Bratcher's open hand across her mouth putting an end to an argument they'd had over a memorial scholarship she'd wanted to set up in her parents' names. Seven years later, she could still taste the metallic tang of blood in her mouth that reminded her she'd made a colossal mistake in inviting the attorney into their lives, falling in love with him, trusting him. Rosemary inhaled a quiet breath and lifted her chin. Richard was dead and she'd become a pro at setting aside those horrible memories and pasting a facade of cool serenity on her face.

"They may look alike, but Howard isn't like his brother. Howard's never laid a hand on me. In fact, I think he feels so guilty about how Richard treated us when I was engaged to him that he goes out of his way to be helpful."

"He's just keeping you close so you won't sue his law firm."

"Maybe." Initially, she'd been leery of Howard's offer to take over as the family's attorney. But he knew more than anyone else about the wrongful death and injury suit Richard Bratcher had filed against the aerospace manufacturer that built the faulty plane her father had flown on that fateful trip, and she couldn't stand to drag the suit out any longer than it had already lasted. Plus, he'd been nothing but a gentleman and rock-solid support through the continuing upheavals in her life. "Howard makes it easier to get in to see you. And he's responsible for keeping you in the infirmary wing to do your rehab instead of you being sent back to general lockup with the other prisoners."

"Don't stick with him because of me. I can handle myself in here. I don't trust him, sis."

Rosemary's smile became genuine. "You don't trust anybody."

Stephen sat up straight and reached for her. At the last second, he remembered the guard at door and raised both hands to show they were empty. Rosemary held up her hands, as well, and got a nod of approval before reaching over the battered tabletop to hold her brother's hands. "I trust you. I'm okay being in here because I know you're safe now. You *are* safe, right?"

Stephen's grip tightened, as if somehow sensing that all was not well in her life. But Rosemary clenched her jaw and continued to smile. The last thing he needed was to worry about her on the outside, when he couldn't do a thing about it. "I am."

She was right now, at any rate.

The assurance seemed to ease his concern. He eased his grip but didn't let go. "That bastard Richard is dead. But it'd kill me if I thought his brother or anyone else was hurting you."

"I'm fine." What were a few obscene phone calls, anyway, after all they'd been through? Her hope had been to find a few answers for herself, not raise doubts in her brother's mind. "As much as we both wanted Richard out of our lives, I know you didn't kill him." Stephen had been in a rehab facility in the middle of a forty-eight-hour lockdown the morning she'd discovered her fiancé dead in bed at his condo, poisoned sometime during the night. She, however, had had no alibi and had spent several months as KCPD's number one suspect until the trail of clues went cold and Richard Bratcher's murder had been relegated to the cold-case files. Rosemary squeezed her brother's hands. "Whoever poisoned him did us a favor. But if you're protecting someone who wanted that reporter dead, or you're taking the blame for her murder because you wished you'd been the one to kill Richard... Please, Stephen. Talk to me."

His eyes darkened for a split second before he shook his head and pulled away. "I was using that night. I pulled the trigger. Now I'm done talking about it. You should be, too."

"Why?"

"Rosemary—" He bit down on a curse and folded his hands together, his finger tracing the marks he'd left in his own skin back in the days when he'd been too stressed-out to cope or on a manic high.

"It's okay, Stephen," she quickly assured him, alarmed by the frantic, self-destructive habit he'd worked so hard to overcome. "I won't mention it again."

This visit, at any rate.

Reluctantly, she acquiesced to his demand and sat back in her chair. She knew there had to be more to Stephen's motive for killing an innocent reporter than simply being high as a kite and not knowing what he was doing, as he'd stated in court. The monster in their own home had been the real threat, and, in her heart, she believed there was a connection between the two murders—a logical reason her brother was going to spend half his adult life in prison and she was going to be alone. But if Stephen wouldn't talk, she wasn't certain how else she could get to the truth about the two murders and finally put the nightmares of the past behind her.

Yet, until that revelation, Rosemary stuck to the role she'd learned to play so well, dutifully taking care of others. "Is there anything you need? I brought the books you asked for, and two cartons of cigarettes." She curled her fingers into a fist, fighting the instinctive urge to reach for the neckline of her dress and the scars underneath. Instead, she arched an eyebrow in teasing reprimand. "I wish you'd give those up. You know they're not good for you."

That earned her half a grin from her brother. "Let me kick one addiction at a time, okay?"

"Okay." A high sign from the guard warned her their time was nearly up. Rosemary blinked back the tears that made her eyes gritty and smiled for Stephen's sake as he stood and waited for the guard to escort him back to his cell. "I wish I could give you a hug."

"Me, too." But that kind of contact wasn't allowed. "I love you, sis. Stay strong."

As if she had any choice. She fought to keep her smile fixed in place. "I love you. I'll keep writing. And it wouldn't hurt you to pick up a pencil every now and then, either. Be safe."

He nodded as he shuffled to the door in front of the guard. "You, too."

Rosemary was alone for only a few seconds before another guard came to the door to walk her out to the visitors' desk. But it was long enough for the smile to fade, her shoulders to sag and her heart to grow heavy.

How was one woman supposed to endure so much and still keep going on with her life? She followed the rules. She'd done everything that was expected of her and more. Why wasn't it good enough? Why wasn't *she* good enough?

"Ma'am?"

With a quick swipe at the hot moisture in her eyes, Rosemary nodded and got up to accompany the guard out that door into an antechamber and then out the next one into the visitors' waiting area. She jumped at the slam of each heavy door behind her, which closed her off farther from the only family she had left. With every slam, her shoulders straightened, her heart locked up and she braced herself to meet the concern that etched frown lines beside Howard Bratcher's eyes when he greeted her. "How are you holding up?"

"I'm fine."

While she waited in line to retrieve the purse she'd checked in at the front desk, Rosemary became aware of other eyes watching her. Not quite the lecherous leer she'd imagined tracking her from the shadows each night she got one of those creepy phone calls. Certainly not the solicitous concern in Howard's hazel eyes.

When the holes boring into her back became too much to ignore, she turned.

"Rosemary?"

But she didn't see Howard standing beside her. She looked beyond him to the rows of chairs near the far wall. The girlfriends, wives and mothers waiting to see their loved ones barely acknowledged her curiosity as her gaze swept down the line. There were a couple of men in T-shirts and jeans. A few more in dress slacks and polo shirts or wearing a jacket and tie like Howard. They were reading papers, chatting with their neighbors, using their phones.

But no one was watching.

No one was interested in her at all.

She was just a skittish, paranoid woman afraid of her own shadow these days.

Hating that any sense of self-confidence and security had once again been stolen from her, she turned back to the guard at the front desk and grabbed her purse. "Thank you."

But when she fell into step beside Howard and headed toward the main doors, the hackles beneath her bun went on alert again. She was suddenly aware of the youngish man sitting at the end of the row against the wall. He wore a loose tie at the front of the linen jacket that remained curiously unwrinkled, and he was texting on his phone.

Was it that guy? Had he been following her movements with that more than casual curiosity she'd felt? Although it was hard to tell if he was making eye contact through the glasses he wore, he seemed to be holding his phone at an oddly upright angle, tapping the screen. He lifted his attention from his work and briefly smiled at her before returning to whatever he found so fascinating on the tiny screen.

Like an image of her?

"Rosemary?" She felt Howard's touch at her elbow and quickly shifted her gaze back to the door he held open for her. "Is something wrong?"

"I don't know." Stepping outside, the wall of heat and humidity momentarily robbed her of breath. But her suspicion lingered. "Did you see that guy?"

"What guy?"

They were halfway across the parking lot now. "The one who was staring at me?"

Howard glanced over his shoulder and shrugged. "They probably don't see a lot of pretty women here."

Pretty? Rosemary groaned inwardly at the sly compliment. She caught a few frizzy waves that curled against her neck and tucked them into the bun at the back of her head. After Richard's abuse, the last thing she wanted was to attract a man's attention. But the curiosity of that man in the waiting room had felt like something different. She shuddered in the heat as she waited for Howard to open the door of his car for her. "I think he took a picture of me with his phone."

"So you don't mean one of the prisoners?"

"No. He was one of the attorney-looking guys out in the waiting area."

"Attorney-looking?" Howard laughed as he closed the door behind her and walked around to his side of the car. He shed his suit jacket and tossed it into the backseat before getting in. "So we're a type?"

"Sorry. I didn't mean anything negative by that. I was just describing him. Suit. Tie. Maybe more on the ball than some of the others waiting to visit friends and family here. He looked like an educated professional."

"No offense taken." He pushed the button, and the engine of the luxury car hummed to life. "Could be a reporter, getting the scoop on Kansas City's newest millionaire visiting the state penitentiary."

Right, as if hearing her picture might be in the paper again was a whole lot better than thinking someone was spying on her. "I wish you wouldn't say that."

He pushed another button to turn on the air-conditioning. "What do you want me to call it? Your brother's in the state pen. It's public record."

"No. 'Kansas City's newest millionaire.'" She supposed the soap opera of her life made her recent wealth big news in a summer where most of the local stories seemed to be about the weather. "I'd give anything if that headline had never hit the papers. I hate being the center of attention."

"Yet you handle it all with grace and decorum." Howard reached for her hand across the seat, but Rosemary pulled away before he made contact, busying herself with buckling up and adjusting the air-conditioning vents. Even as the evening hour approached, the temperature across Missouri was still in the nineties. Seeking relief from the heat was as legitimate an excuse to avoid his touch as her innate aversion to letting a man who looked so much like his late younger brother—or maybe any man, at all—get that close to her again.

With a sigh he made no effort to mask, Howard settled back behind the wheel and pulled out onto the road leading away from the prison. "Hungry for an early dinner? My treat. Jefferson City's got this great new restaurant on top of one of the hotels downtown. You can see the Capitol Building and almost all the riverfront. Day or night, it's a spectacular view."

The answering rumble in her stomach negated the easy excuse to say she wasn't hungry. Instead, she opted for an honest compromise. "Dinner would be great. But, could we just drive through and eat it in the car? I need to get home and let the dogs out. And we still have a two-and-a-half-hour drive to Kansas City ahead of us."

Howard had seen the wrongful death and manufacturer's negligence lawsuit his brother had started for her through to its conclusion. And though she'd trade the 9.2-million-dollar settlement for her parents in a heartbeat, she was grateful to the Bratcher, Austin & Cole law firm that they'd gotten the company to admit its guilt in their construction of the faulty wing struts on the small airplane that had crashed, killing her parents instantly.

And though Howard's interest might have as much to do with the generous percentage his firm had received from the settlement, Rosemary appreciated his attempts to be kind. However, her gratitude didn't go so far as to want to encourage a more personal connection between them. She'd thought Richard Bratcher was her hero, rescuing her from the dutiful drudgery of her life, and she'd fallen hard and fast. Richard had been her first love…and her biggest mistake—one she never intended to make again. But her business relationship and friendship with his older brother, Howard, shouldn't suffer because of it. She glanced across the seat and smiled. "Is that okay?"

Knowing her history with his brother, Howard was probably relieved she hadn't given him a flat-out no. He nodded his agreement, willing, once again, to please her. "Fast food, it is."

Almost three hours later, Howard pulled off the interstate and turned toward her home on the eastern edge of Kansas City. Although it was nearly eight o'clock, the sun was still a rosy orange ball in the western sky when he walked her up onto the front porch that ran clear across the front of her ninety-year-old bungalow.

From the moment the car doors had shut and she'd stepped out, she could hear the high and low pitches of her two dogs barking, and was eager to get inside to see them. She had her keys out and her purse looped over her shoulder when she realized Howard had followed her to the top of the stairs, waiting to take his leave or maybe hoping to be invited in for coffee.

What one woman might see as polite, Rosemary saw as suffocating, maybe even dangerous. As much as she loathed going out in public, she hated the idea of being trapped inside the house with a man even more. No way was she reliving that nightmare. With the dogs scratching at the other side of the door now, anxious for her arrival, Rosemary turned and lifted her gaze to Howard's patient expression. "Thank you for going with me to Jefferson City."

"My pleasure."

"Do I owe you some gas money?"

He chuckled. "Not a penny."

Finally getting the hint that this was goodbye, he leaned in to kiss her cheek. But Rosemary extended her hand instead, forcing some space between them. "Good night, Howard."

He gently took her hand and raised it to his lips to kiss the back of her knuckles instead. "Good night. I'll pick you up tomorrow?" he asked, releasing her from the gallant gesture and pulling away.

Right. More papers to sign. "I can drive, you know."

"But the drive will give me a chance to explain the trust fund and scholarship you'll be setting up before you sign anything." There'd already been plenty of explanation and she'd made her decisions.

"Howard—"

"That way you won't have to spend any longer than a few minutes at the office."

Now *that* was a selling point. Rosemary nodded her acquiescence. "I'll be ready. See you then."

She waited until he was backing out of the driveway and waved before turning around to unlock the door. She typed in the security code to release the alarm, but her hand stopped with her key in the lock. She wasn't alone.

Was *he* watching her? Would there be another vile message waiting on her answering machine?

I see you, Rosemary. Thinking your money can buy you security. Thinking those dogs will keep you safe. One of these days it'll be just you and me. I'll show you how justice is done. I'll take you apart piece by piece.

With her shaking hand still on the key, she glanced up and down the street at the peaceful normalcy of a summer evening in the older suburban neighborhood. There was an impromptu ball game in the Johannesens' front yard across the street. Mrs. Keith was out trimming her shrubs while her husband washed the car in their driveway.

Squinting against the reflection of the sunset in her next-door neighbors' living room window, Rosemary caught the shadowy silhouette of Otis or Arlene Dinkle. The brief ripple of alarm that had put her on guard a moment earlier eased. The Dinkles had lived next door for years, and had been friends with her parents long before Rosemary had moved back home to care for her teenage brother.

Unable to get a good look at which of the couple was eyeing her, Rosemary exhaled a sigh of relief and waved. They'd watched over her for a long time, including that night Richard had attacked her and she'd run to their house to call the police, fearing he'd come back after he'd stormed out. Her wave must have been all the reassurance the Dinkles needed to know she'd arrived home safely. The shadow disappeared and the blinds closed.

Breathing easier now, Rosemary unlocked the door and went inside. "Hey, ladies. Mama's home."

Her smile was genuine as she locked the door behind her and dropped to her knees to accept the enthusiastic greeting from the German shepherd with the excited whine and the miniature poodle leaping up and down around her.

"Hey, Duchess. Hey, Trixie. I missed you guys, too." She spared a few moments to rub their tummies and accept some eager licks before rising to her feet and doing a quick walk through the house with the dogs trailing behind her.

She really should have no worries about an intruder, especially with the yappy apricot poodle and the former K-9 Corps dog who'd been dismissed from the program because of an eye injury on hand to guard the place. If the dogs weren't alarmed, she shouldn't be, either. Still, she checked all the rooms, including the guest suite upstairs, before she set her purse down beside the answering machine on the kitchen counter.

No blinking red light.

"Thank goodness."

Her day had already been long and troubling enough without having to deal with another message from the unwanted admirer she'd picked up the night after news of her settlement being finalized had appeared in the *Kansas City Journal*. And she was certain the police department was tired of her calling in to report the disturbing calls. She knew she was tired of hearing the subtle changes in their tone once she identified herself. The officers were sympathetic when they saw her name in the system as a victim of domestic violence, but seemed to think she was some kind of crank caller when they read her abuser was dead and that she had once been a suspect in his murder. They probably thought she was some sort of paranoid crazy lady—or a woman desperately seeking attention when, in reality, she'd be far more content to fade into the woodwork.

The advice from the officer she'd finally been connected with had been to keep a log of the calls and let her know if she thought they were escalating into something more serious. If she'd known when Richard Bratcher's controlling demands were going to escalate into violence, she might have been spared a split lip, a broken arm and... She ran her fingers beneath the collar of her blouse, resting her palm over the old scars there. Talk about a sudden and unexpected escalation. But when images from that horrific time tried to surface, Rosemary pulled her hand away and stooped down to busy her fingers and brain with the much more enjoyable task of petting the dogs and rubbing their bellies.

After a happy competition for her affection, Rosemary kicked off her sandals and relished the cool tile under her toes. With both dogs dancing around her, she unbolted the back door and opened the screen door to let them out into the fenced-in yard to run around.

The warm breeze wrapped her eyelet skirt around her knees and caught the wispy curls escaping from her bun and stuck them to the warm skin of her cheeks and neck. With the nubby concrete of the patio still warm beneath her feet, she glanced up at the sky and tried to gauge how long they had before nightfall. While Trixie sniffed the perimeter of the yard and the big German shepherd loped along behind her little buddy, Rosemary walked to the edge of her in-ground pool and dipped her toes into the water. As tempting as it might be to cool off in the pool, she hated to be out after dark. Besides, Duchess and Trixie had been on their own for most of the day and deserved a little one-on-one attention. A few games of fetch and tug-of-war before bedtime would do just as much to help her forget these restless urges to prod the truth from her brother, rail against the fear and loneliness that plagued nearly every waking moment and live her life like a normal person again.

Laughing as Duchess barked at a rabbit in the Dinkles' backyard garden, startling Trixie with her deep woof and setting off a not-to-be-messed-with barking from the smaller dog, Rosemary opened the storage unit at the edge of the patio where she kept pool and outdoor pet supplies. One of the shelves was dedicated to a sack of birdseed, grooming brushes and a stash of dog toys.

She pulled out the tennis ball Duchess loved to chase and gave it a good toss, watching the dogs trip over each other in their eagerness to retrieve the faded yellow orb. Then she reached inside for one of Trixie's squeaky toys and gasped.

The last rays of sunlight hitting the nape of her neck could have been shards of wintry ice as she snatched her hand away from the gruesome display inside.

"I don't understand why this is happening," she whispered through her tight throat.

But she couldn't pull her eyes away from the tiny stuffed animal—tan and curly coated like her sweet little Trixie—hanging from a noose fashioned out of twine from the cabinet's top shelf. Nor could she ignore the typed message pinned to the polyester material.

I know what you did.
You don't deserve to be rewarded.
You can't escape justice.

Who would…? Why would…?

Duchess dropped the slobbery ball at her feet, and the dogs buffeted her back and forth, eager for her to throw it again. When she didn't immediately respond, the German shepherd rose up on her hind legs to help herself to another toy inside the cabinet, and Rosemary snapped out of her shock.

"Down, girl. Get down." Rosemary pushed the black-and-tan dog aside and closed the cabinet doors. Then she latched onto Duchess's collar and swung her gaze around the yard.

Was someone watching her right now? Was some sicko out there getting off on just how terrified he could make her feel?

She led the dogs to the side gate with her to check the front of the house. No doubt picking up on her alarm, Trixie barked at nothing in particular. At least, nothing Rosemary could make out. She saw regular, light evening traffic out on the street, with all the cars driving slowly past because of the kids playing nearby. The Keiths had gone inside. There was no visible movement in the Dinkle house next door.

Rosemary's breath burned in her throat. This had gone beyond excusing those calls as some drunk who'd read her name in the paper. Somebody wanted her scared? He'd succeeded.

"Duchess, heel. Trixie?" The German shepherd fell into step beside Rosemary as she scooped up the poodle. "No one's going to hurt you, baby."

She checked the separate entrance that led to the basement apartment where Stephen had lived when he'd gotten older. Good. Bolted tight. Then she took the dogs inside the kitchen and locked both the screen and steel doors behind her before punching in the code to reset the alarm. She flipped on the patio light, gave the dogs each her own rawhide chew and walked straight through to the front door, turning on every light inside and out.

Verifying for a second time that every room of the house was empty, Rosemary returned to the kitchen to brew a pot of green tea and fill a glass of ice to pour it over.

Her hands were shaking too hard to hold on to the frosty glass by the time she'd curled up on the library sofa with the dogs at her feet and the lights blazing. She should turn on the TV, read a book, sort through another box of papers and family mementos that had become her summer project, or get ready for bed and pretend she had any shot at sleeping now.

Rosemary deliberated each option for several moments before springing to her feet and circling around behind the large walnut desk that had been her father's. She opened the bottom drawer and pushed aside a box of photographs to unlock her father's old Army pistol from its metal box. It had been years since he'd taken her and Stephen target shooting out at a cousin's farm in the country, so she couldn't even be sure the thing still worked, much less remember exactly how to clean and load it. Still, it offered some measure of protection besides Duchess and Trixie. She pulled out the gun, magazine and a box of bullets and set them on top of the desk.

Then, even if they thought she was some sad, lonely spinster desperate for attention, she took a long swallow of her iced tea, picked up the phone and called KCPD to report the latest threat.

CHAPTER TWO

DETECTIVE MAX KROLIKOWSKI was a soldier by training. He was mission oriented. Dinkin' around on a wild-goose chase to see if some woman had talked to some guy about a crime that had occurred ages ago, just in case somebody somewhere could shed some new light on the unsolved case he and his partner from KCPD's Cold Case Squad were investigating, was not his idea of a good time.

Especially not today.

Max stepped on the accelerator of his '72 Chevy Chevelle, fisting his hand around the steering wheel in an effort to squeeze out the images of bits and pieces of fallen comrades in a remote desert village. He fought off the more troubling memory of prying a pistol out of a good man's dead hand.

He should be in a bar someplace getting drunk, or at Mount Washington Cemetery, allowing himself to weep over the grave of Army Captain James Stecher. Max and his team had rescued Jimmy from the insurgents' camp where he and two other NCOs been held hostage and tortured for seven days, but a part of Jimmy had never truly made it home. Eight years ago today, he'd put his gun in his mouth and ended the nightmares and survivor's guilt that had haunted him since their homecoming.

Max had found the body, left the Army and gone back to school to become a cop all within a year. Getting bad guys off the streets went a ways toward making his world right again. Following up on some remote, random possibility of a lead on the anniversary of Jimmy's senseless suicide did not.

"Whoa, brother." The voice of his partner, Trent Dixon, sitting in the passenger seat across from him, thankfully interrupted his dark thoughts. "We're not on a high-speed chase here. Slow it down before some uniform pulls us over."

Max rolled his eyes behind his wraparound sunglasses but lifted his foot. A little. He snickered around the unlit cigar clenched between his teeth. "Tell me again why we're drivin' out to visit this whack job Rosie March? She's hardly a reliable witness. Murder suspects generally aren't."

Tall, Dark and Hard to Rile chuckled. "Because her brother—a convicted killer with motive for killing Richard Bratcher—is our best lead to solving Bratcher's murder, and he's not talking to us. But he is talking to his sister. At least, she's the only person who visits him regularly. Maybe we can get her to tell us what he knows. Besides, you know one of the best ways to investigate a cold case like this one is to reinterview anyone associated with the original investigation. Rosemary March had motive for wanting her abusive boyfriend dead and has no alibi for the time of the murder. She'd be any smart detective's first call on this investigation. It's called doing our job."

Max shook his head at the annoyingly sensible explanation. "I had to ask."

Trent laughed outright. "Maybe you'd better let me do the talking when we get to the March house. Somehow, I doubt that calling her a *whack job* will encourage her to share any inside information she or her brother might have on our case."

"I get it. I'm the eyes and the muscle, and you're the pretty boy front man." Max plucked the cigar from his lips as he pulled off the highway on the eastern edge of Kansas City. "I'm not in the mood to make nice with some shriveled old prune of a woman, anyway."

"Rosemary March is thirty-three years old. We've got her driver's license photo in our records, and it looks as normal as any DMV pic can. What logic are you basing this I'd-rather-date-my-sister description on?"

Max could quote the file on their person of interest, too. "Over the years she's called in as many false alarms to 9-1-1 as she has legit actionable offenses, which makes her a flake in my book. Trespassing. Vandalism. Harassing phone calls. Either she's got a thing for cops, she has some kind of paranoia complex or it's the only way she can get any attention. Whatever her deal is, I'm not in the mood to play games today."

"Some of those calls were legit," Trent pointed out. "What about the abusive fiancé?"

"Our murder victim?"

"Yeah. Those complaints against Bratcher were substantiated. Even though someone scrubbed the photos and domestic violence complaints from his file after his death, the medical reports of Miss March's broken arm, bruises and other injuries were included as part of the initial murder investigation."

"But the woman's never married. She's only had the one boyfriend we can verify." Okay, so a fiancé who'd hurt her qualified as low-life devil scum, not boyfriend, in his book. But Rosemary March had money. A lot of it. Even if she had three warts on the end of her nose and looked like a gorilla, there should be a dozen men hitting on her. She should be on the social register donating to charities. She should be traveling the world or building a mansion or driving a luxury car or doing something that would make her show up on somebody's radar in Kansas City. "The woman's practically a recluse. She has her groceries delivered. She's got a teaching degree, but hasn't worked in a school since that plane wreck her parents were in. She's probably a hoarder. Her idea of a social outing is visiting her brother in prison. If that doesn't smack of crazy cat lady, I don't know what does."

"It's a wonder you've never been able to keep a woman."

Max forced a laugh, although the sound fell flat on his eardrums. Somehow, subjecting a good woman to his mood swings and bullheaded indifference to most social graces didn't seem very fair. But there were times, like today, when he regretted not having the sweet smells of a woman and the soft warmth of a welcoming body to lose himself in. Looked as though another long run or hour of lifting weights in the gym tonight would be his only escape from the sorrows of the day. "I make no claims on being a catch."

"Good, 'cause you'd lose that bet."

He wasn't the only cop in this car with relationship issues. "Give it a rest, junior. I don't see you asking me to stand up as best man anytime soon. When are you going to quit making goo-goo eyes at Katie Rinaldi and ask her out?"

"There's her son to consider. There's too much history between us." Trent muttered one of Max's favorite curses. "It's complicated."

"Women usually are."

This time, the laughter between them was genuine.

When Max and Trent both got assigned to the Cold Case Squad, their superior officer must have paired the two of them together as some kind of yin and yang thing—blond, brunette; older, younger; a veteran of a hard knocks life and an optimistic young man who'd grown up in a suburban neighborhood much like this one, with a mom and a dad and 2.5 siblings or whatever the average was these days; an enlisted soldier who'd gone into the Army right out of high school and a football-scholarship winner who'd graduated cum laude and skipped a career in the pros because of one concussion too many. Max and Trent were a textbook example of the good cop/bad cop metaphor.

And no one had ever asked Max to play the good-cop role.

But their strengths balanced each other. He had survival instincts honed on the field of battle and in the dark shadows of city streets. He was one of the few detectives in KCPD with marksman status who wasn't on a SWAT team. And if it was mechanical, he could probably get it started or keep it running with little more than the toolbox in his trunk. As for their weaknesses? Hell, Detective Goody Two-shoes over there probably didn't have any weakness. Trent wasn't just an athlete. He was book smart. Patient. Always two or three steps ahead of anybody else in the room. He was the only cop in the department who'd ever taken Max down in hand-to-hand combat training—and that was because of some brainiac trick he'd used against him. And he was one of the few people left on the planet Max trusted without question. Trent Dixon reminded Max of a certain captain he'd served under during his Army stint in the Middle East. He would have followed Jimmy Stecher to the ends of the earth and back, and, in some ways, he had.

Only Jimmy had never made it back from that last door-to-door skirmish where he and the others had been taken prisoner. Not really. Oh, Max had led the rescue and they'd shipped home on the evac plane together after that last do-or-die firefight to get him out of that desert village. They'd been in Walter Reed hospital for a few weeks together, too. The two men he'd been captured with had been shot to death in front of him. Jimmy hadn't cracked and revealed troop positions or battle strategies, and he'd never let them film him reading their latest manifesto to use him as propaganda. But part of Jimmy had died inside on that nightmarish campaign—the part that could survive in the real, normal world. And Max should have seen it coming. He'd been responsible for retrieving their dead and getting their commander out of there. But he hadn't saved Jimmy. Not really. He hadn't realized there was one more soldier who'd still needed him.

He'd failed his mission. His friend was dead.

Despite the bright summer sunshine burning through the windshield of his classic car, Max felt the darkness creeping into his thoughts. The image of what a bullet to the brain could do to a man's head was tattooed on his memories as surely as the ink marking his left shoulder. He'd known today would be a tough one—the anniversary of Jimmy's suicide.

Trent knew it, too.

"Stay with me, brother." His partner's deeply pitched voice echoed through the car, drawing Max out of his annual funk. "Not everybody's the enemy today. I need you focused on this interview."

Max nodded, slamming the door on his ugly past. He rolled the unlit cigar between his fingers and chomped down on it again. "This is busywork, and you know it." Probably why Trent had volunteered the two of them to make this trip to the suburbs instead of sitting in the precinct office reading through files with the other detectives on the team. Max didn't blame him. Teaming with him, especially on days like this, was probably a pretty thankless job. He should be glad Trent was looking out for him. He *was* glad. Still didn't make this trip to the March house any less of a wild-goose chase when he was more in the mood to do something concrete like make an arrest or run down a perp. "Rosemary March isn't about to confess or tell us anything her brother said. If she knows something about Bratcher's murder, she's kept quiet for six years. Don't know why she'd start gettin' chatty about it now."

Trent relaxed back in his seat, maybe assured that Max was with him in the here and now. "I think she's worth checking out. Other than her brother's attorney, she's the only person who visits Stephen March down in Jeff City. If he's going to confide anything to anyone, it'll be to his sister."

"What's he gonna confide that'll do our case any good?" Max stepped on the accelerator to zip through a yellow light and turn into the suburban neighborhood. Hearing the engine hum with the power he relished beneath the hood, he pulled off his sunglasses and rubbed the dashboard. "That's my girl."

"I swear you talk sweeter to this car than any woman I've ever seen you with," Trent teased. "But seriously, we aren't running a race."

"Beats pokin' along in your pickup truck."

Besides, today of all days, he needed to be driving the Chevelle. The car had been a junker when Jimmy had bequeathed it to him. Now it was a testament to his lost commander, a link to the past, a reminder of the better man Max should have been. Restoring this car that had once belonged to Jimmy wasn't just a hobby. It was therapy for the long, lonely nights and empty days when the job and a couple of beers weren't enough to keep the memories at bay. Or when he just needed some time to think.

Right now, though, he needed to stop *thinking* and get on with the job at hand.

Max put the sunglasses back on his face and cruised another block before plucking the cigar from his lips. "Just because the team is working on some theory that this cold-case murder is related to the death of the reporter Stephen March killed, it doesn't mean they are. We've got no facts to back up the idea that March had anything to do with Bratcher's death. March used a gun. Bratcher was poisoned. March's victim was doing a story on Leland Asher and his criminal organization, and there's no evidence that Richard Bratcher was connected to Asher or the reporter. And Stephen March sure isn't part of any organized crime setup. If Liv and Lieutenant Rafferty-Taylor want to connect the two murders, I think we ought to be digging into Asher and his cronies. The mob could have any number of reasons to want to eliminate a lawyer."

"But poison?" Trent shrugged his massive shoulders. "That hardly sounds like a mob-style hit to me."

"What if Asher hired a hit *lady*? Women are more likely to kill someone using poison than a man is. And dead is dead." Max tapped his fingers with the cigar on the console between them to emphasize his point. "Facts make a case. We should be investigating any women associated with Asher and his business dealings."

But Trent was big enough and stubborn enough not to be intimidated by Max's grousing. "Even if she turns out to be a *shriveled old prune*, Rosemary March is a woman. Therefore, she meets your criteria as a potential suspect. Doesn't sound like such a wild-goose chase now, does it?"

Growling a curse at Trent's dead-on, smart-aleck

logic, Max stuffed the cigar back between his teeth. It was a habit he'd picked up during his stint in the Army before college and joining the police force. And though the docs at Walter Reed had convinced him to quit lighting up so his body could heal and he could stay in fighting shape, it was a tension-relieving habit he had no intention of denying himself. Especially on stressful days like this one.

Feeling a touch of the melancholy rage that sometimes fueled his moods, Max shut down the memories that tried to creep in and nudged the accelerator to zip through another yellow light.

"You know…" Trent started, "you take better care of this car than you do yourself. Maybe you ought to rethink your priorities."

"And maybe you ought to mind your own business."

"You're my partner. You are my business."

Max glanced over at his dark-haired nemesis. Conversations like this made him feel like Trent's pop or Dutch uncle, as if life had aged him far beyond the twelve years that separated them in age. Still, Trent was the closest thing he had to a friend here in KC. The younger detective dealt with his moods and attitude better than anybody since Jimmy. Nope. He wasn't going there.

"Bite me, junior." Max pulled up to the curb in front of the white house with blue shutters and red rosebushes blooming along the front of the porch.

"I know today is a rough one for you." Trent pulled his notebook from beneath the seat before he clapped a hand on Max's shoulder. "But seriously, brother. Did you get that shirt out of the laundry? You know you're supposed to fold them or hang them up when you take them out of the dryer, right? Did you even shave this morning?"

"You are not my mama." Although part of him appreciated the concern behind Trent's teasing, Max shrugged his hand away and killed the engine. "Get out of my car. And don't scratch anything on your way out."

Max set his cigar in the ashtray and checked the rearview mirror, scrubbing his fingers over the gold-and-tan stubble that he probably should have attended to before leaving for work this morning. Although the crew cut was the same as it had been back in basic training, the wrinkled chambray of his short-sleeved shirt would have earned him a demerit and a lecture from Jimmy. What a mess. One beer too many and a sketchy night's sleep had left him ill-equipped to deal with today.

Swearing at the demons staring back at him, Max climbed out, tucking in the tails of his shirt and adjusting the badge and gun at the waist of his jeans as he surveyed up and down the street. Looked like a pretty ordinary summer morning here in middle-class America. Dogs barking out back. Flowers blooming. Kids playing in the yard. Royals baseball banners flying proudly. Didn't look like the hoity-toity neighborhood where he expected a millionaire crackpot to live. Didn't look much like a place where they could track down clues to a six-year-old murder, either.

But he had to give Trent credit for dragging him out on this fool's errand. Driving the Chevy and breathing in the fresh air beat being cooped up in the office with a bunch of paperwork and his gloomy thoughts. Max tipped his face to the sunshine for a few moments, locking down the bad memories before he took the steps two at a time and followed Trent up to the Marches' front porch.

"What is this? Fort Knox?" he drawled, eyeing the high-tech gadgetry of the alarm on the front door, along with the knob lock and dead bolt. "My grandma lives in a brand-new apartment complex and doesn't have this kind of security."

"The woman does live alone," Trent reminded him.

Max peered in through the front bay window while Trent rang the doorbell. The front room was neat as a pin, if stacks of boxes and piles of papers on nearly every flat surface counted. But not a cat in sight. He refused to believe that the noise of dogs barking out back might in any way disprove his theory about crazy Rosemary March.

"Yes?" Several seconds passed before the red steel door opened halfway. He could barely hear the woman's soft voice through the glass storm door. "May I help you?"

Trent flashed his badge and identified them. "KCPD, ma'am. I'm Detective Dixon and this is my partner, Max Krolikowski. We're here to ask some questions. Are you Rosemary March?" She must have nodded. "Could you open the outside door, too?"

"If you step back, I will. I'll disable the alarm and come out."

Max moved to one side while Trent retreated to the requested distance between them.

Max had expected that shriveled-up prune from his imagination to appear. He at least expected to see a homely plain Jane with pop-bottle glasses. He wasn't expecting the generously built woman with flawless alabaster skin, dressed neck to knee in a gauzy white dress, exposing only her arms and calves to the summer heat. Although her hair, the color of a shiny copper penny, was drawn back into a bun so tight that words like *spinster* and *schoolmarm* danced on his tongue, he hadn't expected Rosemary March to be so…feminine. So curvy. He wasn't expecting to see signs of pretty.

He wasn't expecting the Colt automatic she held down in the folds of her skirt, either.

CHAPTER THREE

MAX'S FINGERS IMMEDIATELY went to his holster. "Gun!"

The redhead nudged open the glass storm door and slipped the pistol behind her back as though they wouldn't notice it. "I asked you to step—"

"Damn it, lady. Keep that thing where we can see it." Max put up one hand to swing the door open wide and folded the other hand around her arm, sliding it down over her wrist until he had the barrel of her weapon in his grasp.

"Get out of my house—" The redhead gasped and recoiled, tugging against his grip. "Let go of me."

No way. Even if she didn't mean them any harm, he wasn't trusting that a fruitcake like her wouldn't accidentally fire off a round. "Damn it, lady, relax. We're just here to talk."

She curled both hands around the butt of the weapon now. If her finger reached that trigger… "Please don't swear like that. It isn't polite."

"And pointing a gun at us is?" Two of her hands against one of his was no contest. She stumbled out the door, uselessly trying to hold on while he pried the weapon from her grip. A rush that was more anger than relief fired through his veins when he realized how light it was. "Oh, hell, no." He turned aside, dropping the empty magazine from the handle and opening the firing chamber. "This thing isn't even loaded."

Her gaze was as icy cool as her skin. "May I please have it back?"

Max turned the gun over in his hands. "This thing is Army issue. About twenty years old." He reset the magazine and thrust the Colt back at her, butt first. If she recoiled half a step at his abrupt action and loud voice, he didn't care. "It isn't yours."

"It was my father's."

"Didn't he ever tell you that you damn sure never point an empty weapon at a guy whose gun can really shoot? Hell, what if I'd pulled my sidearm instead of grabbing yours?"

Her eyes were the silvery color of twilight as she angled them up to him, searching for the intent behind his mirrored glasses. She finally took the gun from him and hugged it near her waist. "You're swearing again."

"Looking down the barrel of a gun does that to me."

"I didn't point it at you," she snapped. "You had no reason to—" And then she inhaled a calming breath and turned to Trent, as though raising her voice to Max violated some code of conduct she wouldn't allow. "I was putting away my father's pistol when the doorbell rang. If I had known you were the police, I would have locked it up first. But I thought it was my friend here to give me a ride into the city, and he would understand. He knows I don't keep it loaded."

Jimmy's hand had held an Army pistol that fateful day, too. Max's mind went hazy for a split second as the gruesome image tried to take hold. But he ruthlessly shoved it aside. Of all the stupid, fool stunts for this woman to pull today. "You don't carry a gun around unless you're prepared to use it."

"And you don't just grab a person because you—" Her chin jerked up to give him a straight-on look at the pink stains dotting her pale cheeks before she clamped her mouth shut and dropped her gaze. Well, what do you know? Crazy Dog Lady had a temper.

"Ease up, Max," Trent warned.

Those gray eyes flashed in Max's direction although she turned her body toward his partner, rightly suspecting that Trent would be the one more apt to listen to a reasonable explanation. "You should have called first. I have an appointment this morning with my attorney. I wasn't expecting anyone else to come to the house."

"Maybe we should start this conversation again." Trent raised his notebook between them and intervened, leaving Max wondering if it was his partner's presence or some snobby code of behavior that made her check her tongue when she clearly wanted to lambaste him for putting his hands on her. She turned her full focus on the taller man, dismissing Max. Trent pulled off his sunglasses and tucked them into his chest pocket. "I apologize for my partner here. His PR skills might be a little rusty, but believe me, he's a good cop. You're perfectly safe with him. There's no one else I trust to have my back more. Are you Rosemary March?"

"You already know that or you wouldn't be here."

Trent managed to keep the patient tone Max hadn't been able to muster. "First of all, is everything all right, ma'am? It tends to put us on alert to see someone carrying a weapon. I assure you, Max was only trying to prevent an accident from happening."

Her gaze darted up to his. "Is that true?"

Max shrugged. "I don't like to get shot."

"But that's why you touched me? You thought I was going to…?" Her voice trailed away and her focus dropped to the middle of his chest. "Sarcasm, right?"

"Oh, yeah." With a clear lack of appreciation for his cynical humor, her gaze bounced across the width of Max's shoulders, up to the scruff on his chin, over to the large bay window and finally down to the brass badge clipped to his belt. Prim and proper Miss Rosemary March was hiding something, buying herself time to come up with the right thing to say. Why? Something had her spooked. Was it the badge? His very real, very loaded gun? Was it him? Six feet, two inches of growly first sergeant in need of a shave could be intimidating. Was it Trent? Max's partner was even taller, still built like the defensive lineman he'd once been. And she had to be, what, all of five-five?

A chill pricked the back of his neck. That instant wariness, much like the split-second warnings he'd gotten over in the desert before all hell broke loose, put him on alert. Maybe he and Trent weren't the reason she was carrying that gun. Thinking he ought to be worried about more than that empty weapon, Max rested his hand on his holster and looked beyond her into the foyer. "Is someone in the house with you?"

"No." Too fast an answer.

When he reached for the door, she sidestepped to

block his path. She put her hand up to stop him from opening the door. Max put on the brakes, but with his momentum he swayed toward her, breathing in a whiff of her flowery soap or shampoo. He heard her suck in her breath and felt her fingers push against him before she curled them into a fist and pulled back almost as soon as they made contact with his chest.

"Lady, I'm trying to help—"

"I said no." Although the firm tone drew him up short, the warning was directed to the button on the wrinkled point of his collar.

And she was shivering. In this ninety-degree heat, he could see the fine tremors in the fist clutched to her chest.

Max huffed out a frustrated breath that she turned her face from. He scrubbed his hand over the stubble on his jaw and wisely backed away before he muttered the curse on the tip of his tongue. He wasn't able to read this chick at all. She wasn't wrinkled. She wasn't old. And the only thing prunish about her was the snooty tone that attempted to put him in his place time and again. And, hell, he had to admire anyone who dared to stand up to him on a day like today.

First, she'd been an imposition on his time. Then she was a threat. Now he could smell the fear on her, but she refused to admit to it.

And how could he still feel the imprint of five fingers that had barely brushed against him?

He splayed his hands at his waist and demanded that she start making some sense. "Are you hiding something? Is that why you don't want us inside?"

"No, I just don't like having anyone…" She pressed her pink lips together in a thin line, stopping that explanation. "It's a mess."

The boxes and piles of papers stacked in the room indicated she was telling the truth. Still, there was something off about this woman—about this whole situation. "Nobody comes to the door with a gun because she's embarrassed about her housekeeping. That thing is an accident waiting to happen."

"I'll explain it again." Oh, right. In case the dumb cop couldn't figure it out. "The gun was still out from last night. I've been going through my parents' things for months now and found it in my father's desk. I was putting it away before my ride comes to pick me up this morning. The doorbell rang while I was straightening up. I thought it was my attorney. I didn't want to keep him waiting." Despite the even, articulate tone, her soft gray eyes kept glancing up to him but wouldn't lock on to his questioning gaze. Probably because he wasn't letting her see it. She drifted a step closer to Trent. "I wasn't expecting anyone to come to the house. The officer took a report over the phone last night. I thought someone would come over then. But no one ever did so I assumed KCPD had dismissed my call."

Huh? That comment short-circuited his fuming suspicions. Max traded a look with Trent before asking, "What report?"

"The one I called the police about last night." Last night? He'd missed something here. Had she gone back to making spurious calls to 9-1-1? While Max was wondering if his communication skills had gone completely off the rails, Rosemary March's body language changed. Her free hand went to the stand-up collar of her dress and she puffed up like a banty hen trying to assert herself in the barnyard pecking order. "Would you mind taking off your sunglasses, Detective Krolikowski? It's rude not to let someone see your eyes when you're having a conversation with them."

"What?"

"Take off your glasses. I insist."

"You insist?" Max bristled at her bossy tone. "Boy, you've got to have everything just so, don't you."

"I don't think common courtesy is asking too much."

"Max." Trent nodded at him to do it.

Really? Max pulled off his glasses and hooked them on the back of his neck. She wanted the glasses off? *How about this, honey?* He folded his arms across his chest and glared down into her searching gray eyes until they suddenly shuttered. She must have had her fill of cynicism and impatience because she retreated until her back was pressed against the glass door.

He didn't need to hear the breathy tone of her polite thank-you to recognize the sudden change in Miss Rosie's demeanor or feel like a heel knowing he was the cause of it. What had he done? Most people got in his face or blew him off when he got in a mood like this. But Rosemary March was different. So what if this conversation wasn't making any sense to him. He knew better than to let anybody's odd behavior get under his skin. His presence here clearly agitated her. She breathed harder, faster, and Max topped off his jackassery by noticing her full, round breasts pushing against the gauzy white cotton of that dress.

That little seed of attraction he hadn't expected to feel was clearly agitating him. "Ah, hell. Ma'am, I didn't mean… I wish I could explain where my head is today, but it's too long a story. Are you sure you're okay?"

She nodded, but he'd feel a lot less like a scary bastard if she'd get some color in those pale cheeks or lecture him again. Putting his hand on her and crowding her probably hadn't been the smartest moves. Something about the gun must have drummed up memories of Jimmy and put him on his worst behavior.

But that was a lousy excuse for a man sworn to protect and serve. This was about more than a soldier's or a cop's hardwired reaction to giving anybody a chance to get the drop on him or his men. And he could hardly explain his skepticism regarding her usefulness as a witness on this anniversary of Jimmy's senseless death. He owed her some kind of apology for scaring her. For being a jerk. But the words weren't coming. Not today.

When had words ever been his strong suit?

Thank God, he was part of a team and could rely on Trent's handsome face and friendly smile to salvage this interview. Max cleared his throat and backed toward the front steps. "I'll, uh, just do a quick walk around the place if that's okay with you."

Miss Rosemary gave him a jerky nod, her gaze breezing past his chin again. "I left the message in the cabinet on my patio out back." Message? Trent glanced over his shoulder and traded a confused look, but Max wasn't about to ask. "The dogs will bark, but they don't bite." And then her twilight gaze landed on his. A fine, coppery brow arched in what might be arrogance. Or a warning. "At least, they haven't bitten anyone yet."

Nope. Didn't have to hit him over the head more than once. He had no business trying to make nice with anybody today.

"I'll look." He nodded to Trent. "You talk."

Max trotted down the steps and breathed a lungful of humid summer air into his tight chest while he made another cursory scan of the well-kept front yard. When he realized the lady of the house wasn't answering any of Trent's questions with him still in sight, he muttered a curse and followed the driveway around the side of the house.

Message in a cabinet? Was that code for something? Like *Scram, Krolikowski*? And that thing about the dogs not biting anyone *yet*—was that an attempt at humor to ease the friction between them, or her demure version of a threat?

He peeked through the window of the separate garage to see her sedan parked inside, along with a neatly arranged array of storage boxes and lawn equipment. She was right about the dogs barking. As soon as he came into view, a deep-voiced German shepherd with a cloudy eye and a yappy little bundle of curly tan hair charged the chain-link fence and let him know they knew he was there.

A fond memory of Jax, the big German shepherd who'd served with his unit, made him smile. Jax had died in that Sector Six firefight where the captain had been captured. The victim of a hidden bomb. A single bark had given them their only warning before the blast. Jimmy had taken the dog's death as hard as the loss of his men. "Son of a…"

Really? Just like that, whatever positives he could summon today crashed and burned. Irritated with his inability to focus, Max fixed the friendliest look he could manage on his face and approached the fence.

"Hey, big girl. Do you sit? Sit. Good girl." When the shepherd instantly obeyed his command, he figured the poodle was the one he had to win over. He squatted down and held his fist against the chain-link fence to let the excited little dog sniff his hand. They certainly hadn't had a feisty little fuzz mop like this one with the unit. "Hey, there, killer."

When the poodle finally stopped dancing around long enough to lick his knuckles, Max figured it was safe to open the gate and go inside. Apparently, Rosie March had spent a bit of her newly acquired wealth on more than security. Though this was by no means a mansion, the old house had plenty of room for one woman, and was well taken care of. New roof and shutters. Freshly painted siding and trim. The pool in the middle of her backyard was long and narrow, meant for swimming laps instead of sunbathing beside. Yet there was still plenty of green space for the dogs to roam. He shrugged and petted the pooches, who were leading as much as following him on his stroll around the yard. Nothing looked out of place here, but then his real purpose for volunteering to do recon was so the lady of the house would take the panic level down a few notches and talk to Trent.

And he could get his head together and remember he was a cop. He needed to do better. So far, the only thing he knew for sure about this investigation was that Rosie March smelled like summer and her hesitant touch stayed with him like a brand against his skin.

Max rubbed at the spot on his chest. So what did that mean? He was lonesome enough or horny enough to think he was attracted to Miss Prim & Proper just because she'd touched him? Or was that a stamp of guilt because his big, brusque attitude had frightened the woman when he should have been calming her?

"Idiot!" Max punched the palm of his hand.

The German shepherd barked at the harsh reprimand and darted several paces away. "Easy, girl." He held out his hand and let the big dog cautiously sniff and make friends again. "I'm not mad at you. I'll bet your mama never raises her voice like that, does she." He cupped a palmful of warm fur and scratched around the dog's ears. Who was he to call Rosie the Redhead crazy? He wasn't exactly firing on all cylinders himself today. "Don't you be afraid of me, too."

While the shepherd forgave his harsh tone and pushed her head into the stroke of his hand, the poodle rolled on her back in the grass, completely comfortable with his presence there. Max chuckled. "At least somebody around here likes me."

And then he became aware of eyes on him. Not a shy gray gaze worried about what uncouth thing he'd say or do next. But spying eyes. Suspicious eyes.

With his senses on alert, Max knelt down between the two dogs and wrestled with them both, giving himself a chance to locate the source of the curious perusal. There. East fence, hiding behind a stand of sweet corn and tomato plants. Nosy neighbor at nine o'clock. With a clap of his hands, the dogs barked and took off running at the new game.

Max pushed to his feet and zeroed in on the dark-haired woman wearing a white bandanna and gardening gloves. "Morning, ma'am."

Her eyes rounded as though startled to be discovered, and she tightened her grip on the spool of twine she'd been using to tie up the heavy-laden tomato plants. "Good morning. Are you the police?"

"Yes, ma'am." He tapped his badge on his belt. "Detective Krolikowski, KCPD. And you are…?"

"Arlene Dinkle. We've lived here going on thirty years now," she announced. "There's not going to be trouble with Rosemary again, is there?"

Again? The dogs returned and circled around his legs. Max sent them on their way again. "Trouble?"

Mrs. Dinkle parted the cornstalks that were as tall as she was and came to the fence. She lowered her voice to a conspiratorial tone. "There was a man who used to stay with her sometimes. Don't think the whole neighborhood didn't notice. Things haven't been right at this house for a long time."

Maybe he could pick up some useful information on this recon mission, after all—and make up for the interview he'd botched out on the front porch. Max strolled to the fence to join her. "You mean Miss March's fiancé? He stayed here?"

"A couple of times a week. When he was alive."

The older woman clucked her tongue behind her teeth. "Some folks think she killed him, you know. Between those rumors and her juvenile delinquent brother, she definitely brought down the quality of this neighborhood."

That shy, spooked lady on the front porch brought down the neighborhood? That delicate, feminine facade could be the perfect cover for darker secrets. And if Bratcher had been here on a regular basis, she'd have had plenty of opportunity to slip him the poison that had killed him.

But he was having a hard time aligning the image of a calculated murderess with the skittish redhead who protected herself with an unloaded gun. She wasn't that good of an actress, was she? "You know anything about that murder?"

"I should say not." Unlike Rosemary March, Max could read this woman with his eyes closed. Arlene Dinkle liked to gossip. Although he found her holier-than-thou tone a little irritating, the cop in him was inclined to let her. Judging by the streaks of silver in her black hair, she'd been sticking her nose into other people's business for a long time. "Now there's all that publicity with that legal settlement or wherever her nine million dollars came from. Did you know there were reporters at her house two months ago? One of them even came to our home to find out what we knew about her."

"And you told this reporter about Miss March entertaining her fiancé overnight, what, six, seven, years ago? Did you ever see any indication that Mr. Bratcher was violent with Rosie?"

"Rosie? Oh. You mean Rosemary. Yes, there was that one time she came to our house to use our phone—said her lawyer friend who was getting her all that money after her parents' plane crash—oh, the Colonel and Meg were such good people—I don't understand how their children could turn out so—"

"What did Rosie say about her lawyer friend?" Max cut her off before she rambled away on a useless tangent.

She snorted a laugh that scraped against his eardrums. "*Rosemary* said he'd trapped her inside the house until she agreed to sign some prenuptial agreement and marry him. Made no sense at all. They were already engaged. She pounded on our door in the middle of the night, woke Otis and me both out of a sound sleep. Blubbering about how we needed to call the police." The dogs were circling again. Disapproval seeped into Arlene's tone and she pulled back from the fence. "That's when she got the big dog. Washed out of K-9 training. But I swear that dog would still take a bite out of you if you look at her crosswise. The little one digs in the topsoil of my garden, too. Reaches right under the fence. Rosemary ought to put up a privacy fence. She certainly can afford to do it."

Really? Then how would you spy on her? Max kept his sarcasm to himself and followed up on the one key word that might actually prove useful in an investigation. "You said *trapped*. Was Rosie—Miss March—injured in any way that night? Did you believe her when she told you that her fiancé hurt her? Threatened her?"

"Oh, she had some blood on her blouse and she was

cradling her arm. I thought maybe she'd been in a car accident or had fallen down the stairs. We let her use the phone right away, of course, and sat with her until the ambulance and police arrived. But we saw her fiancé drive away, so I wondered why she just wouldn't use her own phone."

"If Bratcher hurt her, she was probably afraid he'd come back. Getting out of the house would be a smart survival tactic."

Arlene straightened, as though insulted that he would doubt her word against Rosie's. "Richard Bratcher was an upstanding member of the community. Why on earth a handsome, charming man like that would ever have to resort to anything so—"

"Arlene." Max caught a glimpse of movement at the sliding glass door on the Dinkles' patio before another man's voice interrupted the tale. "I'm sure the detective isn't here to chat with you. You let him be."

Arlene whirled around on the man with salt-and-pepper hair who must be her husband. "He asked me questions. We were having a conversation."

"Uh-huh." The lanky older man extended his hand over the fence. "I'm Otis Dinkle. We've lived next door to Rosemary and her family since she was a little girl. Is everything okay?"

At least Arlene had the grace to look a little ashamed that she hadn't asked that. Max lightly clasped the older man's hand, assuming that his presence meant he wasn't getting any more facts or nonsense from his wife. "Max Krolikowski, KCPD. I'm not sure, sir. My partner and I are looking into an old case." Maybe this was as good a time as any to test the veracity of Rosie's claims about receiving threats. "But I understand there may have been a disturbance here yesterday?"

"You mean like a break-in?"

Max nodded. "Or a trespasser on the property?"

"Not that I've seen." Otis tucked his fingers into the pockets of his Bermuda shorts and shrugged. "She was gone all day yesterday. I didn't see any activity after she took the dogs out for their morning walk."

"Her new attorney dropped her off last night," Arlene added. "Her dead fiancé's brother. I knew there was something funny going on. The two of them probably—"

Otis put up a hand, silencing his wife's opinion. "She didn't even let him into the house, Arlene. I don't think it's anything serious."

Max arched a curious brow. So the gossipy missus wasn't the only one watching the March house. "You saw her come home last night?"

Otis nodded. "We keep an eye on each other's place. Maybe chat in the front yard or across the fence when we're both out mowing. Other than that, though, Rosemary keeps pretty much to herself. We used to do stuff with her parents, but now that they're gone, she's just not that social."

"You didn't see anyone lurking around the house who shouldn't be?"

"Her dogs would have raised a ruckus. I didn't hear anything like that."

"They were locked up inside, Otis," Arlene reminded him.

"So, no intruders?" Max clarified. "Nothing you saw that seemed…off to you?"

Otis scratched at his bald spot, considering the question. "No, sir. Other than she didn't go for her regular swim this morning. It's been pretty quiet around here since her brother got put in jail. But then, we're retired. We don't keep late hours."

Yet he spied over the fence often enough to know Rosie's morning routine and when she came home at night. Curious.

"Well, if you do see anything suspicious, give us a call, would you?" Max reached into his back pocket and handed the man a business card with his contact information.

Arlene clutched the ball of twine against her chest. "Are we in any danger?"

"I don't think so, ma'am."

Otis held the card out at arm's length and read it. "I'll be. Cold Case Squad? This isn't about a break-in. Are you investigating her fiancé's murder, Detective Krolikowski? You think she did it?"

If poison wasn't such a premeditated means of murder, he might have been willing to dismiss his suspicions about Rosie as a justified case of self-defense. "Do you?"

"If you'd said Stephen, yes—that kid always was the rebellious sort. Good thing he was in rehab that week or you cops would have come down really hard on him. But honestly, I can't see Rosemary raising a hand to anybody. But what do I know? Like I said, she keeps to herself." He winked as a grin spread across his face. "It's those quiet ones you can't trust, right?"

With Arlene's snort of derisive agreement, Max

reached down to pet the German shepherd, dismissing the Dinkles. He'd stomached about all he could of polite conversation today. "Remember to give me a call if you see or hear anything suspicious."

"Will do."

Max clapped his hands and played one more game of try-to-catch-me with the dogs while the couple went back to their back porch, arguing about people breaking in next door and whether or not the neighborhood was safe anymore. As he watched the two dogs run a wide circle around the perimeter of the yard, Max shook his head. If the Dinkles were his neighbors, he'd probably avoid socializing, too.

So what, exactly, would make a healthy woman of means isolate herself the way Rosie March had? Keeping a low profile was generally rule number one for someone who'd committed a crime. Was it the publicity surrounding the lawsuit and sudden fortune she'd won? There were probably friends and family coming out of the woodwork, trying to get a piece of that nine million dollars. He'd hate that kind of spotlight, too. Was she ashamed because her brother had killed a woman, robbing her for a fix? Nobody knew better than him what it felt like to miss the signs of a loved one spiraling out of control. Or was Miss Rosie March just plain ol' afraid of her own shadow because life had dealt her a raw hand? That could explain the frequent 9-1-1 calls and why she'd unpack her daddy's Army pistol.

Max had a feeling there were a whole lot of secrets that woman was keeping. Ferreting them out would require a degree of insight and patience he lacked. KCPD had better send out someone else from the team, like Olivia Watson, so they could talk woman to woman, or cool and unflappable Jim Parker, or even nice guy Trent—without his bad-cop partner tagging along to make a mess of things.

Max watched the Dinkles settle into patio chairs, shaking his head as Otis plugged in earbuds while Arlene peeled off her gloves and prattled on about too many cops and dogs and reporters for her liking. Max tuned her out, too, and whistled for the dogs to return. "Come here, girls!"

He finally conceded that this outing hadn't been a total waste of his time. He'd done some decent police work, confirming that Rosie had a motive for killing Richard Bratcher. Although Arlene had dismissed the violent details that had soured Max's stomach, a woman who'd been held hostage by her abuser might feel she had no other way out of the relationship than to murder the man who terrorized her.

He liked the dogs, too. As much as the dogs he'd served with overseas had detected bombs and alerted his unit to insurgents sneaking past the camp perimeter or lying in wait out on a patrol, they'd been the unofficial morale officers. There was little that a game of fetch or a furry body snuggled up in the bunk beside him couldn't take his mind off of for a few minutes, at least.

The muscles in his face relaxed with an unfamiliar smile as the shepherd and poodle charged toward him. But the dogs ran right past, abandoning the game. Abandoning him.

Tension gripped him again, just as quickly as it had

ebbed, when he heard the clanking of the gate opening behind him. The mutts were showing their true al-
legiance to their copper-haired mistress by trotting up
to greet her. Rosemary March followed Trent through
the gate and latched it behind her, stopping on the opposite edge of the narrow pool. She knelt down in that
starchy dress to accept the enthusiastic welcome of her
pets, and Max's cranky, used-up heart did a funny little
flip-flop at the unexpected sight of that uptight, upper-
crust woman getting licked in the face and not complaining one whit about muddy, grass-stained paws on
her white dress.

Great. That was the last thing he needed today,
thinking he had the hots for the most viable suspect in
their murder investigation—a good girl, no less, who
seemed to push every bad-behavior button in his arse-
nal, a woman who was all kinds of wrong for him and
his crass, worldly ways. She was a suspect, not an opportunity. He needed to get his head back in the game.

"Miss March was visiting her brother yesterday,"
Trent began, giving Max a heads-up nod across the
narrow width of the pool, indicating that he'd gotten
her to open up to him. Max raised a surrendering hand,
promising to watch his mouth and not blow any progress
Trent had made in his absence, and started a slow stroll
around the pool to join them. "She thinks she spotted a
man paying undue attention to her down at the prison,
and that he may have taken a picture of her—"

"I don't think." Rosie glanced up at Trent, then
pushed to her feet. "I know. He didn't have to stare at
me. He was watching me on his phone."

So, still no news about the Bratcher murder. Max played along. Getting her to talk, period, was the first step in getting her to talk about their investigation. "Did you know this guy?"

"I'd recognize him if I saw him again, but I've never seen him before." She backed up onto the patio, keeping both men in sight as Max closed the distance between them. "You don't believe me." She looked across the yard to her neighbors, probably guessing how he'd spent his time back here. Her chin came up as she glanced over at the tall, plastic cabinet, then trained those accusing gray eyes on him. "You never even read the threat, did you? What did Otis and Arlene say to you? You think I'm making this all up."

"I don't know what I think," he answered honestly.

Apparently, that wasn't a good enough answer. With a frustrated huff that might be her interpretation of a curse, she walked past him and opened the cabinet doors. She backed away, picking up the poodle and hugging the dog to her chest, averting her eyes from the shelves inside. "Look for yourself. This is why I called the police."

Max muttered a real expletive when he saw the message and noose hanging inside. He glanced back and scratched around the ears of the little dog who bore an unmistakable resemblance to the toy on display. "Looks a lot like you, killer."

Miss Rosie's eyes widened along with his when his fingertips accidentally brushed against her arm. A split second later she jerked away, pulling herself and the dog beyond his outstretched fingers. "Her name is Trixie.

Is someone going to hurt my dogs? Is someone going to hurt me?"

"You don't know who sent this?"

She shook her head and backed another step away.

Right. Not his dog. Not his anything. *Do your job already.* Max busied his hands by snapping a couple of pictures with his phone before pulling out his pocketknife. Trent had come up beside him to inspect the cryptic message. Max asked, "You got a bag in that notebook?"

Trent pulled out a small plastic evidence bag and held it open while Max cut down the threat. The sisal looped around the toy's neck reminded him of the spool of twine Mrs. Dinkle had been using in her garden. He peeked around the cabinet door and caught Arlene watching from her back porch. Otis remained oblivious as she quickly glanced away. Could it be that simple? "Any reason why your neighbors might want to scare you?"

"Because Arlene hates dogs as much as she loves the sound of her own voice?" Max almost grinned at the spunky dig of sarcasm. But Rosie clapped a hand over her mouth. "I'm sorry. That wasn't very polite." She was reining her emotions in again, a skill Max envied, especially today. "The Dinkles aren't responsible for this. And they certainly weren't in Jefferson City snapping pictures of me yesterday. I'm guessing the money from the settlement is the reward that creep is talking about. Believe me, it doesn't feel like any kind of compensation with all the hassle that has come with it. I'd rather have Mom and Dad and my old teaching job over millions of dollars any day."

I know what you did.

So, who was close enough to Rosemary March, besides her brother locked away in prison, to know or even suspect that she'd murdered Richard Bratcher? Who else cared that she might be guilty?

He plucked the sealed bag from Trent's grasp and dangled it like a pendulum in front of her face. "Can you prove you didn't put this note out here yourself, Rosie?"

Her face went utterly pale. "What?"

"What are you doing, Max?" Trent cautioned.

"Testing a theory." He closed the cabinet doors and moved a step closer. "Have you gotten other threats, Rosie?"

"Yes. Wait. Rosie?" Instead of recoiling from him, she planted her feet, her hand fisting in the dog's curly hair. "We are not friends, Mr. Krolikowski, so you have no right to be so familiar. Or condescending. Especially when it sounds as though you're calling me a liar."

"*Are* you lying, Rosie?"

"Stop calling me that."

"It's a pretty good diversion to make us think someone's after you."

"Diversion from what?" Her chest puffed out, and a blush crept up her neck as understanding dawned. "I'm such an idiot. This is about Richard, isn't it?"

"It's a reasonable question, considering your history. You're kind of like the lady who cries wolf with all your phone calls to 9-1-1."

"My history?" Her cheeks were as rosy as his new

nickname for her now. "We're finally getting to the point, aren't we? Is KCPD accusing me of killing him again? Are you accusing Stephen? And here I thought the police had shown up because…" She stared at the evidence bag in his hand for a moment, her chin trembling against the tight clench of her mouth. Then her lips buzzed with an escaping breath and she walked to the gate. "Duchess, heel. Sit." The German shepherd settled onto her haunches beside her mistress, staying put as Rosie opened the gate. Rosie shifted the poodle to one arm and pointed down the driveway with the other. "I'd like you two to leave my home. Now. And please don't gun your engine on your way out of the neighborhood. There's already enough gossip about me without hearing complaints about loud cars leaving my house."

"There's not a damn thing wrong with the way I drive, lady. You and your brother had more motive than anybody to kill Richard Bratcher. I think you'd be less worried about my car and more worried about talking to us and trying to prove your innocence."

She shook her head, probably biting down on some unladylike crack about being innocent until proven guilty. But all he got was a succinct dismissal. "If you won't help me, I'm not helping you. If you gentlemen have any further questions about Richard's murder, you may call my attorney."

Man, that woman was the definition of control. No blowing her stack or shedding a tear or slapping his face. No answers. No freaking reason he should be so perplexed or fascinated by her. He walked up to her, letting his six feet two inches lean in close enough to steal a breath of her summery scent. "Gentlemen? Honey, I'm as far from being—"

"Max, shut up." His partner pushed him on out the gate.

"You, too?" Max patted his chest pocket, but there was no cigar there. Damn it. The stress, the suspicion, the guilt—too many emotions were hitting him way too fast to deal with them properly. He shook his head and strode toward the Chevelle. "I should have called in sick. I don't need this kind of convoluted drama. Not today." He spun and pointed a finger at the red-head whose cool eyes had locked onto him. "You really need the cops someday, lady, you come and find me. But you'd better be willing to talk and you'd better make sense." He turned and resumed his march toward the car. "I need a drink before I screw anything else up today."

"Excuse us, Miss March. Thank you for your time." Trent hurried to catch up and fall into step beside him. "You know we're not going to get anything out of her now, right?"

"I know."

"You really think she's making up these threats to make her read like a victim instead of a suspect?"

"She's smart enough to do it. Ah, I don't know what I think."

"Hey, Max." A strong hand on his arm stopped him. "I'm on your side, remember?" The tone of Trent's voice was as full of reprimand as it was concern. "It's a little early for the Shamrock, isn't it?"

"Not today, it isn't." He shrugged out of Trent's grip

and circled around the car. It was probably best for everybody here—that frightened, pissed-off woman; his best friend; this case; this job; Jimmy's memory; him—if he just walked away.

But something drew his gaze over the roof of the car back to Rosemary March. She'd followed them along the driveway toward the porch, catching the end of their conversation. But she froze as soon as his eyes locked on to hers, one arm hooked around the poodle, the other clinging to the shepherd's collar. From this distance she looked smaller, fragile and as painfully alone as he'd ever been. She'd needed someone to make her feel safe, and he'd chosen to play his bad-cop role to the hilt. He deserved the truckload of regret that dumped on top of the guilt already weighing him down.

Max swung open the car door and climbed inside to start the engine. "Not today."

CHAPTER FOUR

ROSEMARY SQUEEZED HER fists around the long straps of her shoulder bag, staring at the steel doors of the elevator while Howard Bratcher rattled on about the trust fund and investment portfolio he and his accountant had put together for her on Stephen's behalf. She'd understood the benefits and restrictions and attorney fees clearly the first time they'd discussed splitting up and managing the settlement money, but it was easier to let him repeat himself than to explain the troubling turn of her thoughts.

Two detectives had come to her home this morning. As if her encounter with that grizzled, grabby, surly Detective Krolikowski and his bigger, quieter partner wasn't upsetting enough, it was dismaying to learn that KCPD had reopened the investigation into her fiancé's murder and considered her and Stephen suspects again. Even six years after she'd found his dead body in his condo, blue faced and frozen midconvulsion, it seemed Richard still had the power to destroy any sense of security and self-worth she'd ever had.

The disturbing phone messages and threat in her own backyard left her as on edge and unsure of the world around her as those last few months with Richard had been. Her morning visit from Detectives Dixon and Krolikowski had only intensified her feelings of losing control over her own life.

Trent Dixon might have looked like a Mack truck, but he'd been businesslike, pseudofriendly. He'd kept his words polite and had respected her personal space. But Max Krolikowski made no bones about their reason for being there. And despite the military haircut that reminded her so of her father, he'd been coarse, forthright, unapologetically male—not a kindly paternal figure in any way, shape or form.

The broad-shouldered detective with the stubbled jaw and wrinkled shirt was as different from Richard's suit and tie and courtly charm as a man could be. He was right to keep his eyes hidden behind the mask of those sunglasses. On first glimpse, those deep blue irises had been full of ghosts and despair. But upon a closer look, a quick shift in attitude revealed a frightening sort of defiance—as though some great pain was crushing in on him before he summoned his considerable strength or pure cussedness or both and crushed it, instead.

He'd grabbed her, sworn his frustration with a vast vocabulary of objectionable words, accused her of lying, gossiped with the neighbors about her, made friends with her dogs and then invaded her personal space and gone vulgar and insulting again. He couldn't be more unsuited to her guarded sensibilities.

But it wasn't the lack of manners or even the not-so-subtle doubts about her innocence that stuck with her an hour after he'd driven away.

She'd forgotten how warm a man could be.

The heat of the summer sun on his skin mixed with temper and muscle—Max Krolikowski didn't have to touch her for her to be aware of the furnace of heat that man could generate. Yet he *had* touched her, singeing her skin with his abundant warmth. Rosemary wiggled her fingers around the strap of her purse, remembering the shock of his rough hand sliding over her arm. No man who wasn't her brother—she sneaked a glance up at Howard—or a brotherly type, had touched her since long before Richard's death. Frissons of white-hot electricity had danced across her skin beneath the sweep of the detective's hand. She'd reacted to his touch.

And then she'd touched him. Her hand had encountered a wall of warm, immovable muscle when she'd pushed against his chest. For a split second, her fear and fortitude had given way to a reaction that was purely female. Surprisingly aware. Completely out of character for her now.

She remembered closeness. Wanting. She remembered she was a woman.

Rosemary twisted her neck from side to side in discomfort, feeling as if the cold steel walls of this elevator were closing in on her. Why would her hormones suddenly awaken and respond to an ill-mannered beast like Max Krolikowski? Did she have no sense when it came to men? She'd never had a thing for bad boys before. Of course, she hadn't had the chance to have much of a thing for any man. But wasn't rule one that she needed to feel safe? Could it be that six years of isolating herself in order to recapture control over her own life had left her so lonely that any man barging past those meticulously erected barriers was bound to trigger a reaction?

It was all very unsettling. Max Krolikowski was unsettling. Knowing she was still thinking about him, wary of him, curious about him, wondering why Trixie and Duchess had taken to him so readily, was messing with her carefully structured, predictable world.

"We're here." The elevator dipped as it came to a stop, startling her from her thoughts as much as Howard's interruption had. But by the time the doors slid open, Rosemary had her chin and armor back in place. She arched her back away from the brush of Howard's hand there, hugged her purse to her side and hurried on out the door.

Rosemary stepped out into the cold, modern decor of the Raynard Building's top floor into the Bratcher, Austin & Cole, Attorneys-at-Law, reception area. Before she reached the granite-topped reception counter, Howard wrapped his fingers around her elbow and pulled her to a stop so he could whisper against her ear. "I thought, perhaps, you'd let me take you to lunch afterward."

She didn't immediately process that he'd asked her out on another date, because her mind was too busy comparing the light, cool clasp of his fingers to the purposeful heat of Max Krolikowski's grasp.

Really? She groaned inwardly. Although she couldn't say if her dismay stemmed from her unwanted obsession with the bullying detective or Howard's puppylike determination to turn their relationship into something more than a friendship. How many ways could she say no without hurting his feelings?

Pulling away, she offered him a wry smile. "I don't think that will work today. I've got so much to do at home. There's still a ton of Mom and Dad's stuff to go through."

Howard's smile dimmed. "I understand. Rain check?"

An office door clicked shut at the north end of the hallway and a woman's shrill voice bounced off the sterile walls. "What's she doing here?"

Rosemary's day went from bad to rotten as she turned to face Charleen Grimes. It was impossible not to feel like a frump in the face of the blonde woman's artful makeup and thoroughbred legs. It was impossible not to feel the resentment licking through her veins, either. "Howard is my attorney. Why are *you* here?"

"You don't have to engage her, Rosemary." Howard put his arm around her shoulders and pulled her to his side. This time, she didn't pull away. Nothing like a run-in with her dead fiancé's mistress to sap her strength. "Charleen, what are you doing here?" he demanded with courtroom-like authority. "I thought I made it clear you needed to find different representation."

"You mean besides your brother? I did. I just had an appointment with Mr. Austin." Charleen sauntered across the gray carpet, bringing a cloud of expensive perfume and vitriol Rosemary's way. "You're the one who's got a lot of nerve, showing your face here. I loved Richard. Why couldn't you just let him go?"

After his first attack, Rosemary had been in shock. But after the second time, when he'd twisted her arm so violently it snapped, she'd been more than willing to push Richard Bratcher out of her life. "I told Richard it was over between us. The two of you could have been together. With my blessing."

"Liar."

Rosemary's shoulders pushed against Howard's arm as indignation kicked in. How many people were going to accuse her of that today?

"He pitied you. He said you needed him too much to ever leave you."

What he hadn't wanted to leave was her money. He'd made it clear that he would continue to have Charleen or whomever he pleased in his bed after their marriage because no uptight, inexperienced, overworked mouse like her would ever be able to satisfy a man's appetite. And if Richard's words weren't cruel enough, the slap across the face had been. She'd pulled off his ring and held it out to him. But he'd twisted her arm and the nightmare started.

Rosemary gritted her teeth, blanking the memory of running for her life yet not being able to escape her own home or Richard's torture until he'd run out of cigarettes and had gone for more. "I don't know what to say, Ms. Grimes. Clearly, you're still grieving."

"Grieving? I'm mad because he's dead, and it's your fault."

Apparently, Richard hadn't treated his mistresses like the punching bag she'd been. Rosemary's love for him had died long ago. Why hadn't Charleen's? "It's been six years."

"Feels like yesterday to me. Maybe because two

detectives—Watson and Parker—came to my boutique this morning and asked me questions about Richard's death. That's why I'm here—to alert my attorney." Charleen towered over Rosemary with her three-inch heels and movie-star figure. She used that height to her advantage to sneer down her nose at Rosemary. "But I told them who I suspected."

"That's enough, Charleen." Howard removed his arm to clasp Rosemary's shoulders with both hands and turn her to face him. "Is that true? Has KCPD started a new investigation?"

Rosemary shrugged out of his grip. "Why are you asking me?"

The tall blonde laughed. "Because he thinks you did it, too."

"Suzy." Howard snapped his fingers at the reception-ist gaping behind her desk. "Escort Ms. Grimes back into Mr. Austin's office."

"But Mr. Austin has a client with—"

"Get her out of here!"

"Yes, sir." The dark-haired receptionist hurried around the stainless counter. "Ms. Grimes, may I take you to the lounge and get you some tea or coffee?"

Rosemary had flinched at Howard's raised voice, but Charleen seemed amused by his anger. "Your brother would never speak to me like that."

"My little brother did a lot of things I didn't approve of." Howard moved his tall body in front of Rosemary, blocking her view of the other woman. "If you want to continue to be a client of this firm, I suggest you learn how to keep your mouth shut and behave like a lady."

"Like boring little Miss March?"

"Do you understand what slander charges are, Charleen? I won't have you accusing Rosemary of something she didn't do."

Rosemary heard a snort of derision. "How do you know she didn't kill Richard?"

Howard's shoulders lifted with a deep breath as Charleen followed the receptionist down the long hallway to the other attorney's office suite. With a hand at Rosemary's back, he escorted her in the opposite direction. Once he closed the door to his inner office behind him, he tried to take Rosemary into his arms. "I'm so sorry the two of you had to run into each other."

But comfort was the last thing she wanted, especially with her temper brewing in her veins. She pushed away from his hug and circled around his desk to look out at the Kansas City skyline. Maybe the world was more normal outside that window. "Six years. I thought…" She crossed her arms in front of her as a shiver ran down her spine. "It was foolish to hope the nightmare of your brother was all behind me. I guess people won't leave me alone until his murder is solved and the real killer is in prison."

Howard shrugged off his suit jacket and draped it over the back of his chair, coming up behind her. "Did the police question you about Richard?"

Rosemary nodded. "Two detectives came to see me this morning, too."

"You should have called me right away. I don't want you talking to the police without me present."

When his hands settled on her shoulders again, Rosemary moved away. "Why? I didn't kill him. I don't have anything to hide." Although she hadn't really answered any of Detective Krolikowski or Dixon's questions once she realized they weren't responding to her complaint about the harassing calls and ugly threat. She stopped her furious pacing and inhaled a calming breath. It was wrong to take her frustration out on her friend. "I'm sorry, Howard. This must all be difficult for you, too. Not knowing who's responsible. I'm guessing the police will be questioning you again, as well."

He waved off her apology and followed her around the desk, where he pushed aside some knickknacks and perched on the corner. "Let them come. My alibi's as solid now as it was six years ago. I'm not worried."

"Still, the memories of your brother—I know you loved him. Our reasons may be different, but you need closure as much as I do."

"I'm so sorry, Rosemary. So sorry for everything. I knew Richard had a temper, but I never knew he was hurting you. Maybe if I had known, I could have done something to stop him. But he was so ambitious, so greedy. He never wanted to put in the time and the hard work to pay his dues and get ahead. He always looked for the shortcut. I guess I thought he'd grow out of it one day. I thought you were a good influence on him, that your marriage would be a success." He glanced toward the door, indicating the confrontation with Charleen Grimes. "You were certainly a better class of woman than those floozies he was always taking to bed. As talented a litigator as he was, he was an embarrassment to the reputation of the firm. Cost us clients. Our father went to his grave thinking Richard was never going to amount to anything worth making him a full partner."

"I don't blame you for anything Richard did. You weren't your brother's keeper."

"Maybe I should have been." He reached for her hand, and she forced herself not to dodge his grasp this time. "I intend to take care of you, though, to make up in some small way for the grief he caused you."

Rosemary managed to drum up a smile of thanks before pulling away. "How about you show me those papers you worked so hard to prepare."

Fifteen minutes later, the papers were signed and she was ready to leave. "I'll drive you home," Howard offered.

But Rosemary slung her purse over her shoulder and urged him back to his chair. "I can call a taxi. I know you have work to do." Besides, she'd already spent most of the patience and socializing she had in her today and needed some time alone to decide how best to manage—or avoid—all this attention suddenly being thrust upon her. She needed to set her emotional armor back into place. "But thank you. And thanks for running interference with Charleen."

He raised her hand to his lips and kissed it. "My pleasure. If you say you didn't kill Richard, then I believe you. And I'll defend your innocence until my dying breath." He tugged her closer and Rosemary put a hand on his stomach to keep him from completing the embrace. Still, he lowered his head to rest his forehead against hers. "Even if you did kill that bastard brother of mine in self-defense or because he deserved it, I'll defend your innocence."

Um, thank you? Her chest tightened at his declaration of support that sounded vaguely as if it wasn't real support at all. Before he could dip his lips to hers, Rosemary pushed away. "I didn't kill Richard."

"Of course not." Why didn't that throwaway remark sound as convincing as it might have even an hour earlier? When Howard circled back to his chair, Rosemary hurried to the door. "I'll talk to you soon."

Not too soon, she hoped. But she kept the thought to herself and closed the office door behind her.

AFTER A WALK with the dogs to maintain their training and give them exercise, several laps in the pool to work her vexation with Howard out of her system, and chicken from her back patio grill for dinner to fill her stomach, Rosemary settled down in the library with a glass of wine to attack another box of family papers and photographs.

Sorting through items from her and Stephen's past, as well as those things that had belonged to her parents, served several purposes. From the most practical—the long-term project gave her something meaningful to do with her time since the suspicion of murder had made it practically impossible to find a teaching job at any certified school. The settlement gave her plenty to live on, but she was a grown woman with two college degrees and a fertile brain. If she couldn't occupy her thoughts and work toward goals, she'd go mad. One of those goals was to possibly sell this place, or at least clear out enough space so she could significantly remodel the interior. There were a lot of good memories here. But there were a lot of bad ones, too. And while the familiarity of her childhood home made it a little easier to cope with the grief, panic and uncertainty of these past few years, there were days like this one when the same-old, same-old felt more like a prison where she was destined to live out her days as the neighborhood pariah—the woman who'd benefited from her parents' deaths, the woman who'd gotten away with murder.

Instead of letting the loneliness and fear take hold, Rosemary plunged into the never-ending—sometimes sentimental, sometimes sad—task of sorting papers, mementoes and heirlooms into piles of things to treasure, items to store or sell and things to throw away.

And so, with the drawn shades and night outside her windows closing her into solitude, Rosemary sat on the thick braided rug in the middle of the library floor, with piles of letters and photographs spread out around her. Duchess stretched out on the cool wood at the edge of the rug while Trixie claimed the couch.

Humming along with the Aaron Copland ballet music playing softly in the background, Rosemary smiled at an image of her father in his Army pilot's uniform, taken a few years before her birth. He'd had that freckled, youthful look for as long as she'd known him, even when his hair had started to gray. Not that the silver strands were that noticeable with his hair cropped so closely to his head. He used to joke that it was time for a trip to the barber if a strand of hair so much as tickled his ear.

Memories of her father drifted to another man with the same broad shoulders and buzz cut. Max Krolikowski was taller than her dad, thick chested and muscular instead of lean and lanky, more tawny haired than strawberry blond. And he certainly lacked that boyish smile. But she could picture the gruff detective dressed in a similar uniform. She could picture him in a gritty, action-packed war movie. What was she thinking? There was nothing fake about Max Krolikowski. She could picture him marching across an asphalt tarmac, boarding a troop transport like the one her father had flown, heading off to fight in a real war.

Rosemary's blood rushed a warning signal to her brain. She shouldn't be picturing the surly detective at all.

With a guilty start, she tucked the tiny snapshot back into the envelope with the letter to her mother. Max Krolikowski was nothing like the quiet gentleman Colonel Stephen March had been. Why couldn't she let her fascination with that rude excuse for a cop go?

Focusing on happier times, she retied the ribbon around the bundle of letters her mother had kept from the correspondence she and her father had traded when he'd been away on his first post after graduating college on his ROTC scholarship. Remembering the love her parents had shared chased away her troublesome thoughts, and Rosemary rose up on her knees to reverently place the love letters in a box marked *Keep*.

She hiked up the wrinkled hem of her dress to crawl over to the box she was sorting and pull out another

stack of bound envelopes. But as she sank back onto
the rug, her smile faded. "What are these doing here?"

In the chaos surrounding Richard's ultimatums and
his subsequent murder, she must have tossed these letters into the wrong box. They weren't correspondence
between her mother and father, but a bundle of envelopes from Richard addressed to her.

With her neckline unbuttoned in deference to the
summer humidity, despite the house's air-conditioning,
Rosemary mindlessly rubbed her knuckles over her collarbone and the neat dots of puckered scar tissue there.
Once, she'd thought it romantic that Richard had sent
her notes and poems and pictures, just as her father had
sent them to her mother. But now she was wondering
why she'd ever kept the tangible reminders of her own
foolishness. He hadn't even written the first letter until
she'd mentioned how her parents had made such an effort to stay connected when they'd been apart. Now she
could see it had all been part of his master plan to make
her fall in love and accept his proposal. Weighed down
by responsibility and sadness, desperate for someone
caring and positive in her life, she must have been an
easy mark for a smooth operator like Richard.

"Idiot," she grumbled, reaching out to toss the entire stack into the trash can beside the desk. But then
she realized that half of the envelopes hadn't even been
opened. A check of the postmarks indicated he'd sent
these in the weeks between her breaking off their engagement and filing a restraining order against him,
courtesy of his older brother, and Richard's death.

Against her better judgment, she opened the first envelope and pulled out the familiar parchment with the letterhead from his father's law firm. Rosemary shook her head as she read his dramatic scrawl. "I'll end the affair with Charleen. I'll work on my weakness with other women. I love you. I still want to marry you."

There was no apology for the arm he'd put into a cast or the cigarette burns that marred her skin. Not even an acknowledgment of the cruel coercion he'd used to force her to sign the prenup guaranteeing him a share of her settlement money. Just a blithe pronouncement of love. Funny, if she'd been thinking clearly back then, she'd have seen that all the sentences were "I" statements. Maybe if she'd picked up on those egocentric clues when they were first dating, she could have spared herself the mistake of giving her heart to the wrong man.

Rosemary returned the letter to its envelope and reached for her wineglass to wash away the taste of disgust with a crisp pinot grigio. The trash was too good for these reminders of that sick relationship, so she dropped it and the rest of his letters into a box and set it aside. This winter, she'd burn them with the first fire in the fireplace. She smiled as she raised the goblet to her lips to take a sip.

But a flicker of shadow in the window behind her reflected off the glass.

Her stomach clenched. Wine sloshed over her hand as she spun around. Nothing. Just the blinds swaying with the current of air blowing from the AC vent. She inhaled a deep breath, willing her heart rate to slow down.

Probably just the headlights of a car driving past.

But then Duchess lifted her head, growling a low

warning in her throat. Trixie jumped to her feet and barked, startling Rosemary. "What is it?"

She set down the wineglass with a trembling hand, running a quick mental check. Doors locked. Windows locked. Alarm system armed. Lights on. Dogs at her—

Rosemary screamed at the explosion of shattering glass outside. Trixie sprang from the couch as Duchess leaped to her feet. Both dogs dashed to the front door. A man-size shadow darted past the blinds. Someone was on her front porch. Why didn't the alarm go off?

The dogs' frantic barking nearly drowned out the second explosion of smashing glass. The translucent light filtering through the blinds suddenly went dark and she realized someone out there was breaking the lights. Pounding on the porch railing and furniture outside.

Avoiding the door. Avoiding the windows. Avoiding doing any damage that would trigger a siren and flashing lights.

Shrinking away from the assault on her house, Rosie screamed again at the crunch of metal on metal. "Stop it." She hugged her arms around her waist. "Stop it!"

But a crystal-clear moment of clarity fired through her brain, snapping her out of her chilled stupor. What if the intruder smashed through the door next and turned whatever weapon he was using on her dogs?

Or on her?

A wailing alarm couldn't help her then.

Rosemary lowered her hands into fists. "Duchess! Trixie!"

The barking paused for a second, then started up

again, warning away the intruder at their door. Rose-mary snatched her cell phone off the desk and ran into the hallway, grabbing their leashes off a foyer chair and joining the canine alarm. "I'm calling the police!" she shouted. "Get out of here! Now!"

Footsteps pounded across the slats of her porch and faded into silence. The man was running away. "Duch-ess, sit. Come here, Trix."

As silence fell outside, Rosemary regained control of the dogs. Kneeling between them, she hooked them up to their leashes and pulled them back from the door. Did she dare unlock it to see what was going on? Trixie, especially, was ready to charge whatever danger was on the other side of that door, and Duchess's low-pitched growl indicated that no one here felt entirely safe. She almost wished it was a random act of vandalism or at-tempted burglary. But she'd dealt with too many threats these past few days to believe she was anything but the intended target. She transferred both leashes to her left hand and pulled out her cell, her thumb hovering above the 9 on her screen.

But was calling KCPD again really an option for her? Was there any cop out there willing to help a mur-der suspect?

Rosemary pocketed her phone and waited a good two minutes, until the growling subsided and she got Trixie to sit beside the bigger dog. That meant whoever had been on her porch was long gone. It was safe to open the door, right?

Ignoring the thumping pound of her heart inside her chest, Rosemary typed in the disarm code, unhooked the chain and dead bolt and twisted the doorknob. Still in her bare feet, she stayed inside the locked storm door to survey the damage. There was shattered glass everywhere. A broken table. The intruder had taken a bat or crowbar or some other heavy object to the lights on either side of her door, plunging her porch into darkness. But there was enough light shining out from the foyer to see the dented black metal mailbox hanging by a screw from the siding beside the door.

Once she was certain the intruder had left, she pulled the leashes taut and nudged open the storm door.

"Oh, my God."

There was enough light to read the note hanging from the flap of her mailbox, too.

Murdering whore.
Justice will be done.

She swayed on her feet, shock making her lightheaded for a moment. Her landline rang in the house behind her and she jerked in surprise, sending the dogs into another barking frenzy.

Avoiding the broken glass beneath bare feet and dog paws, she pulled Duchess and Trixie back into the house and locked the storm door. After the fourth ring, the machine in the kitchen picked up, and a man's garbled voice echoed like a creepy whisper throughout the house. "I can see you, Rosemary. I know you're alone. Those dogs can't protect you. I know you're afraid."

The shiver that shook her body nearly robbed her of breath. She didn't remember slamming the front door or releasing the dogs or pulling her cell from the pocket of her dress.

But some shred of a memory stopped her from completing the 9-1-1 call.

KCPD had blown off her last report of a threat. She didn't need anyone patronizing her fears—she needed to feel safe. She wanted to prove to the police she wasn't lying—that she was the victim now, just as she'd been six years ago. With the dogs at her heels, Rosemary ran to the answering machine at the back of the house. But she had no intention of picking up the phone or even erasing that sick message. She had no intention of dealing with Dispatch and being put on hold or winding up as a footnote on some report.

Instead, she pulled the phone book from beneath the machine and looked up an address.

She knew where she could find at least one cop tonight.

CHAPTER FIVE

MAX SWALLOWED A drink of beer that had lost its chill and set the mug down on the rim of the pool table at the Shamrock Bar. He leaned over, blinking his bleary eyes and lining up the shot, tuning out the drone of conversations around the room and the jingle of the bell over the bar's front door. "Six in the corner pocket."

He tapped the cue ball and grinned as the pink ball caromed off the rail and rolled into its target. Finally, something was going right today.

He'd circled to the end of the table to assess his best angle for dropping the seven ball before realizing the noise level of the thinning crowd had paused in a momentary hush. Even his opponent on the opposite side of the pool table seemed to have frozen for a split second in time.

"She's new." Hudson Kramer, a young cop with a shiny new promotion and the subsequent pay hike burning a hole in his pocket, lay down his cue stick and combed his fingers through his hair as glasses clinked and conversations started up again. Was the game over? Hud's mouth widened with a lopsided grin as his eyes tracked movement behind Max. "Wonder if she's lost. Maybe she needs a friend to help her find her way."

With Kramer's grumble of protest at having his shot at winning back the money he'd lost tonight interrupted, Max turned and saw the last person he'd ever expect to see in a bar. "I'll be damned."

Rosemary March's copper-red hair was pulled back in a bun that wasn't anywhere as neat and tidy and screaming *old maid* as it had been this morning. *Fire and ice.* The unexpected metaphor buzzed through his head at the sight of several loose, wavy red strands bouncing against her pale cheeks and neck as she moved. The idea of her letting all that hair flow freely around her shoulders and tunneling his fingers into a handful of it hit him like a sucker punch to the gut. Max sat back on the edge of the table, propping his cue stick against the floor to hold himself upright as she approached.

He must have had too much to drink and was conjuring up hallucinations. He closed his eyes and muttered a curse, wondering why he wasn't conjuring up images of babes on swimsuit calendars instead of Miss Priss with the sharp tongue and crazy ideas.

He opened his eyes again. Nope. She was real. And she was excusing her way past a couple of tables and a cocktail waitress, heading straight toward him and the pool tables. She'd exchanged the dressy sandals for a pair of flip-flops, but she still wore that white, high-necked dress from this morning, looking as virginal and out of place in a bar at this hour as he'd felt at her house this morning. Didn't mean she didn't look all kinds of pretty to a half drunk, half horny bastard like him.

"Ah, hell," he muttered again, wishing he'd said no to

that last beer so he could control that little rush of misplaced excitement at realizing she'd come to see him.

"Detective Krolikowski?" She stopped a couple of feet in front of him, her fingers tightening around the strap of the purse she hugged in front of her. Mistaking his dumbfounded silence for a lack of recognition, she tilted those dove-gray eyes to his and introduced herself. "Rosemary March? We met this morning? I'm not armed, I promise."

"I know who you are, Rosie. You here for a drink?" When the waitress slid between the redhead and the nearest table, Max automatically reached out. Rosie pried at his hand when he tugged on the strap of her purse to pull her out of the other woman's path. Her hips jostled between the vee of his legs and his thigh muscles bunched in a helpless response to her unintentionally intimate touch there. Max instantly popped his grip open and let her scoot around his leg into the space beside him. Ignoring his body's traitorous response to a warm, curvy woman, he held up two fingers to capture the waitress's attention. "Wait. You probably want something fancier than a beer. Wine? One of those girly things with an umbrella?"

"Nothing, thank you."

Oh, he was in a bad way today. After waving off the drink order, he turned on the edge of the pool table and pulled a long, copper-red wave away from the dewy perspiration on Rosie's neck. Warm from her skin, he rubbed the silky strand between his thumb and fingers. "So is this you lettin' your hair down? You go to a bar, but you don't drink? Or is this a temperance lecture for me? Couldn't get enough of puttin' me in my place this morning, eh?"

"No, I... What are you doing?" She jerked away, snatching her hair from his fingertips and tucking it behind her ear. "This was a dumb idea."

Max pushed to his feet and thumped the tip of his cue stick on the table in front of her, blocking her escape. "Hold on, Rosie Posy. What *are* you doing here?"

Her shoulders lifted with a deep breath and she turned, staring at the collar of his shirt before tilting her wary eyes up to his. "I overheard you and your partner talk about coming here. The Shamrock Bar. I looked up the address in the phone book."

"Do you ever give a straight answer to a question?" He hunched down to look her right in the eye. "That's how you found me. Now tell me what you want. Let me guess—you're a pool hustler, and you're here to win ten bucks off me to spite me for being such a jerk this morning."

Hud Kramer walked up behind her before the shocked O of her mouth could spit out an answer. "I bet she could take you, Max."

Max bristled at the interruption. Why was that kid grinning? "Shut up."

Rosie turned to include both men in her answer. Sort of. If looking from one chin to the other counted. What was that woman's aversion to making direct eye contact? With that tart tongue of hers, he couldn't really call her shy. But something had to be going on to make her subvert that red-haired temper and any other emotion she might be feeling. "I haven't played for a long time.

I used to be pretty decent back in college when I'd go out with friends, but I don't think I'd win."

"I'd be happy to give you a few tips, Red." The younger cop seemed to take any answer as encouragement to his lame flirtations. "Aren't you going to introduce us, Max?"

But when Hud leaned in, Rosie flinched back, maybe sidling closer to what was familiar, if not necessarily what she considered friendly. Max shifted in an instinctively protective response, and her hair tangled with the scruff of beard on his chin, releasing her warm summer scent. His pulse leaped and he was inhaling a deep breath before he could stop himself. Rosie March might be a baffling mix of mystery and frustration, but she exuded a wholesome, flowery fragrance that was far more intoxicating than the beer he'd been drinking.

Max growled, irritated by how much he noticed about this woman. And he was even more irritated that the younger detective had noticed it, too. "Get out of here, Kramer."

A soft nudge to the chest with Max's pool cue backed Hud up a step, but the young hotshot was still smiling. Yes, the woman had rebuffed him in favor of the older detective who needed a shave and an attitude adjustment. But Hud wasn't about to lose to him twice in one night. "Our game isn't finished, Krolikowski. I have a feeling I'm about to make a comeback."

Groaning at the taunt, Max set his cue stick on the table and pulled out his wallet. He reached around Rosie to hand a ten-dollar bill to the young officer. "Here. Take it."

"You're conceding defeat?"

"I'm conceding that you annoy the hell out of me and I'm tired of puttin' up with you. Now scram."

"Yes, sir." Kramer took the sawbuck with a wink and a mock salute and headed straight to a green vinyl seat in front of the polished walnut bar to order a refill.

With more room to avoid him now, Rosie quickly stepped away and moved around the corner of the table. "I'm sorry you lost your money. That wasn't my intention." She pulled open the flap on her purse and pulled out her wallet. "I only wanted to talk to a police officer."

Now she wanted to answer questions? Max scanned the booths and tables around the bar. "Take your pick. The majority of the men and women here work in some kind of law enforcement."

"Could I talk to *you*?"

He looked down to see her holding out a ten-dollar bill. Muttering a curse, he pushed the money back into her purse. At this late hour, every young stud in the place was looking for any unattached females who might be interested in one last drink and a chance to get lucky. They wouldn't know that Rosie was a person of interest in a murder investigation. They wouldn't care about her eccentricities or that she could rub a man wrong in every possible way. Like Kramer, they were noticing the outward appearance of innocence and vulnerability. They were seeing the promise of passion in the red flag of Rosemary March's hair. Maybe they were picturing what it would look like down and loose about her bare shoulders, too.

Even in his hazy brain, Max knew she didn't belong here.

"Let's get out of here. Robbie?" He looked to the Shamrock's bearded owner at the bar, and tossed some bills on the table to pay for his tab. "Come on."

Grabbing Rosie by the arm, he turned her toward the door. Whatever she wanted from him, he wasn't about to go toe-to-toe with some young buck who wanted to pick her up just for the privilege of finding out. Although she hurried her steps beside him to keep up, she tried to shuck off his grip. But Max tightened his fingers around her surprisingly firm upper arm muscles and didn't let go until he'd ushered her out the front door into the muggy haze of the hot summer night.

He took her past the green neon sign in the front window so that curious eyes inside wouldn't get the idea that she might be coming back before he released her. He plucked a fresh cigar from his shirt pocket and leaned back against the warm bricks. "Now talk to me."

Once he released her, she took a couple more steps and turned. "You smoke?"

"Not exactly." He tore off the wrapper and stuffed the plastic into his pocket. Then he held the stogie up to his nose, breathing in the rich tobacco scent until he could rid the distracting memory of fresh summer sunshine from his senses. Light from the street lamps and green neon sign in the window reflected off the oily asphalt of the street behind her, making her seem even more out of place in the dingy surroundings. At least he didn't have to deal with Kramer or anybody else hittin' on her out here. Max set the cigar between his teeth and chomped down on it. "Make sense, and make it fast, okay?"

He watched the reprimand on her lips start and die. Good. He wasn't in the mood for one of her lectures on the evils of swearing and smoking—one of which he hadn't done for years. She seemed to consider his request for brevity and nodded. "Actually, I want you to come to my house. I had a trespasser tonight. I don't know how long he was there before he started vandalizing my front porch. He broke the lights and left a message in my mailbox. It's…disturbing, to say the least." She reached into her purse and pulled out a folded sheet of white paper with just her thumb and forefinger and held it out to him. "It's typed like the one I found on the back patio. No signature to say who it's from."

Straightening from the wall, Max snatched the paper from her fingers and unfolded it. "Somebody threaten your dogs again?"

Her chin shot up and her cheeks dotted with color. "He's not after my dogs. He just knows they're a way to get to me. To scare me."

"You keep saying *he*."

"Or she. I don't know who it was. All I saw was the shadow on my porch and the damage after the dogs' barking scared him away."

Max squinted the words on the note into focus. "Murdering whore. Justice will be done." Anger surged through his veins and he swore around the cigar. "You should have reported this ASAP to 9-1-1 instead of taking the time to track me down."

"I don't want to be brushed off with another phone

call, and I certainly don't want to be accused of making it up again."

"What makes you think I'm gonna believe you?"

Her tongue darted out to moisten her lips, and his pulse leaped with a response that told him he was already far too interested in this woman to remain objective. Probably why he was such a growly butt around her. He didn't want to like her. It didn't make sense to like her. And yet, she was doing all kinds of crazy things to his brain and libido.

"To look at you, and listen to the way you talk… You're military, aren't you? Or you used to be? Not just the haircut. But, the way you stand. The way you move. You recognized Dad's gun as Army issue, and you remind me of him when he was young. Except, he was shorter. More patient. And he didn't smoke."

Hell. Where was she going with this? Suspicion tried to move past the fog of alcohol and put him on alert.

"Dad was in the Army. A career man who retired as a colonel. Isn't there some band of brothers code I can call on for you to help me? Without treating me like a suspect in a murder case?"

Max tilted his face to the canopy of cloudy haze reflecting the city lights overhead. He'd spent the day mourning his fallen band of brothers, cursing his inability to save them all—to save his best friend. He couldn't do this. He couldn't call on that part of him to do his duty and fail again. Not for this woman. Not for a comrade in arms or superior officer he'd never even met. With a self-preserving resolve, he lowered his gaze to hers and handed back the note. "You should have called Trent. He's the reasonable one."

"No one will listen to reason." Her hands fisted in frustration. "I need someone who'll help me out of blind faith in my innocence…or out of a sense of duty. Or honor. Besides, I don't know where your partner is. But I remembered you said you were coming here for a drink."

"That was this morning. What made you think I'd still be here?" A little frown dimple appeared between her eyebrows when she wrinkled up her nose in an unspoken apology. Oh. Her opinion of him was that low, huh? He supposed he'd earned it. And yet she'd sought him out instead of Trent or one of the other off-duty detectives and uniforms inside the cop bar. Maybe he shouldn't alter her opinion of him by telling her he'd gone back to his desk at the precinct and put in his full shift before grabbing a burger and heading to the Shamrock. "How will me going to your place prove you didn't put this note there, too?"

The soft gaze that had held his for so long dropped to his chin. Her skin blanched to a shade of alabaster that absorbed the harsh green color of the neon sign. He didn't like that unnatural color on her. He didn't like feeling like a first-class rat for blanking the color from her skin.

"Hey, I…" Max pulled his cigar from his mouth with one hand and reached for a red tendril with the other. Although she startled at his touch, she didn't immediately pull away this time. Instead, she watched his hand as he sifted the silky copper through his fingers. "I'm sorry, Rosie. I'm having a really sucky day. It's hard to see the good in anything or anybody tonight."

"You're not always like this?"

He chuckled at the doubtful face she made. "Some say I am. But on this one day every year, I'm an extra sorry SOB."

"I wish you wouldn't swear like that. I get that you're angry, already."

Oh, he was angry, all right. At himself. At friends who died. At failing to save them.

"I get that you're hurting. Did something bad happen?"

"Yeah. Something very bad happened. To a friend of mine." She'd tilted her eyes up to his, bravely held his gaze. Maybe it was a trick of the lights and shadows, but from this angle, standing this close, her eyes filled with compassion, maybe even a little of that same odd awareness he'd been feeling about her. A man could lose himself in the deep, soft shadows of her eyes if he wasn't careful. As uncomfortable with her intuition about him as he was with the male interest stirring deep inside him, he pulled his fingers from her hair and retreated. "You said your daddy served?"

She nodded, retreating a step herself. "He flew troop transports and cargo planes until he retired from active duty. Later, he commanded a local unit in the National Guard."

Max thought of the unseen pilots and navigators who'd flown him, Jimmy and the rest of their battered squad from the Middle East into Germany. Another transport had finally brought them and the caskets of their fallen friends stateside. The world was a mighty small place in some ways. "He flew soldiers home?"

"Sometimes. Is that important?"

Those pretty, intuitive eyes snuck right past his survival armor. An image of Jimmy's frozen dark eyes blipped through his thoughts. *Never leave a man behind.* He crushed the memory that left him reeling and grabbed her arm, pulling her into step beside him and striding down the sidewalk. "Where's your car? I'll walk you to it and then follow you back to your house."

But when he stepped off the curb he stumbled. His momentum pulled her against his chest for a split second, imprinting his body from neck to thigh with her warm curves, filling his head with that damnable clean scent he wanted to bury himself in.

"On second thought, maybe you'd better drive."

She was the one who grabbed a fistful of shirt and his shoulder to steady him and guide him back to the sidewalk. "You're drunk, aren't you?"

There was that snappy, righteous tone again. Her eyes had gone cold. "That was my goal, honey. It helps me forget."

Rosie didn't waste any time pushing away. "This was a mistake. I thought you were different."

"You are the most confounding woman…" With his emotions off the chart, his hormones twisted up in a mix of lustful curiosity and a craving for the peaceful solace he'd read in her eyes—not to mention the four beers he'd drunk since dinner—Max tossed his unlit cigar into the gutter and stopped her from walking away. "Did something scare you tonight or not?"

He spun her around and pulled her up onto her toes, bringing her lips close enough to steal a kiss if he wanted to. And, by hell, he wanted to.

Shifting his hands to the copper bounty of her hair, Max tunneled his fingers into the silky waves and pulled her mouth to his. With a gasp of surprise, her lips parted and Max took advantage of the sudden softening of that preachy mouth by capturing her lower lip between his. He drew his tongue along the supple curve, tasting something tart and lemony there. Her lip trembled at his hungry exploration. He felt the tiny tremor like a timid caress and throttled back on his blind need. Another breath whispered across his cheek, and he waited for the shove against his chest. But her fingers tightened in the front of his shirt, instead, pressing little fingerprints into the muscles of his chest, and she pushed her lips softly against his mouth, returning the kiss.

Something twisted and hard, full of rage and regret, unknotted inside him at her unexpected acceptance of his desire. Frustration faded. Anger disappeared. The wounds of guilt and grief that had been festering inside him all day calmed beneath her tender response. He threaded his fingers into the loose twist of her bun, pushing aside pins and easing the taut style until her hair was sifting between his fingers and his palms were cupping the gentle curve of her head. "Your hair's too pretty to keep it tied up the way you do, Rosie. Too sexy."

"Detective Krol—" He kissed her temple, her forehead, reclaimed her lips once more. He'd reached for her in a haze of frustration and desire, but she was holding on with a gentle grasp and angling her mouth beneath his. It wasn't a passionate kiss. It wasn't seductive or stylized. It was an honest kiss. It was the kind of kiss a man was lucky to get once or twice in his life. It was a perfect kiss. Beauty was taming the beast.

Or merely distracting him?

Detective?

Ah, hell. He quickly released her and backed away, his hands raised in apology. "Did something scare you tonight…besides me?"

"You didn't scare me," she lied. Her fingers hovered in the air for a few seconds before she clasped them around the strap of her purse.

Max scraped his palm over the top of his head, willing his thoughts to clear. "Just answer the damn question."

She nodded.

She wasn't here for the man. She was here for the cop. He'd like to blame the booze that had lowered his inhibitions and done away with his common sense, but fuzzy headed or sober, he knew he'd crossed too many lines with Rosie March today. "I think this is where you slap my face and call me some rotten name."

Her eyes opened wide. "I wouldn't do that."

"No, I don't suppose a lady like you would."

Her lips were pink and slightly swollen from his beard stubble. Her hair was a sexy muss, and part of him wanted nothing more than to kiss her again, to bury his nose in her scent and see if she would wind her arms around his neck and align her body to his as neatly as their mouths had fit together. But she was hugging her arms around her waist instead of him, pressing that pretty mouth back into its tightly controlled line. When had he ever hauled off and kissed a woman like that? With her history, she'd probably been frightened by his behavior and had given him what she thought he wanted in hopes of appeasing him, counting the seconds until he let her slip away. She had to be terrified, desperate, to come to him after this morning's encounter. The fact that she wasn't running away from him right now had to be a testament to her strength—or just how desperate she was to have someone from KCPD believe in her. And, for some reason, she'd chosen him to be her hero.

Max scrubbed his palm over his jaw. He hadn't played hero for anybody in a long time. He hadn't been any good at it since Jimmy's suicide. He did his job, period. He didn't care. He didn't get involved. This woman was waking impulses in him that were so rusty from lack of use that it caused him pain to feel himself wanting to respond to her request. "What do you need from me?"

She tucked that glorious fall of hair behind her ears and tried to smooth it back into submission. "I think I'm in real trouble. And I don't know what to do. KCPD thinks I might be a killer, so they're not taking me seriously and won't look into these threats. But I thought that you…maybe you'd set aside your suspicions and do it for my dad. I know it's an imposition, and I know you'd rather be investigating me for murder than deal with some unknown stalker you think I made up, but—"

"You're right, Rosie. I was a soldier. Sergeant First

Class, US Army. A man like your dad brought me and my buddies home from a hell of a fight where we lost too many good men." For the first time in a lot of months, on that flight across the Atlantic, he'd been able to close his eyes and sleep eight hours straight, knowing he and his men were safe from the enemy as long as they were on that plane. "What was your daddy's name?"

"Colonel Stephen March."

"Maybe I don't owe the colonel personally. But I owe." She'd appealed to the soldier in him, tapped into that sense of duty he'd once answered without hesitation. She had him pegged a lot sooner than he was figuring her out. "And I owe you for putting up with me on my worst day."

"Is there something I can do to help? Besides…" She ran her tongue around her lips, maybe still tasting some of the need he'd stamped there. "I'm a very good listener."

He grumbled a wry laugh. So, no offer to repeat that kiss, eh? "Just give me a chance to be a better man than the one you met today."

"You'll come look? You'll help me?"

Either he was the world's biggest sucker, or Rosie March was in real danger and she believed he was her best chance at staying safe. Whether he was doing this for her or her dad or to atone for all the mistakes he'd made today—all the mistakes he'd made in the past eight years—he was doing it. "Yes, ma'am." Wisely keeping his hands to himself this time, he gestured for her to lead the way to her car. "Let's go find this lowlife."

CHAPTER SIX

"WHY DO YOU swear so much?" Rosemary glanced away from the stoplight to the big, looming silence sitting beside her in the passenger seat of her car. Although the beard stubble on his square jaw took on a burnished glow from the lights from the dashboard, Max Krolikowski's craggy face remained hidden in shadows. And while she normally appreciated the absence of any confrontation, ten miles without one word left her questioning the wisdom of this last-resort plan to seek him out as an ally.

"Like you said. I'm angry."

And hurting. He said something bad had happened to a friend. If there was one thing she understood about people, it was the stages of pain and grief a person went through when he or she lost someone or something very dear to them. She'd gone through them with her parents, her brother's drug use and murder conviction. Her relationship with Richard. Denial. Anger. Sadness. Acceptance. Only, Max Krolikowski seemed to be stuck in an endless loop of anger and pain.

The light changed and she drove through the intersection. His fingers drummed a silent rhythm on the armrest of the car door. Was that endless tapping an indication that his temper was still simmering beneath the surface? She remembered those strong fingers tangled in her hair, holding her mouth beneath his. He'd used words like *pretty* and *sexy*—and she'd believed him. For that moment, at least.

Richard had never used words like that with her. She'd looked nice. She'd do him proud at a family dinner or business luncheon. And Richard's embraces had never been so spontaneous, so unabashedly sensual.

When Max Krolikowski kissed her, she'd felt that knee-jerk instinct to flee from the unfamiliar, from the potential danger of the unknown. But she'd felt something else, too. She'd felt need. She'd felt heartache. She'd sensed a hopeless man discovering some shred of hope.

Or maybe she was the one who'd succumbed to the need to be held and wanted and important to someone—even for a few seconds outside a noisy bar. Because once he'd gentled his kiss, once she understood there was something besides anger driving his embrace, she'd become a willing participant. A shyly eager partner. Out of her depth, perhaps, but not afraid.

There was something bold, raw and honest about Max's emotions that was completely foreign in her experience with men. But she'd take that kind of blunt honesty, that disruptive force of nature, over Richard's cool charm any day. Richard's cruelty had been a blindside waiting to happen. At least with Detective Krolikowski, she knew to expect the unexpected.

Which brought her thoughts around to the question she'd really wanted to ask. "Why did you kiss me?"

"I saw the chance. I took it. It seemed like the right thing to do at the time."

And now? Did he still think she was...kissable? Rosemary's hands tightened around the steering wheel as the next question came out in a throaty whisper. "Is that what you want from me?"

The drumming stopped. "You mean like payment for helping you out?" He muttered a succinct curse.

"Language, Detective."

"Wow. Your opinion of me must be lower than I thought." His voice was deep and resonant and laced with contempt. "Don't lecture me on my mouth and insult me at the same time. If you're going to treat me like a degenerate, I might as well talk like one."

Rosemary's grip pulsed around the wheel as a defensive temper flared in her veins. "I wasn't insulting you. I'm just trying to understand what's happening between us. My experience with men is rather limited, and hasn't been entirely positive. I haven't had control over a lot that's happened in my life. And now some creep is trying to undermine what little sense of security I do have." She glanced across the seat and found deep blue eyes bearing down on her. She quickly turned her attention back to the neighborhood streets and took a deep breath to cool her outburst and resume an even tone. "I need to understand so I won't be caught off guard again. As for the swearing? If you need to use those words to get your emotions out, then go ahead, I'll get used to it. But they remind me of someone I'd rather not think of."

"Bratcher? Is that how he talked to you?"

The accuracy of his guess made the scars on her chest burn with remembered terror of her erudite fiancé transforming into Mr. Hyde. She rubbed at her collarbone through the linen dress she wore, willing the memories to subside before they could take hold. Max waited with surprising patience until she nodded. "Ninety percent of the time, Richard was the perfect gentleman. But sometimes, in private, he'd blow up."

"Probably when you had a difference of opinion or you tried to assert yourself?"

Rosemary exhaled a breath that buzzed her lips, her temper cooling to match the facade. Max was sounding more like a cop now. And with the finger of suspicion pointed elsewhere for a change, she found his questions easier to answer. "Once he put that ring on my finger, he changed. I knew then it was just about the money. He didn't love me. I didn't realize just how much he loved that settlement money, though."

"Rosie, I'm not aiming any of those words at you, and I don't mean to offend you. It's just I'm a bull in a china shop and you're a piece of china."

She had the scars, inside and out, to scoff at half of that idea. "I'm not fragile. It's just…I'd rather not hear them."

His disbelieving laugh was a deep, hearty tone from his barrel chest. "Yes, ma'am. I'll try to do better."

Despite the suspicion that he might be mocking her, Rosemary nodded her thanks. "That's all I ask."

They drove an entire block before he surprised her by continuing the conversation. "I wasn't thinking when I kissed you, either. I was just doing what felt right at that moment. Look, I admit, I've had a few drinks, and I'm not that great at filtering my thoughts and emotions in the first place. You smelled good."

She *smelled* good? How could such a simple phrase feel as flattering as being called *pretty* or *sexy*? Frankly, she thought she might need a shower after the stress and heat of the day. But his words made her lips tighten against the urge to grin.

He shrugged, his big shoulders seeming to fill the empty space inside her car as he searched for more of an explanation. She could feel the warmth emanating from his body when he turned in his seat to face her and gripped the wheel more tightly to keep from leaning toward it.

"Rosie, I didn't analyze it. I felt like kissing you. The opportunity was there, so I did."

After this morning's battle of wills, she'd been certain the rather earthy Max Krolikowski wouldn't give her a second look—unless he was throwing darts at her picture. "I didn't think I was your type."

"Neither did I." He sank back into his seat with a low exhale. His eyes drifted shut. "Don't worry. I won't let it happen again. I'm a cop, doing the job I should have done this morning. I'm not expecting any favors from you."

Now, why did that reassurance kill any urge to smile? Ignoring her uncalled-for disappointment, Rosemary turned her car into the driveway and shut off the engine. When she saw the dark expanse of her porch and heard the dogs barking inside, it was easy to remember that she'd asked him here to help with the threats, not the loneliness. "We're here. I didn't touch anything except for the note." She pointed to the street lamp behind them. "There's a little light from the street, but if you need a flashlight, there's one in the glove compartment."

He pulled out the flashlight and tested it before shutting the compartment and climbing out. When he hesitated outside his door, Rosemary did the same. He scrubbed his hand across his jaw, a habit that drew her attention to its firm, square shape and the intriguing mix of tawny, gold and brown stubble there. Richard had always been clean-shaven. But Max's day-old beard had been a sharp contrast against her softer skin. His beard had been ticklish, abrading, stimulating—his lips and tongue had been soothing in the aftermath.

Fortunately, he spoke before she succumbed to the silly urge to run her tongue across her lips, remembering what he'd felt like there.

"You know, if you get mad at me, I'm not going to hurt you like Bratcher did. I know I talk loud and need to clean up my act, but I would never lay a hand on you in anger." His gaze found hers when she didn't immediately respond. "I'm not going to leave, either. I said I'd help, and I promise to do what I can."

"For my dad."

He opened his mouth to say something, but changed his mind and circled around the hood of her car, ending the conversation and slipping into detective mode. "Yeah. For your dad. Hooah."

HUA. Heard. Understood. Acknowledged.

Nodding at the military acknowledgment she remembered her dad using, Rosemary followed him up onto the porch. When Max stumbled over the top step, she instinctively reached out to help him. But he caught her arm instead, urging her back behind him while he swept the beam of light over the upended rocking chair, splintered wood and shattered glass littering her porch. "Son of a—" He bit off the curse and released her. "Somebody was smart enough to avoid triggering the alarm— or else plain lucky. This is a lot of rage. Who blames you for your fiancé's death?"

"Who doesn't?" He swung the light over to her, hiding his opinion of her flippant remark in the shadows. Rosemary shook her head, not understanding how a dead man could still be wreaking so much havoc in her world. "I wasn't holding Richard to any promises. I broke off our engagement. I wanted him out of my life."

"Murder is a permanent way to do that."

She pushed the flashlight aside to look him in the eye. "How many times do I have to say it? I did not kill Richard. The only reason I was at his condo that morning was to tell him to stop threatening Stephen with trumped-up charges. He thought blackmailing me would convince me to take him back, but Howard, my new attorney, helped me get a restraining order. I wanted to deliver it to him myself—prove that he couldn't intimidate me anymore."

"But you didn't get to say any of that. You found him dead?"

She nodded, squeezing her eyes shut against the horrible memory of Richard's dead, discolored body. But his puffy blue lips weren't the only detail she recalled. She hugged her arms around her waist before opening her eyes and looking up at Max again. "I could tell he'd been there with another woman. There were condoms on the nightstand and her perfume was still in the bedding."

"He cheated on you, threatened you, abused you. A jury would see that as a lot of motive to kill a man." At her wounded sigh, Max's big hand clamped around hers before she could storm away. "But I'll start working on the assumption that you didn't. Maybe we can track down this other woman. See what she knows."

She remembered her confrontation with Charleen Grimes that morning. Charleen had been so certain that Rosemary was responsible for ending her lover's life. Could that have been a show to hide her own culpability? There'd certainly been plenty of witnesses to her accusations. Still, why would Charleen want to kill the man she professed to love? Rosemary had a feeling the affair had been a tempestuous one. But poison wasn't exactly a spur-of-the moment weapon.

"Rosie?" Max's growly voice interrupted her thoughts. "If you know who the other woman was, I'm going to need that information. The best way to prove your innocence is to find out who really killed your ex."

Rosemary tugged her hand from his grasp and tried to gauge the sincerity of his words. "You believe me?"

"I promised to help."

Not exactly a rousing vote of confidence. But she was scared enough to take it. She gestured to the mess on her porch. "Do you at least believe I'm not doing this to myself?"

"I think I need a clearer head to make sense of what's

going on here." He swung the flashlight toward the sound of the dogs barking behind the door. "Sounds like they need to get out and run around. You got coffee?"

"I can make a pot."

"Do it. Give the dogs a few minutes outside, then keep them in the house with you. Wait. We'll go in through the back. I want to get pictures of the damage before anything is moved. I want to bag that note of yours, too."

He made no attempt to touch her again but fell into step beside her to walk her down the driveway. With every passing second, he was becoming more cop, more man of duty, rather than the tipsy desperado who'd pulled her into his arms and kissed her because he thought it was a good idea at the time. She should be grateful for his professionalism, for the distance he put between them now. That would make it easier to keep her guard up and stay focused on the problems she needed to deal with.

"You got a toolbox somewhere?" he asked, waiting for her to unlock the back door.

"Yes. Dad's workbench is still out in the garage."

"Then I'll need it open, too." After she gave him the pass code, he waited for her to air the dogs, even tussling a little bit with Duchess and Trixie himself, before urging them all back into the house and telling her to lock the door.

Rosemary fed the dogs a treat, brewed a fresh pot of coffee and pulled the makings for a simple sandwich from her fridge.

An hour later, she carried the last of the coffee to

the front door to refill Max's mug before she washed the dishes. She could do this. She could grab his plate and fill his mug and get back to the kitchen without getting herself into any uncomfortable conversation or unwanted physical contact with the man. Although the dogs were eager to spend more time with their new friend on the porch, she shooed them behind her before stepping out to find Max putting the finishing touches on replacing her mailbox.

"Want the last cup?" she offered.

"Sure. I'm going to have a whale of a headache in the morning, but the food and caffeine help." He nodded toward the empty mug and plate on the bench he'd moved beside the rocking chair to replace the broken table.

"Is that a thank-you?" she asked, wondering if there were any manners lurking under that tough hide of his.

"Yeah." He paused with his hand in her father's toolbox, then faced her. She'd like to think that was a blush of humility on his cheeks, but she suspected the flush of color in the shadows was due to the hard work and the temperature that had barely cooled at one in the morning. "You didn't have to go to the extra trouble, but I appreciate it."

"You're welcome." Relaxing enough to smile at the unexpected compliment, she nodded toward the twin glare of bare lightbulbs on either side of her front door. "You didn't have to go to all this trouble, either. I'm grateful. But that wasn't why I asked you here."

"I've always liked working with my hands. Keeps me out of trouble," he added without any elaboration, before plucking a screw from his pocket and going back to the job at hand. "You'll have to get new globes to cover the bulbs I replaced, but everything is cleaned up and secure. As soon as I finish this."

"Uh-huh." Rosemary didn't move. So much for keeping a polite distance and hurrying back into the house. Max's shirt had come untucked somewhere along the course of the long day. And as he raised his arms to drill in the last screw, his shirttails lifted up and his jeans slipped a tad, giving her a glimpse of his gun and badge and a set of abs that belied the beer he claimed to have consumed tonight. She knew he was brawny. She expected him to be fit working for the police department. But the holstered weapon and strong male body beneath the wrinkled clothes and antisocial attitude made her a little nervous.

Although she couldn't say if the suddenly wary tempo of her heart stemmed from the clear reminder that Max was a cop, and cops ultimately treated her as a suspect rather than a victim—no matter how nice they were being about fixing the vandalism on her front porch. Or maybe those tingles of awareness of a man were a real attraction, fed by the unanswered questions she still had about that kiss. When she realized her gaze was lingering on the thin strip of elastic waistband peeking above his belt, she snapped her gaping mouth shut and turned her attention to refilling his mug.

A relationship was the last thing she wanted, right? Richard had made it perfectly clear that she was too timid, too plain, too boring, to ever turn a man's head to thoughts of passion. She was far better suited to domesticity and duty than she was to warming a man's bed or heart. And though, logically, she knew his cruel words had been used to break her spirit and manipulate her, the sting of self-doubt reared its ugly head whenever she noticed a man as something other than a friend or acquaintance. Why set herself up for disappointment and humiliation when the most attractive quality she had, according to Richard, was the money in her bank account?

A relationship with Max Krolikowski could be especially problematic since he seemed to be even less refined, led more by his instincts and whatever he was feeling at any given moment than Richard had ever been, pushing her even more out of her comfort zone and making him a real enigma in her limited experience with the opposite sex.

Not that Max was offering any kind of a relationship. He wasn't interested in her money. He wasn't particularly interested in being here at all. Max was here because he'd been in the Army like her dad. He was a creature of duty as much as she was. A soldier would do for another soldier or his family.

And a military family would do for a soldier in need.

Rosemary put down the plate she'd retrieved, and set the coffeepot beside it. Far better to clear the air between them than to muddy the waters with some foolish fantasy that wasn't going to happen. Clinging to the rocking chair he'd righted, she faced him again. "What happened to your friend? Is it something that interferes with your work a lot?"

Max removed the bit and carefully laid the drill back in her father's toolbox and closed the lid. For a moment she didn't think he was going to answer. Then he crossed into the shadows near the porch railing and sat, crossing his arms in front of him, looking big and unassailable. "You're determined to talk about this, hmm?"

Rosemary withdrew behind the chair. "I believe, maybe, if we're going to be working together, we need to."

"You think this is going to be a team effort?"

"I know you have more questions for me. I don't expect you to help me for nothing—"

"Relax, Rosie." He dipped his face into the light, his sober blue eyes drilling straight into hers. "I'll help you—you help me. Just go easy on the lectures and the heart-to-hearts and remember—I'm giving you fair warning. You can't fix me."

"Are you broken?"

His eyes narrowed and his head jerked slightly, as if her question surprised him…or struck a nerve. Muttering one choice word, he sat back against the porch post. "You're not the only one who's lost people you care about. Eight years ago today, I lost my best friend. Captain James Stecher. We served together in the Middle East."

"He died in battle?"

"Nope. Stateside. Shot himself. Post-traumatic stress."

"Oh, Max." His blunt answer made her eyes gritty with tears. She reached out to squeeze his hand or hug away the pain she imagined hiding behind that matter-of-fact tone.

"I thought it was *detective*."

The growl of sarcasm and his stalwart posture made him seem impervious to pain—or at least unaffected by her compassion—so she curled her fingers around the back of the rocking chair instead. "I'm sorry."

"For what? I'm the one who screwed up. I should have been able to save him."

He rose and leaned across the chair to pick up his coffee. Rosemary managed not to jump when his body heat brushed past her. But when he straightened beside her—tall, broad, the sleeve of his cotton shirt brushing against her shoulder and raising goose bumps—she couldn't help retreating a step.

"I've decided I'm not going to make the same mistake with you," he said.

"What does that mean?"

"It means I need you to drive me to my car at the Shamrock. Then I'll follow you back here and sit out front the rest of the night." He turned and doffed a salute to the shadow in the Dinkles' window she hadn't noticed until that moment. She gasped as the shadow disappeared, and the blinds swayed with Otis or Arlene's hasty retreat. "You've already got the neighbors' attention by bringing me here. I'm guessing you don't entertain a lot of men."

She lifted her panicked gaze to his. She hadn't even noticed the Dinkles' curiosity, but Max had probably been aware of her nosy neighbor the entire time. "Do you think that's necessary? I just wanted a police officer to see what was happening to me and write a report."

"I intend to do more than that, Rosie."

Her blood ran cold at the ominous portent in his

voice. "Do you think something else is going to happen?"

"I'm not going to give whoever this bastard is a chance to scare you again. Or do something worse. There's only so much guilt a man can live with." He continued to scan the neighborhood from her dark porch, even though the Dinkles' spying had been temporarily thwarted. He picked up the note he'd sealed in one of her plastic sandwich bags. "If Bratcher's killer is behind these threats, he or she could be doing it to divert suspicion onto you. Keeping an eye on you might ferret out the suspect."

"I see." Rosemary understood the logic, even if she didn't relish the idea of playing the part of bait for KCPD. Shivering now, she hugged her arms around her middle. "So watching over me and what happens here helps your investigation?"

"Possibly." He reached out and rubbed his hand up and down her bare arm, eliciting more goose bumps as her skin warmed beneath even that casual touch. "But that's not the only reason. If this guy is someone who blames you for Bratcher's murder and thinks they're meting out some kind of justice…?" He lifted his fingers to her hair, scowling at the lone tendril falling against her neck as if he didn't like that she'd pinned the rest of it up into a practical bun again. His palm settled along her jaw, and, instinctively, against her better judgment, she leaned into his warmth. "Look, the only thing you have to understand about me is this. I'm not losing anyone else on my watch. You're still my team's best shot at solving this case. If something happens to you, chances are, we'll never uncover the truth."

If something happens? Even the heat from his callous hand wasn't enough to erase the chill crawling over her body. So volunteering to watch over her wasn't personal at all. It was a practical move on his part. She should appreciate practicality. But the no-nonsense offer hurt, made her wish she hadn't gone to him for help, after all.

Pulling away, Rosemary crossed to the front railing and looked to the street, picturing Max's car parked beside the curb. A man with a gun and a baby blue muscle car should draw all kinds of attention to her quiet home. Attention she didn't want. "What exactly are you saying? You're going to stake out my house every night until you finish your investigation? You're just going to wait until this guy makes good on one of his threats?"

She felt his breath against her neck as he walked up behind her. Her eyes drifted shut at the unintentional caress. But it wasn't reassurance he was offering. "Actually, I was thinking more along the lines of moving into your basement apartment. Your neighbors, this stalker, and possibly the killer, are already going to question why I'm here. But they might drop their guard a little bit if they think I'm the new tenant."

Rosemary scooted away from the warmth she craved. "But that's Stephen's apartment."

"He's not going to be using it for a few years." He caught her by the wrist and turned her to face him, his stony expression telling her his idea wasn't really up for debate. "We're talking a matter of weeks, maybe even days, that I'd be here. I get that I overstepped some personal boundaries and made you uncomfortable earlier, but my plan makes sense. I'll clear it with my team leader tomorrow."

"What if I say no?"

"Why would you say no?" He leaned in, close enough for the moonlight to pick up the color of his eyes and make them glow like a predatory cat as he glared down at her. "I thought you wanted to uncover the truth as much as KCPD does."

"I do." She tugged her wrist free and folded her hands together, willing him to understand the inviolate need to maintain the one place of sanctuary she had left in the world. "But I'm not comfortable having a man in the house. Even with the separate entrance, it would feel like I'm locked in there with you and I wouldn't be free to come and go when I want to. You're laying down rules. You're taking over my life."

"You came to me for help. Do you want to catch a killer or not?" He pointed to the trash bag with the mess from the vandalism he'd cleaned up. "Do you want this sh—" He caught himself, held up a hand in impatient apology and changed the word. "Do you want this garbage to stop? I don't care how many locks you have on that door, if this guy escalates any further, you won't have time to wait for help to get here."

She dropped her gaze to the middle button on that broad chest and considered how helpless she would be against Max's strength if he ever decided to turn on her the way Richard had. She'd thought she could hide in the sanctuary of her own room, lock Richard out. But even without Max's muscular build and physical training, Richard had been able to kick down her door, destroy her phone before she could call for help and hold her hostage for several hours. Repeated threats against her brother had been enough to keep her from pressing charges later. She absently rubbed her palm over the scars on her chest, drifting back to that horrible night.

But two blunt-tipped fingers sneaked beneath Rosemary's chin and tipped her face up, forcing her back to the moment. Max's stern face hovered above hers. "Rosie, I'm not any good at guessing games or reading between the lines. You look me in the eye and tell me exactly what you want."

A dozen different wishes popped into her head. She wanted the memories of Richard's abuse erased from her mind and body. She wanted Max Krolikowski to kiss her again. No, she wanted the sober detective gently touching her skin to *want* to kiss her. She wanted the self-assurance that Richard had stolen from her so she could tell Max all the wishes running through her mind. She wanted her parents alive and her brother safely home from prison. Ultimately, though, there was only one thing that mattered.

"I want to feel safe."

With a firm nod, Max dismissed any further discussion. He picked up the toolbox and the trash bag and paused in front of her. "Then this guy won't get to you again. I'll need a key. I'll need you to do what I say, when I say it. And I'll need you to trust me."

"I know you mean that to be reassuring, but..." She trudged back into the house and locked the door when he indicated that he was heading around to the garage and she shouldn't remain outside by herself. She whispered against the door as she threw the dead bolt. "That's what Richard said, too."

CHAPTER SEVEN

MAX RECOGNIZED OLIVIA WATSON'S short, dark hair as she waited to get on the elevator at KCPD headquarters to report for their morning shift. Thank goodness. He hated running late.

Despite the throbbing in his temples left over from last night's trip to the Shamrock Bar, Max jogged across the foyer's marble tiles. "Hey, Liv. Hold the elevator."

"Good morning, Max." The brunette detective smiled a friendly greeting as he slipped in beside her and headed to the back railing. He leaned his hips against it, exhaling a deep breath. She pointed to the wraparound sunglasses he was still wearing. "The lights too bright in here for you?" she teased.

Great. Trent must have blabbed about him drowning his sorrows last night. And Liv here, like a mother hen to her boys on the Cold Case Squad, couldn't resist making sure he was all right. Max was a grown man, the oldest member of the team. He didn't need any mama or sister or busybody sticking her nose into his regrets. Time to play the old boyfriend/former-partner-who'd-nearly-ruined-her-career card. "Detective Cutie-Pie giving you any grief? Or do you still need me to punch him out for you?"

But Olivia refused the bait and punched the button for the third floor. "I think I finally got it through Detective Brower's thick skull that I don't love him, nor does he even remotely turn my head anymore." She raised her left hand and wiggled her fingers in front of his face. "Of course, the engagement ring Gabe gave me makes a clear statement as to where my heart and loyalties lie."

Max grabbed her wrist to get a better look at the respectable rock on the plain gold band on her third finger. "Hey, congratulations, kiddo." He let her go and leaned in to kiss her cheek. "So that pesky reporter is finally going to make an honest woman out of you."

"Gabe is not pesky."

Max shrugged. "I suppose he did help us catch a killer and put Leland Asher in prison. But reporters who bad-mouth the department still aren't my favorite people."

She leaned against the back wall beside him and jabbed him with her elbow. "Hey. Gabe has printed some nice things about KCPD now, too. He's honest. Always tells it like it is—whether it's good press or not. It's why I trust him. It's one of the things I love best about him."

He nudged her back. "As long as he makes you happy."

"He does."

If Max had any family besides his grandma, he'd wish it included an annoying "sister" like Olivia. Of course, she already had three big brothers, a father and grandfather looking out for her. If Gabe Knight passed muster with her family and she was genuinely happy with this guy, then so was Max. "Then I guess I'll put up with him."

"Do you own a suit and tie?"

He let his head fall back and groaned. "Why?"

"Because I'm inviting you to the wedding."

"You ask a lot of a man, don't you?"

"Only the ones I care about and respect." She reached over and tapped his cheek. "I like the clean-shaven look this morning. Remember how to do that for the wedding. What's the occasion?"

He was glad the elevator had stopped and the door was opening. He'd shaved for work more than once this week. Or maybe that was last week. Had he spruced up in an effort to redeem himself in the eyes of a certain critical redhead? "Hell."

Olivia followed him out into the morning bustle of the third-floor detectives' division as the shifts changed from third watch to first watch. "So what makes you grouchy with an extra side of cranky this morning?"

Trent Dixon was there to meet them as they checked in at the sergeant's desk. "One too many beers last night, I'll bet." Before Max guessed the younger man's intent, Trent had snatched the sunglasses off his face. "Yep. I swung by your apartment this morning to make sure you got here. But nobody answered."

Max snatched the glasses back and hooked them behind his neck. "Did you break in to see my bed hadn't been slept in?" he groused.

"That's for amateurs." He patted the shield on his belt. "I've got one of these, remember? All I had to do was ask nicely. Your super let me in." Trent and Olivia both grinned as they led the way past their desks to the break room for a morning cup of joe.

But Max knew his partner's concern was real. "I left early. Had an errand to run. I dozed a couple hours in my car."

"In your car?" When Max stopped in the hallway outside the break room, Trent and Olivia did, too. Trent was serious when he came back and clapped a hand on Max's shoulder. "But today's a new day?"

Max nodded. His annual Jimmy funk was out of his system—or at least relegated to the backseat in the carful of sticky issues he had to deal with. He looked from one detective to the other, letting them know this wasn't the hangover talking. "I think I got us a lead on the Richard Bratcher murder case. Not from the source you might expect. I was following up on it. Remember our little interview gone south yesterday?"

Trent snickered. "Rosemary March? Is she suing us? Filing harassment charges against you?"

Max rubbed his knuckles over the unfamiliar smoothness of his jaw. She probably would if he tried to kiss her again. Not that he had any plans to do so. In the sane, sober light of day, he…was wondering if any part of Rosie's gentle response had been real. Man, he was going to have to keep his wits about him and his hormones in check on this mission. "I'm going to be spending a lot of time with her over the next few days."

"Come again?" Trent asked.

They were all in cop mode now, listening.

"Turns out her dad was military, and she's latched

on to that aspect of me. She looked me up last night to help with a problem." He glibly skipped past the whole kissing, sparks flying, guilt trip gone sideways incident outside the Shamrock and filled them in on the vile message and rage-fueled destruction he'd tried to repair for her. "Rosie's stalker is legit. And he's escalating. She could turn out to be a good witness for us, but not if this guy gets to her first."

"Rosie?" Liv asked, looking to Trent for an explanation. "You mean Stephen March's sister?" Olivia had no love for Rosie's brother since his efforts to cover up the murder he'd committed had involved several attempts on Olivia and her new fiancé's life. "When did she become Rosie?"

With a shrug, Trent gestured to Max, indicating he had no clue why his partner would give a cutesy nickname to the person who'd been not only the prime suspect, but the only suspect, period, in the initial investigation of Richard Bratcher's murder six years ago.

"It's just what I call her, okay?" Max wasn't about to explain anything personal to either of them, especially since he couldn't pinpoint why *Rosemary* didn't seem to fit the woman who'd gotten so far under his skin yesterday. *Rosemary* was a murder suspect. A mission objective to be explored and dealt with.

Rosie was, well, he wasn't quite sure. And while part of him wanted to blame last night's kiss and desire to get involved with her problems on an unfortunate mix of beer, lust, loneliness and guilt, Max was afraid his connection to Rosie went a little deeper than a cop doing his duty. That whole band-of-brothers logic she'd used to justify seeking him out had only sealed the deal.

Whether he had his team's backing or not, he'd given his word that he would help Rosie unmask her stalker. But finding the bastard who terrorized a vulnerable woman would be a hell of a lot easier if he had the Cold Case Squad and resources of KCPD backing him up.

Ignoring the question, Max stuck with talking cop-speak to Trent and Olivia. *That* he understood. "The timing of these threats is suspect. Either someone connected to the murder is trying to point the finger at her to keep us from looking at them, or someone who knew Bratcher blames her for his death, and is punishing her for it since we haven't arrested anyone for the crime yet. I documented the evidence last night at her house. Rosie couldn't have done that kind of damage herself unless she was doped up on something. With her brother's history of drug abuse and an aversion to drinking, smoking and swearing, I'm guessing she doesn't get high."

"Wait a minute," Trent interrupted, nudging Max and Liv to a private corner as the hallway filled with A-shift cops reporting to the conference room for Morning Roll Call. "You went back to her house?"

"Would you believe she picked me up at the Shamrock Bar?" Trent's expression indicated not. "Close your mouth, junior." Here was the really incredulous part. "Apparently, Rosie thinks I can be her hero. Watching her house, doing what I can to catch this guy who's terrorizing her, should get me close enough to get the answers we need from her. I think she knows more names linked to Bratcher we haven't found yet. I believe she can give us leads that'll make this cold case hot again. If she can't break open this investigation for us, then I have a feeling the guy who's after her will." Max braced his hands at his waist, looking up to Trent and down at Liv to include them both. "I don't think I can do this on my own, though. I have to sleep sometime. Plus, I'll need a liaison to Katie—" the team's information specialist "—and all her records when I'm out in the field. And somebody has to be with Rosie 24/7 while I'm following up some of those leads."

"Whatever you need, brother," Trent offered. "If Miss March turns out to be the linchpin to this investigation, I'm sure Lieutenant Rafferty-Taylor will want the whole team involved."

Olivia agreed. "I'll go brief Jim." Jim Parker was her partner, another member of KCPD's Cold Case Squad. "Are you sure we can trust her, Max?"

"I didn't think so at first, but yeah. I think she's being straight with me." Max's measurements of the dents in the mailbox and light sconces made him think the perp's weapon of choice had been a metal baseball bat. If he'd chosen to take a swing at Rosie or one of the dogs defending her, KCPD would have been investigating something far more serious than vandalism. "I'm hoping my word is enough for you guys to let me run with this."

Liv nodded. "You guys covered for Gabe and me when we needed backup. So you know I'm there for you." When she reached up to brush an unseen greeblie off the shoulder of his shirt, Max wondered if he'd really needed neatening up, or if—with all the other detectives and uniforms filing into the room across the hall—that was her professional version of a supportive hug. "See you two at the morning meeting."

Max grabbed a cup of coffee and followed Trent into the conference room. Weaving through men and women gathered in conversations between the long, narrow tables facing the captain's podium, they found two open chairs near the back of the room.

Max had barely raised the paper cup to his lips when Trent slapped his leather folder on the table and leaned over to ask, "You sure you can do this? Yesterday, Rosemary March was a whack job, and today the *old prune* you couldn't wait to get away from is *Rosie*, and you're going to be her knight in shining armor. Why the change of heart?"

Max raised his gaze to the curious officer eavesdropping on their conversation from the opposite side of the table. The young man with the nosy intent turned out to be Hudson Kramer from the Shamrock Bar. "Did you score with that redhead last night, Krolikowski?"

"Sit down, junior, and mind your own business."

"You struck out, huh?" Grinning like a schoolkid, Kramer braced his hands on the table and leaned closer. "S'pose I could get her number?"

"No, I don't suppose you could." Raising his hands in mock surrender, the younger detective wisely turned away and took his seat before Max lowered his cup and glanced over at his partner. "You don't think I can handle this mission…er, assignment?"

"Max, you are the toughest SOB I know. You can make anything work if you set your mind to it." Trent rested an elbow on the table and thumped Max in the chest. "But I also know you're a pussycat in there. Your emotions get the better of you sometimes. Hell, if Kramer's razzing can rile you, then I've got to wonder just what Rosemary March means to you."

"She's a solid lead on our case. And somebody's got her in his sights." Max downed another sip of the hot brew. "I'm protecting a potential witness. I'm doing my job."

"Uh-huh. I can deal with the crazy guy once a year on the anniversary of Jimmy's death, and cover for you." The conversations around the room receded into background noise when Trent dropped his voice to a whisper. "But if you don't do some healing, if digging up Rosemary's secrets is going to keep you stressed around the clock and you start flipping out again, the lieutenant is going to order a mandatory psych eval on you. You could get suspended if you wig out on the job again, or you start hitting the Shamrock every night. You're too good a cop for that—too good a man. I don't want to see you lose it."

"That's mostly why I'm doin' it." Yeah, as if stepping up to be that pretty, prickly woman's bodyguard was some kind of therapy for him. More like penance. Still, it felt like the right thing to do. "I didn't save Jimmy." Max sat up at attention, his posture reflecting his resolve. "But I'm damn straight going to save her. I'm gonna make things right in this world for once."

"And solve Bratcher's murder?"

Captain Hendricks took his place at the podium and the room instantly quieted. The black man swept his gaze across the room, greeting them all. "Good morning."

"Yeah. Sure," Max muttered beneath the other officers' responses. "That's the idea."

An hour later Max was on his second meeting of the day and his third cup of coffee, sitting through a Skype call between drug research expert and CEO Dr. Hillary Wells of Endicott Global, a drug company based in the KC area, and the other members of the Cold Case Squad.

The brunette woman with short hair and a white lab coat over the business suit she wore filled up the viewing screen in Ginny Rafferty-Taylor's office. Lieutenant Rafferty-Taylor was the veteran detective who headed up the Cold Case Squad. Dr. Wells and the lieutenant seemed to be about the same age, and both were successful professional women. That was probably why Dr. Wells's answers were all directed to the lieutenant. Everyone else in the room seemed to be beneath her time and interest.

"RUD-317 is a cancer-fighting drug," the woman on the screen explained. She seemed more interested in fiddling with the jar of hand cream on her desk than in the interview. "It's not for recreational use."

"Our victim wasn't a cancer patient, Doctor," the lieutenant clarified. "And if he used drugs recreationally, he kept it private. We have no arrests or complaints on record."

"His file says he was a smoker," Trent pointed out. "Is it possible our guy got private treatment? A diagnosis in a foreign country not in his US records? He had money. Maybe the cure worked."

Dr. Wells barely spared a glance for Max's partner. "It's possible. RUD-317 is available in other countries." She glanced down at her notes on her office desk. "I'd have to double-check the status to see if that was true six years ago." She raised her dark eyes to Lieutenant Rafferty-Taylor again. "We've never seen side effects like you describe with RUD-317. I wonder if your victim had an allergic reaction to something in the formula. Or perhaps there was a bad combination of drugs in his system. We do have specific protocols in place for using the RUD products."

The lieutenant might be a petite little blonde, but she was tough as nails, and Max respected her for it. She wasn't going to let the other woman dismiss their case. "Dr. Wells, there are too many other circumstances related to the death of this particular victim for KCPD to readily dismiss it as an accidental drug overdose. We're looking at it as a homicide."

"I see." Dr. Wells jotted something on her notes. "If you fax me a copy of the medical examiner's report, I'd be happy to take a look at it to confirm her conclusions or add to it if any discrepancies jump out at me."

"We'll do that. Thank you, Dr. Wells."

The brunette woman leaned toward the camera, her face filling the screen. "I'd certainly hate for bad publicity surrounding one of Endicott Global's medical products to get out. Trust me, the board of directors is always on me about maintaining Endicott's public image. If one of our company's drugs was used to commit a murder,

I want to know about it. Its misuse might require altering our product labeling and warnings so it doesn't happen again accidentally. We might even have to pull the drug off the market. You know how prevalent lawsuits are nowadays. People can make a fortune and ruin a company that does good work."

Max shifted uncomfortably in his seat at the mention of lawsuits. They were nothing but trouble. It didn't look as though Miss Rosie Posy's nine million dollars were doing her any good.

"I'll have one of my detectives get in touch with you to follow up."

The lieutenant ended the call and Max was back to justifying his plan to the other members of the Cold Case Squad. "Rosemary March wouldn't give us anything yesterday," he explained. "She's not that comfortable with cops."

Lieutenant Rafferty-Taylor arched a silvery-blond eyebrow at him. "So what's your *in*?"

He looked to the woman sitting at the head of the conference table and shrugged. "I remind her of her dad."

"Ouch." Jim Parker, Olivia's partner and the newest member of the team, made a face across the table. "You're not that much older than she is. That has to be hard on the ego."

Max skimmed his hand over the top of his jarhead haircut. "Former military."

Jim got serious and nodded his understanding. "She trusted her father, and so she trusts you."

"Something like that." Max set his cup down beside the stack of case files in front of him and pulled out a photograph of Richard Bratcher to set on top. "I believe she's as anxious to solve Bratcher's murder as we are. This guy made her life hell when he was alive. He's been dead six years and he's still doing the same."

Olivia Watson rested her elbows on the table and leaned forward. "And she thinks finding the killer will make her stalker go away? Could whoever is after her be the real murderer, trying to frame her?"

"That's one idea I had," Max agreed. "Either that, or we've got an unsub who thinks she did it and got away with killing Bratcher."

"So, we need to be interviewing people who were close to Bratcher besides the Marches." Olivia sat back. "Do we have anyone on that list?"

"I'm working the stalker angle." Katie Rinaldi, the brunette information specialist assigned to the team, looked up from her laptop at the far end of the table. "I've been surfing social media sites, trying to track down the pictures Miss March alleges were taken of her when she visited her brother in Jeff City."

"Find anything?" Max asked, suspecting that Rosie was a private enough woman that she wouldn't willingly put herself out on the internet.

Katie's ponytail bobbed behind her as she shook her head. "Nothing yet except for some newspaper photos related to winning that settlement on her parents' behalf, Mr. Bratcher's death and her brother's sentencing for murder." She lifted her blue eyes to include everyone around the table. "But I'm just getting started. I've got some facial recognition software I'll plug in and run against other sites. If her stalker posted pics anywhere, I'll find them and forward the info to your phones and computers."

"Good idea," Jim said, his expression turning grim. "That's how those crooked cops down in Falls City where I worked undercover tracked down my wife. Through a simple picture from our first date she posted online. This guy ain't playin' if he's gotten that close to your witness."

Lieutenant Rafferty-Taylor agreed. "That's a good strategy, Katie. If there are unsanctioned pictures of Miss March online, I want to know who put them there."

"Yes, ma'am."

The lieutenant turned her attention to the big man sitting beside Max. "Trent, let's get those written threats and telephone messages Miss March has received in for analysis. See if any of them are traceable."

"Will do."

Max nodded, appreciating the team following his lead and treating Rosie as a threatened witness instead of a suspect. He tapped the case files on the table in front of him. "I talked her into coming in this morning to look at some photos from known associates of Leland Asher and the vic. Maybe she can ID the guy she saw that way."

Ginny Rafferty-Taylor was a sharp thinker who'd solved several homicide investigations before accepting the promotion to head up the Cold Case Squad. She allowed her team to run with their instincts but demanded their ideas be backed up with hard facts. "We're still working on the theory that several of KCPD's unsolved cases are related?"

They'd had this same discussion several months earlier, when Olivia had closed the six-year-old murder of Danielle Reese, the investigative reporter Stephen March had killed—the crime he was now serving time for in Jefferson City. Although Max's focus was on one woman and one case, he had to agree the idea of connected murders had merit. "It could have happened that way. The Marches had a strong motive for eliminating Richard Bratcher, yet Rosie lacked the means and Stephen lacked the opportunity. We've got Stephen March for murdering Ms. Reese even though Leland Asher and his organization are the ones with the motive for killing her. Asher had an alibi for the night of that murder."

The lieutenant tucked a short, silvery-blond lock behind her ear. "Does Asher have an alibi for the night of Bratcher's murder?"

"I'd love to ask him," Olivia volunteered. "I hate that he's serving a mere two years in prison. Maybe we can make his stay more permanent. If he's behind any of this, we should be able to get a list of contacts he's had recently. Jim and I can look at the prison's visitor logs."

Jim nodded. "We'll find out who he's close to on the inside, too."

Katie Rinaldi tapped her finger against her lips. "It's like that Hitchcock movie, *Strangers on a Train*—you kill the person I want dead and I'll kill yours, and no one will ever be able to prove a thing."

The possibility of the seemingly unrelated murders having a common link had been Olivia's idea to begin with. "There has to be a connection between Leland Asher and the Marches or Bratcher we can find."

Katie ran with the idea. "What if there's a third murder involved that connects everything? Or a fourth or a fifth?"

Trent rolled his chair away from the table and spun toward Katie. "Why don't we stay away from the movies and focus on reality. If we can get Rosemary March on board, I'm sure we can find facts to solve Bratcher's murder and make our case."

Bristling at the criticism, Katie put her hands back on the keyboard and typed a note. "I'll do the research in my spare time—start cross-checking all unsolved murders from the last decade or so. If I find something… *when* I find where those unsolved murders overlap, I'll let you know."

"When do you have spare time?" Trent grumbled. "You're either working or doing something with Tyler and your family or doing one of those stupid plays."

"It's a hobby." Katie's eyes flashed with temper, although her tone remained politely articulate. "And I've made some new friends by getting involved with the community theater. I'm allowed to have a hobby."

Not when it took time away from any possibility of Trent and the single mom spending time together rekindling their high school sweetheart relationship. Max turned away to hide the shaking of his head, happy to leave the soap opera of young love to those who had the energy and fortitude to deal with it. Cupid could just keep his arrows away from a confirmed ol' bachelor like him, and let him do his job and get from one day to the next without any more hassle than necessary.

And yet... Max looked through the window separating Lieutenant Rafferty-Taylor's office from the main floor and saw Rosie March and a tall guy in a fancy suit following one of the uniforms past the maze of detectives' desks toward a row of interview rooms. He was half-aware of other strategies being discussed around the table, of assignments being given. But he was more aware of how the bright flowers printed on Rosie's black dress warmed the pale perfection of her skin. Although the high neckline and modest hem of the sleeveless dress covered up all the interesting bits of her figure, and that old-lady bun at her nape made his fingers itch to free her hair again, there was a distinctive tightening behind his zipper that couldn't be blamed on the desire to drown his sorrows in alcohol or any willing woman this morning.

Stone-cold sober, the dutiful daughter of a colonel was still gettin' to him like an irritation beneath his skin. Could he be just as distracted by the undercurrents of tension between him and Rosie as those that had flared between Trent and Katie a few moments earlier?

Apparently so. Max's hand curled into a fist beneath the table when Rosie startled and drifted back a step, hugging that long shoulder bag to her chest as Hudson Kramer jumped up from his desk to greet her and the suit guy with the silver sideburns. The irritation running beneath Max's collar felt an awful lot like jealousy when he saw Kramer turning on the charm. What did that kid see in Rosie? Was Kramer into that cougar thing? Did he have a penchant for redheads? Or...

Nine million dollars?

The other hand fisted beneath the table. If Hud Kramer had recognized Rosie from the newspaper and thought he could sweet-talk his way into a few dates and a little payout—

"Brother." Trent clamped a hand down on the arm of Max's chair and shook him out of his glowering stare. His partner was kind enough to point toward Lieutenant Rafferty-Taylor, who'd also noticed his straying focus.

With a nod to Max, silently welcoming him back to the meeting, the petite lieutenant continued her summary. "Let's follow up on the toxin that killed Bratcher, too. Sooner rather than later. Endicott Global is big business. If they're worried about bad publicity that might come from being tied to Bratcher's murder, I don't want to give Hillary Wells or anyone else there a chance to scrub their records from six years ago." The lieutenant glanced at the notes on her computer screen. "And if they can give us new information that might not show up on the ME's report, I want to know that, too. With Jim and Liv on the road to Jefferson City, and Trent on forensic evidence detail, Max, I'll leave that to you?"

He jotted the directive in his notebook. "Yes, ma'am."

The lieutenant closed her laptop and stood. "Very well. You've got point on this, Max. Get whatever you can out of Miss March. Use Trent as your contact, and keep us in the loop for any kind of backup or research you need."

Max nodded, then pushed his chair back the moment

they were dismissed, eager to get to Rosie to verify that the plan they'd agreed to last night was still in place. He scooped photos and reports and stuffed the files into his binder to sort out later.

He hadn't even made it around the corner of the table when he stopped in his tracks. But it wasn't the young stud wannabe chatting up Rosie that rankled this time. "Who does that guy who came in with Rosie look like to you?"

"An attorney?"

Max picked up the photo of Richard Bratcher and tossed it onto the table in front of Trent. "Look again."

Trent picked up the picture and whistled under his breath. "An older version of our vic. Now that's awkward." He rose to his feet beside Max. "They're looking pretty chummy. You think the two of them could have plotted together to kill Richard?"

Max didn't want to think that Rosie had plotted anything. But a partner in crime turning on her could certainly explain the stalker. A man who wanted revenge on the woman he thought killed his brother would, too. "I think I'd better go introduce myself."

Trent grinned as Max headed out the door. "Call me if she throws something at you or threatens a lawsuit."

Hud Kramer took the stack of mug shot books the uniformed officer had been carrying, and led Rosie and the other man to the closest interview room. Max dumped his binder on his desk, ignoring the papers that spilled out, and quickened his stride to catch up to the group when Rosie hesitated in the doorway and the ringer for their dead guy nudged her on inside.

"She's not going to like that little room," Max muttered, catching the door before it closed in his face. He pushed it open and stepped inside, looking first to those pretty gray eyes that zeroed in on him and widened before her gaze shuttered and she looked down at the table that cut the room in half. Hell. He'd agreed to help her, hadn't he? Why was she still shying away from him? More important, why did it bother him so much that she did? Max turned his attention to Kramer. "I've got this."

"I was just doing the heavy lifting." Seriously? The younger detective made a point of flexing his muscles when he set down the thick books. "I was keeping the lady occupied until you got out of your meeting."

Max pointed a thumb over his shoulder. "Get out of here and go do some real police work."

"Yes, sir. Bye, ma'am." He winked at Rosie on his way out, earning a soft smile.

"Thank you, Detective Kramer," she answered. Max's groan of annoyance faded when Rosie lifted her gaze to him again. Better. He liked it when he could see into the cool depths of those pretty eyes. But that look was far from a come-on, and her succinct tone reminded him of the reason she was here. "Good morning, Max."

"Morning. You want to introduce me to your friend?"

"Of course." She gestured to the man beside her. "Detective Krolikowski—this is my attorney, Howard Bratcher."

Max extended his hand but hesitated midintroduction. This guy was definitely going on the suspect list. "Bratcher?"

The attorney sealed the handshake. Firmer than Max

had expected. But Howard Bratcher quickly withdrew his hand to stand beside Rosie. "Yes. I'm Richard's brother. I know KCPD has reopened the investigation into his murder. Believe me, Detective, I'm as anxious as Rosemary to identify his killer and clear her name. Richard was an embarrassment to my father, and our law firm. There was no love lost between us. Rosemary's parents were clients of my father's, and she's been my friend and a client of the firm for several years. I'm here for her, not Richard."

Old family friends, hmm? Or something more? Howard slipped his arm behind Rosie's back, and her shoulders stiffened. Max's brewing suspicions edged into something more protective when she turned out of Bratcher's embrace and wound up facing the corner of the room. She reached out and brushed her fingertips across the back wall, and Max wondered if the word *trapped* was going through her mind again.

"Rosemary? I thought this might be a needlessly upsetting errand." Ah, hell. Was this guy thinking he could manipulate Rosie—and her money—the way his younger brother had? Despite his disclaimer, did Bratcher blame Rosie for his brother's murder and think she owed him some kind of payback? The solicitous attorney reached for her. "Would you like me to take you home?"

She wanted his protection? Max pulled out a chair and propped his foot on it, casually sitting back on the tabletop—purposefully blocking the attorney's path to Rosie. "She told you about the damage done to her house last night?"

The attorney pulled up short, his gaze dropping to the chair, then back up to Max. He was probably trying to figure out whether the lumbering detective was clueless, rude or smarter than he'd given him credit for. *That's right, buddy. It's the last one.* Howard Bratcher backed off a step and faced Max. "Yes. That's why I insisted on driving her here today."

Max's gaze went to the soft gray eyes that watched him from the corner of the room now. "Rosie's got her own car. She's perfectly capable of driving herself."

The attorney's eyes narrowed. "We've been close for several years, Detective. I'm concerned for her welfare."

How close? "Did you see the man who was taking pictures of her at the prison?"

"I didn't see anyone taking pictures."

Rosie stepped forward, grasping the back of the chair. "The man with the cell phone? I pointed him out to you. Described him as a lawyer-type guy?"

"I recall your amusing description, but—"

"You didn't stop to take a good look at the man who upset your close friend?" Max challenged.

"I don't remember."

Rosie's hopeful gaze crashed at Howard's noncommittal answer.

If this self-absorbed wise guy was her ally, no wonder she'd sought Max out for help. Even half-toasted, he'd paid attention to the details this bozo had missed. Unless Howie here had missed them on purpose. Could he be behind this terror campaign? Max's ability to read people might be on the fritz, but logic alone told him that a longtime friend would know best what kinds of things could frighten a woman the most.

For a split second, Max understood Rosie's aversion to being confined inside a small space. Especially with Mr. I'll-support-you-as-long-as-I'm-in-charge using up so much breathable air. With so-called friends like Bratcher here, Max wondered how much of Rosie's isolation had to do with her past, and how much had to do with her fear of getting *trapped* in another relationship with someone who, even without similar looks, had to remind her a lot of her dead ex-fiancé.

Following an instinct as ornery and strong as the urge to kiss her last night had been, Max snatched her hand, kicked the chair under the table and pulled her past the tailored suit. "Come with me, Rosie."

"Where are we going?"

He opened the door, picked up the mug shot books and tightened his grip around her protesting fingers as he led her into the familiar bustle of the main room.

Howard's snort of derision followed them out the door. "Shouldn't you address her as Miss March, Detective?"

Shouldn't you recuse yourself from serving as her attorney, Howie?

Max kept his snarky remark to himself and pulled Rosie around chairs and desks, colleagues and computer towers, suspects and complainants in for questioning and statements, until he reached the two desks pushed together where he and Trent worked. He dumped the notebooks on top of the blotter and pushed aside the mess of notes and files before pulling out his chair for her.

"It can get noisy out here, but you'll have plenty of space to spread out. Move anything you want that's in your way." She paused, tilting her face to his, no doubt questioning his sudden bout of chivalry—maybe even questioning if he was the same man she'd recruited for bodyguard duty last night. But the grief and guilt over Jimmy's death was firmly contained today. He hoped. Taking care of Rosie March—keeping her safe from stalkers and pompous attorneys and wannabe boyfriends—was his mission now. Flattening his hand at the small of her back, he urged her to sit. "I apologize for the clutter, but as you can see, there are no walls here. Those interview rooms are all tiny."

When her lips curved into a serene smile, Max nearly succumbed to the boyish urge to smile in return. "I can work here just fine. Thank you."

The crown of her hair brushed past his nose as she moved into the chair, and Max couldn't help but take a deep breath of her sweet, summery scent. A man could get addicted to Rosie's fragrance. Who was he kidding? Old maid bun and conservative clothes aside, Rosie March turned him on like some kind of crazy aphrodisiac. Maybe because he kept thinking of what she'd be like without the severe hairstyle and all that skin covered up.

Reminding himself that she was an assignment, and that she had more of a relationship with her dogs than she did with him, Max pulled the first mug shot book in front of her. "Here you go."

Her shoulders lifted with a resolute sigh and she flipped over the cover to look at the first six men. "So I just start turning pages to see if I recognize anyone who might have been watching me at the prison?"

"Or anywhere else. Unfortunately, we have even more photos you could look at, but I narrowed down the suspect pool to men with a history of harassment and other predatory crimes who fit the general description you gave." He left out the fact that pictures of Leland Asher and his known associates were scattered throughout the books, as well. If the crime boss was behind Richard Bratcher's murder or the threats against Rosie, she'd have to make the connection herself for any kind of case against him to stick. And if she recognized anyone who might be working for Howie here... Max tossed one of the books over to Trent's neat desk. "There, Howie. You can look through some of our pics, too. See if anyone there jogs your memory from the prison waiting room."

Not that he'd trust Bratcher's recognition, or lack thereof, of anyone in the book. But it would get the attorney farther out of Rosie's personal space.

Instead of taking the hint and moving to Trent's work space, Howard circled behind him to bookend the other side of Rosie's chair. "I don't like your tone, Detective Krolikowski. And I'd appreciate it if you'd show my client more respect."

"I've got nothing but respect for Miss March." Max leaned his hip against the edge of the desk, facing the woman between them. She was picking up the papers of an old report that had fanned across the desk and

tucking them into a neat stack. "You got a key for me?"
Max asked.

Howard put a hand on Rosie's shoulder. "What's he
talking about?"

"This is between the lady and me." Although the
dots of color on her cheeks made him wonder if she
was going to renege on the deal they'd made. "Rosie?
Do you remember my terms?"

Do what I say. When I say it. Trust me. If Jimmy had
trusted him enough to share how bad things really were,
then maybe Max could have gotten him help. He could
have been there for his friend. He could have taken the
gun away from him. He could have saved—

"I haven't forgotten." Rosie interrupted the guilty
gloom of his thoughts and set aside the neat stack of
papers before reaching into her purse. She pulled out
a single key and laid it in his outstretched palm. Her
fingers lingered a little longer, dotting his skin with
warmth. Her upturned gaze locked on to his for a moment, as if she sensed that he'd checked out for a split
second. "This was Stephen's. It will get you in the back
entrance."

With Rosie unexpectedly pulling him back to the
present, Max frowned, curling the key into his palm,
catching her fingers in a quick squeeze before she drew
away. "Not the main part of the house? Do I at least get
access codes?"

The heat faded from her cheeks. "The apartment has
a separate entrance. It's not hooked up to the alarm system. I didn't think you'd—"

"We'll make it work," Max interrupted when he saw

Howard Bratcher leaning in to intervene. "I'll see you there on my lunch break."

"So soon?"

"I'm a soldier, remember? I travel light."

Howie's hand settled on her shoulder. "Rosemary, what is this detective talking about?"

Max stood to face him, squaring off over the top of Rosie's coppery bun. "Didn't she tell ya? We're moving in together."

"Excuse me?" Uh-huh. The touching? The temper? This guy thought he and Rosie were more than friends. He at least thought he could control her actions and influence her decisions.

Shrugging off her attorney's hand, Rosie went to work pulling items from beneath the three mug shot books and straightening the rest of his desk. "Max is moving into my downstairs apartment."

"That's right, Howie. I'm her new tenant." He had his story all worked out. "Good part of town. Use of a pool. My building is being renovated. Renting a couple of rooms costs less than staying in a hotel. And Rosie didn't seem to mind having a little extra security around the house."

"I see. Why didn't you tell me you were taking on a new tenant?"

Rosie's busy hands stopped. "Because it didn't concern you. My name has been in the papers, Howard. You said it yourself. *Kansas City's newest millionaire?* And now these threats?" She tilted her face up to her attorney. "Even with the security system you had me install, I've never really felt safe being there by myself.

Duchess is getting older. Trixie makes a lot of noise but isn't a real threat to anyone. I really didn't think having a cop on the premises at night could hurt."

Howard knelt down beside the chair, pulling Rosie's hand into his. "You know I have connections to private security firms across the city. I could have hired someone if I'd known how truly frightened you were."

"I did tell you. I told Detective Krolikowski, too." She pulled her hand away and glanced over at Max before busying her hands again. "He listened."

Tell him, honey. Rosie March isn't alone and vulnerable anymore.

Howard pushed to his feet. That was not a friendly look. "You know I have only your best interests at heart, Rosemary."

"I know," Rosie answered. "And I'm grateful for all you've done for me. But I need to do this for myself. I need to do more to make decisions and handle my own problems."

"I see."

"Maybe you should go back to your office, Bratcher," Max suggested. "This may take a while. I can give Rosie a ride home. After all, we're heading to the same place."

"I'll be keeping an eye on you, Krolikowski. If you take advantage of Rosemary in any way, I will have your badge. And know I'll be asking around to find out what kind of cop you really are."

"Detective?" a quivering voice asked.

Max propped his hands at his waist, ready to take

whatever threat this blowhard threw at him. "I intend to make sure no one takes advantage of her in any way."

"If you're using Rosemary as some kind of pawn in your investigation—"

"Max."

Rosie's sharp voice demanded his attention. "What is it?"

He braced a palm on the desk and leaned in to see what had alarmed her.

She held a picture that had fallen out of his file on Leland Asher. A picture of Asher and his entourage from a hoity-toity society event at the Nelson-Atkins Museum of Art. Only, Rosie wasn't pointing to the crime boss. She was pointing to the younger, shorter man with glasses standing on the other side of Asher's date.

"I know him. This is the man from the prison."

CHAPTER EIGHT

ROSEMARY WONDERED HOW she was ever going to survive the first night with Max Krolikowski living in her basement.

If she couldn't stop this restless pacing, flitting from one room to the next, she'd never get any sleep. She'd start a project in the library, leave it at the first unfamiliar noise and wind up in the kitchen, refreshing the dogs' water bowls. She'd hear the muffled voices of a television newscast through the floorboards, then head off to the front room to adjust the blinds. She'd peek out a window to look at the clouds gathering in the sky and covering the moon, but she'd hear the rumble of thunder in the distance and go back to the kitchen to make sure it was Mother Nature talking and not her new tenant grumbling about something downstairs. Then the dogs would woof at something outside and the whole anxious cycle would start over again.

Max's Cold Case Squad hadn't been able to immediately identify the man in the picture with Leland Asher, since he didn't have a record and wasn't in their criminal database. But she was certain the narrow-framed glasses and nondescript brown hair belonged to the man who'd smiled and taken her picture at the penitentiary.

Knowing there was a mystery man out there somewhere, bent on terrorizing her, who might or might not
have some connection to organized crime, was upsetting enough. But adding in the disruption of having a
man on the premises once again, a man who seemed
to occupy her thoughts the way Max did, left her unable to find any sense of calm or control. Routine, and
the secure normalcy that went with it, had flown out
the window.

Max had probably only needed a few minutes to put
away the items he'd brought in his backpack and duffel
bag and familiarize himself with the bedroom, bathroom and kitchenette, which he said would serve him
just fine. And why wouldn't the man just go to bed already? One time she'd discovered Max out front, install-
ing the new glass globes on her porch lights.

"The weatherman says we're having thunderstorms
tonight," she warned.

"I know." He continued his work, sounding far too
nonchalant about making himself at home here. "I
want to make sure everything is secure before I head
to bed." He nodded for her to go back inside. "But you
go ahead."

Much later, she peeked out the door to find him re-
clining in her rocking chair, sitting in the dark with his
big booted feet crossed on the porch railing. His shirt
hung unbuttoned and loose from his shoulders, the tails
flapping in the breeze that was picking up as lightning
flashed in the clouds overhead. He still wore his gun
and badge on his belt, and a stubby, unlit cigar that made

him look like the gruff Army sergeant he'd once been was tucked into the corner of his mouth.

"Go to sleep, Rosie," he'd ordered, before removing the cigar and turning those watchful blue eyes to catch her spying on him. "You're safe."

Safe from her stalker, maybe. There'd been no phone call, no threat, no visit from anyone who wanted to hurt her for twenty-four hours now. But she wasn't so safe from the curious attraction she felt toward the unrefined yet inarguably masculine detective. And she certainly wasn't safe from the troubling memories of being alone with another man who'd turned her home into a prison where he'd inflicted pain and fear until fate alone had allowed her to escape.

"You won't bring that cigar into the house, will you?"

"No, ma'am."

Her fingers curled and uncurled around the edge of the door. "You need your sleep, too."

"Good night, Rosie."

Rosemary locked herself in her bedroom after that, counting down the hour until she heard the apartment door open and close at the back of the house. Duchess sat up from her cozy pillow beside Rosemary's bed, and Trixie yipped at the unfamiliar sound.

Lightning flashed and thunder rattled the window panes. A few seconds later the rain poured down, whipping through the trees and drumming on the new roof, finally drowning out the sounds of the house and the man in the room below hers.

"Settle down, girls," she whispered. "It's just a storm." The dogs curled into their respective beds and fell asleep long before Rosie turned out the bedside lamp and crawled beneath the sheet and quilt.

But it was hard to follow her own admonishment. Normally, the sounds of a summer storm lulled her into relaxing, but her sleep was disrupted by memories of the moonlight gleaming through the golden hair that dusted Max's muscular chest, and the desire to run her fingers there to discover the heat only hinted at when she'd touched him through his shirt. She remembered that kiss, too, and the way his hands had moved with such urgency through her hair. Maybe he'd put his hands in other places, skim them over her skin and pull her against all that brawny strength and heat. Maybe he'd kiss her again, and this time he wouldn't hold back. Maybe she wouldn't hold back, either.

Later, the bold wishes that filled her dreams and left her perspiring and uncomfortable in her crisp cotton sheets mutated into darker, more disturbing images.

Max's tawny jaw and imposing shoulders gave way to a shadow that was taller, slimmer, darker than the night. Rosemary squirmed in the tangle of covers as the shadow darted past her window. The black figure swirled around the walls of her bedroom, spinning closer, moving so fast that the sea of black miasma soon surrounded her bed. She moaned in her sleep as the blackness closed in all around her, stealing away the light, robbing her of warmth.

Her breathing quickened as the chill permeated her skin. But her arm was too weak to push it away. The darkness consumed her, reached right into her very heart and ripped it from her chest. Then she was burning, bleeding, begging for a reprieve.

A tiny circle of light flared in the darkness and a voice laughed. The tiny light was a fire, glowing brighter, hotter with every breath. She was powerless to move, powerless to do anything but anticipate the coming pain. Laughter rang through the darkness as the fire moved closer and closer, until the hot ember hissed against her cold skin, branding her.

Rosemary came awake screaming. She shot up in bed, her hand clutching at the scars on her collarbone, her heart pounding in her chest. In the instant she realized the torture had been a dream, the instant she realized the shadows were no more than one of the Dinkles' trees, silhouetted by lightning against her window shade, the instant she realized she was perfectly fine and lowered her hand, she realized the laughter was real. High-pitched. Distorted. Distant.

The threat was real.

Duchess was on her feet, growling at the window. Trixie jumped onto the bed and barked. The repetitive laughter, fading in and out like a clown running in circles, was coming from outside in the storm.

"Max?" Fear hammered her pulse in her ears. She needed Max.

A clap of thunder slammed like a door in the distance, and Rosemary jumped inside her skin. "Rosie?" She heard a rapid knocking, like gunshots at her back door. "Rosie!"

"Max?" Rosemary quickly kicked away the covers twisted around her legs and slid off the edge of the bed. She pulled her sleep shirt down to her thighs and crossed to the door. "I'm coming!" But the laughter started up again behind her and she froze. It grew louder, tinnier. The knocking at her back door stopped and a chill skittered down her spine.

Grabbing Duchess's collar as she walked past, Rosemary went to the window. With her heart in her throat, she pulled back the curtain and peeked between the shade and the sill. Lightning flashed and she jumped back from the faceless figure in a black hood standing there.

She screamed again.

A deeper voice shouted outside in the storm. "KCPD! Get on the ground!" The laughter stopped abruptly and when the next bolt of lightning flashed, her window was empty. She saw a blur of movement in the blowing rain as she dropped the curtain and backed away. She heard a familiar grumble of curses.

"Max!" she shouted. What was he doing? If the intruder could threaten her dogs and terrorize her, what would he do to Max? What if he bashed in Max's head with that baseball bat? Would he kill the detective guarding her? Then who would stop him from coming after her? Saving Max was imperative to saving herself. Saving Max was imperative, period. "Max?" Tripping over the excited barking dogs, Rosemary turned and ran. Her fingers fumbled with the stupid lock on her door before she finally opened the thing and slung it open. "Max!"

The wood floor was cold beneath her bare feet, the kitchen tile even colder. She ran through the darkened house but skidded to a stop and abruptly changed course at the furious sound of knocking at her front door now. "Rosie!" He was safe. She would be safe. "Open the damn door! Rosie! Answer me!"

"I'm here. Is he out there? Did you catch him?"

"Rosie!"

She punched in the alarm code, unhooked the chain and dead bolt, turned the knob. Max jerked the storm door from her grasp the moment she'd turned its lock. The blowing rain whooshed in sideways around him, splashing her face and shirt before he pushed her back inside the foyer.

"You've got too many damn locks. I couldn't get to you." While he griped away, she ran straight into his arms, pressing her cheek against the wet skin of his chest, sliding her hands beneath his soggy shirttails and linking them together at the back of his waist. He walked her back another couple of steps, shutting the steel door behind him. "I lost him. You have to answer me when I call you. You can't scream like that and not answer… Okay." Once the adrenaline was out of his system, once he realized how she shuddered against him, clinging tightly to his strength and heat, he curled one arm behind her back and set his gun on the front hall table with the other. His growly tone softened. "Okay, honey." He reached behind him to throw the bolt yet never let go. Then he came back to wrap both arms around her and nestle his jaw at the crown of her hair. She willingly rocked back and forth as his chest expanded and contracted against her after the exertion of chasing a shadow through the storm. "I'm gettin' you all wet."

She shook her head against the strong beat of his heart. "I don't care."

He pulled her sleep-tossed hair from the neckline of her pink T-shirt, smoothing it down her back in gentle strokes. "You're okay. He's gone."

"Did he hurt you?" A crisp wet curl of chest hair tickled her lips. A muscle quivered beneath the unintended caress.

"Me? Nah, I'm too tough for that kind of thing. Are *you* hurt?" He sifted his fingers through her hair until his warm, callous palm cupped the nape of her neck. "Ah, hell, honey. Your skin's like ice." He shifted his stance then, curling his shoulders around her, rubbing his hands up and down her back. "I heard a noise and saw that guy outside your window, but I lost him in the rain once he jumped the Dinkles' hedge out front. And it's way too dark to be firing blindly into shadows. I didn't want to take the time away from you to do a search, in case he doubled back and broke in. I couldn't risk leaving you alone."

Rosemary's shirt and panties were slowly soaking up the moisture from his rain-soaked clothes. But the furnace of heat on the other side of those wet jeans and unbuttoned shirt that he must have hastily tossed on seeped right through the layers of damp material, warming her skin and easing her panic.

Once they were both breathing normally again, he pressed his lips against her temple before easing some space between them, although he continued rubbing his hands up and down her back and the arms she crossed between them. "Tell me what happened."

She watched the rain from his scalp run in rivulets down to his scruffy jaw, pooling at the tip of his chin before dripping onto her arm. "I had a nightmare."

His hands stopped their massage and squeezed her shoulders, demanding she meet his concerned gaze. "Uh-uh. That guy was real. Standard-issue hoodie and dark jeans. At least six feet tall. Wish I'd taken the time to grab my flashlight so I could have seen his face."

The cop was returning. The warmth was leaving. Rosemary hugged her arms more tightly around her waist, suddenly self-conscious to be standing toes to toes in a puddle in her foyer wearing little more than her long pink T-shirt. A wet T-shirt now. Not that she had any illusions about turning Max's head, but she didn't want to embarrass him, either. "I was dreaming of things Richard did to me. When I woke up, that man was at my window. For a split second, I thought…" She shrugged away from Max's touch and shivered. "It was the same man who vandalized my porch. I'm sure of it."

"Your scream woke me. When I got outside, I heard that crazy caterwauling." He picked up his gun and tucked it into the back of his jeans before scrubbing his fingers over his chin and wiping the moisture on the front of his shirt. Was she really still standing there, staring at the glistening wet skin of his chest? "Sorry," he apologized, mistaking her fascinated longing for some kind of effrontery. His big fingers fumbled to pull the soggy cotton together over the hills and hollows of muscle and hook a few buttons to the placket.

"He's long gone. There were footprints beneath the sill. I went back to snap a picture, but they're washing away." Max reached into his shirt pocket and pulled out a little red plastic box. "I found this out there in the grass." He pushed a button, and a warped recording of laughter played.

Rosemary recoiled from the sound. "That's what I heard."

"It's cheap. A noisemaker from a party store. Sounds as though there's water in the mechanism. With the storm, there's no way we're getting fingerprints off this thing. Maybe on the inside, though. Looks like there's something wedged in there. Do you have a plastic bag?" Although she missed the warmth of his body pressed against hers, she knew this businesslike interchange was more important than her own foolish cravings for physical contact. Tucking her hair behind her ears, she nodded. The dogs fell into step beside her, joining their little parade to the kitchen. Max brought up the rear, stopping in each doorway along the hall, checking inside the rooms to make sure everything was still secure. "Sorry about your floor. I'm making a mess."

She stopped at the bathroom to pull her robe from behind the door and shrugged into it, adding another layer of warmth and modesty now that she was done throwing herself at her downstairs tenant. "It'll clean up. I believe you think I'm a prim-and-proper prude. A little mud and water don't bother me." Stepping into the kitchen, Rosemary flipped on the light and eyed the path of water and big muddy prints from Max's bare feet that marked her hallway. "The dogs have tracked in worse. I just like knowing the rules and what's expected of me—and what to expect from other people." She crossed to the bank of drawers beside the oven but hesitated. "I hope I didn't put you in an awkward position before. I don't normally wrap myself around a man while I'm in my pajamas." The burn of embarrassment crept up her neck and into her cheeks at that rather suggestive description of seeking refuge in his arms. "I mean, I don't…not without asking first. But I was scared. And I was worried about you."

Rosemary glanced up as he leaned his hip against the countertop beside her. "Do you hear me complaining?"

She was relieved, and more disappointed than she should be, to see him dismissing her panicked indiscretion with a wry grin. She tried to match his easy smile. "You *are* very good at vocalizing what you're thinking and feeling, aren't you, Detective?"

His smile disappeared and he reached over to catch a tendril of hair that stuck to her damp cheek and tucked it behind her ear. "I thought I'd earned a Max from you by now."

Her gaze drifted to the front of his shirt and the three buttons that he'd fastened into the wrong holes. Rosemary couldn't stop the smile from curving her lips again. This man was a tornado blowing through her controlled, predictable world, upsetting her routine, ignoring her personal barriers, waking wants and needs she thought had died long ago. And yet he was growing more dear to her, more necessary as a protector, a friend and maybe something more, with each encounter. Even if all he ever wanted from her was a drunken kiss and the chance to solve Richard's murder, she was glad that he'd barged into her closed-off, humdrum life. She opened a drawer and pulled out a box of plastic storage bags for him. "Here. Max."

Nodding his approval, Max pulled a pocketknife from the front of his jeans to pry open the red box. "Looks like our perp took it apart to modify it somehow. Even with industrial glue, though, it didn't reseal completely. That's probably how the water got inside."

"That horrible sound reminded me of Richard. Of that night. He laughed when he…" The scars on her chest seem to throb and she tied the robe more snugly around her damp T-shirt.

"Who would know about him laughing that night?" Max asked, pulling out a chair at the table to tinker with the box. "Somebody had to know it would rattle you."

"I'm not sure. It's probably in the police report."

"That's public record if somebody looks hard enough. Who else?"

Rosemary considered herself a very private person, but after that night, she'd been desperate to find someone who could help her escape Richard's tyranny. "My brother, Stephen. A couple of friends."

"What friends?" Max glanced up from unscrewing the back of the box. "Crimes are solved in the details. I need you to tell them to me."

Rosemary wondered if the storm outside could somehow cool the air inside the house, as well. "Otis and Arlene, when I went to their house to call the police afterward. Howard."

"Your attorney?"

She nodded. "I told him everything when he was putting together the restraining order."

What about a statuesque blonde who blamed her for Richard's death?

"You got a suspect for me?" he prompted, sensing her thoughts turning.

Rosemary pulled out another chair and sat kitty-corner from him. "Richard could have told one of his mistresses. I ran into one of them at Howard's office the other day."

"*One* of…?" Max's curse was short and pungent. "Sorry. I know you hate that."

"Not as much as I hate not knowing who's doing this to me. Her name is Charleen Grimes. She said your friends Detectives Watson and Parker had shown up at her boutique to ask her questions. She was pretty ticked off." Rosemary remembered the hate and pain spewing from Charleen's perfectly painted lips that day. "She accused me of killing Richard."

"And getting away with it? Like that first note?"

Rosemary nodded. Charleen's verbal attack in Howard's office that day still rankled. But the memory of the blonde woman striding across Howard's office and towering over her was triggering a different memory. "Charleen is tall for a woman. Could she pass for a man at night, in the shadows?"

"It's possible. The guy I chased tonight was wearing clothes so baggy and nondescript I'd be hard-pressed to confirm a gender. I just assumed it was a guy." He wedged the tip of his pocketknife into the seam around the box. "I want to meet this Charleen… Finally." With one more twist of his knife, the box popped open and a soggy piece of paper fell out and plopped to the floor.

"What's that?"

He put out a hand to keep her from picking it up. "Don't touch it. I'll bag it for prints and have Trent take it to the lab tomorrow."

"You know it's not there by accident. I want to know what it says."

He used the plastic bag to retrieve it from the floor and gently shake it open. "Ah, hell."

It was a black-and-white photocopy of a picture. Of her.

Her thoughts instantly went to the mysterious photographer who'd snapped a picture of her in the visitors' room at the state prison. It was even more disturbing to see her wearing a different outfit than the flowered blouse she'd worn that day. She didn't have to move any closer to see the candid image of her climbing into a cab outside Howard's office building. "How long has he been watching me?"

When Max would have slipped the note into the bag and hidden it away, she grabbed his wrist and insisted on seeing every last gruesome detail.

Her eyes and heart had been x-ed out on the picture. Someone who was very angry with her had drawn a noose around her neck in black ink and typed a message neatly across the top.

I want to feel my hands around your throat, your pulse stopping beneath the pressure of my thumbs. You will burn for what you've done.
There will be justice for Richard.
Ha. Ha. Ha.

But the creepiest part was the five black marks dotting the top of the white dress she wore—five dots right across her collarbone where the burn scars Richard had inflicted upon her lay.

"How could he know? How could anyone know?"

Rosemary was only vaguely aware of Max moving as the room swirled around her. With her hand at her throat, she sank into the back of the chair and closed her eyes.

"Rosie?"

She heard the gruff voice calling to her in the distance. Someone knew her darkest secrets. Someone was using those secrets against her. To terrorize her. To punish her. To plunge her into a nightmare from which she could never escape.

"Rosie."

Rough hands grabbed her shoulders, shook her. She was cold. So cold.

Then the hands closed around either side of her head and she fell forward until her mouth ran into something firm, hot. Something warm and moist pressed between her lips, parting them. The world gradually took the shape and form of fingers tangled in her hair, tugging lightly at her scalp. The pressure on her mouth became pliant lips that tasted of salt and heat and toasty tobacco. The taste was familiar yet new. Potent, with a tickle of sandpapery stubble on the side. Max. Max was kissing her. His hands were holding her. His tongue was sliding against hers. In one moment, she was the stunned recipient of bold passion—in the next, her tongue darted out to catch his and she leaned into the kiss. Deepened it. Came alive with it. Her throat hummed with anticipation. She stretched to fit her mouth more fully against his.

But when her hands came to rest against his chest, he pulled away. The room was still swaying when her eyes fluttered open and she looked into the damp, craggy face of the man kneeling in front of her chair. "Max?"

He stroked his thumb across her tender lips, brushed her hair behind her ears. "You checked out on me there. Don't scare me like that, okay? Stay with me."

The disorienting fear and helplessness faded. Other emotions—confusion, hope, desire—grew stronger. She touched the lines of concern crinkling beside his eyes. She brushed her thumb across the masculine line of his bottom lip, absorbing the heat from his skin into hers. She could hear her heart beating over the drumbeat of rain outside. "Another opportunity you couldn't pass up?" But there was no humor in her laugh, no answering humor in his eyes. "You shouldn't kiss me like that unless it means something to you."

Max's lip trembled beneath her thumb. A deep groan rose from his chest. And then he was pushing to his feet, pulling her with him. His mouth covered hers, hot and wet and full of a driving need she answered kiss for kiss.

He lifted her onto her toes and she wound her arms around his neck, leaning into his sheltering strength. There was little finesse to Max's kiss. But then, she had little to compare it to beyond Richard's smooth, practiced seduction that left her feeling unsatisfied and inadequate.

Rosemary liked this infinitely better. There was little to second-guess about a man sliding his hands down her back to squeeze her bottom and lift her off her feet into his hard thighs and the firm interest stirring in between. Max's cheek rasped against hers as his lips scudded across her jaw and pulled at her earlobe.

His words were basic. "Your skin's so soft. Your hair smells like summer and rain. It's the cleanest scent. I could breathe it in all night long."

When he reclaimed her lips, his tongue was bold, his hands were bolder. Rosemary gasped when she felt his palms branding her skin beneath her shirt. The tips of her breasts tingled, grew heavy and tight as they rubbed against the hard wall of his chest. She wanted his hands there, soothing their needy distress, exciting them more. This kiss was the wildest, most unexpected, most perfect embrace of her life. She was an equal partner, giving, taking. She slipped her hands up into the prickly crop of his military-short hair, turning his head to the angle of kiss she liked best.

"Rosie…honey…" His fingers dipped beneath the elastic of her panties. Yes. She wanted his touch there, too. She was forgetting the past. She was unafraid of the future. There was only Max and this moment and feeling safe and desired.

But when she curled her leg around Max's knee, instinctively opening herself to the need arcing between them, he pulled his lips away with a noisy moan. Her mouth chased after his to reclaim the connection, but his hands were on her shoulders now, pulling her arms from around his neck. Her toes touched the cold tile floor again, jarring her back to common sense. Suddenly, the water that had soaked through her clothes seemed just as cold. She rested her hands at his shoulders a moment to steady herself but curled her body away from his. One moment she was alive and on fire, the next, she was shivering and confused.

Rosemary grasped the back of the chair to keep herself standing as Max determinedly backed away. "That's not why I'm here. I've got a mission. I made a promise." His chest expanded with a deep, ragged breath. "Ah, hell. Quit looking at me like you either want to shoot me or eat me up. I'm trying to do the right thing here."

Max's rejection instantly sent her back to the times in her relationship with Richard when he'd rebuffed her advances. "I wasn't very good, was I? I'm sor—"

"Do *not* let that man come between us." Max swiped his hand over his mouth and jaw and spun away. Just as quickly he faced her again and grabbed her wrist. "You call me whatever crass SOB you want to." He pulled her hand to the front of his jeans and cupped it over the unmistakable warm bulge behind his zipper. "This is what you do to me. I don't know why you and me fit together this good. If I could take you to bed right now and finish this, I would." He released her and backed away, raising his hands in apology. "But that's not what I'm here for. Neither one of us needs that kind of complication in our lives. I have to keep the mission in mind. I'm a cop. I have to think like a cop, not a..."

"Not a what?" she asked, her voice barely a whisper.

But he didn't fill in the blank. "It's not your job to deal with me. I'm damaged goods, Rosie. You can do better than me."

"Now who's apologizing?"

With a shrug of his massive shoulders, he scooped up the noisemaker and message that had sent her into shock and slipped them into plastic bags. "I'm going back outside to give everything a once-over—make sure our friend hasn't come back. I need to call this in to my team, too. My description of the perp is pretty vague, but it's a place to start. I'll have a black-and-white swing through the neighborhood, just in case he's hiding out somewhere." He headed to the back door. "I'll be right downstairs. Just a scream away."

Rosemary shook off her stupor and ran after him, grabbing his arm. "You're leaving me?"

He looked down over the jut of his shoulder at her, his growly voice calming. "I don't want to push my luck by overstaying my welcome."

Right. He was being all noble, doing this for her, respecting the boundaries she'd forgotten herself. She released her desperate grasp and stepped away, rubbing her hands up and down her chilled arms. "You better go call your team. I'll be fine."

"You're gettin' pale again. I'll stay if you want me to."

Rosemary shook her head. "No. You have a job to do. I'll be fine. You're here for me to draw out Richard's killer, not to babysit me."

"You know that's not the only reason I'm here."

"For my dad? You said you owed something to a man like him."

Max exhaled a grumbling sigh. "I doubt your dad would make me ten kinds of crazy the way you do. Would you really be okay with me here in the house? Because, frankly, running up and down those basement stairs and breaking through all your locked doors makes me feel like I'm miles away. What if that guy wasn't content to stay outside your window? If he'd gotten inside the house I'd have had to shoot my way in to get to you."

She was so confused—coming to terms with the idea that she could have feelings and desire for a man again, wanting to solve Richard's murder as quickly as possible, evaluating the false boundaries of her reclusive life that had at least given her the illusion of being safe— what was she supposed to choose? "I don't think gunfire in the house would be safe for Duchess and Trixie."

"Or for you. Would you feel safer if I stayed tonight?"

"I don't know."

"Yeah, you do. Everything else aside, would you feel safer?" He tapped his cheek to ask her to look him in the eye and answer. "Up here, honey."

She did look up into those expectant blue eyes. Yes. In every way that mattered, she felt safe with Max. Rosemary nodded.

"Say it, Rosie. Don't make me think I'm bullying you into this."

"I'm not inviting you into my bed. But you are awfully warm, and I can't seem to shake this chill and…" She hugged her arms around her waist but bravely held his gaze. "I don't want to be alone tonight. Would you stay with me?"

The taut line of his mouth relaxed. "I like a clear set of rules, too. So no hanky-panky, but you wouldn't be adverse to a little cuddling? You know, so I can keep an eye on you and you could borrow some body heat?"

"That would be enough for you?"

He brushed a copper tendril off her cheek and tucked it behind her ear. "That would be perfect."

Rosemary smiled. "Then I can live with those rules, too."

"You know the drill." He opened the door. The wind had shifted, blowing rain beneath the patio roof and through the screen, getting their damp clothes wet again. "Lock up. Keep the dogs with you."

"Yes, sir."

Max hurried over to the apartment entrance to make his phone calls and she locked the door behind him. Plucking the wet cotton knit away from the goose bumps on her skin, Rosemary whistled for the dogs. "Come on, girls."

She changed into a fresh sleep shirt and gathered a sponge and some towels, and dropped to her hands and knees to mop up the mud and water in the foyer and hallway. By the time Max returned, she had a load of soiled towels going in the laundry, the dogs settled in with rawhide treats and her quilt pulled off her bed to wrap around her shoulders as a makeshift robe until her own clothes dried.

Max toweled himself off and changed into a dry T-shirt and jeans he'd brought with him before wandering into the library to find her sitting on the rug, going through another box of her parents' things. He took a sip of the hot decaf coffee she'd fixed for him. "I'm willing to take the couch, but I've slept on enough hard bunks and sandy ground to want to avoid the floor if that's okay."

Rosemary grinned and pointed to the sofa where Trixie had climbed on top of the pillow and blanket she'd set out for Max. "Just push her off. She's got plenty of rugs and pillows around the house to sleep on."

While she finished sorting through an envelope of photographs from a family vacation, tossing the blurry pictures and duplicates in the trash, Max sat. Instead of jumping down, Trixie climbed into his lap and lifted her paws for a thorough tummy rub. When Duchess abandoned her treat and came over to share a little bit of the action, Max reached down to rub the German shepherd's tummy, too.

But then he clapped his hands and shooed both dogs away to turn his full attention on Rosemary. "It's late. We have meetings tomorrow, a couple of leads I'd like to pursue. And in case you thought it was up for debate, it's not—you're coming with me."

When she reached for another envelope of photographs, Max cleared his throat. "Honey, you need some sleep. So do I. Either go to bed or come here."

The teasing command overrode any shyness or second thoughts she was feeling. Clutching the quilt around her shoulders, Rosemary turned off the desk lamp. Max turned off the lamp beside the sofa and set his gun and badge on the table beside his coffee mug. Rosemary sat down beside him, watching the diminishing lightning flicker through the blinds in the front window.

A voice, equally dark as the room now, spoke beside her. "The rules I agreed to included some cuddling." He draped his arm over the back of the couch behind her shoulders, reminding her of the body heat she craved. She curled her feet beneath the quilt beside her and leaned into him, resting her head against his shoulder. His arms folded around her and the quilt, tucking them both to his side. "That's better."

Without a visible clock to keep track of the time, she

wasn't sure how long it was before the warmth of the quilt and man holding her seeped deep into her bones and she was drifting off to sleep. "Max?"

"Hmm?"

"You called me honey tonight. More than once."

"I guess it just slipped out. I wasn't trying to over-step—"

"I like it. I like that you call me Rosie, too. Nobody else calls me Rosie. It makes me feel…normal."

"Normal?"

"You know, not an unemployed millionaire murder suspect who talks to her dogs more than she does to people?" She rested her palm above the deep-pitched chuckle that vibrated his chest. "I'm sorry to be so much trouble. I'm glad you're here. But if I wig out on you at some point during the night, just know it's nothing personal."

"Uh-uh." Max slipped his fingers under her chin and tilted her face to his. "You don't apologize for anything. Whatever you have to say to me, don't be afraid to say it. I'm not Richard. What you see is what you get. You know what I'm thinking or feeling at almost any given moment. It isn't always pretty, but there are no surprises."

"I don't like surprises, anyway."

"You, lady, are the biggest surprise of all." He pressed a chaste kiss to her forehead before swinging his legs up onto the couch and stretching out beside her, pulling the quilt up over them both. "Now, go to sleep. That's an order."

Feeling toastier and more tired by the second, Rosie curled up against Max and drifted off to a deep, nightmare-free sleep.

MAX AWOKE TO sunlight streaming through the blinds, a dog licking his elbow and feeling incredibly hard.

He supposed a creamy thigh wedged between his legs did that to a man. And while there might have been a woman in his past he'd have undressed and gotten busy with to start the new day, this was Rosie March. And there were rules with Rosie. Keeping her safe, proving her innocence, earning her trust and fighting to make sure he was worthy of whatever affection she threw his way meant following those rules as surely as he'd follow an order from a superior officer. Still, while she snored softly on his chest, he raised his head and breathed in the sweet, clean scent of her copper-red hair that reminded him of coming home and leaving battlefields behind him. He wasn't a saint, after all.

But a bigger pair of deep brown eyes were staring at him now. Between Duchess's stoic plea and Trixie's eager tongue rasping along his arm, Max got the message. He reached down to scratch around the poodle's ears. "Need to go outside, girls?"

When Duchess jumped to her feet and the little dog started dancing around, Max tried to calm them. "Shh. Mama's sleeping. I'm coming. Give me a sec."

Sometime during the night, the quilt had ended up on the floor, and Trixie had claimed it for a bed, so there was nothing but the woman herself he needed to extricate himself from. Max palmed Rosie's hip and gently lifted her so he could pull his legs from beneath hers. Then he turned onto his side to pull his shoulder from beneath her head. But his efforts to carefully free himself from the woman draped on top of him without waking or embarrassing her halted when the neckline of her

T-shirt gaped open and he shamelessly took a peek at the plump, heavy breasts that had pillowed against his side and chest most of the night.

But that little rush of lust quickly dissipated when he saw the puckery burn scars along her collarbone, marring Rosie's beautiful skin. He tucked his finger beneath the stretchy cotton and pulled the material aside to get a better look.

"Son of a..." Five perfect white circles the size of a cigarette tip. That explained the high necklines. He dropped his knees to the floor and pulled his arm away as his temper brewed. He vowed then and there to give up the cigars completely—not even a stress-relieving chomp for old times' sake. Nobody did that kind of damage to themselves. That was done to her. He'd have been tempted to pull the trigger on Richard Bratcher himself if he'd known that bastard had trapped her inside the house and tortured her like that.

Jimmy had been tortured. Physically, mentally, emotionally. Had Rosie endured the same?

Jimmy hadn't survived the aftermath of all that had been done to him, all he'd seen. In the end, he'd died alone. If there'd been anything in Max's power he could do to save his buddy, he would have.

Rosie was all alone in this house. But she wasn't going to cope with Bratcher and his cruelty by herself anymore. For Rosie, for her father, for his own sanity and redemption, Max intended to capture a killer and put a stop to anyone or anything that tried to hurt this woman again.

Perhaps sensing his unblinking stare and darkening

mood, Rosie stirred on the couch. She smiled before opening her eyes. "Good morning."

Max didn't trust himself to speak. He curled his fingers into a fist and pulled it away from her.

Rosie's smile disappeared in an instant and she was wide-awake. When she saw the direction of his gaze, she sat up and scooted to the far end of the couch. "What are you doing?"

"Trying not to put a fist through your wall."

"Ugly, aren't they?" She pulled her oversize shirt back into its modest place and picked up the quilt, draping it over her shoulders and covering everything between her chin and her feet. "I suppose with nine million dollars, I could afford to get some plastic surgery and make them disappear. They're there to remind me that I've never really been safe, I've never really been free since that man entered my life. I can never drop my guard or give my heart again. Not until the rumors are put to rest and that crazy stalker—"

When she pushed to her feet, Max was there to stop her from bolting from the room. He caught her face between his hands and dipped his head to kiss her. It was brief, it was passionate, it was full of the unspoken promise he'd made to her moments earlier.

When he released her, she wasn't quite so set on running from him. "What was that for?"

"I saw the chance to do it, so I did."

Shaking off his show of support, his vow to protect her, she headed for the hall anyway. "I don't think I can do this, after all, Max. You need to go."

"Did Bratcher put those marks on you?"

She stopped, pulling the quilt more fully around

her. Her huddled silence was answer enough. Hell. No wonder she'd checked out last night when she saw that sick, doctored-up picture. That kind of graphic accuracy about her past abuse had no other function but to remind her of her worst fears. To make her feel as powerless and alone now as she had back then.

He wasn't giving Rosie the chance to ever feel that way again. "Shower and get dressed and grab some breakfast—or whatever your morning routine is. You're coming with me today."

"But you have to work." Her shoulders lifted with a heavy sigh and she turned, gesturing to the boxes and books all around them. "And I'm still going through Mom and Dad's papers. You don't think I'm safe here during the day? I'll have Duchess and Trixie with me. Send one of your uniformed officers over to keep an eye on me." She shrugged the quilt higher onto her shoulders and hugged it tight around her neck, hiding even more of herself from him—as if his body hadn't already memorized the shape and weight of those generous hips and breasts. "Won't I just be in the way?"

"You aren't a prisoner in this house anymore, Rosie. We talked about this last night. Staying here by yourself isn't an option. I don't want to wait until Trent or someone else from the team gets done with morning roll call to take over the watch here—and I won't trust you with anyone else. We have secrets to uncover, a murder to solve."

"And you think I can help?"

"This morning I have a meeting at Endicott Global. I'd like you to come along on the off chance we see your guy from the picture, or anyone else you might recognize there. In fact, I want you to keep your eyes open anyplace we go, in case he's following you." KCPD still hadn't identified the young man yet. But Max had a feeling in his gut that the man was key to linking Bratcher's murder to Leland Asher's organization and a host of other crimes. "Before we do that, we're going next door. Your neighbors are always peeking at you and seem to have an opinion on everything. Maybe they saw something last night."

"Oh, joy."

Good. Sarcasm beat that self-conscious guilt and avoiding him. "You're the key to my investigation, Rosie. Maybe the key to my redemption over Jimmy's death, too."

"That wasn't your fault."

He put up a hand to stop that argument. "You fight your demons your way, and I'll deal with mine on my own terms. I want you in my sights 24/7 now. Okay? I promise to knock off at five when my shift is over, and I'll bring you back to do your paperwork thing here."

"You're not really giving me a choice, are you?"

"If you don't go, neither do I. And that means we'll never find Bratcher's killer."

A beat of silence passed before she nodded and turned. "Put the dogs in the backyard on your way out. I'll get ready."

CHAPTER NINE

"BRACE YOURSELF," MAX WARNED, pressing the doorbell. "And remember, the idea is to keep them talking."

Rosemary inhaled a steadying breath and hugged her shoulder bag closer to the navy blue animal-print dress she wore. "That shouldn't be hard."

Arlene Dinkle wasn't smiling when she answered the front door. But then, neither was Max.

With a clean shave and a fresh shirt tucked into his jeans, there was little left of the man who'd held Rosemary so tenderly and securely through the night. This guy wore a gun and a badge and an attitude that outgrumped Arlene's early-morning mood.

"Good morning, Mrs. Dinkle." Max flashed his badge but not a smile. "You remember me, don't you?"

"Detective Krolikowski." Arlene carried pruning shears and a small bouquet of cut roses in her gloved hands. "I remember you. Did you catch that trespasser?"

"The department's working on it. I'm following up on what might be a related crime. There was an attempted break-in at Miss March's house last night, and I was wondering if you or your husband saw anything. May we come in?"

"Strange men at all hours, that old car parked in your

driveway, and now this?" Arlene's dark gaze slid over to Rosemary. "You draw a bad element to this neighborhood like a magnet, don't you?"

Bristling at the catty remark, Max's hand clenched at the small of Rosemary's back. But his tone remained good-ol'-boy professional. "Let's get one thing straight, Mrs. Dinkle. You do not get to speak to Miss March like that. She's a victim, not a criminal. You'll give her the same respect you would this badge."

The older woman's petite frame puffed up. "Well, I've never been spoken to—"

"Rosemary. Good morning." Otis strolled out of the kitchen in a pair of track pants and a muscle shirt, carrying a ball cap and bottle of water. He reached around his wife to push open the screen door. "Detective. Please, come in."

There was no offer of a cup of coffee, not even an offer to sit. The fragrance from the roses Arlene had been trimming overwhelmed their small foyer and tickled Rosemary's sinuses. But Otis's welcoming smile seemed genuine. "Trouble next door again?"

"I'm afraid so, sir."

"A man peeked in my window last night," Rosemary explained, trying to keep her tone as even and uncowed by Arlene's rudeness as Max's had been. "He left a threat that indicated he wanted to kill me."

"Oh, my. That's terrible." Otis's smile faded. He swung his gaze over to Max. "Did you catch him?"

"The police haven't caught anybody," Arlene groused. "Now we have Peeping Toms making death threats running around our neighborhood? You know if they can't get into your house, Rosemary, they'll try to break into ours." She thumped her husband's arm. "We can't afford the same kind of high-tech security she has. I told you we should have sold this house and moved ten years ago." She swung her arms out, indicating the rest of the house, inadvertently drawing Rosemary's attention to at least five more vases of roses scattered across the living room. "You never listen."

"Is there a flower show coming up, Arlene?" Rosemary asked. The woman certainly loved her gardening, but the overwhelming smell of attar in the house was giving her a bit of a headache.

"I'm trying to save my prize roses," Arlene explained. "That storm last night nearly did them in. At least I can dry these and save the perfume for potpourri. Unless, of course, some gang person breaks in and robs us. Or kills us in our sleep."

"We're perfectly fine here, Arlene." Otis's quiet, almost monotonous voice was such a contrast to his wife's shrill tones. "Rosemary's the one who's been hurt, not you. It was probably some crackpot who wanted to see what a millionaire looks like."

"Or someone casing the homes in the neighborhood to rob us," she insisted. "I told you about that fancy truck I've seen cruising up and down the street at all hours of the night. And don't think I haven't asked. No one around here owns it."

Otis shrugged. "I would have heard anyone poking at our windows. The game was on until one in the morning." He scratched the bald spot on top of his head.

"Now that I think of it, I did hear some shouting last night. I figured it was someone caught out in the storm."

Arlene clutched the roses to her chest. "They were probably sending signals, telling each other how to get in. Otis, you should have called the police."

"Why? I couldn't make out any words."

Max held up a hand to end the marital debate. "It was probably me shouting. The perp never said a word. Could you tell me a little more about this 'fancy truck,' ma'am?"

The woman could certainly be counted on for details. "I don't know models and makes, but it was one of those extended cab trucks, with a backseat for passengers?" Max pulled a pen and notebook from his pocket and jotted the description. "It was dark green—almost looked black, but I saw it under the street lamp a couple of nights ago and it was definitely dark green. The trim around the wheel wells was black, though."

"Did you happen to get a license plate?"

She thought for a moment. "I don't think it had one. It had those stickers in the window—the ones the dealer puts on when you first buy a car?"

"That helps."

Arlene almost smiled at the morsel of praise.

But her sour frown returned when Otis reached out and patted Rosemary's shoulder. "Are you all right, dear?"

She nodded. "But understandably, seeing the man gave me a good scare. I'm lucky Max was there."

Arlene crossed her arms with a noisy harrumph. "Your parents would have been mortified to know you're alone in their house entertaining a man overnight."

Her parents would have been glad to know that Max had kept her safe. "Not that it's any of your business, Arlene, but Max is renting Stephen's old apartment downstairs."

"Oh." That seemed to deflate Arlene's judgmental superiority a bit. "I misunderstood. So the police are providing extra protection for dangerous neighborhoods like ours?"

The only danger zone on this block seemed to be Rosemary's house. But until she could prove her innocence, she supposed Arlene would continue to believe she lived next door to a murderess and a hive for illegal activities. "It's nice to have a cop living nearby, isn't it?" Rosemary choked out the polite words in the name of neighborhood peace and getting the Dinkles to answer Max's questions.

Max didn't waste time with making nice. "Did you see the green truck last night, ma'am?"

Arlene pursed her lips together, thinking. "No."

"When the truck was here before, did you happen to look at the driver?"

"Not really."

"Did either of you see or hear anything around midnight last night?" Max asked.

Otis crossed his arms and shrugged. "We had that big thunderstorm blow through about that time. Pretty noisy. I didn't hear anything."

"But you were awake watching the ball game?" Max clarified. "I pursued the suspect in the direction of your yard. He crashed through the hedge out front and took off between the houses. I lost him in the storm."

"My hawthorn bushes?" Arlene set the stinky roses on the nearby credenza and pushed between Rosemary and Max. "First my roses and now the hedge? I've been training those bushes for years now." When she hurried out the door and across the yard, Rosemary, Max and Otis followed. "If you arrest this Peeping Tom person, I'm suing him for property damage, too." The older woman stopped in front of the gap of crushed branches in her leafy green hedge. Her shoulders sank with dismay. She picked up one of the broken stems, still full of green leaves and long thorns. "This is ruined. I'll have to plant a whole new shrub and trim the others down to match."

"I'll pay for the new bush, Arlene," Rosemary offered.

"Of course you will. This is your fault. And it's not as though you can't afford it."

For a split second, when Max reached around Arlene, Rosemary thought he was shoving her out of the way for being such a witch. Instead, he pulled loose a scrap of soggy black sweatshirt material that had caught on one of the bush's long thorns. He showed the tatter to Rosemary before holding it up for the Dinkles. "The man I chased wore a black hoodie. Have you ever seen anyone like that around here? The driver of that truck, perhaps?"

"Don't be ridiculous," Arlene answered first. "It's too hot to wear a sweatshirt, even at night. Ours are all packed up until the fall."

Max closed the torn material in his hand and stuffed it into the pocket of his jeans. "I didn't ask if you owned a black sweatshirt, Mrs. Dinkle. I asked if you'd seen anybody wearing one."

The dark-haired woman glanced up at her husband. But was that a plea for help out of talking herself into an awkward corner or the remembrance of something familiar in her eyes?

Otis, oblivious to any underlying message, threw up his hands. "Don't look at me. I have no idea where my old hoodie is."

"I don't suppose you could produce that hoodie, could you, Mr. Dinkle? Let me check to see if there's a chunk of cloth torn out of it?"

"You think my husband is spying on Rosemary, Detective? That he would threaten her?"

"Like I said, ma'am. I'm just here looking for some answers." Max wrapped his fingers around Rosemary's arm, indicating the interview was over. "If you two find that hoodie, or spot anyone else wearing one in the area, give me a call. Let me know if you see that truck again, too. Thank you for your help."

Rosemary hurried her steps to keep up with Max's long strides around the end of the hedge and across her yard to climb inside his blue Chevelle and head to their next appointment. As she buckled herself in, she waited for him to finish texting on his phone and asked, "We didn't find out anything useful from them, did we?"

"I'm asking Trent to see if he can run down the owner of that truck. It's a long shot, but it could be significant." He tucked the phone into his pocket before starting the car's powerful engine and backing out of the driveway. "We also found out that Otis was awake when our unsub was running through his yard. I can't believe that neighbors as curious as they are didn't go to the window when they heard me shouting. Unless one or both of them are hiding something. And we found out he owns a black hoodie—even if he claims to not know where it is."

"We've been friends and neighbors for years. Why would Otis want to kill me?"

"I don't know. Maybe he doesn't. But I can't imagine he's a very happily married man. I'm guessing he's got all sorts of hobbies to distract him from that shrew. Listening to music, running."

"You think scaring me to death qualifies as a hobby?"

Max reached across the center console to squeeze her hand. "The Dinkles' information might not mean a thing except that you need to find better neighbors. I'm figuring out all the pieces to the puzzle right now. Pretty soon we'll be able to discard the ones that don't fit, and put the right ones together and find our answers. We'll get this guy. Whoever it is. We'll clear your name. I promise." He released her to shift the car into Drive. "Want to have a little fun?"

"I thought we were focusing on finding those puzzle pieces."

He grinned. "Not all day long. Hold on."

He gunned the souped-up engine and spit out a cloud of exhaust right in front of the Dinkles' house before speeding away.

Rosemary laughed when she saw, in the side-view

mirror, Arlene's hand fly up and the woman launch into a tirade that had no place to go except at her poor husband. But Otis didn't put up with it for long. Arlene was probably still complaining about ruined hedges and smelly exhausts and who knew what else when Otis plugged in his earbuds, pulled his cap over his head and took off on his morning jog.

She turned and relaxed in the car's bucket seat. "You're naughty, Detective Krolikowski."

Max slid his mirrored sunglasses on. "Yep. I kind of am."

But her smile quickly faded when she considered the idea that turning her life upside down and forcing her to live like a recluse might be someone's idea of a hobby.

ROSIE STROLLED THE grand hallway on the executive floor of the Endicott Global building, studying the oil paintings and watercolors displayed on the paneled walls. Max stood close by, studying her.

The drive to the industrial park area north of downtown Kansas City had given Max the chance to get the Cold Case Squad up to speed on events from the past twenty-four hours. He'd dropped off the party-store recording device and the sick threat buried inside it at the precinct with Trent to see if the lab could get anything useful off the water-soaked items. Liv and her fiancé, Gabe Knight, who thought he recognized the society event in the photo with the young man Rosie had ID'd, were using his connections at the *Kansas City Journal* to track down a name. Trent had given the information about the dark green truck cruising Rosie's neighborhood to the team's information guru, Katie Rinaldi. If anyone could track down the owner of a truck with no license plate or VIN number, it was Katie and her magic computer tricks.

Right now, Max was playing a waiting game—his least favorite part of police work. Waiting for information from his team, waiting for the appointment that was running late…waiting for these feelings he had for Rosie to start making sense.

He'd been with a few women most of the world would consider prettier, and certainly more outgoing and daring than Rosie. But this was more than a pickup in a bar—a one-night stand before he moved on in the bright light of day. This was more than repaying a debt he owed an Army pilot he'd never met, more than an assignment Lieutenant Rafferty-Taylor had given him. Whatever was happening inside him, it was even more than doing for her what he hadn't been able to do for Jimmy. Whatever was going on between him and Rosie Posy was complicated and messy, unlike any sort of relationship he'd toyed with before.

Sure, her needy grabs and shy kisses could turn him inside out. A man could lose himself in her cool eyes and the warm scent of her hair. They'd talked. She'd listened. *He'd* listened. When the hell had that ever happened? He was no lothario, but her responses to his touch, whether it was a drunken kiss or a platonic cuddle, made him feel powerful, male—as if he might just be a decent catch for the right woman, after all. But how could a woman who was so wrong for a guy like him ever be the right one?

And since when did he get so philosophical about a woman or wanting to understand his feelings, anyway?

He had a job to do. Period. HUA. He wasn't going to let any distracting emotions cloud his judgment or get in the way of solving this murder again.

In a few long strides, Max caught up to Rosie. She seemed to like these paintings of farms and fruit and people he didn't know, hanging in gaudy gold and heavy wood frames that seemed more about showing off how much money Endicott Global made in a year rather than the art itself. Or maybe Rosie was just more capable of being patient and feigning interest than he'd ever be.

She'd stopped in front of a life-size oil painting of a white-haired man with a wizened face, standing in front of a fancy marble mantel. The old geezer's posture was surprisingly straight, which made Max think the guy was former military. But with his pin-striped suit, and thumb tucked into the watch pocket of his paisley vest, Max got the idea that the guy was more of a politician or businessman than anybody who'd gotten his hands dirty down in the trenches.

"He looks important," Rosie said, staring up at the painting.

Nope, he wasn't any good at pretending to be interested in something he wasn't. He went for prettier works of art himself. Like the woman draped over his randy body when he'd woken up this morning. He reached over and brushed a curling copper tendril off her cheek. She shivered when his fingertip circled around her ear. Yep, this lady was more responsive to his touch than she probably ought to be. "Why do you wear your hair like this? Don't tell me it's in deference to the summer heat."

She shrugged and moved a step beyond his reach. "It keeps my naturally wavy hair under control."

"You'd turn more heads if you lost a little bit of that control."

"I'm not interested in turning heads. I've been in the spotlight far more than I ever wanted to be. I already have bright red hair and pasty white skin." Warm copper silk and unblemished alabaster that was finer than the marble in that pretentious painting was a more accurate description in his mind. "It's calmer, easier to get through life, to be more subdued or conservative—whatever you want to call it—and not draw attention to myself."

"That's Bratcher's doing, not yours."

Rosie swiveled her gaze up to him. "That makes you angry?"

"Yeah. He's been dead six years. It pisses me off that that man can still hurt you."

"Wearing my hair in a bun hurts me?"

"Thinking you've got to have a certain look or act a certain way or else somebody's going to hurt you. Being afraid like that isn't right." He tugged at the tendril that had sprung back onto her cheek. "Be yourself. Tell the world what you want and go for it. I think there's some fire hiding under that ladylike facade of yours. Wear your hair down and loose if that's the way you like it, or shave it off in a buzz cut—which I hope like hell isn't what you really want."

"Max. Your language," she chided in a whisper,

glancing over at the receptionist at the main desk. "We're in a public place."

Instead of apologizing, he fingered the top button of her blue-and-white dress. "Unhook a few of these. Good grief, woman, it's ninety-three degrees out there and it isn't even noon yet."

She swatted his hand away. "No."

His resentment of Richard Bratcher quickly gave way to a lopsided grin. "Told you there was fire in there."

And then he thought of the real reason she wore those high-necked dresses and his mood shifted again, raising her concern. "What is it?"

"Those scars are badges of honor. You survived. That takes real strength." Jimmy Stecher's worst wounds were far less visible. "I'd bet money you've got some form of PTSD, just like Jimmy did. I think of all the pain and guilt and fear Jimmy kept locked up inside him. Maybe if he hadn't believed he was all alone…if he'd known he could rail at me or talk or whatever he needed, I'd have been there for him. He shouldn't have tried to control every little thing. Clearly, he couldn't handle the pressure. No one can."

"Max. I'm not going to kill myself." Her soft voice pierced the heavy thoughts that had blurred his vision. She brushed her fingers against his, down at his thigh. "I've seen a therapist. I'm coping. Besides, I'm not alone. You're with me."

He turned his hand and captured hers in a solid grip. "Good. You're growing on me, Rosie. I'd hate to finally figure you out one day and then lose…"

Ah, hell. Max's thoughts all rolled together in a jumble. Lose what? Her? After just a few days, he wouldn't do anything so dumb as…anything that felt so right as… He'd fallen for Rosie March.

Max pulled his hand away and stuffed it into the back pocket of his jeans. Well, of course he had. When had he ever done anything the easy way? This was sure to come back and bite him in the butt. Because Rosie March probably had no plans to ever fall in love again, and certainly not with a boorish, potty-mouthed tough guy like him.

Perhaps mistaking the source of his uncomfortable silence, Rosie changed the conversation to a more neutral topic. She pointed to the white-haired man in the painting. "Who do you think this is?"

The tapping of high heels on the marble flooring thankfully interrupted them. Dr. Hillary Wells walked up. "That is Dr. Lloyd Endicott. The founder of our company." Although Max recognized the older woman from the computer screen at the Cold Case Squad meeting, she was taller than he'd imagined. Her short, dark hair and high cheekbones were even more striking in person. She wore a pricey skirt and blouse beneath her stark white lab coat and, as Max remembered the preferential treatment from the meeting, he wasn't surprised that she extended her hand to Rosie first. "Hi. I'm Dr. Hillary Wells. You're here for an appointment?"

"Yes," Rosie answered.

He flashed his badge before shaking her hand. "Max Krolikowski, KCPD. This is my associate, Miss March."

Hillary gestured to the double doors behind the receptionist's desk, and they fell into step beside her.

"Come into my office. I apologize for running late. Even though I'm overseeing the entire company now, I still like to keep my hand in the lab where I started— before Dr. Endicott discovered my talents and promoted me. Keeps a girl humble, you know. I was following up on some experiment results. If I'm recommending to the board that they up funding for a new product line, I want to make sure I know what I'm talking about."

After ordering coffee from her assistant and showing Rosie and Max to two guest chairs, she hung up her lab coat and pulled on a jacket that matched her skirt, instantly switching from scientist to CEO. She came back to her desk and opened a tub of hand cream. As she rubbed the cream into her skin, she pointed to the door, indicating the portrait of the distinguished gentleman Rosemary had asked about. "Lloyd started his research in a small lab not far from our location. Brilliant man. He developed a viable oral chemotherapy treatment with minimal side effects. A dozen patents later, he had multiple labs doing the research for him, he was building production facilities around the world, and Endicott Global went public." She sat in her chair behind the desk, her tone growing wistful. "The man died a billionaire, but he was always happiest puttering around in the lab."

"He sounds like a father figure to you," Rosie suggested.

"Very much so," Hillary agreed. "He was certainly a mentor of mine. We worked closely together for a number of years. I suppose that's why he handpicked me to succeed him. He had no children of his own and had been a widower for some time."

"I was close to my father, too. You must miss him."

"I do. Lloyd was an elderly man, but he was always young at heart." Her assistant brought them each a coffee and slipped out as quietly as he'd come in. Dr. Wells took a few moments to drink a sip and compose herself. "He was taken from us far too soon. Terrible car accident."

Rosie cradled her mug in her lap, probably feeling real empathy for the other woman, or maybe just thinking about how much she missed her own dad. "I'm so sorry."

"Thank you." Hillary swallowed another sip, then set her mug aside. She grew more businesslike and turned her attention to Max. "Now. How may I help you, Detective? You're following up on the report KCPD sent me?"

"Yes, ma'am." Hopefully, he'd be able to uncover a more useful puzzle piece here. "The Richard Bratcher case? The ME found a toxic amount of RUD-317, a drug your company produces, in his system. Can you tell us about it?"

Dr. Wells picked up a pair of reading glasses and opened a folder on her desk to skim the file. "Ah, yes. After reading your ME's report, I asked my assistant to pull the pharmaceutical file. So what are your questions about the drug?"

Rosie moved to the edge of her seat and set her coffee mug on the desk. "You keep calling it a drug. But it poisoned Richard. Surely, it's not still on the market."

"RUD-317 is used for the treatment of certain cancers. It targets and reduces malignant tumor growth. In some applications it eradicates the cancerous growth completely. In others, it contains the malignancy." Dr. Wells thumbed through her file and pulled out a thick set of papers stapled together. "Six years ago it was brand-new on the market. These are the drug trials immediately preceding that time to tell us who had access to RUD-317 outside of the lab. Our staff, of course, is all bonded, with signed confidentiality agreements. It would be impossible for one of them to get the drug out of the lab. Every shift goes through a security check when they leave."

Max bit down on the urge to argue her point. Nothing was impossible if you knew the right person and had the right leverage.

"Richard was never sick a day in his life. If he had cancer, he never told me." Was that distress he heard in Rosie's voice? Did she really care that that monster might have been battling cancer?

"You knew Mr. Bratcher personally?"

"Yes."

"Not every patient chooses to share with his loved ones when he has a serious illness."

Rosie sank back in her chair, her confusion and unease with this conversation making her press her pretty mouth into a grim line and her eye focus drop to that self-conscious, don't-notice-me level she used as a defense mechanism.

Max reached across the space between their chairs to squeeze her hand. When that gray gaze darted over to meet his, he winked, silently encouraging her not to give up the fight. Then he released her and turned his attention back to Dr. Wells. "If you read the ME's report again, Doctor, you'll see he wasn't being treated with the drug. Bratcher wasn't sick." Not physically sick, at any rate. "Either he had access to the drug himself, or someone on your list there had a motive for killing him."

The dark-haired CEO sat up ramrod straight, clearly displeased with him questioning her authority. She held up the packet of paper. "All I can tell you is that there is a Bratcher in this study. He could have been part of the placebo group, or he could have been a legitimate patient who was cured and continued to use the drug against our advisement."

Dr. Wells set the packet down, rested her elbows on top of it and steepled her fingers. Here it came. The lecture telling Max that he, the Cold Case Squad and ME's office had to be wrong. Because Dr. High-and-Mighty there was always right.

"Our report, in conjunction with the ME's autopsy, indicates that your Mr. Bratcher had consumed a far bigger dose than recommended, or multiple doses over a short period of time. There was a huge quantity of RUD-317 in his system. More than enough to trigger the convulsions, aspiration of stomach contents and suffocation that led to his death." She sat back in her chair, blithely unaware or uncaring of how the gruesome details surrounding Bratcher's death made Rosie go pale. "If Mr. Bratcher was murdered, then you have to prove how all that medication got into his system. Someone could have opened the capsules and slipped the RUD-317 into his food or drink, or replaced some other medication he regularly took without his knowledge. But unless you can prove any of that, all you have is a drug overdose, and Endicott Global is not responsible."

Max pushed to his feet. This interview was done. Dr. Wells had gone CEO on them, more interested in protecting her company and its profits from a potential lawsuit than in helping them solve a murder.

Max thanked her for the coffee and little else. "I'll need a list of all the patients in that clinical trial, and any staff, researchers or salespeople who would have had access to the drug six years ago. Maybe one of them had a grudge against Bratcher. It could be a disgruntled client, or somebody he took for a lot of money."

Dr. Wells closed the file and stood, also. "I'll have my assistant forward the staff contacts later today. Patient names are confidential, however. You'll need a warrant for me to share that."

"My lieutenant's already working on it."

"Then as soon as my office receives it, I'll get you a list of everyone who had contact with the drug."

Max was ready to leave, but Rosie was a class act all the way. "Thank you for your time, Dr. Wells."

"Glad to help." The CEO followed Max and Rosie to the door. "Detective Krolikowski, I can't believe that anyone employed by Endicott Global or its affiliates would abuse our drugs and knowingly hurt someone. We take too much pride in our work, in our mission to save lives."

"Nonetheless, I want that list."

"Very well." She caught the door before Max could close it behind them and extended her hand to Rosie again. "Rosemary? Perhaps I'll see you at one of the museum's upcoming fund-raisers. I sit on the city's cultural arts board. We're always looking for new donors to support the arts in Kansas City."

Rosie shook the doctor's hand and nodded her thanks to the invitation. But when he would have expected her to quickly pull away, Rosie continued to hold on for an awkward length of time. What was that redhead up to?

"Dr. Wells, did you have access to RUD-317 six years ago?"

The two women locked gazes. To her brave credit, Rosie wasn't the first one to look away. Hillary ended the handshake and gave the door a nudge, herding them out. "Of course I did. I helped Lloyd create it. But I never even met your Mr. Bratcher. Why on earth would I want to kill him?"

The door snapped firmly shut in their faces. Suddenly, Dr. Wells's assistant was there to walk them to the elevator. Max glanced down at Rosie. "I guess our meeting's over."

Once the elevator doors closed behind them and they were alone, Max sat back against the railing and asked, "What was that handshake thing about?"

"I can't be certain. Maybe it's a woman's intuition, or perhaps an old memory is trying to surface."

"I need a little more to follow what you're getting at."

She thrust her right hand at his face. "Smell that."

"Whoa." Max grinned and ducked to one side to avoid an accidental punch to the chin. But he caught a whiff of what Rosie was talking about. He laced his fingers together with hers and drew her hand to his nose again. He breathed in the floral scent of Hillary Wells's hand cream. "You said you smelled perfume on the sheets in Bratcher's hotel room that day."

Rosie nodded. "I just assumed it was Charleen Grimes who'd spent the night with Richard. But maybe there was someone else there, a different woman." She pulled her hand away and wrapped it around the strap of her purse. She leaned against the back wall beside him. "Six years is a long time to try to pinpoint an exact scent, and it's probably not anything that could help you make an arrest—"

"But it's another potential piece of the puzzle."

CHAPTER TEN

ROSEMARY FOLLOWED MAX off the elevator onto the top floor that housed the office suites of Howard's law firm. The day had been a long one. She was hungry for dinner. She'd love a long swim to ease the tension from her muscles. Duchess and Trixie were probably dancing around the house to be let out to do their business. She was done talking to people who wouldn't give her straight answers.

And ever since the idea of Otis Dinkle spying on her had been put into her head, she'd felt as though someone had been following her all day as Max carted her from interview to interview—keeping her in sight, keeping her safe. Max assured her they were gathering useful clues, expanding KCPD's list of suspects and crossing others off the list who either had an alibi or lacked a motive to kill Richard and threaten her.

More than anything, she wanted to go home to her quiet little house and be surrounded by her parents' things and her beloved pets. Maybe she and Max would get to talk. Maybe he'd see the chance to steal another kiss and take it. And maybe, if her scars and the self-confidence that sometimes failed her hadn't been too much of a turnoff, he'd offer another night in his shel-

tering arms and she'd know a second night of blissful
sleep. He'd said she had to be bold and ask for what she
wanted—that he was no good at reading between the
lines and guessing. Well, what she wanted was to go
home. With him.

But when she opened her mouth to say as much,
Charleen Grimes unfolded her long legs from the couch
in the center of the room and crossed the floor in her
three-inch heels.

"That's Charleen Grimes," she whispered, instead.

"The mistress?" Max clarified. Rosemary would
have turned around, gone back downstairs and walked
home if Max's hand hadn't been at her back, drawing
her forward beside him. He dipped his face beside her
ear and whispered, "The woman needs some meat on
her bones. Your ex must have had a thing for making
love to sticks." He turned his fingers to pat the swell of
Rosie's hip. "I'll take a real woman any day."

"Bless you, Max." Rosie's chin lifted a little higher
at the praise. "Good evening, Charleen."

"Well, if it isn't the little murderess herself."

Howard stepped out of his office at the end of the
hallway and hurried to join them. "Charleen, you are
way out of line." He snapped his fingers to the receptionist for her to notify Mr. Austin that his client had
arrived for her KCPD interview. "Remember our conversation about slandering my client."

"*I'm* out of line?" She ran her painted nails along the
lapel of her blue silk jacket. "Which one of us is here
to be questioned as a murder suspect?" Charleen's blue

eyes narrowed. "You and your nine million dollars took Richard from me. I will never forgive you."

A sad realization washed over Rosemary. "You really loved him, didn't you?"

"A lot more than you ever did."

Most certainly. "Did you love him so much that you'd rather see him dead than with anybody else?"

"How dare you, you little mouse. I'm the only one who wants justice for Richard. All you're concerned about is saving your own skin."

"Justice?" Rosie's blood turned to ice in her veins. How many of those crude threats had mentioned justice for Richard? Were Charleen's words a horrid coincidence? A slip of the tongue? Or was there something much more ominous and far too familiar in the accusation?

Charleen took another step and Max's hand shot between them to keep the woman from coming any closer. "Stay with me, Rosie." His blue eyes met hers with a pinpoint focus, probably checking to make sure she didn't slip into another one of those trancelike states where she was paralyzed with fear. She blinked, nodded, silently reassured him she wasn't so upset by the other woman's words that she couldn't function. "Maybe I'd better handle this interview on my own," he suggested.

Howard was instantly at Rosemary's side. "Perhaps so, Detective. I don't know why you have her out doing your job."

Max's shoulders came back at the irritation in Howard's voice. Thankfully, he didn't take the bait and continue the argument. "Just get her someplace safe for twenty or thirty minutes, okay?"

"My pleasure." Howard's cool hand cupped her elbow, pulling her away from Max. "You're welcome to wait in my office while your friend conducts his business."

"Thanks." While Howard tucked Rosemary's hand into the crook of his elbow and led her to his back corner office, Max escorted Charleen in the opposite direction to Mr. Austin's suite at the end of the hallway. "What's that perfume you're wearing?" he asked. "It's sexy as all get-out."

"Don't try to charm me, Detective Krolikowski. You haven't got the chops for it."

The man wasn't as clueless as he pretended to be. "So I can't buy that scent for my girlfriend?"

Charleen stopped and leveled a glare at Rosemary. "No."

Girlfriend? Was that part of his investigative bag of tricks to get a suspect talking—using her as the proverbial burr that could get Charleen agitated underneath her saddle? Or could there be a grain of truth in that one word? Rosemary's pulse did a funny little pitterpatter at the hope that he might be halfway serious about claiming her as his.

But Charleen's hateful gaze was a painful reminder that Rosemary needed this part of her life to be over. Charleen pouted her ruby-red lips into a smile and linked her arm through Max's, figuratively taking from Rosemary what Charleen claimed Rosemary had taken from her. The tall blonde sashayed her hip into Max's as their voices faded down the long hallway, and Rosie's nostrils flared with an emotion that was far closer to feeling possessive about Max than feeling inadequate lined up next to a woman whose beauty she couldn't match. "It's a personal scent, designed especially for me. Back in my modeling days—"

"Don't let her get to you. Charleen's a bitter, vindictive woman." Howard closed the outer office door and followed Rosemary into his private office, locking the door behind him. Was he that worried about the tall blonde causing a scene that would upset her? "In her own way, I think she truly loved Richard. But she didn't handle all the other women and one-night stands as well as you did."

Rosemary's laugh held little humor. "I don't think I handled his cheating well at all." She dropped her purse into one of the guest chairs and sat in the other, leaning back and closing her weary eyes. "It does devastating things to a woman's ego and ability to trust when she finds out she's not enough for her man."

"Are you enough for Krolikowski?"

Her eyes fluttered open at the unexpected question. "Excuse me?"

Howard shrugged and crossed to the wet bar in the corner. "I couldn't help but notice how chummy the two of you have gotten these past few days."

She sat up straighter. "We're working together. I finally have someone at KCPD treating me like the victim, not a prime suspect."

"Seemed friendlier than that to me." He held up a mug. "Coffee?"

"Please."

Friendlier? Certainly Max had become important to her these past few days. He'd been the only one to believe that the threats against her were real and not some scam to gain sympathy or divert attention onto another suspect in KCPD's Cold Case Squad investigation. Okay, so it had taken a little blackmail in the form of appealing to his military roots to finally get him to listen. But once he saw the damage to her front porch and read the notes, he believed. He protected. He upset her small, familiar world in frightening, exciting ways, and yet he made her feel safe. So, yes, they'd become friends—an opposites attracting, differences complementing each other kind of thing. But something in her heart wanted them to be much more.

Once this case was solved, however—assuming they could piece all the old secrets together to complete the puzzle and finally solve Richard's murder—would she be enough to interest a man like Max? Would there be other reasons he might want to remain a part of her life?

"Here you go." Howard handed her a mug of the steaming brew and took a seat on the corner of his desk, facing her. He swallowed a drink, then splayed his fingers and looked at his hand before rubbing his knuckles against the leg of his lightweight wool slacks. "Is he making any progress? Getting the job done?"

Rosemary cradled the warm mug between her hands. "You know how important it is to me to clear my name. It's the only way to convince Charleen and my neighbors and the rest of the world that I didn't get away with murder. Maybe I could get a job teaching again. Max is helping change people's opinion of me. He's expanded the list of suspects so that my name's not the only one on it for a change. He makes it more comfortable for me to interact with people." She shook her head. "I still can't claim that it's easy—my trust issues make it hard to socialize for long with big groups or certain people, of course—but he makes it easier to try."

"Good for him." Howard set his mug on the desk and scratched at a trio of welts on his left hand. "I made life easier for you, too, if you remember. I kept you from ever being formally charged for Richard's murder by reminding the police they didn't have enough evidence to take the case to the DA for prosecution."

"I appreciate that, Howard. I don't know how I would have gotten through the last six years without you. You were so helpful with Stephen's case, too." When she saw how badly the red marks were irritating him, she set her mug on the desk, too, and got up to cradle his big hand between hers. "Where did you get those nasty scratches? I think you need some hydrocortisone or calamine…"

Puncture wounds. A dermatitis reaction to a foreign substance, like leaf sap or pollen.

Rosemary released his hand and backed away as if his skin had burned her. He'd grappled with a hawthorn bush. "You?"

The dark eyes looking back at her were anything but friendly, patient or professional. That hard, cold, disappointed look was a lot like…his brother's.

"The canned laughter was a little theatrical, but that scream of yours was worth every penny."

Rosie glanced at the door. Did she need to run? Would he really hurt her? "I thought you were my friend."

Howard's voice was laced with contempt. "And I thought you were smart."

Rosie dropped her chin and shivered. So talking was out. Ingrained habits from an abusive relationship were hard to break. She felt herself tensing, bracing, preparing herself for whatever cruel words would spew from his mouth. She inched away as the dimensions of the locked room closed in on her.

He'd trapped her.

Just like his brother had.

Only, she wasn't alone in her house with a dangerously unpredictable man. She wasn't alone at all. Max was right down the hallway. Okay, about a hundred feet down that hallway. With at least three closed doors in between them.

Rosie's chin shot up as she shook off the crippling fears of the past. She grabbed her purse and dashed to the door.

But Howard beat her to it. Moving surprisingly fast for an older man, he planted himself between her and escape. She quickly circled behind his desk and leather chair, scanning the room for an available weapon if she needed to defend herself.

"I lost my brother because of you," Howard accused.

"I didn't kill him."

"I don't care who did. I'm just glad he's gone." He moved to the desk and Rosie backed up to the window. "He was blowing through the family fortune, ruining the firm with his indiscretions. That's why he latched on to you—for the money and respectability."

"You're not like him, Howard. Please. You were kind to Stephen. You took care of our legal and financial needs. You helped me get Richard out of my life."

"Damn right, I did. You owe me. I've been there for you every step of the way. I was patient with you and all your little idiosyncrasies." As he came around the desk, she countered his path, keeping as much distance as possible between them. The wary beat of her pulse nearly choked her. If he laid a hand on her the way Richard had… "You depend on me," he reminded her. "When you started getting those threats, when your mysterious stalker knew so many intimate details about you and Richard and said he wanted to kill you, I knew you were afraid."

"I was terrified. Why would you do that to me?"

He pounded his fist on the desk and she jumped. "So you would come to me for help. Not to some uncivilized thug of a cop. Good grief, I heard you picked him up in a bar. You're my class of people, Rosemary, not his."

"That uncivilized thug is right down the hall, Howard. I'll scream and he'll throw you in jail so fast—"

"He can't hear you through soundproofed walls. And I have a feeling Charleen won't be a very cooperative witness and that her interview will take a while. Long enough for you to come to your senses and remember who your real hero is."

Her gaze darted from the thick walls lined with books to the tenth-story window and locked door that offered her only means of escape. "I'm not that frightened mental invalid beaten down by grief and abuse anymore. The real me is coming back. Max!"

When she charged toward the door, Howard shifted direction and snatched her arm, pulling her against him and slapping his other hand over her mouth to silence her. "You won't scream, because I'll have his badge if you do."

Rosie froze in his painful grip and he moved his sweaty palm off her lips. "You'd do that? You'd ruin his career?"

Howard laughed. "It'd be easy enough. Krolikowski is already on thin ice with the department. Public drunkenness. Anger issues—"

"He's not like that—"

"—a blatant disregard for regulations and comportment. He'd probably come in here and beat me up if he could hear you. Imagine the mileage I'd get out of that with the commissioner."

She tugged against the hand on her arm. "I'd tell his superior officers the truth. You're crazy."

"Oh, *I'm* crazy? Says the thirty-something recluse who lives inside a fortress, dresses like an old maid and is afraid of her own shadow? You think they'd take the word of a murder suspect over a respected member of the court?" His moist breath spit against her ear. "Whatever you think you have with him is done. *I'm* the man you need. You're going to marry me."

Her hips butted against his desk. His thighs trapped her. "Never. You threatened to kill me, Howard."

"I would have married you and made the threats all go away. That was the plan. I wanted you so scared that you'd have to come out of that cave you hide in and turn to someone for help. And it was working until Krolikowski came along." He flattened his hand against his chest. "It was supposed to be me. For six years I've planned how we would be together. I showed you more patience than any normal man could. I set it up so that *I* was the man in your life."

"You were my friend."

"People have married for less."

"I don't love you."

"That doesn't matter. We could have a successful business partnership. I'm more mature than my brother ever was. I wouldn't make demands on you."

She lowered her chin and shook her head. "That damn money."

"Now that's hardly ladylike. Krolikowski's bad habits are rubbing off on you." He spoke to her cowed head. "I've earned you, you freak. I sided with you against my brother's memory. I was loyal to you. I did everything I could for your loser brother. Who else would have you?"

"If that's the deal you're offering, I'd rather be alone." When she zeroed in on his Italian loafers, she felt a flare of red-haired temper flooding through her. She was done being the Bratcher brothers' victim.

She brought her heel down hard on his instep and shoved her shoulder into his chest, freeing herself. Howard stumbled back into a bookshelf and she ran for the door. "Max!"

All she had to do was scream if she was in trouble, and he'd come running. No matter how many floors or doors were between them. He'd promised.

"Max!" Ignoring Howard's threat, she threw open the door.

"Your choice. His career is over. You will not leave me for him."

"I was never yours."

He cinched his hands around her waist and tossed her toward the desk. She bruised her hip against the corner, but he was there before she could scramble away, capturing her against the solid oak. "He's rough, exciting, animalistic, I bet."

"What is wrong with you?" Rosie clawed at his neck, beat at his chest. "Get your hands off me. He's going to arrest you."

Howard bent her back over the desk, his thigh sliding between hers. She slapped at the hand that skimmed her breast. "Is that how you like it? Rough? I don't have to be a gentleman. All these years I thought that was what you wanted. But I could send you a few more love notes if you want."

"Get. Off. Me." Her shoulder hit a coffee mug, sloshing the hot liquid onto her arm. Forget the Colonel's empty Army pistol. She reached up, closed her hand around the mug and tossed the hot liquid in his face. She wasn't the only one screaming when she ran for the door. "Max!"

But she'd only riled the beast. Before she made it to the door, Howard caught her and shoved her up against the bookshelf. He closed his hands around her neck in a choke hold that cut off her voice and her breath and stuck his red, scalded face near hers. "I always wondered what it was like when Richard got rough with you."

Rosie twisted, gouged, kicked. She tried to suck in a breath, but the sound gurgled in her throat. Her chest constricted. Ached. Howard had lost it. There was no reasoning with him now.

"Rosie!" A fist pounded on the locked door.

Maybe Howard hadn't heard the same angry shout she had. He tightened his grip around her neck. "There *is* a little rush to this, isn't there? I can feel the pulse points beneath my thumbs. Does it hurt? Do you feel like doing what I ask now?"

Pound. Pound. "Rosie!"

She scratched at his injured hand, but she was getting weak. She needed air. White dots floated across her vision and the room tilted.

"If you don't say yes to me, I'll make sure you go away for Richard's murder. I know enough details about your relationship to make you look guilty as sin. I'll even defend you…and, sadly, lose your case." He nuzzled her ear. "What will it be? Boyfriend or me? Prison? Or marri—"

The frame around the door splintered and the heavy oak swung open beside her. Max rammed Howard like a linebacker, tearing his grip off Rosie, freeing her. The two men flew across the desk and Rosie collapsed to her knees. She sucked in a deep breath that scratched her throat and filled her deprived lungs with precious oxygen. A chair toppled, another broke.

"Max." Her voice came out in a hoarse croak. His

fist met Howard's jaw with a thud, and the attorney's head snapped back. "Max!"

"You keep your hands off her. Understand?"

Howard laughed in response, not putting up any fight. "Temper, temper, Officer. Oh, I am so reporting this. Cop Attacks Attorney."

"The attorney's a nut job." Max flipped Howard face-down on the carpet, put his knee in the man's back and cuffed him.

His grizzled jaw was tight when he reached over to touch Rosie's bruised neck and arm. "He hurt you."

"I'm okay. I'll be okay." Her voice was getting stronger. The room blossomed with color again after she'd nearly passed out. Max's blue eyes. The red blood at the corner of Howard's mouth. Rosie pushed to her feet, leaning on the shelves for support. "Howard sent those threats. It makes sense. He knew the details of my relationship with his brother. He wanted to scare me so I'd turn to him. Fall for him, maybe." Howard giggled like a child as Max helped him into a chair. She averted her gaze from those crazy cold eyes and looked to the man who had saved her. Again. "I turned to you, instead."

"You're sure you're okay?" He palmed the back of her neck and pulled her onto her toes for a quick, hard kiss that left her a little breathless again. His chest expanded in quick, deep inhales after the brief fight and sprint down the hallway. "Thank God you can scream, woman. I don't want to think about what could have happened if I'd been even a few seconds late. I had the receptionist call 9-1-1. Uniformed officers should be here any minute."

In the meantime, Rosie didn't complain when he hooked his arm around her shoulders and pulled her against him. She was quickly learning that this was where she felt the safest. "He was no better than Richard. How do I keep attracting these winners?" she added, the sarcasm clear, even in her husky tone.

Max went quiet for a few seconds, then covered the silence with a wry little laugh. "I'll throw his butt in jail for a very long time."

But Rosie tugged on his shirt, stopping him midreport. "Howard didn't kill Richard. He's hardly a perfume kind of guy. And how would he get his hands on RUD-317?"

"He could be the Bratcher in that pharmaceutical trial Dr. Wells is holding on to." He tapped the shoulder of the curiously subdued man sitting on his cuffed hands. "Hey. How about it, Bratcher?"

Howard grew more subdued as the manic thrill he'd discovered when he'd been choking her subsided. She could tell he was thinking more like a lawyer than the man with the violent obsession who'd brought a baseball bat and terror to her home. "I don't know what you're talking about."

"Can I at least book him for making terroristic threats to you?"

"Be my guest." Rosie nodded, wishing she felt more relief at finally identifying the man who'd preyed on her darkest fears.

Max didn't seem to think this was over yet, either. "We've got two perps—Howie here and the woman who killed his brother six years ago. Ah, hell." Max pulled her toward the broken door to look out into the lobby but stopped when he realized he'd be leaving Howard unguarded if he went any farther. "Charleen Grimes just left with her attorney." He pulled out his cell and punched in a number. "I'm calling the team. We're gonna end this thing."

MAX LEANED AGAINST the Chevelle's front fender while Rosie finished giving her statement to Olivia Watson. He nodded to Jim Parker, walking past with a large evidence bag holding the black sweatshirt hoodie with the torn sleeve he'd found in the trunk of Howard Bratcher's car.

A car. Why couldn't the attorney drive a fancy green pickup truck like the one Arlene Dinkle had reported seeing in the neighborhood? Now that would make the puzzle come together all neat and pretty. But Bratcher didn't own a truck. Maybe it was nothing but coincidence that an unidentified vehicle would show up in the same time frame as each of Bratcher's visits to Rosie's house. But, like most of the cops he knew, Max didn't like coincidences. If a good cop looked hard enough, there was almost always a rational explanation out there somewhere. Did the green truck mean someone else was watching Rosie's house? Their killer, perhaps? Or had Arlene made the whole thing up?

The truck wasn't the only piece to the puzzle that was bothering him. The summer night was still plenty warm, but Rosie kept running her hands up and down her bare arms as she and Liv talked over by Liv's SUV, as though she had a chill she just couldn't shake. Max wanted to put his hands there and warm her up. No, what he really wanted was to get her out of here— away from the flashing lights and endless questions and Howard Bratcher locked in the back of Trent's SUV to someplace quiet where they could be alone. Where he could hold her long enough to chase away that chill.

"Did you send a unit to keep an eye on Charleen Grimes?"

Max pulled away from the car at the approach of his lieutenant, Ginny Rafferty-Taylor, straightening to a civilian version of attention as his team leader came up beside him. "Yes, ma'am. If she goes anywhere besides home or her shop, or does anything suspicious, we'll know about it."

"In the meantime, we got a copy of that list of drug test patients and research and production staff from Endicott Global. Katie's going over it with a fine-tooth comb to see if Charleen's name pops—or any other family or business associate who could have gotten her access to the drug." The lieutenant tucked her short, silvery-blond hair behind her ears and leaned her hips back against the car the way he had a moment earlier. "You did good work today, Max."

He slid his fingers into the back pockets of his jeans and shrugged his frustration. "I haven't solved our case yet."

"Take the compliment. We've been working this murder for six years now. This is the first forward progress we've made in almost that long." She nodded toward the conversation wrapping up near the building's front door. "Miss March filled me in on the threats

Howard Bratcher made against your badge, too. Don't worry. I've got your back. I didn't settle for just anybody on my squad. You were all handpicked for your various expertise."

"I gave Bratcher a fat lip." He eyed the purple bruises already appearing on Rosie's pale skin as she paused beneath a streetlight before crossing the street to join them. He felt his fingers curling into fists again. Was that supposed to be his area of expertise? Laying a guy out flat for nearly squeezing the life out of a woman? "I suppose I have an anger management class in my future?"

"You were protecting someone you care about." The lieutenant leaned in and whispered, "Besides, didn't I ever tell you I have a soft spot for big guys who are good with their hands?"

"No."

She squeezed his arm before walking away to her car. "You should meet my husband sometime."

Max chuckled. "Yes, ma'am."

Rosie exchanged good-nights with the lieutenant before joining Max at the car.

"Cold?" Max brushed his hands over the goose bumps dotting her arms.

She shook her head and shivered anew. "Confused, maybe. Disappointed in my inability to function out in the real world."

"That's harsh."

"Tonight made me feel like I'm not meant to be anything more than a prize to be stolen or swindled. Howard was so angry. Just like Richard." She raised her gaze to his. "Why couldn't I see it? Why did I think Howard was my friend?"

"Because you've got a heart, Rosie March." He opened the car door and pulled his black leather jacket from the backseat to drape around her shoulders. "Here. I think it's human nature to trust people, to want to see the best in them. Especially if that's the way they want you to see them. Most people keep their deepest thoughts and insecurities and shortcomings hidden. Good people and bad." He freed a couple of tendrils from the collar of the jacket. "I'm glad the bad things in this world haven't warped you like me yet."

She linked her fingers with his and held on when he would have pulled away. "I'm always going to believe you're a good guy, Max. Thank you. I can never repay you for listening to me, believing me. Jimmy would have been proud of you for standing by me and helping me get Howard out of my life."

"Just promise me if you meet anyone else named Bratcher, you'll run the other way instead of making friends."

At last, she smiled. "I promise." She braced her free hand against his chest and stretched up to kiss his cheek. "You did great, Sergeant. Thank you."

"Why does that sound like goodbye?" He tugged on her fingers and led her around to the passenger seat. "I live in your basement."

"But I thought—with Howard under arrest…"

This mission wasn't over yet, as far as he was concerned. "There's still a killer out there I'm looking for. And we've stirred up enough of a hornet's nest today that I'm not letting you out of my sight until we identify the woman who was in Bratcher's bedroom that night and I can close my case." He opened the car door for her to get in. "Buckle up."

Her smile eased his concern a fraction. "Yes, sir."

By the time he'd circled back to the driver's side, Trent was jogging up to meet him. "Hey, brother."

"What is it, junior?"

His partner handed him a DMV printout of Glasses Guy, the man Rosie had ID'd from the society page photo. "Meet Leland Asher's nephew, Matthew."

"Son of a gun." He handed the printout over to Rosie. "Look familiar?"

"That's him. Is he part of his uncle's organization?" She handed the paper back. "What's his connection to me?"

"It may not mean anything. We can't tie him to any criminal wrongdoing," Trent answered. "But he does visit his uncle in prison."

"So he could be a courier for getting his uncle's messages in or out of Jeff City." Max quickly skimmed the rest of the information on the page and muttered a curse. Matt Asher drove a Chrysler sedan, not a green pickup. "So he doesn't have a connection to the Bratchers, either."

Trent shook his head. "He's got an alibi for most of the nights the stalker was at Rosie's house."

"Which is?"

"Believe it or not—therapy. He sees a clinical psychologist. I'm guessin' he's got family issues. We'll keep an eye on him to see if any messages are passed between him and Uncle Leland when he visits him in prison. But right now, we've got nothing on him. We can't touch him. Plus, the kid's only twenty-two. He was barely old enough to drive when Bratcher was murdered."

Max looked up to his partner and thanked him.

"Not a problem. Anything else?"

"Yeah. Send somebody over to watch Rosie's house tonight. I need some solid shut-eye."

Trent waved to Rosie to reassure her, as well. "I'll be there myself as soon as I process Bratcher."

"I owe ya."

"Don't worry, brother. I'll collect."

MAX AND THE DOGS heard the quiet whimpering over the rainfall sounds of the shower coming through the bathroom door. He didn't know about Duchess and Trixie, but he wasn't sure how long he could stand that heartbreaking little mewl before he busted down another door to get inside and do something about it.

The house couldn't be locked up any tighter. He had his Glock strapped to his belt. The blinds throughout the house were drawn to dissuade the Dinkles' and anyone else's curiosity about the copper-haired recluse, and he knew Trent was parked in his truck out in the driveway tonight. So no way had anyone gotten past all those lines of defense to hurt her.

Still… He knocked softly at the door. "Rosie? Honey, are you okay?"

"Just a minute." Although he could easily jimmy the old door lock, he scrubbed his hand over his stubbled jaw, waiting impatiently through some sniffling and shuffling noises. Then the running water stopped.

A few seconds later, the latch turned and the door opened.

"You girls, stay," he ordered. Not waiting for an invitation, he slipped inside the white-and-black-tiled bathroom and closed the door behind him.

"What is it?" Rosie asked, clutching the lime-green towel that hung from the scalloped swells of her breasts down to the top of her thighs. His pulse rate kicked up in hungry awareness, so he wisely hung back by the door. "Is something wrong?"

"I hope not." Ignoring the long, wavy strands of wet copper that clung to her shoulders and sent tiny rivulets of water down her arms and into the shadowy cleft between her breasts, Max focused on the ugly marks marring the skin around her neck. He brushed his fingers across the blue-and-violet bruises there. "Are you in pain? Is your throat still sore? The paramedic said that gargling would help." He ran through the checklist of possible complications related to her assault. "Are you having any trouble breathing or swallowing? Maybe I should have run you to the ER instead of bringing you home."

She offered him an unconvincing smile. "I'm okay. I'm sore. But the hot water helps."

So, no physical pain. That would have been easier to deal with. With the pad of his thumb, he wiped away a tear that lingered on her cheek. "And this?"

She turned her head and pressed a kiss into his palm. "You once said that I could tell you anything, that you'd listen."

"That's right." He made a valiant effort to avert his gaze from all that creamy bare skin peeking out above and below the edges of the towel. But the burn scars and bruises at her neck were a sobering reminder to his traitorous body that she wanted to have a serious conversation here. "Is everything okay?"

"You said I should look you in the eye and ask for what I want." She tilted those soft gray eyes to his and he lost his heart to her a little more. "I want you to stay."

"I wasn't planning on going back to the basement."

"No. I'm not saying this right." Her gaze dropped to his chin, then bounced right back. "Stay here. With me."

The walls of restraint that were keeping his libido in check took a serious hit. But he didn't want to misunderstand. "Honey, don't tease a man. Are you asking me to take you to bed?"

She nodded and reached up to trace her fingers along the line of his jaw, waking dozens of very interested nerve endings there. "I want to do more than cuddle tonight, Sergeant. I want to feel like a normal, desirable woman. I want to feel good hands, safe hands...*your* hands on me. I want to erase—"

"I get the message." Max already had her in his arms. His mouth was on hers, his tongue driving inside to claim her taste for his own. He drove her back against the tile wall, imprinting her curves against his harder body. Her hands slid up to his face and hair and his slid down to grasp her hips and pull them into the cradle of his thighs.

His jeans felt thick. His shirt was an impediment. And that towel definitely had to go.

With their lips clinging to each other, their hands explored places that were tender and hard. Silky and soft. Cool and hot. He got his belt off and his holster safely set aside on the vanity before she reached for the zipper of his jeans.

"Not yet, honey." He caught her wrists and moved her hands to his chest, encouraging her to go after the buttons on his shirt while he shucked out of his boots and jeans.

By the time he was as naked as she was and he'd fished a condom out of his wallet, her lips had discovered the taut, eager nipples of his chest and a bundle of nerves behind his left ear. He'd feasted on her lips and filled his hands with the heavy weight of her breasts. He tongued his way from one curve to the next, stopping only to turn the shower back on and adjust the temperature to a soothing warmth before he palmed the back of her thighs and lifted her into the shower with him.

"Max," she gasped, her thighs clenching when the water first hit her skin.

"Easy, honey." He pulled her into the heat of his body and switched positions, taking the brunt of the spray on his back. "I want to make this as good for you as I can."

Then he grabbed the bar of soap and really went to work. She wanted to forget that Howard had touched her? That Richard had abused her? Max wanted to imprint himself all over her body. He put his hands every place he could touch—her feet, her legs, that sweet round bottom. He washed her stomach and back and arms and breasts, running the creamy soap over her beautiful skin. Then he moved the soap between her legs to wash her there.

Her thighs clenched around his hand. Her fingers dug into his shoulders. Her forehead fell against his chest. "Oh, Max. Max." She said his name, over and over, in breathless whispers against his skin. Soon, he set the soap aside. With the heat of the water and the heat of his hand pressing against her most tender flesh, he felt her tighten, quiver. And when he slipped a finger inside her, then two, she cried out his name and convulsed around his hand.

How could any man not think this brave, vibrant, responsive woman was anything but sexy and desirable?

But it wasn't enough. For either of them.

The shy siren with the beautiful body slipped her arms around his neck and pressed every decadent inch against his hot, primed body. Not even the water sluicing over his head and shoulders could come between them as she pulled her mouth down to his and asked for what she truly wanted.

"You, Max. I want you inside me. Now."

His fingers shaking with the need of his body, he reached around the shower curtain and ripped open the condom packet. All he remembered were her hands learning his body, her lips demanding kiss after kiss. He happily obliged her exploration until he could take no more.

"Now, honey."

"Yes."

He picked her up and her legs wrapped around his hips as he eased himself inside. He held his breath for a moment, filling her, expanding her warm sheath to accommodate his desire. With his strong hands holding her securely between the tile wall and his body, he began to move inside her. Slowly, at first. A thrust, a kiss. A thrust, a nibble of her ear. His lips moved lower with each thrust and she arched her back, offering him her body. He closed his mouth over the proud peak of her breast, swirled his tongue around her pearled nipple and she gasped.

His body demanded faster, harder, and hers accepted, welcomed, blossomed with his need.

The one glitch came when he pressed a kiss to the scar on her collarbone. Her fingers tried to push his lips away. "Don't," she whispered. "They're ugly."

But Max insisted on gently kissing each mark. "Every inch of you is beautiful to me."

And then the need became too great. The rhythm between their bodies synced and moved together. The water ran, the heat consumed him. And with a final thrust that blinded him to all but the crazy, inexplicable love he had for this woman, Max poured himself out inside her.

A few minutes later, after catching their breaths and another quick rinse in the cooling shower, Rosie turned off the water. He wrapped a towel around his waist and another around her, then lifted her into his arms and carried her to bed.

He shoved a pair of bed-hog dogs onto the floor and laid her down. Max climbed in beside her, pulled the covers up over them both. Spooning his damp, spent body next to hers, he pulled Rosie to his chest, buried his nose in the sweet scent of her hair, and they drifted off into a deep, healing sleep together.

CHAPTER ELEVEN

MAX AWOKE TO a dog licking his ear and an empty pillow beside him.

A brief moment of panic—that Rosie had somehow been taken from him while he slept, with that dreadful sense of finality he'd felt the morning Jimmy hadn't shown up for their fishing weekend—roused him completely. But the panic quickly ebbed when he smelled the coffee brewing in the kitchen and heard the strains of an orchestra playing softly from another part of the house. Rosie was fine. Just an early riser, eager to get a start on a new day. Hopefully, not a woman who was having regrets about the night before.

And then there was the poodle who'd taken such a shine to him. Pushing aside Trixie's tongue, Max sat up. She switched the licking to his hand until he spared a minute to give her a tummy rub. "Really? Is this going to be a thing with you?"

He set the fuzzy morning greeter on the floor and got up to use the bathroom, retrieving his shorts and jeans and pulling them on. He tucked his holster into the back of his belt and pulled out his phone to put in a quick call to Trent to get a status report.

"Morning, sunshine," Trent teased. "How'd you sleep?"

"Better than you, I'm guessin'. Anything I need to know about?"

"Everything's quiet out here. I got a call five minutes ago from Jim. He said Charleen Grimes left her condo, drove through a coffee shop, then went to work. Apparently, they're having a big summer clearance sale at her boutique if you're lookin' for a new dress."

"No, thanks." Max shook his head and went to the kitchen to pour himself a mug of coffee. Even after a stakeout, the younger detective was too chipper in the morning for his tastes. "Anything else?"

"You need to call Katie. She's got some information you'll want to hear."

"Got it. I've got my coffee now, so you can leave. Thanks for keeping an eye on things."

"Not a problem."

Max drank half his coffee and ate a cinnamon roll that he hoped Rosie had left out for him before dialing Katie's number.

"Good morning, Max." Was everyone he knew a morning person?

"Morning, kiddo. Trent said you had something for me?"

"You bet. I tracked down a short list of dark green, extended cab pickup trucks with black trim—sold in the KC area in the past month, so it would still have dealer stickers and not a registered license plate yet."

"How short is the list?"

"Three trucks. Here's where it gets interesting."

Normally he was amused by Katie's flair for drama, but this morning he just wanted to get the info and get back to Rosie. "Tell me, sunshine."

"All three were purchased as fleet vehicles for Endicott Global."

Max opened his mouth to swear but decided Katie didn't need to hear him any more than Rosie did. But that Wells woman had lied to them with a straight face. The CEO fit two of the three puzzle pieces—she had access to the drug that killed Richard Bratcher, and a company vehicle had been spotted near Rosie's house. "You did good, kiddo. Thanks."

More awake and on guard and ready to face whatever reaction Rosie had to that steamy shower they'd shared, he sought her out and found her sitting on the braided rug in the library. He needn't have worried about her having regrets or feeling self-conscious about her beautiful body or feeling pressured to turn one night into a full-blown relationship. She jumped up from the boxes and papers she'd been sorting and hurried across the room, smiling.

The jeans she wore kind of caught him off guard. He wouldn't have thought she even owned a pair with that wardrobe of dresses she usually wore. But he couldn't help but smile back—or cling to the kiss she rose up on tiptoe to give him. "Morning, Rosie Posy."

"Max, look what I found." She hadn't pinned her hair up yet, either, which distracted him from the stationery and envelopes she juggled in her hand. "I was going through some old letters Richard had written me. I felt like I was starting a new life today so I wanted to get rid of my past. I mean I'm thinking of myself as Rosie instead of Rosemary now. I'm not afraid some creep will come to my house every night anymore. I was going to throw away all these old letters he sent me."

He put a hand up to stop the philosophical discussion he wanted to hear more about—later—and urged her to get to the point. "What did you find, Rosie?"

"This." She tossed most of the letters she held into a box, then unfolded one stamped with the Bratcher law firm name at the top. A rock settled in Max's gut. This couldn't be good. "Richard must have stuck this letter in the wrong envelope. It's to his mistress, not me."

He took the letter. "You know, for a man I've never met, I sure do dislike him."

Rosie pointed to the salutation at the top of the paper. "Look who it's written to."

Max drew in a satisfied breath as the third piece of the puzzle fell into place.

Charleen Grimes wasn't the only woman Richard had cheated with.

"We've been looking for the wrong mistress."

It was a love letter to Hillary Wells.

"I'M TIRED OF WAITING."

"Sir, I told you she was on a conference call… Sir?"

Rosie nodded to the sputtering assistant at the front desk as Max flashed his badge and marched right past him into Hillary Wells's office at the Endicott Global building.

She plowed into Max's back when he suddenly stopped. He spun around to catch her hand and keep her from tumbling, but she could see what had stopped him. The office was empty.

"Is there a back door to this room?" Max asked. "She's not here."

The assistant stepped into the office and looked around, too. He threw up his hands as if surprised to see his boss had left.

Max clapped him on the shoulder and pushed him out of his path. "Nice stall, kid. You hear from the boss lady, tell her KCPD wants to have a conversation with her."

"Yes, sir."

While they were driving down the highway, Max alerted the Cold Case Squad that Hillary Wells was in the wind. She'd skipped out on her appointment with Max and Rosie and hadn't left her contact information with her assistant. She wasn't answering any of her phones, and, according to Katie, who'd tried to locate her via GPS, Dr. Wells's cell phone had been turned off.

"Wait a minute." Katie hesitated, probably reading something off one of her computer screens. Rosie had put Max's cell on speaker and held it up for him to speak and hear while he drove the Chevelle.

"What is it, kiddo?" Max prompted.

"It looks like she has a cabin down by Truman Lake. I've got a ping off her vehicle's smart system there."

"Give me a twenty." Once Katie gave them the cabin's location and directions to get to it, Max made his way to the south end of the city and drove over to one of Missouri's most popular recreation areas.

An hour later, after a scenic drive through the northern edge of the Missouri Ozarks, they pulled into a gravel driveway behind a dark green pickup truck.

"Son of a gun." Katie's research was right on the money. "She's here," Max announced, nodding toward the windows along the front of the cabin that had been opened to let in the warm summer breeze. He took Rosie's hand and pulled her into step beside him and they walked to the front door. "Today, maybe you'd better let me do the talking. I have a feeling the good doctor won't be such a cooperative witness this time." He knocked on the door. "KCPD. It's Detective Krolikowski, Dr. Wells. I'd like to ask you a few more questions."

When the woman didn't immediately answer, Rosie asked, "How does this work, exactly—you ask her if she killed Richard?"

Max grinned. "Well, the direct approach doesn't usually work for most suspects."

"It worked for me."

He reached over and sifted his fingers through the ponytail hanging down the back of her T-shirt. "You, Rosie March, are the exception to most rules."

After more than a minute with no response, Max knocked again. "KCPD." He motioned Rosie to stand back to the side as he pulled his weapon.

His wary posture put her on guard, too. "Do you think something's wrong?"

His shoulders lifted with a deep breath. "I hope she hasn't done anything stupid like take some of her own drugs to get out of doing prison time."

"Suicide?"

Max's jaw trembled before he knocked on the door one last time. He was thinking of his friend Jimmy. "I'm comin' in, Dr. Wells."

Rosie clung to the safety of the wall while Max turned the knob and pushed open the door.

A gunshot exploded close to Rosie's ear and Max went flying back off the front step. "Max!"

He hit the ground with a horrible thud and pulled his knees up, groaning, rolling from side to side as the front of his shirt turned red with blood.

Hillary Wells marched out of the cabin, shifted the aim of her gun at Rosie and warned her, "Don't move."

Rosie clung to the cedar planking of the cabin while Hillary picked up Max's weapon, which had been jarred from his hand when he'd landed.

She unloaded the magazine of bullets from his gun and tossed the weapon one direction into the woods surrounding the house, and the magazine into the trees in the opposite direction.

Hillary turned back to Rosie, using her gun to give succinct directions. "Now handcuff his wrists together. Then get his keys and load him into the backseat of his car. You're driving."

ROSIE SWIPED AWAY the tears the spilled from the corner of her eye, not sure if they were tears of fear that Max's head kept lolling from one side to the other as he bled out into the backseat, or pure, white-hot anger for the woman sitting in the passenger seat, calmly giving driving directions while training her gun at Rosie to ensure her cooperation. She suspected it was a little of both. Hillary Wells had killed one man Rosie had thought she loved, and now the woman was going to kill Max. And that would be a loss from which Rosie was certain she'd never recover.

Rosie glanced down at the typed suicide note Hillary had forced her to sign by threatening to shoot Max again. The Endicott Global CEO had written an essay of pure fiction, where Rosie confessed to murdering her abusive ex-fiancé by filling a bottle of champagne with RUD-317, seducing him in his condo and sneaking out after he'd overdosed on the drug. When the Cold Case Squad detective unmasked her as the killer several years later, she shot him before her secret could be revealed. But she'd fallen in love with the detective and, regretting her rash action, killed herself.

Rosie shifted her grip on the wheel and tried to think of a way she could escape and get Max to an ER for medical treatment. He kept sliding in and out of consciousness. His breathing was labored and his skin was far too pale.

"No one who knows me will ever believe that note."

Hillary smirked. "They won't believe you're a strong enough woman to commit cold-blooded murder?"

"No. They won't believe I'd ever want to seduce Richard."

The deep-pitched chuckle from the backseat infused her with renewed strength and determination. "That's my girl," Max rasped.

But Hillary didn't appreciate the humor. "I knew you were going to be trouble. You couldn't be content, could you? Nobody could prove you murdered Richard, but as long as you were the police's prime suspect, no one was looking at me, either." She indicated a narrow side road and ordered Rosie to turn. "Richard was a scumbag—greedy, self-centered, violent—the world is better without him. It was a win-win situation. You weren't in jail and he was out of your life. But you had to know the truth, didn't you?"

"He's never been out of my life since I met him. Clearing my name is the only way I can finally say goodbye to his influence over me."

Sheer will seemed to fuel the grumbling voice from the backseat. "Why did you kill him, Doc? You didn't like that he cheated on you, too? Or are you just a man hater?"

"It was purely business." She pointed to a gravel road among the trees. "Turn here." Rosie obeyed, following Dr. Wells's directions deeper into the forested recreational area dotted with remote cabins around the dam and creeks that fed them. "Richard was a two-night stand. I picked him up in a hotel bar."

Rosie glanced in the rearview mirror. Max opened his eyes and nodded. He remembered it, too. Rosie had picked him up in a bar and recruited him into helping her. She hadn't regretted a moment of their time together since.

"How is murder a business deal?" Rosie asked, concentrating on the narrowing road. They were dropping in altitude, too. They were approaching a remote cove off the main lake.

"I needed someone else dead and out of my way before he cheated me out of my life's work and rightful position at the company."

"Lloyd Endicott?" Max guessed.

"Yes." The woman was completely unapologetic about the death of her so-called friend and mentor. "I knew I'd be the first person the police would look at if it was proved Lloyd's death was anything but accidental. So I made a deal with a colleague to arrange for his death, and in exchange, I was asked to eliminate Richard."

"Strangers on a Train," Max muttered.

"What?"

"Nothing. I have a couple of friends who like old movies."

Turning up her nose as if polite chitchat was beneath her, Hillary used the gun to give Rosie the next direction. "Pull up over there at the old boat ramp. Leave the engine running."

"Who wanted Richard dead?"

"I'm not allowed to say. A deal's a deal."

"Killing us can't be part of the deal. Isn't the trick to getting away with murder that you have an airtight alibi while someone else does the dirty work for you?"

"Hence, the signed confession. When your bodies are found, they'll find the letter and file your deaths away as a murder-suicide."

Rosie's heart squeezed in her chest at the pained expression on Max's face. She knew it wasn't just the bullet hole in his gut, but the memory of his best friend's suicide that was tearing him up.

Forcing Max to suffer like this, taking away the man

who'd given her a few days of happiness simply wasn't fair. Not after everything else she'd been through. She wasn't exactly sure what that feverish sensation flowing through her veins was, but Rosie was thinking that Max had been right about her. She wasn't that quiet, demure, fragile woman by nature—that was a persona she'd taken on to survive her life with Richard and the terrible years that followed. Rosie had a redheaded temper firing through her blood.

She shifted the Chevy into Park and looked straight ahead at the gray-green water and whitecaps below. "Dr. Wells, I think you should know that I would never commit suicide. I've fought too hard to survive and to find happiness. No one will believe the story. There'll be an investigation."

She found Max's questioning gaze in the mirror and darted her eyes twice to the right. *I've got a plan. It's a crazy one. But I'm not giving up without a fight.*

Max nodded. "Hooah." HUA.

Heard. Understood. Acknowledged.

Clutching his stomach, he sat up a little straighter. "I love you, Rosie."

"I love you."

"Isn't that just sickeningly sweet," Hillary sneered. "You know what to do. As soon as I get out, shift the car into Drive. I'll make your boyfriend's death as painless as possible—a shot to the head. Then you drive the car into the lake. Unless you'd rather me wait to put the gun in your hand after I shoot you, too?" The dark-haired woman laughed. "Personally, I'd choose drowning in this deep part of the lake. That way, at least, I'm giving you a sporting chance at surviving."

Rosie took a deep breath and shifted the car while Hillary unbuckled her safety belt and reached for the door handle. "I know you love this car, Sergeant."

His expression turned as grim as she'd ever seen it. "Do it!"

Rosie stomped on the accelerator as Hillary turned to shoot Max. The car jerked forward, toppling the woman off balance. When she tumbled back against the seat, Max surged forward with a feral roar, looping his hand-cuffs around Hillary's neck as the gun fired.

"Max!" She heard his grunt of pain, saw the red circle appear on his shoulder and stain the front of his shirt.

His stranglehold on Dr. Wells went slack. "What are you doing? Stop!" she cried, struggling to free herself from the noose of Max's arms.

There was nothing Rosie could do but hold on and pray as the Chevy leaped the top of the boat ramp and hit the old concrete and rocks farther down. The car bottomed out, threw its passengers up to the ceiling. The gun bounced out of Hillary's hand and skittered along the floorboards. The other woman screamed as the car hit the water and plunged, nose first, in a slow-motion dive to the bottom of the lake.

The bruising wrench of the seat belt stunning Rosie quickly gave way to panic as the gray-green water rushed in. She was ankle-deep in the cool water before her brain kicked in. She quickly unhooked her seat belt and climbed up onto her knees to help Max escape.

"Max?" No answer. "Sergeant, can you hear me?" she shouted in a firmer voice. When his groggy eyes blinked open, she softened her command. "Can you unhook your seat belt?" She unlooped his arms from the headrest where he'd caught Hillary, then scrambled over the seat when the water rushed over his lap and his bound hands made it impossible to find the release.

Rosie spared a brief glance for the woman who'd tried to kill them, but at some point of impact, Hillary had struck her head and she was floating, unconscious, off her seat. Worrying more about the man she wanted desperately to save, Rosie took a breath and sank below the water that was pouring over the seat to release Max. When he, too, started to float, she pushed his body up to the ceiling where there was still air. "Breathe, honey. Take a deep breath."

She took several breaths herself, filling her lungs as deeply as she could before the translucent water hit the corner of her mouth and she sputtered.

She tipped her mouth to the ceiling. "Let me do the work, okay? Just don't fight me. You saved me, and now I'm going to save you."

He nodded his understanding before his eyes closed and the water rushed over his head. After snatching one last breath from a pocket of air, Rosie dove beneath the water to unlock Max's door and push it open. The changing water pressure made the car sink faster, but sucked them both out of the car when she grabbed onto his shirt and pulled him with her.

Then it was a series of kicks, a pull of her arm and ignoring the panicked need to breathe before she broke

the surface of the water. Refilling her lungs with re-
viving air, she pulled Max's heavy body onto her hip
and held his head above water as best she could while
she fought the wind-tossed waves and swam in a side-
stroke to shore. She was near exhaustion by the time she
reached a shallow enough depth that she could stand.

"Stay with me, Max," she urged, wiping the water
from his face and hair and dragging him to shore.

She slipped a couple of times trying to push him
up onto the dry ground between the rushes, grass and
rocks. He was conscious, at least, thank God, because
once he could get his legs beneath him, he helped
push himself higher onto the bank. But then she lost
her footing on the slick, mossy rocks and fell into the
water again, swallowing a mouthful as she sank beneath the surface. When she pushed herself back up,
a hand latched onto hers. Relief swept through her as
she surfaced.

"Max…" Stunned, she would have fallen again, but
the man who pulled her from the water didn't release
his grip. "You."

When the young man with the glasses finally let
go, she scrambled away, crawling over Max's legs and
kneeling in front of him to provide some sort of protection for her wounded hero. The young man who'd
taken her picture at the prison that day picked up the
suit jacket he'd tossed into the grass.

"You do good work, Miss March," he said, shrugging into his jacket.

"Who are you?"

"A friend of a friend who's looking out for you." He

turned his gaze out to the water where there weren't even bubbles left to show where the car had sunk. "Dr. Wells was becoming a bit of a problem for us."

Max's big hand grazed her knee and held on, comforting her as some of his strength returned. "You're Asher's man."

"No, Detective. I'm my own man." Without any more explanation than that, the mysterious Glasses Guy climbed the hill toward a black Chrysler parked at the top. "I already called 9-1-1. An ambulance is en route. I surely hope you don't bleed to death, Detective." He climbed inside his car and started the engine. "Ma'am. I think you'll understand that I'd rather not be here when the police arrive."

And with that, he drove away.

Rosie heard sirens in the distance and started to stand. But Max pulled her back to her knees. "Come here."

Without regard for modesty, she pulled off her T-shirt and wadded it up to stanch his wounds.

He splayed his fingers on her bare stomach and grinned. "Honey, I'm afraid I can't help you with that right now. Maybe later?"

How could he joke and flirt when she was so afraid? "Max. You're bleeding. Maybe dying. I don't want to lose you."

"Come. Here." He grabbed her and pulled her down into the grass beside him. He pressed a kiss to her temple and rubbed his grizzled cheek against hers. The sirens were getting closer. Glasses Guy hadn't lied. Help was coming. "Are you okay? Are you hurt?"

"I'm fine. You're the one who got shot. Twice."

"I'm gonna live through both. I'm a tough guy, re-member?"

"Damn it, Max—"

"Rosemary March. Did you just swear? You know I don't like hearing that from you," he teased. He pulled her in for a kiss that lasted until a groan of pain forced him to come up for air. "You get under my skin, Rosie."

"Like an itchy rash?" she teased, pushing the wad-ded T-shirt back into place over his stomach wound.

"Like an alarm clock finally waking me up to the life I'm supposed to have. With you." So when did the tough guy learn to speak such beautiful things? Tears stung her eyes again as she found a spot where she could hug him without causing any pain. "I know I'm not the guy you expected to want you like this, and I know you weren't the woman I was looking for. Hell, I wasn't even looking."

"Neither was I."

"But we found each other."

"We're good for each other."

"I'm not an easy man to live with. I come with a lot of emotional baggage."

"And I don't?"

"You can do better than me."

Rosie shook her head, smiling. "I can't do better than a good man who loves me. A man who encourages me to be myself and to be strong and who makes me feel safer and more loved than I have ever felt in my life."

"I do love you, Rosie."

"I love you, Max." They shared another kiss until

she realized the ambulance and two sheriff's cars were pulling to a stop at the top of the boat ramp.

"What are we going to do about these feelings?" Max asked.

"What do you want to do?"

"Let's give the Dinkles something to talk about."

"You're moving in upstairs?"

"And opening all the windows."

Rosie smiled. "Oh, I hope we give them plenty to talk about."

* * * * *

KANSAS CITY CONFESSIONS

For my dear friend and fellow author, Laura Landon.

She's a sweetie to travel to conferences with,
and a tough ol' bird when it comes to motivating me.
Love her!

Oh, and she writes wonderful historical romances, too.

CHAPTER ONE

"'GOD BLESS US, every one.'"

Katie Rinaldi joined the smattering of applause from the mostly empty seats of the Williams College auditorium, where the community theater group she belonged to was rehearsing a production of Charles Dickens's *A Christmas Carol*. The man with the white hair playing Ebenezer Scrooge stood at center stage, accepting handshakes and congratulations from the other actors as they completed their first technical rehearsal with sound and lights. The costumes she'd constructed for the three spirits seemed to be fitting just fine. And once she finished painting the mask for the Spirit of Christmas Future, she could sit back and enjoy the run of the show as an audience member. Okay, as a proud mama. She only had eyes for Tiny Tim.

She gave a thumbs-up sign to her third-grade son and laughed when he had to fight with the long sleeves of his costume jacket to free his hands and return the gesture. His rolling-eyed expression of frustration softened her laugh into an understanding smile.

She mouthed, *Okay. I'll fix it.* Once he was certain she'd gotten the message, Tyler Rinaldi turned to chatter with the boy next to him, who played one of his older

Cratchit brothers. One of the girls joined the group, bringing over a prop toy, and instantly, they were involved in a challenge to see who could get the wooden ball on an attached string into the cup first.

Although extra demands with her job at KCPD and the normal bustle of the holidays meant Katie was already busy without having to work a play into her schedule, she was glad she'd brought Tyler to auditions. The only child of a single mother, Tyler often spent his evenings alone with her, reading books or playing video or computer games after he finished his homework. She was glad to see him having fun and making friends.

"Note to self." Katie pulled her laptop from her lime-green-and-blue-flowered bag and opened up her calendar to type in a reminder that she needed to adjust the costume that had initially been made for a larger child. What was one less hour of sleep, anyway? "Shorten sleeves."

"I think we might just have a show." Katie startled at the hand on her shoulder. "Sorry. I didn't realize you were working."

Katie saved her calendar and turned in her seat to acknowledge the slender man with thick blond hair streaked with threads of gray sinking into the cushioned seat behind her. "Hey, Doug. I was just making some costume notes."

The play's director leaned forward, resting his arms on the back of the seat beside her. "You've done a nice job," he complimented, even though she'd been only one of several volunteers. His professionally trained voice articulated every word to dramatic perfection. "We're down to the details now—if the gremlins in this old theater will give us a break."

"Gremlins?"

Doug looked up into the steel rafters of the catwalk two stories above their heads before bringing his dark eyes back to hers. "I don't know a theater that isn't haunted. Or a production that feels like it's going to be ready in time. Those were brand-new battery packs we put in the microphones tonight, but they still weren't working."

"And you think the gremlins are responsible?" she teased.

Laughing, he patted her shoulder again. "More likely a short in a wire somewhere. But we need to figure out that glitch, put the finishing touches on makeup and costumes, and get the rest of the set painted before we open next weekend."

"You don't ask for much, do you?" she answered, subtly pulling away from his touch. Doug Price was one of those ageless-looking souls who could be forty or fifty or maybe even sixty but who had the energy—and apparently the libido—of a much younger man. "It's a fun holiday tradition that your group puts on this show every year. Tyler's having a blast being a part of it."

"And you?"

Katie smiled. Despite dodging a few touches and missing those extra hours of sleep, she'd enjoyed the creative energy she'd been a part of these past few weeks. "Me, too."

"Douglas?" A man's voice from the stage interrupted the conversation. Francis Sergel, the tall, gaunt gentleman who played the Spirit of Christmas Future, had a sharp, nasal voice. Fortunately, he'd gotten the role because he looked the part and didn't have to speak onstage. "Curtain calls? You said you'd block them this evening."

"In a minute." Doug's hand was on her shoulder again. "You want to go grab a coffee after rehearsal? My treat."

Although she knew him to be divorced, Doug was probably old enough to be her father, and she simply wasn't interested in his flirtations. She had too many responsibilities to have time to be interested in any man besides her son.

"Sorry. I've got work to finish." She gestured to her laptop and saw the screen-saver picture had come up—a picture of Trent Dixon, a longtime friend and coworker. Trent, a former college football player, was carrying her son on his big shoulders after a fun day spent in Columbia, Missouri, at a Mizzou football game. Dressed in black-and-gold jerseys and jeans, both guys were smiling as if they'd had the time of their lives—and she suspected they had. Trent was as good to Tyler now as he'd been to her back in high school when she'd been a brand-new teenage mom and she'd needed a real friend. As always, the image of man and boy made her smile... and triggered a little pang of regret.

Katie quickly pushed a key and sent the image away before that useless melancholy could take hold. She'd made her choices—and a relationship with Trent wasn't one of them. She needed the brawny KCPD detective as a friend—Tyler needed him as a friend—more than she needed Trent to be a boyfriend or lover or even something more. She'd nearly ruined that friendship back in high school. She'd nearly ruined her entire life with the foolish impulses she'd succumbed to back then. She wasn't going to make those mistakes again.

Katie pointed to the small brown-haired boy onstage. All her choices as an adult were based on whatever was best for her son. "It's a school night for Tyler, too. So we need to head home."

But Doug had seen the momentary trip down memory lane in her lengthy pause. He reached over the seat to tap the edge of the laptop. "Was that Tyler's dad?"

The scent of gel or spray on his perfectly coiffed hair was a little overpowering as he brushed up beside her. Katie leaned to the far side of her seat to get some fresh air. "No. His father signed away his rights before Tyler was born. He's not in the picture."

She realized the tactical error as soon as the words left her mouth. Doug's grin widened as if she'd just given him a green light to hit on her. She mentally scrambled to backtrack and flashed a red light instead.

Easy. She clicked the mouse pad and pulled up the screen saver again, letting Trent's defensive-lineman shoulders and six feet five inches of height do their intimidation thing, even from a picture on a small screen. "This is Trent Dixon. He's a friend. A good friend," she emphasized, hoping Doug would interpret her longtime acquaintance with the boy who'd grown up across the street from her as a message that she wasn't interested in returning his nightly flirtations. "He's a cop. A KCPD detective."

If Trent's imposing size wasn't intimidating enough, the gun and badge usually ensured just about anybody's cooperation.

"I see. Maybe another time." Doug was king of his own little company of community theater volunteers and apparently didn't accept the word *no* from one of his lowly subjects. "I'll at least see you at the cast party after opening night, right?"

For Tyler's sake, she'd go and help her son celebrate his success—not because Doug kept asking her out. Katie lowered her head, brushing her thumb across the bottom of her keyboard, studying Trent's image as plan B popped into her head. Trent was Tyler's big buddy—the main male role model in her son's life besides her uncle Dwight, who'd taken her in when he'd married Katie's aunt Maddie nine years ago. Trent would be at the show's opening night. She'd make sure to introduce the big guy to Doug and let the handsy director rethink his efforts to date her. Katie was smiling at her evil little plan when she looked up again. "Sure. All three of us will be there."

"Doug?" Francis Sergel's voice had risen to a whiny pitch. "Curtain call?"

"I'm coming." The director waved off the middle-aged man with the beady dark eyes. "By the way, Tyler's done a great job memorizing his lines—faster than the other kids, and he's the youngest one."

Katie recognized the flattery for what it was, another attempt to make a connection with her. But she couldn't deny how proud she was of how her nine-year-old had taken to acting the way she once had. "Thanks. He's worked really hard."

"I can tell you've worked hard with him. He stays in character well, too."

"Douglas. Tonight?" Francis pulled the black hood off his head, although his dark, bushy beard and mustache still concealed half his face. "I'd like to get out of this costume."

"Coming." Doug squeezed her shoulder again as he stood. "See you tomorrow night." He clapped his hands to get everyone's attention onstage and sidled out into the aisle. "All right, cast—I need everybody's eyes right here."

But Francis's dark gaze held hers long enough to make her twitch uncomfortably in her seat. The man didn't need the Grim Reaper mask she was making for him. With his skin pinched over his bony cheeks and his eyes refusing to blink, he already gave her the willies. When he finally looked away and joined the clump of actors gathering center stage, Katie released the breath she hadn't known she'd been holding. What was that about?

Dismissing the man's interest as some kind of censure for keeping the director from doing his job, Katie turned to Tyler and winked. She tilted her head to encourage him to pay attention to Doug before she dropped her focus back to the computer in her lap. Francis was a bit of a diva on the best of nights. If he had a problem with Doug trying to make time with her, she'd send the actor straight to the source of the problem—aka, not her.

Feeling the need to tune out Doug and Francis and the prospect of another late night, Katie turned back to her computer. Blocking the final bows and running them a few times would take several minutes, leaving her the opportunity to get a little work done and hopefully free up some time once she got home and put Tyler to bed.

With quick precision, she keyed in the password to access encrypted work files she'd been organizing for the police department—sometimes on the clock, sometimes in her own spare time. Katie had spent months scanning in unsolved case files and loading the data into the cross-referencing computer program she'd designed. Okay, so maybe her work as an information specialist with KCPD's cold case squad wasn't as exciting as the acting career she'd dreamed of before a teenage pregnancy and harrowing kidnapping plot to sell her unborn son in a black-market baby ring had altered her life plan. But it was a good, steady paycheck that allowed her to support herself and Tyler single-handedly.

Besides, the technical aspects of her work had never stopped Katie from thinking, imagining, creating. She loved the challenge of fitting together the pieces of a puzzle on an old unsolved case—not to mention the satisfaction of knowing she was doing something meaningful with her life. She hadn't had the best start in the world—her abusive father had murdered her mother and been sent to prison. Helping the police catch bad guys went a long way toward redeeming herself for some of the foolish mistakes she'd made as an impulsive, grieving young woman trying to atone for her father's terror. Working with computers and data was a job her beloved aunt Maddie and uncle Dwight, Kansas City's district attorney, understood and respected. She would always be grateful to the two of them for rescuing her and Tyler and giving her a real home. Although she knew they would support her even if she had chosen to become an actress, this career choice was one way she could honor and thank them for taking her in and loving her like a daughter. Plus, even though he didn't quite grasp the research and technical details of her job, Tyler thought her work was pretty cool. Hanging out with all those cops and helping them solve crimes put her on a tiny corner of the shelf beside his comic book and cartoon action heroes. Making her son proud was a gift she wouldn't trade for any spotlight.

Katie sorted through the first file that came up, highlighting words such as the victim's name, witnesses who'd been interviewed, suspect lists and evidence documentation and dropping them into the program that would match up any similarities between this unsolved murder and other crimes in the KCPD database. The tragic death of a homeless man back in the '70s had few clues and fewer suspects, sadly, making it a quick case to read through and document. Others often took hours, or even days, to sort and categorize. But she figured LeRoy Byrd had been important to someone, and therefore, it was important to her to get his information out of a musty storage box and transferred into the database.

"There you go, LeRoy." She patted his name on the

screen. "It's not much. Just know we're still thinking about you and working on your case."

She closed out his information and pulled up the next file, marked *Gemma Gordon*. Katie's breath shuddered in her chest as she looked into the eyes of a teenage girl who'd been missing for ten years. "Not you, too."

The temperature in the auditorium seemed to drop a good twenty degrees as memories of her own kidnapping nightmare surfaced. This girl was seventeen, the same age Katie had been when she'd gone off to find her missing friend, Whitney. Katie had found her friend, all right, but had become a prisoner herself, kept alive until she could give birth to Tyler and her kidnappers tried to sell him in a black-market adoption scheme. Thanks to her aunt and uncle, Tyler was saved and Katie had escaped with her life. But Whitney hadn't been so lucky.

She touched her fingers to the young girl's image on the screen and skimmed through her file. The similarities between the old Katie and this girl were frightening. Pregnant. Listed as a runaway. Katie had fought to save her child. Had Gemma Gordon? Had she even had a chance to fight? Katie had found a family with her aunt Maddie and uncle Dwight and survived. Was anyone missing this poor girl? According to the file, neither Gemma Gordon nor her baby had ever been found.

"You must have been terrified," Katie whispered, feeling the grit of tears clogging her throat. She read on through the persons of interest interviewed in the initial investigation. "What…?" She swiped away the moisture that had spilled onto her cheek and read the list again. There was one similarity too many to her own nightmare—a name she'd hoped never to see again. "No. No, no."

Katie's fingers hovered above the keyboard. One click. A few seconds of unscrambling passwords and a lie about her clearance level and she could find out everything she wanted to about the name on the screen. She could find out what cell he was in at the state penitentiary, who his visitors were, if his name had turned up in conjunction with any other kidnappings or missing-person cases. With a few keystrokes she could know if the man with that name was enjoying a healthy existence or rotting away in prison the way she'd so often wished over the years.

When a hot tear plopped onto the back of her knuckles, Katie startled. She willed herself out of the past and dabbed at her damp cheeks with the sleeve of her sweater. Beyond the fact that hacking into computer systems she didn't officially have access to without a warrant could get her fired, she knew better than to give in to the fears and anger and grief. Katie straightened in her seat and quickly highlighted the list of names, entering them all into the database. "You're a survivor, Katie Lee Rinaldi. Those people can't hurt you anymore. You beat them."

But Gemma Gordon hadn't.

After swiping away another tear, Katie sent the list into the database before logging out. She turned off the portable Wi-Fi security device on the seat beside her and shut down her laptop. She squeezed the edge of her computer as if she was squeezing that missing girl's hand. "I'll do whatever I can to help you, too, Gemma. I promise."

When she looked up, she realized she was the only parent left in the auditorium seats. The stage was empty, too. "Oh, man."

How long had she been sitting there, caught up in the past? Too long. Her few minutes of work had stretched on longer than she'd thought, and the present was calling. She stuffed her equipment back into her flowered bag and stood, grabbing her wool coat off the back of her seat and pulling it on. "Tyler?"

Katie looped her bag over her shoulder and scooted toward the end of the row of faded green folding seats. As pretentious and egotistical as Doug Price could be, he also ran a tight ship. Since they were borrowing this facility from the college, there were certain rules he insisted they all follow. Props returned to backstage tables. Costumes on hangers in the dressing rooms. Rehearsal started when he said it would and ended with the same punctuality. Campus security checked the locks at ten thirty, so every night they were done by ten.

Katie pulled her cell phone from her bag and checked the time when she reached the sloping aisle—ten fifteen. She groaned. The cast was probably backstage, changing into their street clothes if they hadn't already left, and Doug was most likely up in the tech booth, giving the sound and light guys their notes.

Exchanging her phone for the mittens in her pocket, Katie hurried down the aisle toward the stage. "Tyler? Sorry I got distracted. You ready to go, bud?"

And that was when the lights went out.

CHAPTER TWO

"Ow." DISORIENTED BY the sudden darkness, Katie bumped into the corner of a seat. Leaning into the most solid thing she could find, she grabbed the back of the chair and held on while she got her bearings. "Hey! I'm still in the house."

Her voice sounded small and muffled in the cavernous space as she waited several seconds for a response. But the only answer was the scuffle of hurried footsteps moving over the carpet at the very back of the auditorium.

She spun toward the sound. "Hello?" She squeezed her eyes shut against the dizziness that pinballed through her brain. Only her grip on the chair kept her on her feet while her equilibrium righted itself. She heard a loud clank and the protesting squeak of the old hinges as whoever was in here with her scooted out the door to the lobby. Opening her eyes, Katie lifted her blind focus up the sloping aisle. "Tyler? This isn't a good time to play hide-and-seek."

Why weren't the security lights coming on? They ran on a separate power source from the rest of the theater. "Did we have a power outage?"

Why wouldn't anybody answer her? Panic tried to

lock up the air in her chest. The dark wasn't a safe place to be. She'd been reading those old case files, had lingered over the pregnant teen whose kidnapping and unsolved murder would have been Katie's story if she hadn't been lucky—if her aunt and uncle hadn't moved heaven and earth to find her. Why did it have to be so dark? Maybe that had been Doug or the security guard or some other Good Samaritan rushing out to get upstairs to the tech booth in the balcony. She just needed to be patient.

Only it felt as though several minutes had passed, and the lights still weren't coming on. Maybe it had only been seconds. But even seconds were too long in a blackout like this. She swayed against the remembered images of hands grabbing her in the night, of her dead friend Whitney and a teenage girl whose life and death had been relegated to a dusty cold case file.

"Stop it." Rubbing at the bruise forming on her hip, letting the soreness clear her mind, Katie forced her eyes open, willing her vision to focus in the darkness and her memories to blur. Her work took her to the past, but she lived in the here and now. With Tyler. He'd be frightened of the pitch-black, too. She had to find her son. "Think, woman," she challenged herself. "Tyler?"

But the only change in the shroud of blackness was her brain finally kicking into gear.

"Ugh. You're an idiot." Rational thought finally returned and she pulled out her phone, adjusting the screen to flashlight mode to make sure someone could see her before shining it up toward the tech booth in the balcony and shouting again. "Lights, please? Doug?"

Her light wasn't that powerful, but the booth looked dark, too. "Is anybody up there? I'm on my way out. My son's here, too. Please."

She waited in silence for several more seconds before she heard a soft click from the stage. She turned and saw the ropes of running lights that marked the edge and wings of the performance space had come on. *This way*, they beckoned. Really? That was the help she was going to get? Put in place to help the actors find their way offstage during a blackout at the end of a scene, the small red bulbs barely created a glow in the shadows.

"Thanks! For nothing," she added under her breath, pointing her phone light to the floor to illuminate the stairs she climbed to get onto the stage. Somebody with a twisted sense of humor must be trying to teach her a lesson about her tardiness. Up here, at least, she could follow the dimly lit path the actors did, and she ended up pushing through the side curtains to get to the back-stage doors and greenroom and dressing areas beyond.

Her stomach twisted into a knot when she pushed open the heavy firewall door. It was dark back here, too. Her annoyance with Doug turned to trepidation in a heartbeat. "This isn't funny," she called out. Where had everybody gone? Where was her son? "Tyler? Sweetie, answer me."

She kicked the doorstop to the floor to prop the steel door open. Okay. If somebody wanted to spook her, wanted to teach her a lesson about keeping others late at the theater, he or she had succeeded.

But with her son missing, she couldn't allow either fear or anger to take hold. Katie breathed in deeply, waiting until she could hear the silence over the thumping of her heart before following her light into the greenroom, or cast waiting area. Turning her phone to the wall, she found the light switch and lifted it. Nothing.

Had someone forgotten to pay the light bill? Was the college saving money by turning off the electricity after ten? She glanced back toward the stage. The running lights were still glowing. Even if they were battery-powered, someone had to have turned them on. And she knew she hadn't imagined those footsteps earlier. She wasn't alone.

"Tyler, honey, if you're playing some kind of game, this isn't funny." She shouted for the security guard who worked in the building most nights. "Mr. Thompson?"

Was Doug Price playing a trick on her for turning him down again? Did he think she'd be freaked out enough that she'd run to him and expect him to be her hero? If that was what this was about... Her blood heated, chasing away the worried chill. Oh, she was so never going out with that guy. "Tyler? Where are you?"

Why didn't he answer? Had he fallen asleep? Had something happened to him?

Uh-uh. She wasn't going there.

Katie shined her light into the men's dressing room. Lights off. Room empty. She sorted through the costumes hanging on the rack there, peeked beneath the counter. Nothing. She opened the door to the ladies' dressing room, too, and repeated the search.

"Tyler Rinaldi, you answer—"

A boot dropped to the floor behind the rack of long dresses and ghostly costumes. Katie cried out as the layers of polyester, petticoats, wool and lace toppled over on top of her. Hands pushed through the cascade of clothes, knocking her down with them. "Hey! What are you…? Help! Stop!"

She hit the tile floor on her elbows and bottom, and the impact tingled through her fingers, jarring loose her grip on the phone. Her assailant was little more than a wisp of shadow in the dark room. But there was no mistaking the slamming door or the drumbeat of footsteps running across the concrete floor of the work space and storage area behind the stage.

Katie's thoughts raced as she clawed her way free through the pile of fallen clothes and felt around in the darkness to retrieve her phone. Had she interrupted a robbery? There were power tools for set construction and sound equipment and some antiques they were using as props. All those things should be locked up, but an outsider might not know that. Was this some kind of college prank by a theater student? Could it be something personal? She wouldn't have expected Doug to get physical like that. Had she offended someone else?

Her fingers brushed across the protective plastic case of her phone and she snatched it up. She pushed to her feet and smacked into the closed door. "Let me out!" She slapped at the door with her palm until she found the door handle and pulled it open. "Stay away from my son! Tyler!"

But by the time she ran out into the backstage area in pursuit of the shadow, the footsteps had gone silent. The exit door on the far side of the backstage area stood wide open and a slice of light from the sidewalk lamp outside cut clear across the room. After so long in the darkness with just the illumination from her phone, Katie had to avert her eyes from even that dim glow. She saw nothing more than a wraithlike glimpse of a man slipping through the doorway into the winter night outside.

Following the narrowing strip of light, she stumbled forward, dodging prop tables and flats until the door closed with a quiet click and she was plunged into another blackout.

She stopped in her tracks. The one thing she hated more than the darkness was not knowing if her son was safe. And since she couldn't find him...

She pushed a command on her phone and raised it to her lips. "Call Trent."

Inching forward without any kind of light now, she counted off each ring of the telephone as she waited for her strong, armed, utterly reliable friend to pick up. She thought she could make out the red letters of the exit sign above the door by the time Trent cut off the fourth ring and picked up.

"Hey, sunshine," he greeted on a breathless gasp of air. "It's a little late. What's up?"

Oblivious to the current irony of his nickname for her, Katie squeezed her words past the panic choking her throat. "I'm at the theater... The lights..." She bumped into the edge of a flat and shifted course. "Ow. Damn it. I can't see..."

A warm chuckle colored the detective's audible breathing. "Did you leave your car lights on again? Need me to come jump-start it?"

"No." Well, technically, she didn't know that, but she didn't think she had.

"Flat tire? Williams College is a good twenty minutes from here, but I could—"

"Trent. Listen to me. There is some kind of weird…" As his deep inhales and exhales calmed, she heard a tuneless kind of percussive music and a woman's voice laughing in the background. *The man is breathless from exertion, Katie. Get a clue.* "Oh, God," she mumbled as realization dawned and embarrassment warmed her skin. "I'm so sorry. Is someone with you?"

Instead of answering her question, Trent's tone changed from winded amusement to that steely deep tone that resonated through his chest and reminded her he was a cop. "Weird? How? Are you all right? Is Tyler okay?"

Trent Dixon was on a date. He might be in the middle of *more* than a date. She'd forgotten about setting him up with that friend from the coffee shop a few weeks back. Trent wasn't her knight in shining armor to call whenever she had a problem she couldn't fix. He wasn't Tyler's father and he wasn't her boyfriend. Trent was just the good guy who'd grown up across the street and had a hard time saying no to her. Knowing that about him, because she was his friend, too, she'd worked really hard not to take advantage of his good-guy tendencies and protective instincts. "Is that Erin Ballard? I'm sorry. I wasn't thinking. You have company."

"I dropped Erin off an hour ago after dinner. I stopped by the twenty-four-hour gym because I needed to work off some excess energy. And it's too cold to go for a run outside." He paused for a moment, wiping down with a towel or catching his breath. "Apparently, I'm not the only night-owl fitness freak in KC."

He felt energized after his date with Erin? Was that *excess energy* a code for sexual frustration? Had he wanted something more from Erin besides dinner and conversation? Or had he gotten exactly what he wanted and was now on some kind of endorphin high that wouldn't let him sleep? The momentary stab of jealousy at the thought of Trent bedding the willowy blonde she'd introduced him to ended as she tripped over the leg of a chair in the darkness. "Damn it."

"Katie?"

"I'm sorry." She should be thinking of her son, not Trent. Not any misplaced feelings of envy for the woman who landed him. Tyler was the only person who mattered right now. And a panicked late-night call to a man she had no claim on wasn't going to help. "Never mind. I'm sorry to interrupt your evening. It's late and I need to get Tyler home to bed. Tell Erin hi for me."

"Katie Lee Rinaldi," Trent chided. "Why did you call me?"

"I'll handle it myself."

"Handle what? Damn it, woman, talk to me."

"Sorry. I don't need you to rescue me every time I make a mistake. Enjoy your date."

"I'm not on a… Katie?"

"Good night." She disconnected the call, ending the interrogation.

Seconds later, the phone vibrated in her hand. The big galoot. He'd called her right back. Not only did she feel guilty for interrupting his evening, but now she realized just how crazy she'd sounded. Practically perfect Erin Ballard would never panic like this and make a knee-jerk call to a friend for help.

Pull it together and think rationally. She should simply call 9-1-1 and report a break-in or say that an intruder had vandalized the lights in the theater. She could call Uncle Dwight. But as Kansas City's DA, it would only be a matter of minutes before half the police department knew that she'd lost her son and wasn't fit to be his mother.

Katie inhaled a deep breath, pushing aside that option as a last resort. She didn't ever want to be labeled that impulsive, needs-to-be-rescued woman she'd been as a teenager again. Katie Rinaldi stood on her own two feet. She took care of her own son. The two of them would never end up like the girl in that file again.

"Tyler!" With her phone on flashlight mode once more, she hurried as quickly as she dared toward the exit sign. "If you are playing some kind of game with me, mister, I'm grounding you until you're eighteen."

Silence was her only answer.

Had Tyler gotten tired of waiting for his flaky, work-obsessed mother and headed on out to the car? Or was he still inside someplace, trapped in the darkness like she was? Why didn't he answer? *Could* he answer?

First that damn case file and now this? She couldn't stop the nightmarish memory this time. Her feet turned to lead. Katie didn't have to close her eyes to remember the hand over her mouth. The prick of a needle in her arm. Her limbs going numb. Cradling her swollen belly and crying out for her baby as she collapsed into a senseless heap. The night she'd been abducted she'd gone to help Whitney and wound up in the same mess herself. A few weeks later, she'd given birth to Tyler in a sterile room with no one to hold her hand or urge her to breathe, and she'd nearly given up all hope of surviving.

But the tiny little boy the kidnappers laid in her arms for a few seconds had changed everything, giving her a reason to survive, a reason to escape, a reason to keep fighting.

If anything happened to her son...

If he'd been taken from her again...

Finally. Her palm flattened against ice-cold steel. Burying her fears and summoning her maternal strength, Katie shoved open the back door. A blast of bitter cold and snowy crystals melting against her nose and cheeks cleared her thoughts. "Tyler!"

It was brighter outside the theater, even though it was night. The campus lights were on, and each lamppost was adorned with shiny silver wreaths that shimmered with the cold, damp wind. The rows of lights illuminated the path down into the woods behind the auditorium and marked the sidewalk that led around the back of the theater to the parking lot on the north side. New snow was falling, capturing the light from the lamps and reflecting their orange glow into the air around her.

There were dozens of footprints in the first layer of snow from where the cast and crew had exited out to their cars. But there was one set of man-size prints leading down the walkway into the trees, disappearing at the footbridge that arched over the creek at the bottom of the hill. Good. Run. Whoever had been in the darkened building with her was gone.

But the freezing air seeped right into her bones when she read the hastily carved message in the snow beside the tracks.

Stop before someone gets hurt.

She shivered inside her coat. "Gets hurt?" She looked out into the woods, wondering if the man who'd trapped her in the dressing room was still here, watching. "Stop what? What do you want? Tyler?"

Confusion gave way to stark, cold fear when she zeroed in on the impression of a small, size-five tennis shoe, left by a brown-haired boy who hated to wear his winter boots. She hoped. The prints followed the same path as the senseless message. "Tyler!"

Thinking more than panicking now, Katie searched the shadows near the door until she found a broom beside the trash cans there. She wedged the broom handle between the door and frame in case the footprints were a false hope and she needed to get back inside the theater and search some more. She followed the smaller track down the hill. Had the man taken her son? Convinced him to come along with him to find his missing mother? Had she been stuck inside the building for that long?

But suddenly, the boy-size footprints veered off into the trees. Katie stepped knee-deep into the drift next to the sidewalk, ignored the snow melting into her jeans and headed into the woods. "Tyler!"

She heard a dog barking from somewhere in the distance. Oh, no. There was one thing she knew could make her son forget every bit of common sense she'd taught him. The boy-size prints were soon joined by a set of paw prints half the size of her fist. Both tracks ran back up the hill toward the parking lot, and Katie followed. "Please be chasing that stupid dog. Please don't let anyone have taken my son. Tyler!"

The trail led her back to the sidewalk and disappeared around the corner of the building. Katie broke into a run once she cleared the snow among the trees and followed the tracks into the open expanse of asphalt and snow. She was almost light-headed with relief when she spotted the boy in the dark blue parka, playing with a skinny, short-haired collie mix in the parking lot. "Tyler!"

A blur of tan and white dashed off into the woods, followed by clouds of hot, steamy dog breath and a boy's dejected sigh.

Thank God. Tyler was safe.

Sparing one moment of concern for the familiar collarless stray disappearing into the snowy night, Katie ran straight to her son and pulled him into her chest for a tight hug. She kissed the top of his wool stocking cap, hugged him tighter and kissed him again. "Oh, thank goodness. Thank goodness, sweetie."

"Mo-om," Tyler whined on two different pitches before pushing enough space between them for him to tilt his face up to hers. "You scared him away."

Katie eased her grip around her son's slim shoulders and brought her mittened hands up to cup his freckled cheeks and look down into those bright blue eyes that matched her own. "I was so scared. There was a blackout inside the theater and I couldn't find you." Since running across the parking lot in panic mode and hugging the stuffing out of him had probably already worried him enough, Katie opted to leave out any mention of the cryptic message in the snow or the man who'd pushed her down in the dressing room. "I kept calling for you, but you didn't answer. What are you doing out here?"

"Feeding Padre. Doug told me he was out here again tonight, so I came to see him."

"Doug did?" Why would the director send her child out of the theater on such a bitter night?

"He said he'd tell you where I was." But Doug hadn't. "I think Padre's hungry, so I saved my peanut butter sandwich from lunch for him."

Still feeling uneasy, her breath came in ragged puffs while Tyler knelt down to stuff an empty plastic bag into the book bag at his feet. Katie looked all around the well-lit but empty lot to verify that her red Kia was the only vehicle there and that no one else was loitering about. If Doug had meant to tell her Tyler's whereabouts, he'd forgotten amid the busyness of shutting down a tech rehearsal and had apparently gone home without giving her mother's concern a second thought. Maybe the mix-up was all perfectly innocent. But if he'd done it on purpose...

"Come on, sweetie. We need to go." Katie draped her arm around Tyler's shoulders when he stood back up and hurried him along beside her to the car. "Didn't you eat your lunch?"

"Most of it. But I can always have a bowl of cereal

when we get home, and Padre doesn't have anybody to feed him."

"Padre?" She swapped her phone for the keys in her coat pocket and unlocked the car.

Tyler opened the passenger door and climbed inside on his knees, tossing his book bag into the backseat. "Did you see the ring of white fur around his neck? It looks like the collar Pastor Bill wears, and everybody calls him Padre."

Katie closed the door and hurried around the front of the car to get in behind the wheel. Naming a dog she knew he couldn't have was probably a bad thing, but she was more worried about blackouts and intruders and not being able to find her son. She placed her bag in the backseat beside Tyler's, locked the doors and quickly started the engine so she could crank up the heat. "Why didn't you wait for me? Or come get me as soon as you'd changed? I'm sorry I got distracted, but I was sitting out in the auditorium. I would have come to feed the dog with you. You shouldn't be out here by yourself, especially at night."

Tyler turned around and plopped down into his seat. "I know. But I wanted to see Padre before one of the other kids got to him first. He likes me, Mom. He lets me pet him and doesn't bite me or anything. Wyatt already has a dog, and Kayla's family has two cats. So he should be mine."

She grimaced at the sad envy for two of the other children in the play. "Tyler—"

"When everybody else started to leave, I tried to get

back in, but the door was locked. So I stayed outside to play with Padre."

"Is that the real story? I don't mean the dog. Doug sending you outside? Getting locked out?" She pulled off her mitten and reached across the car to cup his cheek. Chilled, but healthy. She was the only one having heart palpitations tonight. "There wasn't anyone left in the cast or crew to let you back in?"

"Maybe if I had my own cell phone, I could have called you."

"Really?" She pushed his stocking cap up to the crown of his head and ruffled his wavy dark hair between her fingers. "I was scared to death that something had happened to you, and you're playing that card?"

He fastened his seat belt. "I put a phone on my Christmas list."

"We talked about this. Not until middle school."

"Johnny Griffith has one."

"I'm not Johnny Griffith's mom." Katie straightened in her seat to fasten her own seat belt. "You're up past your bedtime. Let's go home before your toes freeze."

"Did Doug ask you out again?" Tyler asked. "Is that why he wanted to get rid of me?"

She glanced over at the far too wise expression on her son's freckled face. "He did. I told him no again, too."

Tyler tugged off his mittens and held his pink fingers up in front of the heating vent. "I thought maybe you were still in there talking to him. He's a good director and all, but I don't want him to be my dad."

Katie reached for Tyler's hands and pulled them between hers to rub some love and warmth into them. "He won't be." Not that he'd had a chance, anyway. But endangering her son certainly checked him off the list. "I can guarantee that."

"Good." When he'd had enough of a warming reassurance, Tyler pulled away and kicked his feet together, knocking snow off his shoes onto the floor mat. "Do you think Padre's toes will freeze out there tonight? Dogs have toes, right?"

"They do. But he must have dug himself a snow cave or found someplace warm to sleep if he's survived a whole week outdoors in the wintertime. I think he'll be okay. I hope he will be." Katie smiled wryly before turning on the windshield wipers and clearing away the wet snow. She shifted the car into gear, but paused with her foot on the brake to inspect the empty parking lot one more time. Maybe Tyler hadn't been in any danger. Maybe she hadn't really been, either. But why leave that message? And if the intruder had run along the pathway, had Tyler seen him either sneak into the building or run out of it? The man could easily have parked in another area of the campus so she wouldn't be able to spot him. But could Tyler have gotten a description that might put him in some kind of future harm? Her grip tightened around the steering wheel. "Did anybody talk to you while you were out here by yourself?"

"Wyatt and Kayla said goodbye. Kayla's dad asked me if you were still here. I told him as long as the car was, you were, too."

She'd make a point to thank Mr. Hudnall for checking on her son tomorrow night. "I meant a stranger.

Anybody you didn't know? Was anyone watching you or following you?"

Tyler dropped his head back in dramatic groan. "I know about stranger danger. I would have shouted really loud or run really fast or gotten into the car with Kayla's dad because I know him."

"Okay, sweetie. Just checking."

He sat up straight and turned in his seat. "But if I had a phone—"

"Maybe later." She laughed and lifted her foot off the brake. "I need to talk it over with Aunt Maddie and Uncle Dwight first. We're on their phone plan."

And now the sulky lip went out. "Am I going to get anything that's on my Christmas list?"

"There are already some presents under the tree."

"None of them are big enough to be a dog. And none of them are small enough to be a phone. They're probably socks and underwear."

"I'm sure you'd be really good with a pet, sweetie, but you know we can't have a dog in our apartment." She pulled the car up next to the sidewalk at the corner of the theater building. "Hold on a second. I propped the door open in case I couldn't find you out here. I need to go close it so we don't get in trouble with the college. Sit tight. Lock yourself in until I get back."

After pulling her lime-green mittens back on and tying her scarf more tightly around her neck, Katie climbed out, waited for Tyler to relock the doors and hurried back to the exit. She glanced through the woods and walkway for the stray dog or a more menacing figure, but saw no sign of movement among the trees and shadows. But she slowed her steps once she shifted her full attention to the door. It was already closed, sealed tight. Had she not wedged the broom in securely enough?

Pulling her phone from her pocket again, Katie checked the time before turning on the camera. She'd only been gone a few minutes, hardly enough time for the security guard to make his rounds. And if he'd been close by already, why wouldn't he have answered her shouts of distress or turned on a light for her to see?

Who had closed this door? The same unseen person who'd flipped on the running lights and hidden in the dark theater?

The man who'd run off into the woods after knocking her off her feet?

No matter what the answers to any of those questions might be, Katie worked around enough cops to know that details mattered. So she moved past the door and angled her phone camera down to take a picture of the disturbing message.

Her breath rushed out in a warm white cloud in the air, and she couldn't seem to breathe in again.

The message was gone.

The marks of her heeled boots were clear in the new layer of snow. But the rest of the footprints—boy-size tennis shoes, paw prints, the long, wide imprints of a stranger running away from the theater—*Stop before someone gets hurt*—had all been swept away.

A chill skittered down the back of her neck. She was bundled up tight enough to know it wasn't the snow getting to her skin. This was wrong. This was intentional. This was personal.

Katie backed away from the door. The man inside the theater had come back. He could still be here—hiding in the trees, lurking on the other side of that door, watching her right now. Waiting for her.

She glanced back and forth, trying to see into the night beyond the lamplights and the snow. Nothing. No one. She hadn't seen the man who grabbed her the night she'd been kidnapped, either.

She was shaking now. Katie didn't feel safe.

Her son wasn't safe.

"Tyler." She whispered his name like a storm cloud in the air as she turned and raced back to the car, banging on the window until Tyler unlocked the door and she could slip inside. She relocked the doors and peeled off her mittens before reaching across the seat and cupping his cheek in her palm again. "I love you, sweetie."

His skin was toasty warm from the heater, but she was shivering inside her coat as she shifted into gear and sped across the parking lot to the nearest exit.

"Mom? What's wrong?"

Tyler's voice was frightened, unsure. She was supposed to be his rock. She was a horrible mother for worrying him with her paranoid imagination. She was putting him in danger by not thinking straight.

"I'm sorry, sweetie. I'm okay. We're both okay." She shook the snowflakes from her dark hair, smiled for him, then pulled out onto the street at a much safer speed. "Why don't you tell me more about Padre."

"CONFOUNDED WOMAN." TRENT slowed his pickup to a crawl once he saw that the parking lot outside the Williams College auditorium had nothing but asphalt and snow to greet him after his zip across Kansas City to get to Katie and Tyler.

As he circled the perimeter of the empty lot, just to make sure he hadn't misunderstood the location of the distress call, and the tiny Rinaldi family truly wasn't stranded someplace out in the bitter cold, Trent admitted that Katie Lee Rinaldi knew how to push his buttons— even though she never did it intentionally. It was his own damn fault. If he hadn't felt especially protective of Katie ever since she'd decided back in high school he was the one friend she could rely on without question, and if all the hours he'd spent with Tyler didn't make him think he wanted to be a father more than just about anything—more than making sergeant, more than playing for the Chiefs, more than wishing he didn't have the time bomb of one concussion too many ticking in his head—then he wouldn't charge off on these fool's errands to protect a family that wasn't his.

He pulled up at the sidewalk near the auditorium's back entrance and shifted the truck into Park. He'd left before finishing a perfectly good workout to find out what Katie's phone call had been about when he'd barely been able to work up a polite interest in lingering on Erin Ballard's doorstep and trading a good-night kiss. Erin was an attractive blonde who could carry on an intelligent conversation, and who'd made it perfectly clear that she'd like Trent to come in out of the cold for some hot coffee and anything else he might want. Erin wasn't impulsive. Her wardrobe consisted of beiges and browns, and nothing she'd said or done had surprised him. Not once. Cryptic phone calls, leading with her heart and putting loyalty before common sense were probably foreign concepts. If it wasn't on Erin's planner in her phone, it probably wouldn't happen. Erin wasn't interesting to Trent.

She wasn't Katie.

No woman was.

The proof was in the follow-up buzz in his pocket. Trent checked his phone again, admitting he was less frustrated to read the Are you mad at me? text from Erin than he was to see that he hadn't heard boo from Katie since she'd called about witnessing something *weird* and had sounded so afraid.

No. Busy. With work, he added before sending the text to Erin. Maybe the woman would get a clue and stop pestering him. He'd already turned down her efforts to take a couple of dates to the next level as gently as he could, and he was done dealing with her tonight.

But he wasn't done with Katie.

After pulling his black knit watch cap down over his ears and putting his glove back on, Trent killed the engine and climbed out for a closer look. Because he was a cop and panicked phone calls about something *weird* happening at the theater tended to raise his suspicions, and because it was Katie, who was not only a friend since high school but also a coworker on the cold case squad, Trent wasn't about to ignore the call and drive home without at least verifying that whatever problem had prompted her call was no longer anything to worry about.

Not that he really knew what the problem was. Trent pulled a flashlight from the pocket of his coat and shined the light out into the foggy woods at the edge of the lot before clearing his head with a deep breath of the bracing air. The snow drifted against the brick wall of the building and crunched beneath his boots as he set out to walk the perimeter and do a little investigating before he followed up with Katie to find out what the hell she'd been babbling about.

Katie had been frightened—that much he could hear in her voice. But she'd never really answered any of his questions. He didn't know if she was having trouble with her car again, if something had happened to Tyler, if she was in some kind of danger or if she'd gone off to help a friend who needed something. With his interrogation skills, he could get straight answers from frightened witnesses with nervous gaps in their memories and lying lowlifes who typically avoided the truth as a means of survival.

But could he get a straight answer from Katie Rinaldi?

He checked the main entrance first but found all the front doors locked. He identified himself with his badge and briefly chatted with the security guard, who reported that the campus had been quiet that evening, that the on-campus and commuter students alike had pretty much stayed either in the buildings or made a quick exit in their cars as soon as evening classes had ended. Nobody was hanging out any longer than necessary to tempt the weather or waste time in these last days before finals week and Christmas break. After thanking the older man and assuring him he was here on unofficial police business and that there was no need to call for backup or stop making his rounds, Trent followed the lit pathway around the rest of the building. Other than the campus officer's car, the staff lot to the south was empty, too.

Unwilling to write the call for help off just yet, Trent circled to the back of the auditorium. But when the chomp of snow beneath his steps fell silent, Trent looked down. "Interesting."

What kind of maintenance crew would take the time to clear a sidewalk at this time of night when the snow wasn't scheduled to stop falling for another couple hours? Trent knelt and plucked a bristle broken off a corn broom from the dusting of snow accumulating again beneath his feet. And what kind of professionals with an entire campus to clear would bother with a broom when they had snowblowers and even larger machinery at their disposal?

Had there been a prowler near the building who'd swept away any evidence of lurking on campus? Was that what Katie had called him about? Had she seen someone trying to break in? Had the perp seen her? With his hackles rising beneath the collar of his coat, Trent pushed to his feet, noting where the new snow had been swept away—around the locked back door and down the sidewalk into the trees. He'd qualify that as *weird*. The scenario fit some kind of cover-up.

"Katie?" There'd better not be an answer. He raised

his voice, praying the woods were quiet because the Rinaldis were safely home, asleep in their beds. "Tyler?"

His nape itched with the sensation of being watched, and Trent casually turned his light down along the path between the trees. Was that a rustle of movement in the low brush? Or merely the wind stirring the branches of a pine tree? The lamps along the sidewalk created circles of light that made it impossible to see far into the woods. With his ears attuned to any unusual sound in the cold night air, he moved along the cleared walk down toward the frozen creek at the bottom of the hill. "KCPD! You in the trees, show yourself."

His deep voice filled the air without an answer.

"Katie?" His gloved fingers brushed against the phone in his pocket. Maybe he should just call her. But the hour was late and Tyler would be in bed and a phone ringing at this hour would probably cause more alarm than reassurance. Besides, if she wouldn't give him any kind of explanation when she called him, he doubted she'd be any more forthcoming when he called her. He'd give this search a few more minutes until he could say good-night to the suspicions that put him on guard and go home to get some decent shut-eye himself.

When he reached the little arched bridge that crossed the creek, *weird* took a disquieting turn into *what the hell?* Trent stopped in the middle of the bridge, looking down at both sides—the one that had been deliberately cleared from the back door of the theater down to this point, and the two inches of snow on the sidewalk beyond the creek marked by a clear set of tracks. There were two skid marks through the snow, as if someone had slipped on the bridge and fallen, then a trail of footsteps leading up the hill on the opposite side. One set of tracks. Man-size. More than that, the distance between the steps lengthened, as though whoever had left the trail had decided he needed to run. A man in a hurry—running from something or to something or because of something. A student in a hurry to get to his dorm or car? Or a man running away from campus security and a cop who might be curious about why he'd want to erase his trail?

Where had this guy gone, anyway? The snow was coming down heavily enough that those tracks should be nothing but a bunch of divots in the icy surface if they'd been there when classes had been dismissed or Tyler's rehearsal had ended. These were deep. These were recent. These were—

Trent spun when he heard the noise crashing through the drifts and underbrush toward him. He'd pulled up his coat and had his hand on the butt of his gun when a blur of tan and white shot out between the trees and darted around his legs. "What the...?"

Four legs. Black nose. Long tail.

After one more scan to make sure the dog was the only thing coming at him, Trent laughed and eased the insulated nylon back over his holster. "Hey, pup. See anybody but me out here tonight?"

The dog danced around him, whining with a mixture of caution and excitement. Apparently, Spot here was the only set of eyes that had been watching him through the trees. The poor thing wore no collar and needed a good brushing to clean the twigs and cockleburs from his dark gold fur. Feeling a tug of remembrance for the dogs his family had always had growing up, Trent held out his hand in a fist, encouraging the dog to get familiar with his scent. "You've been out here awhile, haven't you, little guy?"

Of course, standing six foot five made most critters like this seem little, and once the dog stopped his manic movements and focused on the scent of his gloved hand, Trent knelt to erase some of the towering distance between them and make himself look a little less intimidating. When he opened his hand, the dog inspected the palm side, too, no doubt looking for food, judging by the bumpy lines of his rib cage visible on either side of his skinny flanks. The stray wanted to be friendly, but when Trent reached out to pet him, the dog jumped away, diving through a snowdrift. But as if deciding the big, scary man who had no food on him was more inviting than the chest-deep cold and wet, he came charging back to the sidewalk, shaking the snow off his skinny frame before sitting down and staring up at Trent.

"What are you saying to me?" Trent laughed again when the dog tilted his head to one side, as though making an effort to understand him. "I'm Trent Dixon, KCPD. I'd like to ask you a few questions." The more he talked, the more the dog seemed to quiet. He thumbed over his shoulder toward the auditorium. "You know what happened here? Have you seen a curvy brunette and a little boy about yea high?" When he raised his hand to gesture to Tyler's height, the dog's dark brown eyes followed the movement. Interesting. Maybe he'd had a little training before running away or getting tossed out onto the street. Or maybe the dog was just smart enough to know where a friendly snack usually came from. "Your feet aren't big enough to make those tracks on the other side of the bridge. And I'm guessing you spend a lot of time around here. What do you know that I don't?"

The dog scooted forward a couple inches and butted his nose against Trent's knee. When he got up close like that, Trent could see that the dog was shivering. With his stomach doing a compassionate flip-flop, he decided there was only one thing he could do. Katie Rinaldi might not need rescuing tonight, but this knee-high bag of bones did.

"Easy, boy. That's it. I'm your big buddy now." Extending one hand for the dog to sniff, Trent petted him around the jowls and ears with the other. When the dog started licking his glove, desperate for something to eat, he grabbed him by the scruff of the neck. Other than jumping to his feet, the dog showed no signs of fear or aggression. Maybe the mutt had made friends with enough college students that he didn't view people as a threat.

"I'm afraid I'm going to have to take you in," Trent teased, standing and lifting the dog into his arms. Craving either warmth or companionship, the dog snuggled in, resting his head over Trent's arm and letting himself be carried up the hill to Trent's truck. "I'll get you warmed up and get some food in you. Maybe you'll be willing to tell me what you saw or heard then."

The dog was perfectly cooperative as Trent loaded him into the cab of his truck and pulled an old blanket and an energy bar from his emergency kit behind the seat. "It's mostly granola and peanut butter but…okay."

Taking the bar as soon as it was offered, the dog made quick work of the protein snack. "Tomorrow I'll get you to the vet for a checkup and have her scan to see if there's an ID chip in you." He got a whiff of the dog's wet, matted fur when he leaned over to wrap the blanket around him. "Maybe they can give you a bath, too."

Trent shook his head as the dog settled into the passenger seat, making himself at home. "This is temporary, you know," Trent reminded him, starting the engine and cranking up the heat. "I'm a cop, remember? I'll have to report you."

Stinky McPooch raised his head and looked at Trent, as though translating the conversation into dogspeak. His pink tongue darted out to lick his nose and muzzle and he whined a response that sounded a little like a protest.

"Don't try to sweet-talk your way out of this. You owe me some answers. So what's your story? No warm place for the night? Anybody looking for you?" The dog tilted his head and an ear flopped over, giving his face a sad expression. Trent turned on the wipers and shifted the truck into gear before driving toward the street. "Sorry to hear that. I'm a bachelor on my own, too. You can call me Trent or Detective. What should I call you?" When he stopped at the exit to the parking lot, Trent reached over the console to pet him. Pushing his head into the caress of Trent's hand, the dog whimpered in a doggy version of a purr. "All right, then, Mr. Pup." He pulled onto the street. There wasn't much traffic this time of night, so it was safe enough to take his eyes off the road to glance at his furry prisoner. "Did you see anything suspicious at the theater tonight?"

The dog barked, right on cue.

When Trent moved both hands to the steering wheel, the mutt put a paw on his arm, whimpering again. Trent grinned and scratched behind the mutt's ears, loving how the dog was engaging in the conversation with him. "Tell me more. I like a witness who talks to me. I think you and I are going to get along."

His interrogation skills were intact.

Now if he could just get a certain brunette to tell him what the hell had panicked her tonight.

CHAPTER THREE

TRENT WAS A man on a mission when he stepped into his boss's office at the Fourth Precinct building. Lieutenant Ginny Rafferty-Taylor was out somewhere, but he'd spotted Katie going in earlier and wanted a few minutes of face-to-face time with her before the morning staff meeting started.

Instead of asking a pointed question about last night's phone call, however, he paused, unobserved, in the doorway as she dropped to the floor.

"Where did I put that stupid pencil?"

He did a poor job of keeping his eyes off the bobbing heart-shaped curves of Katie Rinaldi's backside as she crawled beneath the conference table in search of the accursed writing instrument. Thank goodness Lieutenant Rafferty-Taylor was nowhere to be seen, because he was failing miserably at professional detachment. He stood there like a man, not a cop, admiring the view, savoring the stronger beat of his pulse until Katie's navy blue slacks and the mismatched socks on her feet disappeared between two chairs.

With temptation out of sight, Trent's brain reengaged and he swallowed a drink of his coffee. The hot liquid burned a little more common sense down his throat, reminding him that he was at work, the fellow members of KCPD's cold case squad were gathering in the main room outside with their morning coffee and case files, and Katie had made it clear that—no matter how she twisted up his insides with this gut kick of desire— she only wanted to be friends.

I love you, Trent. I always will. But I'm not in *love with you.*

Man, had that been a painful distinction to make.

He'd felt an undeniable pull to this woman since he was fifteen years old and she'd moved in with her aunt across the street from the home where he'd grown up. Although he'd been a jock and she'd been into the arts, proximity and a whole yin and yang thing of opposites attracting had played hell with his teenage libido. When she'd gotten pregnant their senior year, his idealistic notions about the dark-haired beauty had dimmed. But when she disappeared, and he'd played a small role in helping her get safely home, an indelible bond had been forged between them, deeper than anything raging teenage hormones could account for.

After her return, she'd talked him into singing in a musical play with her and he'd discovered he liked driving her back and forth to rehearsals and hanging out with her. They'd dated a few times their senior year of high school. Well, he'd been dating, hoping for something more, but Katie had always pulled back just when things were getting interesting.

She didn't mean to be a tease, and had always been straight with him about her feelings and concerns. It just wasn't easy for her to trust. He understood that now better than he had ten years ago. She'd grown up with an abusive father, witnessed her mother's own murder at his hand. She'd survived a kidnapping, but lost the good friend she'd been trying to help when she'd gotten involved with the kidnappers in the first place. She'd had an infant son before graduation and had to learn about being a mother.

Katie had every right to be cautious, every right to insist on standing on her own two feet, every right to protect herself and her son from getting attached to someone who'd thought he was going to make a career for himself in another city. She wouldn't risk the stability she provided for Tyler. She wouldn't risk either her or her son possibly getting hurt. He'd admired her for her stubborn strength back then. Still did. Understanding why she wouldn't give them a chance, Trent had accepted the dutiful role of friend and gone off to play football in college and take his life and dreams in a different direction. Some dreams died or morphed into other goals. He'd come back to Kansas City, come home to be a cop.

He might be a different man than the teen he'd once been. But the rules with Katie hadn't changed. One wiggle of that perfectly shaped posterior, one flare of concern that all was not right in her world, shouldn't make him forget that.

Besides, a man had his pride. Yeah, being built to play the defensive line made him a little scary sometimes. But he wasn't completely unfortunate in the looks department. He had a college degree and a respectable job, and his parents had taught him how to treat a lady right. He didn't have to pine away for any woman. He dated. Okay, so a lot of those dates—like Erin Ballard last night—had been set up by Katie herself, but he could get his own woman when he had to. He'd even been in a couple of long-term relationships. It wasn't as if he was a saint—he enjoyed a woman's company.

Trent drank another, more leisurely sip of coffee, cooling his jets while he remembered his purpose here. He anchored his feet to the carpet, bracing himself. From the grumbling sounds beneath the table, Katie was on a tear about something this morning. A civilized conversation might not be possible. But he'd gotten information from less cooperative witnesses in an interrogation room. He just had to stay calm and make it happen.

A chair rolled across the utility carpet as she popped out on the other side of the table. "You and I need to talk," Trent stated simply.

Her head swiveled around and her blue eyes widened with a startled look, then quickly shuttered. She knew he was talking about last night. But she blithely ignored the issue between them. "I have to find that pencil first." It was hard to feel much resentment when her bangs flew out in a dozen adorable directions after she raked her fingers through the dark brown waves and stood. "It's the second one I've lost today. I don't have time for this. I'm making my presentation to you guys this morning and—"

Trent tapped the back of his neck, indicating the bouncy ponytail where an orange mechanical pencil had been speared through her hair.

She buzzed her lips in a frustrated sigh and pulled the pencil from her hair. "Thanks."

He stepped into the room to keep their conversation private from their friends gathering outside the office. "You called me—"

"Trent, please." Katie gestured to their team leader's empty desk. "I have to get everything ready for the meeting before the lieutenant gets back."

Fine. He'd ease into the questions he had for her. As long as he could get her talking to him. Trent glanced over at the empty desk where the cold case squad's team leader usually sat. "Where is she?"

"The lieutenant got called into Chief Taylor's office for an emergency meeting. She said she'd be back in time for the team briefing."

"Emergency?" That word and news of an impromptu meeting with the lieutenant's cousin-in-law, aka the department's top brass, wasn't something a cop wanted to hear at the beginning of his shift. He eyed the other members of the team through the glass window separating Lieutenant Rafferty-Taylor's office from the maze of detectives' desks on the building's third floor. Max Krolikowski, his partner, along with Jim Parker and Olivia Watson, stood together chatting, apparently as unaware as he as to what the emergency summons might be. Katie's frenetic movements weren't exactly reassuring. "Any idea what's up?"

"Not a clue." She unplugged a cord, inserted a zip drive and pulled up a file on her laptop. When she looked up at the dark television screen at the opposite end of the conference table, she groaned and circled around the table to fiddle with the TV. "It's not my job to keep track of every bit of gossip that comes through the KCPD grapevine. The lieutenant was heading out when I came in. She told me to go ahead and set up for the staff meeting. So, of course, the wireless connection is on the fritz, and I had to track down extra cords. Then I realized I left one of the files in my bag and hadn't uploaded the pictures yet, so I had to go back for that. And now the stupid TV—"

"Take a breath, Katie."

"*You* take a breath," she snapped, spinning to face him.

"Really? That's your witty repartee?"

"I mean…" Her eyes widened like cornflowers blooming when her gaze locked on to his.

Accepting the remorse twisting her pretty mouth as an apology, Trent crossed the room to inspect the closed-circuit television. He tightened a connector on the side of the TV and turned the screen on for her. "There. Easy fix."

"Thanks." She bent over her laptop, resuming her work at a more normal pace. "I'm sorry. That was a dumb thing to say. I was going on like a chatterbox, wasn't I?"

"There's something buggin' you, I can tell. But it's just me, so don't sweat it."

"I'm not going to take advantage of your cool, calm collectedness. You didn't come to work so you could listen to me vent."

"But I do want to hear about last night."

She arched a sable-colored brow in irritation. Okay.

Too soon to press the subject. Just keep her talking and eventually he'd get the answers he needed.

Trent reached around her to set his coffee and notebook in front of the chair kitty-corner from hers. Although Katie was of an average height and curvy build, she'd always seemed petite and fragile. It didn't help that she'd kicked off her shoes beneath the table, while he'd tied on a pair of thick-soled work boots this morning to shovel his sidewalks, blow the snow off his driveway and walk the dog he'd taken in around the block. Despite her uncharacteristic flashes of frustration and temper, and the static electricity that made the strands of her ponytail cling to the black flannel of his shirt, she seemed pretty and dainty and far too female for the cells in his body not to leap to attention whenever he got this close to her.

"You seem a little off your game this morning." He spoke over the top of her head, backing away from the enticement of making contact with more than a few wayward strands of hair. "You know something about the lieutenant's emergency meeting that you're not telling me?"

"Nope. She was business as usual."

"Is Tyler okay?"

"He's fine. I swear." Katie tilted her gaze up to meet his, confirming with a quick smile that that much, at least, was true. Then she went back to work on her laptop. She swiped her finger across a graphic on her screen and loaded the image of several mug shots up onto the larger screen. "I guess he's a little ticked at me. There's this stray dog that he's gotten attached to running around the theater this past week. He wants a dog so badly, it's at the top of his Christmas list. But our landlord won't allow pets. I mean, the dog is friendly enough, but he's skin and bones. I feel so bad for him, especially in this weather. Apparently, Tyler's been feeding him."

"A tan dog with a white stripe around his neck?"

"Yes. How did you…?" Her cheeks heated with color as she tilted her face up to his. "You went to the theater last night. I told you everything was fine."

Trent propped his hands at his waist, dipping his head toward hers. He matched her indignant tone. "No, you told me you'd *handle* whatever it was. If everything is fine, you wouldn't need to handle anything."

"Well, I don't need you to rescue me every time something scares me."

"What scared you?"

She paused for a moment before waving off his concern and turned back to her computer. "That's not what I meant."

"Then give me some straight answers. Something hinky was going on outside that theater. Either you saw something, or you at least suspected it." He wrapped his fingers around the pink wool sleeve of her sweater and softened his tone. "Something that *scared* you, and that's why you called me."

She hesitated for a moment before shrugging off his touch. "You were on a date."

"The date was over."

"Because of me?" She turned in the tight space between the table and chair, her forehead scrunched up with remorse.

He tapped the furrow between her brows and urged her to relax. "Because I wanted it to be."

She batted his hand away, dismissing his concern. "Trent, I don't have the right to call you whenever I need something. I'm not going to wimp out on being a strong woman and I don't want to take advantage of our friendship. We shouldn't have that you're-the-guy-I-always-call-on kind of relationship, anyway. You need to…find someone and move on with your life."

"I'll make my own decisions, thank you. I call you when I need something, don't I?"

"Sewing a button on your dress uniform is hardly the same thing."

"Look, you and I know more about each other than just about anybody else. We've shared secrets and heartaches and stupid stuff, too. That's what people who care about each other do. Now—as a friend who doesn't appreciate phone calls that make him think something bad has happened and he needs to drop everything without even taking a shower and speed across town in a snowstorm—"

"You didn't—"

"—I need you to tell me exactly why you called last night. And don't tell me you were frightened of that sweet little dog, who, incidentally, is spending the day at the vet's office while the Humane Society is checking to see if he's been reported missing."

Her eyes widened again. "You rescued the dog?"

"You wouldn't let me rescue you. Now answer the question. What scared you last night?"

"Nothing but my imagination. I'm sorry I worried you. The dog's okay?"

She changed topics like a hard right turn in a high-speed chase.

Trent shrugged. This woman always kept him on his toes. "I fed him some scrambled eggs and gave him water. He spent the night whimpering on a blanket in my mudroom, but he didn't have any accidents. Don't know if he's housebroken or just too scared he'll get into trouble and get dumped out someplace again. I took him to the vet's this morning for a thorough checkup and a much-needed grooming. My truck still smells like wet, stinky dog."

"Thank you." Her lips softened into a beautiful smile. When she reached out to squeeze his hand, he squeezed right back. "Thank you for saving him. I wanted to, but I'm not sure Tyler would understand having to take him to a shelter instead of taking him home."

"It looks like I'll be fostering Mr. Pup for a while. Until the Humane Society can find out if there's an owner or put him up for adoption. Maybe Tyler can come visit him."

Katie shook her head, whipping the ponytail back and forth. "Don't tell him that. He'd be at your house every day after school."

"You know I don't mind having Tyler around."

"I know. But… Mr. Pup? Tyler calls him Padre."

Trent nodded. The name fit. "Like a priest's collar. That's what I'll call him, then. Now, about last night…"

He could do the sharp right turns, too. But her frustrated huff warned him he'd have to coax the answers out of her, just like he'd coaxed Padre into trusting him. "You have to give me something, Katie. You know I won't quit."

"I know." Her blue eyes tilted up to meet his briefly. Her gaze quickly dropped to the middle button of his shirt, where she plucked away what was most likely a couple of dog hairs. The nerves beneath his skin jumped as her fingers danced against his chest. But he couldn't allow himself to respond to the unintended caress. This was distraction. Nervous energy. Something on her mind that kept her from focusing. There was definitely something bothering Team Rinaldi this morning. "I have to get ready for the meeting."

"Every morning, you've been bragging about Tyler and the play you guys are doing. This morning, all you're doing is apologizing and fussing around like it's your first day on the job." Outweighing her by a good hundred pounds wasn't the only reason he wasn't budging. He covered her hand with his, stilling her fidgeting fingers. "Talk to me. Use words that make sense."

"Calling you was an impulse," she conceded. "Once I got my act together, I realized I shouldn't have bothered you."

Nope. He still wasn't budging.

Trent felt the whisper of her surrendering sigh against his hand. "They didn't need me backstage last night, so I was doing some work on my laptop out in the theater auditorium. I found a connection between an old double missing-person case and some new stuff we're working on. I got caught up following the trail through the reports and I lost track of the time."

This was remorse talking, maybe even a little fear, he thought, as she slowly tilted her gaze to his again. "I couldn't find Tyler when I was done. I mean, eventually I did. He was by himself in the parking lot, waiting for me. Everyone else had left and he was locked out of the building. And then I thought I heard... I swear someone was..."

"Someone was what?" He gently combed his fingers through her scattered bangs, smoothing them back into place.

"I thought someone was watching me. The lights went out, so it was pretty dark, and while I was looking for Tyler in the dressing rooms, some guy pushed me down and ran outside."

Trent's fingers stilled. His grip on her hand against his chest tightened. "A man attacked you? Are you hurt?"

She brought her other hand up to pat his, urging him to calm the blood boiling in his veins. "This is why I don't tell you things. It wasn't an attack. The dark always freaks me out a little bit, and my imagination made things seem worse than they were. Once I found Tyler with Padre, everything was fine."

"You don't know what that guy was after."

"He wasn't after me. Maybe I interrupted a break-in. Or some homeless guy snuck in to get out of the cold and he got scared by the blackout, too. He just wanted me out of his way so he could escape. Doug Price is going to give me grief tonight for not picking up the mess I left in the dressing room, but I wasn't hurt. I was more worried about Tyler."

He didn't care about whoever Doug Price was, but if he gave Katie grief about anything, he'd flatten him. "Did you report it?" She hadn't. "Katie—" His frustration ebbed on a single breath as understanding dawned. "You called *me*." Hell. He should have investigated inside the building instead of letting the dog distract him from his purpose. He should have gone straight to Katie's apartment when he didn't find her and Tyler at the theater, even if it was the middle of the night and he woke them out of a sound sleep. "I'm sorry. If I'd known what kind of danger you were in—"

"It wouldn't have done any good. By the time I found Tyler and went back to take a couple of pictures, anything suspicious I'd seen was gone." Katie quickly extricated her hands from his and nudged him out of her way. "I wasn't in any real danger. I was being a lousy mom last night. Guilt and reading that file about the missing teen and her baby made me imagine it was something more." She picked up a stack of briefing folders and distributed them in front of each chair around the table. "Except for that message."

Oh, he had a bad feeling about this. "What message?"

She tried to shrug off whatever had drained the color from her face. "Some prankster wrote something creepy in the snow behind the theater."

"And then he swept it away."

Katie spun to face him. "Yes. But how did you…? Right. You were there. And you don't quit."

He propped his hands at his waist. "What did the

message say? Something about breaking in to the theater?"

She hugged the last folder to her chest. "I don't know if it was even intended for me."

"What did it say?" he repeated, as patiently as he'd talked to Padre.

"'Stop or someone will get hurt.'"

He dug his fingers into the pockets of his jeans, the only outward sign of the protective anger surging through him. "Stop what? Who'll get hurt?"

Her shoulders lifted with silent confusion. She didn't have those answers. "Maybe he thought I was chasing him. I wasn't. The darkness freaked me out and kept me from thinking straight, and all I wanted to do was find Tyler to make sure he was safe. If I hadn't panicked, I'd have handled things better, and I wouldn't have ruined your evening."

Trent plucked the folder from her grasp and set it on the table. "You lost track of your son. That's supposed to frighten a parent. Don't beat yourself up about it. You said he's okay, right?"

She nodded. "We're both fine. Thanks for worrying."

"Thank you for sharing. Now maybe I won't worry so much."

She moved back to her computer and manipulated the pictures again. "I'll believe that when I see it."

They *did* know each other well. "Honey, you know I'm always going to worry—"

"You shouldn't call me *honey*." Katie glanced toward the window to the main room. "The rest of the team is here. I need to finish setting up."

CHAPTER FOUR

IF THAT WOMAN worked any harder at pushing him away, she might as well slam Trent up against the wall. "At least promise me you'll keep a closer eye on the people around you. If somebody was lying in wait for you—"

"I promise. Okay? Just let it go." Katie stepped around him as Max, Olivia and Jim came in, their animated conversation masking the awkward silence in the room.

"You're killing me here, Liv," Trent's partner, Max, groused. "A Valentine's Day wedding? You're already making me shave and rent a tux."

Olivia breezed past the burly blond detective, the oldest member of their team, taking her seat at the table. "Just because you and Rosie eloped to Vegas doesn't mean the rest of us don't want to share that special day with friends and family."

Max jabbed his finger on the tabletop, defending his choice in wedding arrangements. "Hey. I wanted to make an honest woman out of Rosie. And you know how her last engagement turned out. She wasn't interested in dragging out the process any more than I was."

Max's new wife had barely survived the nightmare of her first engagement to an abusive boyfriend and had become a recluse as a result. Meanwhile, Max had been fighting his own demons when the two had first met and clashed during the investigation into her ex-fiancé's unsolved murder. Mixing like oil and water, it was a wonder the prim and proper spinster and the rugged former soldier had ever gotten together at all. But Trent had never met two misfits who were a better match for each other. Max brought Rosie out of her shell, and she'd uncovered a few civilized human qualities that Trent's rough-around-the-edges partner had lost in the years he'd been dealing with post-traumatic stress. Max had been shot twice and Rosie nearly drowned solving that case. But the close calls had made them willing to risk everything and seize the love they'd found.

Trent might be a little envious of his older friend settling into the sort of relationship he'd once wanted with Katie Rinaldi, but he was happy for his partner. And he had been honored to fly out to Las Vegas to stand up for the couple.

"As soon as the doctor cleared me to travel, I made the reservations. There wasn't time to send out invitations." Max reached over to thump Trent's shoulder as he pulled out a chair to sit beside him. "At least I took the big guy with us."

Trent grinned, thinking he'd better join the teasing banter before anyone questioned the tension between him and Katie. "And then you put me on a plane back to KC twenty minutes after the ceremony so you two could get started on the honeymoon."

Max grinned. "Hey, I'm ugly. Not stupid."

Olivia was smiling suspiciously, working her cool

logic on Max. "Maybe, since you cheated Rosie out of the whole white-wedding thing, she'd like to put on a fancy gown and see you all dressed up for once in your life. I've yet to see a man that a tuxedo couldn't make look good."

"I'd love to see her in a beautiful dress like that." Was the old man on the team blushing? Who'd have thought? Still, Max grumbled, "You're determined to make me miserable, aren't you?"

Jim Parker grinned and pulled out the chair beside his partner. "Maybe he's worried you're going to make him dance with you at the reception, Liv—after Gabe, your dad and your brothers, of course."

"And Grandpa Seamus," Olivia added. She pointed to Max. "But you are definitely on my dance card after that." She wiggled her finger toward Trent. "You, too, big guy. You all agreed to be our ushers, so it's tuxes and boutonnieres for everyone."

Max put up his hands in surrender. "There's only so much froufrou a man can take, Liv."

Jim propped his elbow on the arm of his chair, leaning over to back up Olivia. "I don't know, Max. There are few things I like better than slow dancing with my wife. Natalie's pregnant enough now that when we're close, I can feel the baby kicking between us."

Max scrubbed his palm over the top of his military-short hair and muttered a teasing curse. "Okay, Parker. Now you've gone too far, buying into all of Liv's romantic mush." Knowing full well he was going to eventually buy into it, too, Max turned back to the lady detective. "I thought you were a tomboy."

Olivia smiled wistfully. "My wedding day will be the exception. I'm the only female in my family. You don't think those boys all want to throw a big party for me? Dad insists on me wearing the veil of Irish lace that Mom wore at their wedding, and I want to. It's a way of honoring her memory and making me feel like she's there with us." The mood around the entire table quieted out of respect for Olivia's mother, who had died when she was just a child. But the detective with the short dark hair didn't let the room get gloomy. "Besides, Gabe looks gorgeous in a tux, and I refuse to have him looking prettier than me."

"Impossible," Max teased. "But if you're going all formal, then I guess I can put on a tie."

"Thank you for your sacrifice." Olivia smiled before turning her attention to Trent. "What about you? Will we see you dancing the night away at the reception?" She snapped her fingers as an idea struck. "You should bring Katie."

The brown ponytail bobbed as Katie's head popped up from her laptop screen. "Me? Like a date?"

Trent groaned inwardly at the pale cast to her cheeks. Did she have to look as if the possibility of attending a friend's wedding together was such an out-of-left-field idea?

"If you want." Olivia chided the low-pitched whistle and sotto voce teasing from Jim and Max before smiling at Katie. "Stop it, children. Believe me, I understand better than most about the department's no-fraternization policy. But even though we're part of the same team, technically, you work in two different branches—

information technology and law enforcement. Besides, I was thinking practicality. Trent's an usher and you're still going to be one of my bridesmaids, right?"

"Of course. I was honored you asked me to be a part of the ceremony, but…" Katie's apologetic gaze bounced off Trent and back to the bride-to-be. "I was going to bring Tyler as my date."

Olivia seemed pleased by that answer. "Even better. I'd love to see the little man again. All three of you should come together."

Even though they hadn't gone out on a date together in nine years, it seemed as though everyone thought of Trent and Katie as a couple. Maybe the others even took it for granted that they were destined to be a family unit one day. The only people who knew it was never going to happen were Trent and Katie themselves.

Sinking into his chair, Trent took another long swallow of his coffee. He watched the strained expression on Katie's face relax as the two women talked about Tyler. Her round face and blue eyes animated with excitement as they wagered whether her nine-year-old son would make as much of a fuss about dressing up for the special occasion as Max had. Katie was a different woman when she talked about her son. Her eyes sparkled and the tension around her mouth eased into a genuine smile.

No wonder she'd been so upset about losing track of Tyler last night. Tyler was her joy, her reason for being—her number-one excuse for shunning Trent and any other relationship that threatened to get in the way of taking care of her son. It wasn't that she didn't care about Trent as a friend, but she'd given her heart to another male nine years ago.

Max's fist knocked on Trent's chair below the edge of the table. Trent took another drink before meeting his partner's questioning look. "You okay, junior? You're pretty quiet this morning."

"You're loud enough for the both of us."

Max grinned at the joke as he was meant to, but his astute blue eyes indicated he wasn't buying the smiles and smart remarks. "There's that whole tall, dark and silent thing you do, and then there's stewing over in the corner. You two were duking it out in here before we came in, weren't you?" His gaze darted over to Katie and back to him. "Seriously, what's the problem? Is it you? Katie? Is the kid okay?"

Trent swore under his breath. There was no subtlety to Max Krolikowski, no filter on his mouth. When he saw a problem, he fixed it. When he cared about something or someone, he went all in. Hell of a guy to have backing him up in a fight, but best friend or not, Trent wasn't sure the man he'd been partnered with on the cold case squad was the guy he wanted to confide his frustration and concerns about Katie to. "She basically told me to mind my own business."

Max dropped his voice to a low-pitched grumble. "You think something's up?"

Even if Trent wanted to share his suspicions about blackouts and prowlers and threats in the snow, he wouldn't get the chance to. All conversations around the table stopped as Lieutenant Ginny Rafferty-Taylor rushed into her office. "Are we all here?" The petite blonde officer set her laptop and a stack of papers at the head of the table before going back to shut the door. "Sorry I'm late."

Trent set down his coffee and turned everyone's focus to the police work at hand. "Ma'am. Katie said you had an emergency meeting with Chief Taylor?"

The older woman nodded. "Seth Cartwright from Vice and A.J. Rodriguez from the drug unit were there, too. I'll get right to it since it affects investigations in each of our divisions."

"What affects us?" Jim asked.

"Leland Asher."

Trent's mouth took on a bitter tang at the mention of the alleged mob boss whose name kept popping up in several of their unsolved investigations.

Olivia leaned forward at the familiar name. "What about him? Gabe's first fiancée was writing a newspaper exposé about Asher when she was killed." Olivia and Gabe had solved that murder, but they hadn't been able to prove Asher had hired the man who'd shot the reporter.

Even Katie, who had never dealt with Asher directly, knew who he was. "His name shows up as a person of interest in several investigations in the KCPD database. Has he been arrested for one of those cases?"

"Not likely," Max said. "He has a great alibi for any recent crimes. He's currently serving a whopping two years for collusion and illegally influencing Adrian McCoy's Senate campaign."

"Not even that, I'm afraid." Lieutenant Rafferty-Taylor shrugged out of her navy blue jacket, hanging it over the back of her chair before sitting. Her back remained ramrod straight. "Asher's case went to appellate court on a hardship appeal. The chief just got word that Asher is being released from prison early, on parole. That's what good behavior and a pricey lawyer will do for you."

A collective groan and a few choice curses filled the room.

"Any chance the judge made a mistake?" Trent asked.

Their team leader shook her head. "It's the holidays, Trent. I think Judge Livingston was feeling generous. Chief Taylor wanted to alert us that Mr. Asher will be back on the streets, albeit wearing an ankle bracelet and submitting to regular check-ins with his parole officer, sometime tomorrow or Thursday."

"Well, merry Christmas to us," Max groused, folding his arms across his chest. "Just what we need, a mob boss heading home to KC for the holidays. I bet the crime rate doubles by New Year's."

For a moment, the petite blonde lieutenant sympathized with her senior detective, but then she opened her laptop, signaling she was ready to begin their morning meeting. "I know we believe Leland Asher is the common link to several of the department's unsolved or ongoing cases. The chief wanted us to be fully informed so we can keep an eye on him. Without our efforts turning into harassment, of course," the lieutenant cautioned.

"I'm willing to harass him," Olivia volunteered with a sarcastic tone. Max pointed across the table and nodded, agreeing with the frustration-fueled plan. "What's the point of solving these old cases if a judge is going to let the perpetrators go with little more than a slap on the wrist?"

Trent could feel the tension in the room getting thicker. Cold case work wasn't an easy assignment. Sometimes evidence degraded or got lost. Witnesses passed away. Suspects did, too. Memories grew foggy with age. And perps who'd gotten away with murder or other crimes that hadn't yet reached their statute of limitations grew confident or complacent enough over the years that they weren't likely to confess. So when the team built a solid enough case to convict someone, it sure would be nice if they'd stay behind bars for a while.

"Are we moving any cases we think Asher might be a part of to our active files?" Trent asked.

The lieutenant nodded. "We should at least give them a cursory glance to see which ones to follow up on. I believe we can use this to our advantage. Katie, will you flag those files and send each of us copies for review?"

"Yes, ma'am." Katie's head was down and she was already typing. By the time she looked up to see Trent grinning at her geeky efficiency, she was hitting the send button. She smiled back before turning to the lieutenant. "I just ran a search for Mr. Asher's name, and all those files should show up on your computers by the time you get back to your desks."

Trent gave her a thumbs-up before turning back to the others. "It'd be a hell of a lot easier to prove Asher's connections to those crimes by seeing who he interacts with on the outside."

Lieutenant Rafferty-Taylor nodded to him, probably appreciating how his suggestion cooled the jets of the others in the room, especially his perennial Scrooge of a partner, Max. Then she gestured to Katie at the opposite end of the table. "Speaking of connections, Katie, you said you've come up with something we need to look at in your research? Shall we get to work?"

"Yes, ma'am." Katie shoved her bangs off her forehead and glanced around the table as everyone waited expectantly. Trent winked some encouragement when their gazes met. She smiled her thanks for his support before looking down at her laptop. She highlighted the first picture on the television screen and turned to point to the gathering of mug shots she'd posted there. "Detailed information is in the folder in front of you, but you can follow the gist of what I think might be a significant discovery up on the screen." As Trent settled in to listen to the presentation, the rest of them did, too.

"As you all know, Lieutenant Rafferty-Taylor has had me copying and downloading all of our old print files of unsolved cases into a database and cross-referencing them. There are still more boxes in the archives, but those are cases that are thirty years or older. I'm focusing on more recent crimes where the perpetrator and potential witnesses are likely to still be alive."

Max whistled. "You've already been through thirty years of open and unsolved cases? Hell, you're making the rest of us look like a bunch of goldbricks."

"Not a chance, Max." She laughed at the gruff man's teasing compliment. "I've been doing this pretty steadily since spring. And I didn't get shot up and have to go on sick leave, either."

Trent nudged his partner. "Or run off to Vegas to get

married before reporting back for active duty." Katie's dedication explained a lot of her late nights and the pale shadows under her blue eyes. But was all this unpaid overtime she'd put in the reason she had no time for a relationship? Or was it the thing she chose to do to fill up the empty hours in her life so she wouldn't miss those relationships? "What did you find out?"

Katie curled a leg beneath her to sit up higher in her chair. "When Olivia was investigating Danielle Reese's murder last spring, she came up with her *Strangers on a Train* theory, and it got me to thinking."

Olivia nodded. "*Strangers on a Train*, as in the Alfred Hitchcock movie where two people meet and agree to commit murder for the other person."

Her partner, Jim, continued, "But since they've never met before and don't run in the same social circles, the one with the motive can arrange for an alibi, while the one who actually commits the crime won't pop as a suspect on the police's radar because he or she has no motive to kill the victim."

"That's why we arrested Stephen March for Dani Reese's murder." Olivia braced her elbows on the table and leaned forward. "The evidence says he's good for it. But he had no motive. I still believe he was blackmailed into doing it, or—"

"He murdered her in exchange for somebody else killing Richard Bratcher," Max finished. Trent reached over and rested a hand on his partner's shoulder. March and Bratcher were sensitive subjects for the stocky detective because Stephen March was his wife's younger brother, and Bratcher had been the bullying fiancé who'd abused Rosie Krolikowski. Max nodded his appreciation at the show of support. "We got Hillary Wells for Bratcher's murder, even though she barely knew the guy." He turned his attention back to Katie. "Are you saying that you did your brainy thing and finally found where March and Dr. Wells could have met and set up their murder bargain?"

"Not exactly."

"What exactly are we talking about, then?" he asked.

"I designed a program to search for commonalities between cases by looking for key words or names or places. What I discovered is a pattern between several crimes that occurred over the last ten years."

"A pattern?" the lieutenant asked.

Katie nodded. "I haven't been able to prove that they're all linked to one particular case, or even to just one person, but I've made some interesting connections between these six suspects and—" she swiped her finger across her laptop, changing the images "—these six victims."

Trent recognized the pictures of both Dani Reese and Richard Bratcher, the victims Stephen March and Hillary Wells had killed. He also recognized the stout cheeks and receding hairline of Leland Asher. "It's not an exact swap where Suspect A kills Victim B while Suspect B kills Victim A. It's more as though they're links in a chain."

The lieutenant urged her to continue. "Do you have specific examples of those links?"

"Yes, ma'am." Katie adjusted the display to bring the twelve images up side by side before she twirled her chair to the side and got up to touch the television screen. Her ease in front of an audience reinforced Trent's suspicion that whatever had had her so flustered earlier had to do with the details about last night, maybe something that she still hadn't shared with him—not a presentation to her boss and coworkers involving multiple murders. "It's a painstaking process, but as I put in more information from the reports, I've come up with links from unsolved cases to people or events from murders you all have closed earlier this year. Some of these seem pretty random, but in a place the size of Kansas City, the fact that these people may have come into contact with each other at all seems compelling to me."

Olivia tried to follow Katie's line of reasoning. "Some of the connections are obvious. Stephen March killed Danielle Reese. Dani was investigating Leland Asher. Hillary Wells murdered Richard Bratcher, and he was the man who was abusing Stephen's sister, Rosie March."

Max swore under his breath. "Don't remind me."

She pointed to the photo of a distinguished white-haired gentleman. "This is Dr. Lloyd Endicott, Hillary Wells's former boss and mentor. He died in a suspicious car crash that has yet to be solved. We suspect he's the man Dr. Wells wanted to have killed, since she took over his company and the millions of dollars that went with it."

Although Trent sometimes worried that Katie's knowledge of all these dusty old cases bordered on the obsessive, he couldn't deny how useful it was to have a walking, talking encyclopedia working on their team.

He pointed to the image of a professional woman with short dark hair. "Does Hillary Wells or any of those other suspects or victims connect to Leland Asher?"

Katie nodded. "You might be surprised to know that before she died, she worked out at the same gym Matt Asher does."

"Leland's nephew?" Trent shifted his gaze to the image of a young man in a suit and tie who wore glasses and bore a striking resemblance to Leland Asher. "You think the two of them knew each other?"

She shrugged. "I can't say for certain unless I dig into the gym's schedule, class and personal trainer files, but the opportunity to meet was certainly there."

"It would be easy enough to go to the gym and ask some general questions to see if anyone ever saw the two of them together," Trent offered.

The lieutenant nodded. "Make a note to do that."

"Yes, ma'am."

"I don't have any evidence that Hillary Wells and Leland Asher ever met." Katie pointed to the nephew and then to Leland Asher. "But Max discovered that Matt regularly visits his uncle in prison."

Olivia nodded. "I'm guessing he's in the family business, although we haven't been able to prove that he's guilty of anything illegal. But he's down in Jefferson City nearly every week, so you know he must be passing messages to and from his uncle. Leland could have ordered Hillary to kill Richard Bratcher."

Jim Parker agreed. "It'd make sense for Matt Asher to keep the family business running while Uncle Leland is incarcerated. Where are his parents? Is his father involved in any of Leland's criminal activities?"

"There's no father in the picture. I did a little research through Social Services and found what I could on his mother. She's Leland's sister—never married. It's in your folders. Isabel Asher overdosed when Matt was eleven—ten years ago." Katie pointed to the image of a blonde woman who had probably once been a knockout before the blank, sunken eyes and sallow skin in the photograph marred her beauty. "That's why she was in the system—she was fighting an ongoing addiction to crack cocaine, was in and out of rehab. There were several calls from teachers about neglect. After Isabel's death, Matt Asher went to live with his uncle."

Max tipped his chair back and said what they all suspected. "The dope was probably supplied by her brother's import business. If not, he'd certainly have the money to buy her whatever she wanted."

Jim concurred. "Access to her brother's wealth would make her a prime target. Let me guess, there's a boyfriend she used to shoot up with. Asher blamed him for his sister's death and that guy's in one of your dead files?"

"Well, Francisco Dona did have a couple of arrests in his packet, but he can't be involved in any of our more recent crimes." She highlighted the mug shot of a dark-haired lothario with long, stringy hair and a goatee. "He died in a motorcycle accident shortly after Isabel's death."

"Are we sure it was an accident?" Trent asked.

Katie drew a line from Francisco Dona to Lloyd Endicott. "Well, even though one rode a motorcycle and the other drove a luxury car, the sabotage to the engines was similar."

"As if both crimes had been committed by the same person?" Max sat up straight, his gruff voice incredulous. "Wow, kiddo. You're thorough."

"It's a thing I do. I like to poke around. Solve puzzles. It's just a matter of getting access to the right database."

Lieutenant Rafferty-Taylor threw a note of caution into the mix. "And having the legal clearance to access that database?"

"Yes, ma'am." Katie's lips softened with a sheepish smile. "Either I've got departmental clearance or it's public access. I haven't needed a warrant to put together any of this information, although there are places I could dig deeper if I did have one. I've sent out feelers to businesses, doctors, private citizens and so on to update our records. Some are eager to answer questions and help. Others don't even respond. Of course, I could find out more if..." She twiddled her fingers in the air, indicating her hacking skills. Trent had no doubt that Katie could access almost any information they needed—but the way she'd obtain it wouldn't stand up in court and no conviction would stick.

The lieutenant smiled. "We'll work within legal means for now. Continue with your report. This is already good stuff we can follow up on."

Trent read through the slim report on the dead socialite. "Says here the detectives assigned to the case suspected foul play in Isabel Asher's death. They thought it might be a hit by a rival organization to send a message to Asher. So you think Francisco Dona made a deal with someone to kill her?"

Katie nodded. "There was no conclusive evidence in her KCPD case file, although that's an angle the detectives in the organized crime division investigated before it was closed out as an accidental death."

Olivia thumbed through the information in her folder. "You *have* been busy. These deaths all happened within a general time frame, six to ten years ago. It makes our *Strangers on a Train* theory plausible."

Jim dropped his folder on the table, shaking his head. "But there are six murder victims here. And we've only solved two of them. And we haven't linked either of those conclusively to Leland Asher ordering those murders. You said this guy is getting out this week. If we can't pin something solid on him, we'll never get him back in prison." The blond detective looked from the lieutenant back to Katie. "Is there any place else where all of their killers could have met with Asher? Even randomly?"

"You mean like sitting together at a ball game? I haven't found anything like that yet, but…" Katie sat back in her chair and drew lines from one picture to another on her computer screen, giving them all a visual of her extensive research. "Leland Asher was diagnosed with lung cancer two months ago. The doctors suspect he's been suffering longer than that."

Their team leader nodded. "That probably helped prompt his early release as well—so the state doesn't have to pay for his medical treatments. What else?"

"Either Matt Asher or Leland's girlfriend, Dr. Bev-

erly Eisenbach, have been to see him every week while
he's getting radiation treatments and chemo shots."
Katie drew another line. "Matt and Stephen March
both saw Dr. Eisenbach as teens for counseling. Hillary Wells ran Endicott Global after Dr. Lloyd Endicott's
death, and Dr. Endicott belonged to the same country
club as Leland." The grumbles and astonished gasps
around the table grew louder as the links of this twisted
chain of murder fell into place. "Isabel Asher was Leland's sister and Matt's mother, of course. Roberta Hays
was the DFS social worker assigned to Matt's case.
And…"

Trent looked up from the notes in his folder when
she hesitated. "What is it?"

She circled the image of a haggard-looking man with
graying hair. "I found a connection to me in here."

"What is it, kiddo?" Max asked, voicing the others'
surprise and concern.

"Roberta Hays's brother is Craig Fairfax."

Ah, hell. Trent recognized the name from Katie's
past. *That* was what had truly scared her. He sat forward, extending his long arm to the end of the table.
He reached for Katie, his fingertips brushing the edge
of the laptop where her hands rested on the keyboard.
But she curled her fingers into a fist, refusing his touch.
That didn't stop him from asking the question, "You
discovered Fairfax in your research last night?"

Her gaze landed on his, and she nodded before explaining the significance of that name to the others.
"He's the man who kidnapped me when I was seventeen. He tried to take Tyler from me as part of an ille-

gal adoption ring. He and his sister Roberta—who used her position with Family Services to scout out potential candidates like me—are both serving time now."

No wonder she'd gotten obsessed with her work and lost track of both Tyler and the late hour last night. Trent was already sending a text of his own, verifying that Craig Fairfax was still locked up in a cell in Jefferson City and not running loose on the Williams College campus.

"What's his connection to cold case?" the lieutenant asked, gently reminding Katie of the focus of the team's investigation. "Does he fit in with our *Strangers on a Train* theory? Can we tie him to Asher's criminal organization?"

Katie nodded. "Mr. Fairfax was diagnosed with prostate cancer earlier this year." She drew one last line on the computer screen from one sicko to another. "He's in the same prison infirmary with Leland Asher."

CHAPTER FIVE

"YOU NEED ME there to back you up?" Max Krolikowski's voice was a deep growly pitch over the cell phone Trent slipped beneath the edge of his black knit watch cap as he climbed out of his truck at the Williams College auditorium.

"Nah, brother," Trent answered, flipping up the collar of his coat against the clear, cold night. He turned his back to the bitter wind blowing from the north and strode across the cleared pavement toward the massive brick building. "This is personal. We're off the clock."

"Doesn't mean I won't be there in a heartbeat. I owe you for helping me keep an eye on Rosie this summer." Max chuckled. "Besides, I decided I like ya. I'd hate to have to break in a whole new partner."

Trent laughed, too. "Nobody else would have you, you grumpy old man."

"Bite me, junior."

"Love you, too." Stretching out his long legs, Trent stepped over the snow piled between the sidewalk and curb. He noted that the parking lot was crowded with cars and the pavement and sidewalk had been cleared from one end to another by plows. There'd be no footprints to follow tonight unless the perp he believed had been spying on Katie was dumb enough to trek through the drifts. But if the guy who'd shoved her to the floor was that kind of dumb, Trent intended to be here to have a conversation about keeping his distance from the Rinaldi family. "Hey, did you ever hear back from the gym Matt Asher belongs to?"

"I thought we were off the clock."

"I'll stop thinking about these unsolved cases when you do."

Trent's booted feet quickly ate up several yards walking around to the front lobby doors of the building while Max grinched around in the background. When his partner came back to the phone, Trent knew he'd been checking the facts in his notebook. "Since the manager didn't seem to know much when we visited this morning, I stopped by on my way home and chatted up the after-work crowd. Several people recognized Matt Asher and Hillary Wells, but couldn't remember if they'd ever seen them in a conversation with each other."

Trent figured with the discrepancy between their ages—Matt barely being twenty-two and the late Dr. Wells being a professional woman in her forties—that any conversation more intimate than a polite greeting between the two of them might stand out enough to make an impression on at least one of the other gym members. When he suggested the idea, Max concurred. "Asked and answered. No one I spoke to could recall either Matt Asher or Hillary Wells being in the same room together, much less sharing that they were looking for a way to have someone killed."

The sharp wind bit into Trent's cheek when he turned

to the front doors. He hunched his shoulders to stay warm. "So that's not our connection between the two of them. Still, eliminating the gym doesn't mean she didn't have some other connection to Leland Asher."

"So we keep digging."

Trent nodded. "I'll ask Katie if she's come up with anyplace else that can tie the two of them together."

"Or tie Dr. Wells directly to Asher." Trent heard a soft voice in the background, then something that sounded suspiciously like lips smacking against each other. Max's gruff tone softened. "Rosie says to tell you hi—"

"Hey, Rosie."

"—and invite you over for dinner sometime before Christmas."

"I accept. Will you be there, too?"

"Wiseass." Trent grinned at the reprimand he heard in the background. "Um, the missus says I need to mind my manners. Maybe Friday before we all go see the little man in his play?"

"Sounds like a plan."

"Give me a call sometime to let me know if anybody else tries to bother Katie. She's part of the team, too. I don't like the idea of anybody messin' with one of us."

"That's why I'm here. If nothing else, I'm going to make sure she and Tyler aren't the last ones here and walking by themselves to their car again." Trent held open one of the glass front doors for a pair of chattering, bundled-up coeds who must have been leaving an evening meeting or practice in one of the fine arts classrooms. He barely saw their bold smiles and flirty eye contact. He silently bemoaned the idea that their interest in him sparked amusement rather than any fraction of the pull that a few ponytail hairs clinging to his shirt had that morning. "Ladies," he acknowledged to some silly giggles before they hurried past him and he signed off on his call to Max. "I'll keep you posted."

As soon as he stepped into the lobby out of the wind, Trent pulled off his cap and stuffed it into a coat pocket along with his phone. He removed his gloves and unzipped his coat before heading across the worn marble floor to the auditorium's dark red doors.

He stooped a little to peer through the cloudy glass window near the top of the door and saw a hazy tableau of the Cratchit family lifting their pewter mugs in a toast. He smiled when he spotted the little boy with the old-fashioned crutch tucked beneath his arm. Tyler's smudged face was easily the most animated of all the children onstage as he said his lines. There was a lot to admire about Katie's son. Trent didn't remember having that much confidence at that age, except maybe playing sports—but certainly not speaking in front of an audience. "Way to go, Tyler."

Trent shifted his gaze to the sloping rows of seats in the shadows between the lobby and the brightly lit stage. There wasn't much of an audience to be nervous about tonight. There was a skinny, graying man in a turtleneck pacing back and forth between the curved rows of seats. There were some obvious family of the cast scattered around, one running a handheld video camera, another snapping pictures with her phone. And there sat Katie beside a pile of coats in a chair in the middle of it all. Her downturned head made him think she was working on something in her lap instead of watching the rehearsal. Her laptop? Didn't that woman ever take a break from work? Was there something obsessive about learning the truth about that long-missing girl? Or was Katie reading more about Craig Fairfax, the man who'd tried to steal an infant Tyler from her and murdered her high-school pal Whitney Chiles?

"Come on, Katie Lee." His low-pitched whisper reverberated against the glass. She carried the weight of too much life experience on those slim shoulders. She didn't need to take on any more trouble. "Just enjoy the show."

If Katie was going to put in overtime making sense of the cases the team was working on, then he should do the same. Remembering his main reason for driving out here tonight, Trent detoured up the stairs to the tech booth in the balcony. He pulled out his badge before knocking on the door. The two men inside running lights and sound seemed willing enough to chat.

"Detective Trent Dixon," he identified himself, learning the men's names were Chip and Ron. "You guys know anything about a power outage here in the auditorium last night?"

"Yeah, I heard about the blackout," Chip, a balding man in metal-framed glasses, answered. "And how Katie foiled a break-in. But that's not on me. I locked up the booth when I left. And the work lights in the auditorium and backstage were still on. I walked out with Doug Price, the director. He turns everything off when he leaves—after the cast and crew are gone."

Only an innocent woman had been left behind in the dark. "Is there a way to turn off the work lights but turn on the rope lights to see backstage?"

Chip pulled down the lights at the end of the scene, then raised them slightly for the stage crew to come on and change the set for the next scene. Then he nodded. "The rope lights just plug in. Unless there was a power outage and everything in the building was dead, it'd be easy enough to throw a few switches backstage yet leave those on."

So the details Katie had shared about last night meant the blackout was deliberate. But whether the intent had been to trap her inside the theater or to cover up an intruder's escape, it was impossible to tell. "Did you see any signs of someone tampering with your light board?"

"It was just like I left it."

Ron, the sound guy with his cap sitting backward on his head, agreed. "The booth was locked up tight when I came in at six to set the microphones for rehearsal tonight. If anybody was in here, he had to have a key."

"And the director is the only person in the play with a key?" Trent would make a point of introducing himself to Doug Price.

Ron shrugged. "Except for campus security. Or maybe someone in the theater department. But all their productions are done for the semester. That's why we can be in here now."

The crew left the stage and both Chip and Ron went back to work. "Lights up."

Trent thanked them for their cooperation and went back down to the auditorium, sneaking in the back while

Ebenezer Scrooge and the ghostly Spirit of Christmas Future walked onstage. After his eyes adjusted to the semidarkness, he spotted Katie's hot-pink sweater and headed down the aisle toward her. When he got closer, he could see that she was looking at a crumpled piece of paper instead of the flat screen of her laptop.

So she wasn't working. But her head was down and she was rubbing her fingers back and forth against her neck beneath the base of her ponytail, as if a knot of tension had formed there. She was so intent on whatever she was reading that she jumped when he slipped into the seat beside her.

"Sorry." He nudged his shoulder against hers to apologize for startling her, then nodded toward the paper she was quickly folding up. "What's that?"

"What are you doing here?" She dropped her voice to a whisper to match his before turning to the coats beside her. "Oh, shoot. I left my bag backstage." Without missing a beat, she stuffed the paper inside the pocket of her coat.

Okay. So that wasn't suspicious. He eyed the navy wool coat where the letter had disappeared. If that was some kind of threat... "Everything okay?"

"What? Oh." She pulled her lime-green scarf from the pile and folded it neatly on top of the coat, burying the missive beneath another layer. Right. So they were back to her keeping secrets and suffering on her own when he knew damn well he could help. "It's Tyler's letter to Santa. He said he doesn't believe in Santa Claus anymore but that he wrote the letter for my sake.

I've always sent one out for him…mostly so I can read it and see what's tops on his wish list."

It was a plausible explanation for the frown between her brows. "That's a hard transition to go through the year they stop believing in the magic and hope of Christmas."

The frown eased a tad and she leaned toward him so they could talk without their voices carrying up to the stage. "He's still got plenty of hope, judging by the extent of that wish list. But other than some bad grammar, he sounds…" She sank back against the chair on a whispery sigh. "In a lot of ways he's still my little boy. But in some ways he's growing up way too fast."

Trent stretched out and slipped a friendly arm across the back of her seat. "That growing-up stuff is inevitable. You do know that, right, Mom?"

She gave his ribs a teasing tap with her fist. "I know. And it certainly beats the alternative." That brief glimpse of a smile quickly faded. "When I think of some of those cases I've read through this year, like that missing teenage girl and baby—like my friend Whitney back in high school—I know we're lucky to be here. But I can't help thinking I've cheated him somehow, that I haven't given him everything he needs, that he feels he has to be all grown-up to take care of me. He doesn't, of course. But maybe he doesn't believe that I can take care of him."

"You're a terrific mom, and he knows that. All little boys want to try on being a man for a while, especially when they know they've got someone there to back them up in case the experiment isn't as exciting or safe as they thought it would be." Trent dropped his arm around her shoulders and pulled her to his side in a friendly hug. "Tomorrow, he'll be a kid again. I promise." When she leaned against him, her fresh-as-a-daisy scent drew his lips to her hair and he pressed a kiss to her temple.

"Don't do that." Her hand at his chest pushed him away and she sat forward in her seat, moving away from the touch of his arm, as well. "If Tyler sees, I don't want him to get the wrong idea about us."

"The wrong idea?" Well, hell. "That peck was just a show of support between friends. A woman is damn well gonna know when I intend my kiss to mean something more."

She turned with a surprised gasp. "Trent, I didn't mean to insult—"

He put up his hand to silence her apology. Yet when his gaze fell on the naturally rosy tint of her lips and lingered, the spike of resentment firing through his blood blended with a yearning he hadn't acknowledged in years. She shouldn't draw that pretty mouth into such a tightly controlled line, and he shouldn't have this urge to ease it back into a smile beneath his own lips. Maybe he had crossed a line without realizing it. Because, right now, every male cell in his body was wishing for a little privacy so he could kiss her just once the way he'd always longed to. But he hadn't had the skills as a teenager, and as an adult he didn't have the permission to even try.

For a long time now, he'd imagined if they could share one real, passionate kiss, he'd find out that this desire simmering in his blood was just the remnants of a teenage fantasy. He'd discover the spark wasn't really there. He and Katie would share a laugh over the awkward encounter, and he'd finally be able to get this useless attraction out of his system. Inhaling a cautionary breath, Trent pulled his hand back to rest on the arm of the seat, letting his shoulder form the barricade she wanted between them.

"It won't happen again." At least, he hoped he could keep that promise. "I'd never do anything to jeopardize my friendship with you or Tyler."

But as Trent faced the stage again, adjusting his long legs in the narrow space between the rows of seats, his eyes were drawn to the show's director, Doug Price. The pacing had stopped and the older man's dark eyes were trained on the seats where he and Katie sat. Tyler wasn't the only one she needed to worry about seeing and misinterpreting a quick kiss.

So, did the temperamental artiste simply dislike the hushed tones of a whispered argument near the back of the theater interfering with him watching his play? Or was there something more personal in the territorial sneer he aimed at Trent and Katie? Did this guy have a thing for Katie?

The flare of jealousy was fleeting, there to acknowledge but quickly dismiss. If there was one thing Trent understood about Katie Lee Rinaldi, it was that it wasn't *him* she was loath to have a relationship with. She didn't want a relationship with any man.

There was no competition here. Trent acknowledged the man's displeasure with a nod and scrunched down in his seat in an unspoken assurance that he wouldn't disrupt the rehearsal again.

But there were even curiouser things afoot when he noticed the Grim Reaper wannabe onstage repeatedly tugging on his mask, using the adjustment of his costume to peer out at the director. And, though it was impossible to track the exact direction of the actor's glare beneath the black hood and mask, Trent would bet money that the guy was taking note of Doug Price's interest in Katie, too.

Trent leaned his head toward Katie and whispered, "Who's the guy onstage?"

She guessed he wasn't talking about Mr. Scrooge. "Christmas Future is Francis Sergel. I made his costume. He's probably getting ready to complain about something that itches or doesn't fit him." She finally relaxed and settled back into the seat beside him. "He's good at that."

"Complaining?"

"Oh, yes." He grinned at the subtle sarcasm that bled into her tone. Although it still rankled that she would have such a strong reaction to that innocent kiss, Trent appreciated her attempt to return them to their normal footing with each other. He wasn't about to completely drop his guard and relax, though, not with the director and twitchy man onstage each sliding them curious looks. "So what's on Tyler's list? You know I like to get the little guy a present every year."

He felt the momentary stiffening in her shoulder where it brushed against his, but she didn't try any awkward evasion of the question this time. "A bunch of video and computer games. I'll give you a list. And a dog. If I'm not careful, he's going to run away from home and move in with you now that you're fostering Padre. That's *his* dog. In his nine-year-old brain, anyway. He barely talks about anything else."

"You know I've got two extra bedrooms at my house. And a fenced-in yard. Tyler is welcome to come over to visit anytime. They can play outside. That dog loves jumping and snuffling around in the snow. I think the cold in his nose makes him a little hyper. He needs somebody Tyler's age who can keep up with him. Heck, maybe I'll even put Ty to work picking up Padre's messes in the backyard."

Katie laughed out loud, then quickly slapped a hand over her mouth when Doug Price swung around to glare at her again. She quickly dropped her voice back to a whisper. "Do it. That'd be the reality check Ty needs to understand that owning a pet is a lot of work and responsibility. It's not just the landlord's rules or me being mean."

"I'll make the offer."

"Douglas!" Trent sat up straight when Francis Sergel jerked the black hood off the back of his head and stepped out of character and walked to the edge of the stage. "I can't work like this."

For a split second, Trent instinctively went on the defensive, worrying that his accusatory whine was targeted at Katie. It wasn't until he felt her hands through the thick sleeve of his coat that he realized he'd thrown his arm out in front of her.

Now, *that* was a look that warned him he'd over-stepped the boundaries between them again.

Francis pulled the mask off his face and shook it at the director. "This needs another elastic strap sewn in. It keeps shifting on my face and I can't see."

Doug Price turned his face toward the catwalk near the ceiling and griped, "Spare me from working with these dime-store divas," while the actor playing Eb-enezer muttered something similar. Then the director swung around and snapped his fingers. "Katie. Grab your sewing kit and take care of that."

The squeeze of her hands around his forearm kept Trent from answering back about talking to her in that dictatorial tone. Apparently, Katie hadn't been singled out, because the director used the same tone with the actor onstage. "Give your mask to one of the crew, Fran-cis, and finish the scene."

"I need the mask to get into my character." The bearded man with black circles drawn around his eyes needed more than that Grim Reaper robe and makeup to get his creepy on?

"All you have to do is hit your blocking marks and point. Rise to the challenge." Doug gestured to the tem-peramental actor, then turned again. "Katie? Sooner rather than later, if you would. I'm trying to get an ac-curate running time on the show tonight."

"My sewing kit is in my bag in the greenroom."

"Then get it." His gaze slid past her to Trent. "And this is a closed rehearsal. Tell your boyfriend to buy a ticket if he wants to watch."

That's it. The need to stand up to that idiot jolted

through Trent's legs. But Katie's hand on his shoulder and a warning look kept him in his seat. She stood and beamed a smile at the director. "He already has."

Trent could have choked on the honey dripping from her voice, but the sweetly veiled retort seemed to appease Mr. Price. With a nod to Katie, the director turned back to the actors onstage. "All right. Let's take it back from your entrance, Francis."

He hissed a whisper behind her back as she moved in front of him toward the aisle. "So kissing you on the head is off-limits, but letting your director think I'm your boyfriend is okay?"

"That's Doug's interpretation, not mine. He saw your picture with Tyler on my computer and…" She looked down at him, her mouth twisted with another apology. "I didn't correct his mistake. Misleading Tyler is one thing. But sometimes, Doug is a little friendlier than I—"

"How friendly? Someday you're going to have to explain the rules—"

"Mom?"

Trent heard the loud whisper from the corner of the stage and peeked around Katie to see Tyler's smudged face peering from the edge of the heavy velvet curtain. The tiny dimple of a frown appeared between his feathery eyebrows, reminding him of Katie when she was stewing over a problem. Had he heard Price yelling at her? Had he seen the two of them arguing? Did he think he needed to protect his mama?

"Douglas? Now I have to deal with this?" When Mr. Death up there pointed to the little boy showing his face onstage, Trent shot to his feet, grabbing Katie on either side of her waist and moving her to his side. If he turned that snooty temper on Tyler...

But Katie Lee Rinaldi had already made it clear she could protect her son her own self, thank you, very much. "It's okay," she said in full voice. She stayed Trent's charge to her defense with a hand at the middle of his chest. She nodded to the actors and stopped the director before he could open his mouth. Then she curled her thumb and finger into an okay sign and winked to her son. "I'll be right there."

When she tapped either corner of her mouth and modeled a smile for him, Tyler's moment of concern disappeared and he smiled back at her. The boy smiled at Trent and thrust his hand out at waist level, sneaking a not-so-subtle wave to him. Trent put his fingers to his forehead and returned a salute, offering his own reassurance that the child didn't need to worry about his mom or anyone else while he was here.

As quickly as he'd popped out, Tyler disappeared behind the curtain.

"And this hobby is fun for you?" Trent dipped his chin to meet Katie's whispered thanks.

"The creative part of it is. But on this production, some of the people..." Katie's gaze shifted back and forth between Price and Sergel. "Not so much. But don't go all alpha on me. I can handle Doug and Francis. I already know how to deal with children."

His throat vibrated with a chuckle at her sarcasm. "Yeah, but yours behaves better."

Her fingers tangled together with his in a quick

squeeze. "Duty calls. Thanks for stopping by. I know Tyler is happy to have you here to watch him. Although I think you make him a little nervous."

Trent tightened his grip to stop her as she scooted past him, surprised at the admission. "I do? I don't mean to. The whole team is coming to opening night. Will he be okay with that?"

She smiled away his concern. "Relax. Having a few nerves onstage is a good thing. Seeing you will keep him on his toes. He wants to do a good job for you."

Katie made it impossible not to smile back. "Tyler's always first-string in my book."

"He knows that."

"Katie!" Doug yelled. "I need this fixed before the next scene." Trent released Katie's hand and straightened to all six feet five inches of irritated man before shrugging out of his coat and hanging it on the back of his seat, making it clear without saying a word that he was staying and that the lashing out at her needed to stop. The director seemed to rethink whom he could push around by adding a succinctly articulate, "If you please."

"Trent…" She knew what he was doing.

"Go on. I'm doing this very beta style, I promise. I'm just going to sit here until the show's done so I can give Tyler my critical opinion."

"And make sure these guys mind their manners?"

"It's what a boyfriend would do, isn't it?" Trent doffed her a salute, too. He also intended to be here to walk her to her car after rehearsal was done and to make sure nothing *weird* happened tonight. He folded his big body into the seat as if it was the most comfortable chair in the world. "I know Tyler will be my favorite thing about the play."

"Thank you." She turned into the aisle and hurried down to the stage.

Frankly, he wouldn't put up with the bossy overlord and the whiny string bean onstage. But he was here to support Katie and Tyler, not to audition or volunteer backstage for anything himself. All the more reason to find out who had trapped her in the theater and separated her from her son last night. If it was just one of these bozos trying to intimidate her, his presence could put a stop to that. And if it was something more sinister, then the scene of the crime was the best place to look for the answers Katie wouldn't give him.

Like what was in a letter to Santa that could upset her like that?

Once Katie took the mask from the stagehand and disappeared behind the curtain, Trent reached across the empty seat into her coat and pulled out the letter that had dented a worried frown on her smooth forehead. If that story had all been a lie and it was some kind of threat related to last night, and she didn't think she needed to tell him, then... He read the addressee on the envelope out loud. She hadn't lied. "Santa Claus?"

He pulled out the crumpled letter and smoothed it against the thigh of his jeans before reading.

Dear Santa,
I think you might not be real. My friend Wyatt says that his mom is Santa Claus but I know you are not

a girl. I'm writing this letter just in case because Jack says your real, and because Mom asked me to write you a letter and it makes her happy when I do what she says. If you do come by on Christmas Eve, I want a dog, a cell phone, the action figures from the movie I saw this summer, gamer cards and a dad. Uncle Dwight is fun to do stuff with, but he is cousin Jack's dad. Jack is in second grade at my school and is fun to play with. Jack's not really my cousin, but it's weird to have an uncle younger than me and Dwight's more like a grandpa. Mom says our family dynamite is complicated. I want a dad who can play baseball and computer games, but I don't want him to be so good that he beats me all the time. Mom won't let me play any battle games, but I like the racing games and the ones where you have to collect stuff and get speshul powers. I found a dog named Padre at rehersal. He can be mine if you want. If you can catch him. He likes peanut-butter sandwiches. A dad with a dog would be the best.
Your friend,
Tyler Rinaldi
PS: I live in an apartment, so you will have to come in the front door because we don't have a chimney. I can leave it unlocked.
PSS: Jack wants a racing car set and boxing mitts.
PSSS: I don't want one of those little girlie dogs with a bow in her hair.

A dad? Tyler had asked Santa for a dad? No wonder Katie had fretted over the letter. There were at least two things on this list she couldn't give her son, and that had to be difficult for a single mom who wanted to give the world to her child. And yeah, Tyler did sound a little like a cynical grown-up in a couple places. But this was still the voice of a little boy speaking from his heart.

Trent felt a few sentimental pangs pulling on his heart, too. He'd known Tyler since the boy was an infant and his neighbor Maddie McCallister—now married to DA Dwight Powers—had taken the rescued baby in to care for him until she and Dwight had tracked down the missing Katie and broken up that illegal adoption ring.

The illegal adoption ring headed by Craig Fairfax.

Craig Fairfax, the man who'd ordered the murder of their high school classmate Whitney Chiles. The man who'd tried to kill Katie, and Maddie and Dwight, too.

Craig Fairfax, the man who shared a prison infirmary with reputed mob boss Leland Asher, the prime suspect in several of the unsolved cases their team was investigating.

If Katie's thoughts had taken the same dark trail, then she was probably more worried, unsure and afraid than she was letting on.

Trent's nostrils flared with a deep, quiet breath as the cop in him took over once more. He was here to keep Katie and Tyler as safe as they'd let him and to put a name to any threat that might mean them harm. Whether that threat was a frightened intruder; a cast or crewmate with some kind of bitter feelings or obsession toward Katie or Tyler; a convicted killer who might be using a mob boss and his connections to take revenge on the family who'd put him away for life; or even the mob boss himself, who was taking advantage of the inside knowledge he could gain on Katie in some bizarre plan to thwart the cold case squad's investigation into him and his activities—he couldn't leave the family alone and unguarded. No matter how awkward things got between him and Katie, no matter how angry she got at his interference—no matter how painful it was for him to be close and not have what he'd once wanted—he wasn't going anywhere.

The Rinaldis and finding answers to this complicated mix of unsolved cases were his number-one assignment now.

Trent carefully returned the letter to the pocket of Katie's coat and smoothed everything back into place. Then, while the Spirit of Christmas Future and Ebenezer Scrooge resumed their journey through the bleak future that awaited a man who refused to change his miserly ways, Trent pulled out his phone and sent a couple of queries to the KCPD database, checking to see whether Doug Price or Francis Sergel had any kind of criminal record or had been listed as a person of interest in any ongoing cases.

Interesting. Francis Sergel's name didn't show up anywhere until about ten years ago on a DMV app, and the guy had to be in his late forties or fifties. That most likely meant a legal name change for any number of reasons, from annoying enough people in his previous life and needing a fresh start to entering witness protection or something more nefarious. A man with only a recent past also meant a search through databases that Katie would have to access for him. But who would change his name to Francis? Or Sergel? Unless there was some kind of personal significance to the name. That was something else Katie could find quick answers to if he put her on the hunt.

And then there was Douglas Price. His fingerprints were in the system because he used to be a public school teacher. But there was nothing more than a few speeding tickets in his history.

Scrooge was dancing a jig with his nephew's wife and celebrating Christmas when a shadow fell over Trent.

"Don't get on my case about working when I'm off the clock if you're going to do it, too." Katie plopped down in the seat beside him, hugging her bulky canvas carryall bag in her arms. "Did something come up?"

Trent brushed his finger over his phone to darken the screen. "I was doing a little background check on a couple of your friends here." The dent between her delicate eyebrows instantly appeared. But he wasn't going to lie to her about his concerns. "Did you know Francis doesn't show up in the system until around ten years ago?" He nodded toward her bright green-and-blue bag. "You got something in that magic computer of yours that can tell me why he changed his name and who he used to be? Or at least give me an idea why he'd pick that name?"

"Francis?" She opened the flap of her bag and pulled out her laptop. "You think he's suspicious?"

"I'm a cop, Katie. I'm suspicious of everyone until I have an explanation that makes sense." He clipped his phone back onto his belt and rested his forearm on the chair between them. "I just want to make sure we've got nothing to worry about from any of the people around you."

"I told you last night I probably got in the way of an intruder."

"Then why mess with the lights? Why go to the extra effort to threaten you?"

"You think someone here... That Francis would...?" She pulled out a smaller remote gadget, turned it on and set it on the chair beside her. Then she dropped her bag to the floor and set her laptop on her knees. "Okay. What do you want me to look up? Legal cases? Witness relocation? Criminal profiling reports?" She reached over and tapped the back of his hand as she turned her open laptop toward him, urging him to look at the display screen. "Trent?"

"Son of a bitch." Trent felt his temperature go up, even as her fingers chilled against his skin.

There was a message scrawled in lipstick across the screen.

Stop what you're doing.

"That message last night *was* meant for me."

CHAPTER SIX

MAX KROLIKOWSKI STRODE onstage to join Katie, Tyler and the other members of the production company Trent had gathered to ask a few questions. Max dangled a plastic bag with a tube of lipstick inside. "I found this in the makeup supplies in the dressing rooms. The tip's worn flat and it looks like a match to the color on Katie's laptop. The case has been polished up, though." He glanced down at Katie, sitting in one of the dining table chairs on the set. "Either you guys are fanatics about cleaning up, or somebody's wiped it for prints."

She appreciated Trent's partner answering the call as soon as Trent had phoned and requested backup— "Somebody got to Katie again."

But right now she was wishing Max wasn't such a good cop and that the evidence relating to that disturbing message hadn't been so easy to find. Katie shook her head, not liking the implication. "We're not fanatics."

There was no longer a plausible option to dismiss the weird things that had happened to her at the theater. Someone was watching her. Someone was taking advantage of the opportunity to frighten her. And he was succeeding. She'd made a life for herself behind the scenes now—at work, at the theater—putting her son first. Being thrust into the spotlight by an anonymous stalker didn't feel so good.

Trent thanked the mother who'd been taking pictures with her phone and dismissed her and her daughter. "Let's take the tube, anyway. Maybe the lab can get a latent or DNA off it or the laptop." His big shoulders lifted with a shrug that Katie didn't find very reassuring. "So far, everybody's been cooperative, but no one saw anyone or anything that seemed out of place backstage. That makes me suspect someone here, whose presence wouldn't be questioned. Someone who's better at lying than I am at detecting it. I'm not sure where to take this next."

"You'll figure it out, junior. We just keep asking questions," Max advised, dropping the lipstick into the paper sack where her computer had already been tagged and bagged as evidence. He rolled up the top of the sack, then paused when he saw Katie watching him. "You're okay if I do this, kiddo? Will you need this for work tomorrow? I know you and your computer are attached at the hip."

Attached at the hip, hmm? Apparently, not closely enough.

"It's okay, Max," she assured him. "I ran a quick diagnostic myself. It doesn't look as though anyone messed with any of the files or programs, and I have everything backed up on a portable hard drive. Plus, I have a desk computer at home and at work."

Katie rubbed her hands up and down her arms, trying to erase the chill beneath her cardigan and blouse.

She couldn't help but let her gaze scan the faces of the remaining cast and crew sitting onstage or in the audience seats. Had the makeup kit from the dressing rooms merely been an item of opportunity for an outsider? Or was someone involved with the play a better actor than anyone suspected? And what did any of this have to do with her?

Trent's cool gray eyes passed over her, winking a silent version of *hang in there* before he turned to Doug Price and repeated the question he'd already asked. "Did you see anything that looked out of place earlier this evening? Anyone you didn't recognize?"

Doug's grayish-blond eyebrow arched up with disdain. "Besides you?"

Max folded his arms over his sturdy chest. "Answer the question."

Perhaps thinking better of crossing the detectives who'd taken over his rehearsal, Doug eased his taut features into an imitation of a smile. "Look, I'm as concerned about Katie's safety—about the safety of everyone here—as you are, Detective. The entire cast and crew were here tonight. In fact, I think it's the first time since we started rehearsing that no one's been absent because of illness or a conflict. The kids all have a parent or guardian who comes to rehearsals with them, too. I won't allow any of the little minions to be unsupervised."

"So you're saying there were more people than usual here tonight," Trent clarified. "And you knew all of them?"

Doug considered his answer for a moment before

crossing to the edge of the stage and pointing to the back corner of the auditorium. "There was a man here filming the scenes with the children. I'd never seen him before. I assumed he was a father who'd come instead of the moms who are usually here."

"Oh, my God." Katie's stomach twisted into a knot. There'd been a strange man filming Tyler and the other children? She instantly sought out her son, playing a card game with Wyatt on the stairs leading down to the seats. He must have felt her concern because he looked up at her and frowned. Damn it. She was worrying him again. Better than most, she knew what it was like to be afraid for a mother's safety. She shouldn't be scaring him.

A large hand closed over her shoulder. She glanced up at the sudden infusion of warmth and support. But Trent was asking her for information as much as calming her fears. "Did you recognize this man?"

Her gaze drifted out of focus, trying to visualize the man she'd only glanced at in passing. "I didn't know him. But I assumed the same thing—that he was someone's dad."

"Can you describe him?"

"The camera was in front of his face when I saw him. Brown hair. Brown wool coat. Um, dress shoes instead of snow boots." She blinked her eyes back into focus. "His camera was a digital Canon with a mini zoom lens. Black woven strap around his neck. Sorry, that still doesn't give you a name or face."

Trent grinned. "Leave it to you to notice the tech. And don't apologize. This is a lot more than I knew a

second ago." Even as he jotted down the limited description, she saw him checking the people remaining
in the theater. Katie didn't see anyone who matched her
vague description, either.

"Trent?"

A tug on Trent's sleeve turned him away from her.
Katie watched her son's eyes tip up to the man who
towered above him.

"What is it, buddy?" Trent dropped to one knee,
putting himself closer to eye level with Tyler. "Do you
know the man I'm asking about?"

Tyler shook his head. "There wasn't any dad here
except for Kayla's. She gets to stay with him this month,
and it was his turn to watch us backstage. He doesn't
have much hair at all."

Trent nodded at the matter-of-fact explanation.
"What's Kayla's dad's name?"

"Mr. Hudnall."

When Trent glanced back at Katie, she filled in the
blank for him. "Willie Hudnall. We all signed up to take
different nights to supervise the children backstage. He
was in the greenroom with the kids when I went back
to fix Francis's mask."

"So he was there when your laptop was unprotected.
He could have written that message there."

She hated to think the man she'd been grateful to for
checking on Tyler twenty-four hours ago might now be
a suspect. "My point is, I would have recognized him
if he'd been the man in the audience. We all would
have. Plus, Mr. Hudnall was wearing hiking boots, not
dress shoes."

Max nodded to Trent and pulled out his phone. "I'll give the description we have to campus security. Find out if they've seen anyone like that."

While Max took a few steps away and made the call, Katie gestured to the others remaining for this official Q and A. "There are more than two dozen people backstage at any given time. More if you count the crew. Any one of them could have…" She pulled Tyler onto her lap and hugged her arms around him. She looked again. Looked closer. Maybe the enemy was right here. A friend in disguise. One of the people she trusted— one of the people she trusted with her son.

Trent rose in front of her, reading her distress. "Any one of them could have left you that message."

"But why? What am I doing that's such a threat to anyone? I'd rather think it was that stranger. I know these people. I've been hanging out with them almost every evening for weeks now. Some of them have become friends." She shoved her fingers through her bangs, willing some sort of clarity to reveal the truth. "What does it mean? What am I doing that I have to stop?"

A noisy harrumph from the front row drew Trent's attention. "You got something to say, Mr. Sergel?"

Francis might have cleaned off his makeup, but wearing street clothes as black as the costume he wore in the play, and taking the stairs two at a time on his long, spidery legs, he still bore an ominous look that would keep Katie from ever trusting the man. "Just that Ms. Rinaldi keeps flirting with our director."

"Excuse me?" What was wrong with this guy to give

him such a petulant mean streak? "I don't flirt with anybody."

Although he spoke to Trent, his beady, dark eyes were focused squarely on Katie. "Maybe someone resents that she's drawing attention to herself and trying to make her or Tyler Doug's favorite."

Katie shot to her feet, holding on to Tyler's shoulders to keep him from tumbling to the floor. "Are you kidding me? I haven't done anything to make Doug think—"

"Doug's the one who keeps hitting on Mom," Tyler piped up.

The director's head swung around, as if he'd dozed off during the part of the conversation that didn't concern him. "I beg your pardon?" He took a step closer. "I was simply being friendly. You keep to yourself so much, I wanted you to feel included."

"My mom doesn't even like you, and you're too old to be a dad," Tyler argued. "You should leave her alone."

"Tyler!" More shocked by her son's choice of defense than by Doug lying about his interest in her, Katie turned him to face her. "What do you know about men hitting on women?"

"Mo-om." Tyler rolled his eyes. "I watch TV. I know stuff. And I watch you, too. Doug's always asking you to go somewhere after rehearsal."

"And I always say no."

Trent stopped the mother-son conversation with a hand on her arm and turned their attention back to Francis. "Are you jealous, Sergei?"

"I only have the best interests of this production in mind."

"If the boss is paying more attention to the pretty lady than to the show onstage, that bothers you?"

"Well, of course it does. I think it bothers all of us."

"So you have a problem with Katie and Mr. Price being friends," Trent reasoned. "Would you like her to stop doing that?"

Francis lifted his pointy chin. "I am not answering any more questions without my attorney present."

"Have you done something to make you think you need an attorney?" Francis was tall. But Trent was taller. And bigger. He forced Francis to take a step back just by leaning toward him. "Did you deface Katie's computer? Maybe wanted to teach her a lesson? Remind her of her place? You were backstage for most of the play."

"Stop twisting my words around."

But Trent Dixon didn't back down. "I saw you snap at more than one person tonight, including Tyler and Katie. Maybe you're the one who wants to be the director's favorite."

"I refuse to answer any of your accusations. I only want the best show possible, and these two amateurs—"

"We're all amateurs, Francis." Doug Price pulled Francis back beside him. "Stop talking before you say something you'll regret." He turned to the others watching from the audience. "Everyone, please. Detective Dixon, there are children here and it's late. May I send them home? This is all very upsetting and counterproductive to putting on a successful play, and opening night is Friday. I don't think you'll find out anything more tonight. You can get everyone's contact information from Katie's cast-and-crew list if you have more questions. No one knows who this man with the camera was, but I promise you, if he shows his face again, I'll demand he identify himself."

"I want to know what he took pictures of, too."

"Of course." Doug clapped his hands, ensuring that everyone was following his directions and moving toward the backstage exit. "Shall we? I'm sure campus security is waiting to lock up after us."

Trent nodded. "Tell them to go ahead. We'll be right out. Thank you to everyone for your cooperation." Although his smile included the cast, crew and parents filing past them, he had nothing but *I'm watching you* in his eyes for Francis, who didn't move until Doug gave him a nudge and a warning glare.

Doug himself was the last one of the interview group to leave the stage, but he paused and brushed his fingers against Katie's elbow. When she flinched, his grip tightened in a paternal squeeze, and she looked up into light brown eyes that seemed genuinely concerned. "I'm sorry this is happening to you, dear. I hope you'll do whatever is necessary to stay safe."

"Thank you, Doug."

He released her to give Tyler's chin a playful pinch. "Be sure to keep our Tiny Tim safe, too."

"I will."

Trent urged the director to follow the rest of the cast and crew. "Good night, Mr. Price."

Doug's cajoling smile disappeared. "Good night, Detective."

As soon as Doug had disappeared offstage with the others, Tyler rubbed his knuckles back and forth across his chin. "I hate when he does that. He treats me like I'm a little kid."

Salty tears stung Katie's eyes as her *little kid* showed yet another sign of growing up too fast. Despite his token grumble, she pressed a kiss to the crown of his hair and ruffled the dark curls before nudging him to the stairs. "Get your coat on and gather your things. Don't forget your library book for school."

She felt Trent's compassionate gaze on her but couldn't look up to meet it. Not without the tears spilling over. Refusing to turn into an emotional basket case of fear, fatigue and regret, Katie picked up her own coat off the back of the chair and slipped into it.

She was pulling her knit cap on when Max ended his call and rejoined them. "Campus security hasn't seen anybody matching Katie's description of the unknown man tonight, but they'll keep an eye open for anyone matching his general description. I took the liberty of encouraging them to track Sergel and Price's whereabouts when they're on campus, as well. I gave them the plates, make and model of their cars and texted the same to you, in case either one shows up someplace they shouldn't."

Trent was bundling up to face the wintry night, too. "You read my mind, brother. I'll follow up with Katie's list to see if anybody else jumps out as having some kind of motive." He thrust out his hand. "Thanks."

"I'm keepin' tabs on what you owe me, junior. Don't worry." Max laughed as he shook Trent's hand. "I'll make sure everybody else has left before I head to the lab." His goodbye included Katie. "See you two in the morning."

"Good night, Max. Thanks."

The burly detective dropped a kiss on her cheek. "Take care, kiddo." He exchanged a couple of fake boxing moves with Tyler. "You be careful, little man."

"I will. Bye, Max."

By the time the work lights were out and they said good-night to the security guard, Katie's car and Trent's pickup truck were the last two vehicles in the parking lot. Trent set Tyler's book bag in the backseat and knelt down in the open doorway to buckle him in and steal a quick hug while Katie stowed her own bag and started the engine. "You did a good job tonight, Tyler. For a while there, I forgot it was you onstage and thought you were Tim Cratchit. I can hardly wait to watch the whole show on Friday. I'll be sure to tell Padre what a good job you did, too."

"Padre?"

Trent grinned. "Yeah. Your mom told me that was the name you gave him. I picked him up last night. He's going to be staying with me for a little while, until he gets some meat on his bones."

Tyler made no effort to hide his gap-toothed smile—or stifle the yawn that followed. "Tell Padre I said hi. And that I want to come see him Saturday. And don't give him away to anybody until I get there, okay?"

"I won't. I'll tell him you're coming."

Katie looked across her son to the big man kneeling there and mouthed, *Thank you*. Even though his eyes had drifted shut, her son was still smiling. She buckled herself in. "Good night, Trent."

But when Trent started to leave, Tyler's eyes popped open. "Mom? Do you think anything scary will be written on your computer at home?"

He must have been more aware of tonight's events—and more frightened by them—than she'd realized. She reached across the console to cup his cheek, hating that a nine-year-old should have a worry mark on his forehead. "No, sweetie. I don't see how anyone could get into our apartment. We'll be fine."

He roused himself from his sleepy state and sat up straight. "What if that man who took pictures of us is there? Can we call Trent if we see him?"

Katie was at a loss. How could she make Tyler's fears go away when she wasn't sure what was happening around her and whom she needed to be afraid of? "Sweetie, if you see that man…or anyone who… Of course, we'll call the police. I don't want you to be afraid. I—"

"And you'll stop doing whatever is making him so mad?"

She looked past those wide blue eyes into Trent's, wishing she knew how to answer Tyler's question. Trent's eyes had darkened like steel at the worried timbre in Tyler's voice. He reached into the car and palmed the top of Tyler's head. "Tell you what. I'll follow you and your mom home. Give the place a good once-over before you lock up. I'll make sure nobody's there who shouldn't be." He pulled his gloved hand into a fist and held it out to Tyler. "Sound like a plan, buddy?"

With a nod, Tyler bumped his small fist against Trent's and settled back into his seat.

Trent's gaze sought hers this time. "Are you okay with that?"

Okay with Trent reassuring her son and making sure they were both safe?

Katie nodded. "I'll see you at home."

CHAPTER SEVEN

TYLER'S HEAD HAD lolled over onto his shoulder and he was snoring softly in a deep sleep when Katie pulled into her parking space at the apartment complex where the two of them lived near the Kauffman and Arrowhead stadium complex. Trent had pulled into a visitor's space and joined them by the time she had her and Tyler's bags looped over her shoulder, and she was leaning into the car to unbuckle her son.

"Wait." A gloved hand closed around her arm and pulled her aside. "Let me." Trent took her place at the open door and reached in to lift her sleeping child into his arms. "Lock up and lead the way."

With a nod of thanks, she closed the door and locked the car. Then she reached up to tug Tyler's scarf and collar around his face to protect him from the cold night air. Katie was just as aware of Trent's bulky frame blocking the wind as he followed behind her as she was his constant scanning back and forth to ensure that no one seemed unusually interested in the trio coming home late at night. Trent's intimidating stature and the gentle surety with which he carried Tyler against his chest made her feel at once protected and a little nervous. She'd known the teasing Trent, the caring Trent, the solid-as-the-earth Trent most of her life, and there was a deep comfort in that familiarity. But there was a harder edge to the cop who didn't back off from asking tough questions, his quick ease at taking charge and asserting an authority that allowed no argument, a staunchness under fire that was both exciting and a little unsettling.

Still waters run deep.

The observation lodged in her head and refused to recede as she tapped her key fob against the lobby's automatic door lock, and again to get inside to the bank of elevators that would take them to the second floor. The elevator doors closed and her nose filled with the crisp scents of snow and cold on their clothes, the sweeter scent of a little boy who'd eaten red licorice backstage in the greenroom, and a muskier scent that was male and sexy and not any kind of *boy* next door or old-friend-like in the least.

What was wrong with her tonight? Had those threats stripped away a layer of composure she needed to keep her world in order? Why couldn't she stop analyzing the subtle changes she'd noticed in Trent tonight? He'd matured into a powerful Mack truck of a man who bore little resemblance to the lanky teen she'd once hung out with. The shadow of his late-night beard emphasized the angles and hollows along his cheeks and jaw. He moved with the easy yet purposeful stride of a predator guarding his territory. She'd gotten a glimpse of his temper tonight and been reminded that he was more complex than the nice guy who could make her laugh or make her feel safe. Had she just not allowed herself to analyze his size and scent and changeable demeanor before? Why had she overreacted to a simple kiss to her hair earlier? Why should her curious mind be so fixated on the man riding silently in the elevator beside her?

Even seeing Trent step out of the elevator first to look up and down the hallway to make sure it was clear felt different than all the times she'd had him over for a home-cooked meal or a bit of mending in exchange for putting together a bike for Tyler's birthday or teaching him how to hit a pitched ball or helping her replace a headlight on her car. And when had his jeans started hugging those muscular thighs with every long, sexy stride? *Stop looking!*

Feeling something very close to lusty attraction, and uncertain she wanted to feel anything like that for any man, Katie darted around Trent with her key to get the door open. Her soft gasp of breath at the rustle of her wool sleeve brushing against his nylon coat was like a mental alarm clock, waking her from this ill-timed fascination with the man.

"Make sure it's locked before you insert the key," Trent whispered. "Any sign of a break-in and we're turning around."

Feeling less sure of her relationship with this version of Trent Dixon, Katie obeyed his direction. She twisted the knob and felt the solid connection there. "It hasn't been tampered with."

After unlocking the door and pushing it open, she waited for a few seconds after he carried Tyler past her and inhaled a deep, senses-clearing breath before bolting the door behind her. She bought herself another second to shake off this discomfiting awareness that fogged her brain by taking off her gloves and cap and tossing them on the kitchen table with their bags before following Trent down the hallway to the two bedrooms there.

Trent had Tyler's gloves and hat off and had her son half sitting on the edge of the bed, half leaning against him. Smiling at the sweet picture of man and boy, and refusing to acknowledge the pang of feminine awareness that instantly warmed her body, Katie knelt beside them. With Tyler's head resting on Trent's ample shoulder, Katie peeled off his jacket and clothes and changed him into the superhero long johns he wore for pajamas.

Katie tucked Tyler under the matching bedspread and sheets and bent over to kiss his soft, cool cheek. "Good night, sweetie. Pleasant dreams."

"G'night, Mom," the sleepy boy muttered. "'Night, Trent."

"Good night, buddy."

Katie turned on his night-light before joining Trent at the open doorway. They watched Tyler for a minute or so until he sighed and rolled over, fast asleep, secure in his own bed. Exhaling her own sigh of relief, Katie backed out of the room and pulled the door to behind them. "Thank you for helping with him," she whispered.

"Never a problem." Trent stuffed his cap and gloves into the pockets of his coat as he followed her to the kitchen. She pulled out a stool at the counter and invited him to sit while she hung her coat, along with Tyler's, over the back of a chair. Then she opened the top of Tyler's book bag and pulled out his homework folder and the remnants of his lunch. Trent unzipped his coat and settled onto the stool while she checked to make sure Tyler had completed his schoolwork at rehearsal.

"Is it too late to offer you a cup of coffee?" she asked, making the effort to sound as normal as she would on any other night Trent visited, despite battling the disquieting urge to shoo him on out of the apartment so she could sort through all these feelings buzzing to the surface tonight and get herself back in order again. "A couple of cookies, maybe? We baked Christmas cookies with Aunt Maddie this past weekend."

"I'm not hungry." He took out his notepad and pen. "I thought of this on the drive over. Before I leave, I want you to check your bag again. Tyler's, too. I want to make sure I've got all the details before I write up my report."

Katie squeezed the brown lunch sack in her fingers and turned to him. "You don't think this is about me? You think he got into Tyler's stuff, too?"

Trent's eyes had cooled from that intense storm cloud from earlier in the evening to an ordinary, calming gray. "I've got no evidence to think that, but I know the best way to get to you is to do something to that little boy. So humor me, okay? I want to make sure I cover all my bases."

Any last chance at reclaiming normalcy vanished at the idea of Tyler receiving one of those disturbing threats. She immediately dumped the squished sack and sorted through a sandwich bag with bread crusts and pretzel bits and an empty applesauce container. She thumbed through the folder of papers, scanning each page to make sure there were no extra messages or bright red lipstick scribbled on one. Checking each pocket of the bag, she found the deck of gaming cards he had been playing with earlier at rehearsal. All the children took books and games to keep them occupied when they were backstage waiting to go on. "This looks like the normal mess I unpack every evening."

"Now yours. Is there anything missing? Anything that's been tampered with besides your laptop? Anything been added that wasn't there before?"

"Some loose things spilled to the bottom of the bag when he pulled the computer out. But it's all my junk." Katie opened the matching navy, white and lime-green billfold and fingered through some ones and a twenty, along with the receipts she'd tucked in with them. She checked her debit and credit cards, pulling the cards halfway out of their pockets and pushing them back in. "I don't think whoever it was stole any..."

Katie's mind sorted through several snapshots of memories that hadn't meant anything at the time. She touched the clear plastic window where she kept her driver's license and a couple of punch cards for a local coffee shop and pretzel cart. Her shoulders tensed. Oh, no. No, no.

"What is it?" The wood stool creaked as Trent rose to stand beside her. "Katie?"

"These two punch cards are switched around, and the corner of this one is bent. I'm sure it wasn't before. And my license isn't centered like it was before. I think he pulled them out and stuffed them back in. He searched through my things."

"He pulled out your driver's license?" He reached

around her to lift the billfold from her grasp and inspect the cards.

"Maybe." She looked up at him over her shoulder. "Do you think he was looking for my home address? If it was someone from the play, our numbers and addresses are already on the cast-and-crew list. Why would he need to check my license?"

"To throw us off the scent? Because he was gone the day Price handed out the contact list? Because he isn't a part of your show?" Trent muttered something under his breath. "Maybe because this twisted perp has some kind of obsession with you?"

Like the bitter wind blowing outside her windows, a chill swept through Katie, freezing her right down to the bone. "Obsession?" Hugging her arms across her waist, Katie shivered. "My father was obsessed with my mom. He didn't like her to be with anybody when he wasn't around. He barely tolerated her being with me. And when she tried to get away from him, to help me get away..." Joe Rinaldi had killed her mother. Katie's vision blurred with tears. "What if this guy shows up here or does something to Tyler?"

Katie was rattled. She was exhausted. And she was afraid. When Trent put an arm around her shoulders, she turned in to his hug. Pressing her cheek against the soft nap of his flannel shirt and the harder strength underneath, she slid her arms around his waist beneath his jacket and let the heat of his body seep into hers.

The other arm came around her at the first sniffle. "I won't let him hurt you, sunshine. I won't let him hurt Tyler, either."

She nodded at the promise murmured against the crown of her hair. But the tears spilling over couldn't quite believe they were truly safe, and Katie snuggled closer. Trent slipped his fingers beneath her ponytail and loosened it to massage her nape. "What happened to that spunky fighter who got her baby away from Craig Fairfax and helped bring down an illegal adoption ring?"

Her laugh was more of a hiccup of tears. "That girl was a naive fool who put a lot of lives in danger. I nearly got Aunt Maddie killed."

"Hey." Trent's big hands gently cupped her head and turned her face up to his. His eyes had darkened again. "That girl is all grown-up now. Okay? She's even smarter and is still scrappy enough to handle anything."

Oh, how she wanted to believe the faith he had in her. But she'd lost too much already. She'd seen too much. She curled her fingers into the front of his shirt, then smoothed away the wrinkles she'd put there. "I'm old enough to know that I'm supposed to be afraid, that I can't just blindly tilt at windmills and try to make everything right for everyone I care about. Not with Tyler's life in my hands. I can't let him suffer any kind of retribution for something I've done."

"He won't."

Her fingers curled into soft cotton again. "I don't think I have that same kind of fight in me anymore."

"But you don't have to fight alone."

"Fight who? I don't know who's behind those threats. I don't even know what ticked him off. It's just like my dad all over again."

"Stop arguing with me and let me help."

"Trent—"

His fingers tightened against her scalp, pulling her onto her toes as he dipped his head and silenced her protest with a kiss. For a moment, there was only shock at the sensation of warm, firm lips closing over hers. When Trent's mouth apologized for the effective end to her moment of panic, she pressed her lips softly to his, appreciating his tender response to her fears. When his tongue rasped along the seam of her lips, a different sort of need tempted her to answer his request. When she parted her lips and welcomed the sweep of his tongue inside to stroke the softer skin there, something inside her awoke.

Katie's fingertips clutched at the front of Trent's shirt, clinging to the warm skin and muscle beneath. She tried to keep things simple, to indulge herself in a little comfort without forgetting the rules that kept her world in order. But with fatigue, charged emotions and the history between them to combat, the rules suddenly didn't make much sense, and the friendly embrace gave way to a real, passionate kiss.

Sliding her hands up, she smiled at the ticklish arousal of her palms skimming over the scruff of his beard. Trent tasted the width of that smile with his tongue before touching his padded thumb to the corner of her mouth and demanding she open fully for him. With a breathless moan in her throat, she obeyed. As he plunged his tongue inside to claim her, she was quickly consumed by the searing heat of his kiss.

Trent unhooked the band of her ponytail and sifted

the falling waves through his fingers. For a moment, Katie thought they were falling. But she quickly found the anchor of Trent's shoulders as he sank back onto the stool at the counter and pulled her between his legs. Drawn to the heat that instantly flared between them, she pushed the cool nylon of his coat down his arms and moved in closer. He released her only long enough to shrug the coat off and let it fall to the floor before he gathered her close again. Katie wound her arms around his neck, and his hands slipped down to palm her butt, lifting her squarely into his desire, letting her body fall against his.

Katie melted into his strength. Tears were forgotten as she surrendered to the shelter of his arms and the forthright desire in his kiss. Each tentative foray between them was welcomed, rewarded. Surrounded by Trent's arms and body, cogent thought turning to goo by a sudden craving for his lips on hers, Katie felt her fears and a lifetime of worry and regret slipping away until there was only a man and a woman, and Trent's heat chasing away the chill of the long night. Such strength. Such gentleness. Such patient seduction. The mother in her went away. The weariness diminished. The loneliness disappeared.

Katie had been kissed before. She'd been kissed by Trent. But he'd been a teenage boy then. She'd been little more than a girl herself. This Trent was all grown man, with hard angles and knowledgeable hands. Her breasts grew heavy and pebbled at the tips, rubbing in frustrated need against the layers of clothing between them. His fingers tugged at the hem of her sweater and blouse, then slipped beneath to sear her skin. He palmed the small of her back, dipped his fingertips beneath the waistband of her jeans and panties to brand the curve of her hip. Denim rasped against denim as he adjusted her between his strong thighs and bulging zipper, stirring an answering need deep within her. This was a different kiss. A deeper kiss. It was a kiss that sneaked around her defenses and made her forget that she was anything other than a woman who hadn't been kissed or held for a very long time.

She reveled in his strength. The passion arcing between them jump-started her pulse and refueled her energy. His raw desire renewed her own confidence and strength. She needed this. She needed Trent.

"Katie," he gasped against her mouth. Her lips chased his to reclaim the connection. This wasn't the time for talking. She heard the deep-pitched chuckle in his throat even as he nipped at the swell of her bottom lip. "Sunshine. The counter's digging into my back. Can't we find someplace a little more comfortable?"

A woman is damn well gonna know when I intend my kiss to mean something more.

Her fingers stilled in the tangle of his hair. This wasn't right. Trent Dixon wasn't supposed to be so all-fired manly and irresistible. She wasn't supposed to want him like this. Katie turned her mouth from the sting of his lips and a kiss brushed across her cheek instead. She brought her hands down to brace them against his shoulders and put a little space between them. Her nerve endings seemed to be short-circuiting. She slid down his body until her toes touched the floor, but she wasn't sure her legs would hold her upright. There were reasons a kiss like this had never happened between them before. She'd forgotten what was important. She'd forgotten Tyler.

She'd forgotten the threats.

Katie needed the cop. She needed the friend. She couldn't afford to lose either one from her life right now.

Finally coming to her senses, Katie blinked his grinning mouth into focus and shoved at Trent's chest. "What was that?"

She would have staggered away if his hands hadn't settled at either side of her waist to steady her. "Maybe it's the way things should be between us."

"No." Her hands dropped to the bulk of his biceps and pushed again. "I'm not going to make any more mistakes."

Trent's grip on her tightened, as if sensing her instinct to bolt. "Where's the mistake, Katie? I know you have feelings for me. And I've never made any secret—"

"I care about you, Trent. But I'm not—"

"In love with me." What was left of his smile disappeared. He set her away from him and reached down to snatch his coat off the floor. He towered over her when he stood. The drowsy timbre of his voice hardened like his posture. "Trust me, I know the difference." She hugged her arms around her waist and stepped out of the way as he shot his arms into the sleeves and shrugged the coat over his shoulders. "That wasn't the kiss of a woman who only cares about a friend. Deny it all you want, but there's something between us."

"Don't do this, Trent. Please. Not now. I don't want to fight."

"This is an adult discussion, not a fight. Maybe I've

been reading you wrong all these years, thinking you were just too scared, too wounded to trust anyone completely—that you just needed time to heal. Maybe patience doesn't pay off." He stalked across the kitchen and foyer to the front door.

Katie followed, hating that he saw her like that, like some kind of small, wounded bird. "I don't need you reading me at all. I just need you to leave before I say something I'll regret."

He halted with his hand on the knob and spun around, startling her back a step. "What would you regret, sunshine? You regret having my help tonight?"

"No."

He leaned in closer. "You regret kissing me?"

"Like that, I do. Yes." Katie put up a hand to ward off his advance and planted her feet. "I regret being impulsive."

Trent walked right into the palm of her hand, forcing a connection between them. When she would have pulled away, he caught her hand against his chest. He reached out to brush her hair off her face, his callused fingertips stroking her skin as he smoothed the wayward waves behind her ear. "That's one of the things I've always liked about you. You may be a brainy chick, but you always follow your heart." He laughed, but there was no humor there. "Except with me."

Katie tugged her hand free and backed away from the taunt she felt in his touch. "I can't afford the luxury of being impetuous anymore. I'm not the same person I was when I was seventeen and I thought I could save the world. I can't afford to be. Not with Tyler in the picture." She crossed to the table and picked up the remains of Tyler's lunch and carried it around the island to stuff it into the trash. "You know how many mistakes that's gotten me into in the past. It's what got me kidnapped by Roberta Hays and Craig Fairfax. It's what got Whitney killed."

"Caring about people isn't why you and Whitney—"

"If someone is targeting me for a reason we haven't figured out yet, then it's all the more important that I keep my head about me and not lose my focus and put Tyler at any kind of risk."

"I would never hurt Tyler. I love him—you know that."

"Yes, and he loves you, too." Funny, the big brute didn't look one bit smaller or any less irritated with her with the quartz counter and width of the kitchen between them. She gripped her own edge of the counter and willed him to understand why she couldn't handle another kiss like that. "What if you and I try to be a couple and it doesn't work out? Other than Uncle Dwight, who's like a grandfather to him, you're the closest thing Tyler has to a dad."

"A dad?"

"You know you're a natural at it. You're that perfect mix of buddy-buddy and making sure the rules get followed. You make him feel safe. And I know what it's like to be a child who doesn't feel safe. I won't put him through that." She blanked her mind to the memories of her father's violent rages against her mother before the remembered fear and helplessness could latch on and draw her back to the past. "If you and I take a stab at a serious relationship and it doesn't work out, then it's going to ruin our friendship and you won't be part of our lives anymore. If that happened, Tyler would be crushed. So would I."

"Why are you so sure we wouldn't work?" Trent crossed to his side of the island. "How do you know?"

"Because I screw things up, Trent." There. He knew that about her, but he'd forced her to say it, anyway. He straightened at the bald statement, his quiet rigidity sucking the charged energy from the room. It was a clever trick she'd seen him use in an interview room, creating an uncomfortable silence that a person felt compelled to fill with an explanation. "It's my fault Mom died. And because I failed her, I thought I could redeem myself by saving Whitney. I jeopardized the life of my own unborn child to help a friend, and she ended up dead, anyway. I nearly did, too." Katie raised her hands in a supplicating gesture. "I can live with my guilt and grief. I might even be able to handle a broken heart if I had to. But that's me. I would never ask Tyler to pay for my mistakes."

His eyes darkened like the shadows of the dimly lit room. "And you think you and me would be a mistake?"

"I can't afford to find out." Her arms flew out as the depth of her concerns pushed aside reason. "Get mad. Storm out of here. I'm sorry I can't be what you want me to be, but please… Think about where I'm coming from and try to understand. I need you to be my friend, Trent. I need you to be the rock in my life you always have been. Tyler needs that, too."

He nodded, as if finally seeing her point. But the man wasn't an interrogator for nothing. He set down his gloves and stepped back from the counter to zip his coat. "What if it *did* work out between us? What if you're robbing us of the chance to be happy—to be a family? I could be a real father to Tyler. And you know I'd be a damn sight better husband to you than your father was to your mom."

Katie carefully considered her answer. She had no doubt that Trent would make a wonderful parent to her son or any other child. And that kiss? She circled the counter and crossed to the door to throw open the dead bolt and usher him out before those lingering frissons of desire could catch hold again. Common sense had to prevail. She had to make the right choices this time.

"One thing about us, Trent, is that we've always been honest with each other. Screwing up relationships is all I've ever done. And I don't want to fail at us. It would hurt too much. I forgot myself tonight. I was afraid and you were there for me. But I have to think about the future. I'd never want to mislead you, and I would never forgive myself if Tyler got hurt."

"You're asking a hell of a lot from me."

"I know. And it isn't fair. But maybe if we never give in, if we never start…"

She splayed her fingers on the closed door in front of her, feeling as though she'd been caught in a trap of her own making. They already had given in. The mistake had already been made with that little make-out session. Maybe the hurt was inevitable.

"You aren't a screwup, Katie Lee Rinaldi." She felt the heat of Trent's body behind her. "I'm not storming out of here in a temper, I'm not going to abandon you and Tyler when you need me, and I'm sure as hell not going to hit you."

"I know you would never—"

"For what it's worth, your mother's murder wasn't your fault."

"But it was." She spun around, seeing nothing but a wall of dark gray coat. The grit of unshed tears rubbed at her eyes. She hadn't blanked the memories, after all. It had been cold that night, too. There'd been so much yelling, so much pain. So much blood. "If I hadn't skipped my curfew that night, Mom wouldn't have been out looking for me. I was the reason Joe got so mad, the reason he blamed her. And when he slapped me and she said that she'd had enough and we were going to leave him—"

A large hand palmed the nape of her neck, lifting her onto her toes. Then Trent's mouth was on hers again. This kiss was hard and quick, a forceful stamp that drove away the nightmare. His face hovered near hers when he pulled away, and Katie couldn't look away from those dark gray eyes. "Your father was a bully and a bastard, and I'm only sorry that there was no one to stop him from hurting you and your mother back then. But it was *not* your fault."

"Trent—"

He pressed a thumb to her lips to silence any further discussion. "*Not* a screwup," he repeated before nudging her to one side and pulling open the door. Maybe as stunned by his unflinching support as she was by the power of that kiss, Katie hugged her arms around herself, trying to hold on to the warmth he'd instilled in her while he tugged on his cap and gloves. "I have to go home and let the dog out. Lock up behind me. Try to get some sleep. I'm going to put you to work on some research in the morning. In the meantime, I'll make sure someone's watching the building through the night."

"Have I scared you off with my neurotic fruitcake-iness?"

"You won't get rid of me that easily, sunshine." He stepped out into the hallway. There was a trace of the familiar grin she'd grown up with when he glanced back over his shoulder. "Who'd have thought you'd be the one to come up with so many rules? But I'll follow them. For now. You and Tyler will be safe."

The door closed behind him and she threw the dead bolt. But she sagged against the painted white steel when the full promise of Trent's words registered.

For now.

What happened when her by-the-book cop stopped following the rules she'd set down for their relationship? If Trent's patience ran out and he finally started pursuing her in earnest, how would she be able to resist the security and comfort he offered? Where would she get the strength to turn away from that simmering attraction that had bubbled to the surface tonight?

Katie pushed away to turn off the light and head back to her bedroom. She desperately needed some rest so she could be 100 percent in the morning when she saw Trent again—so she could keep their relationship at the normal she needed. If those anonymous threats didn't break her resolve to remain alone and avoid the temporary security of a relationship that was doomed to fail, Trent Dixon's seductive, unflinching determination would.

CHAPTER EIGHT

"COME ON, PADRE." Trent downed the last of the tepid coffee and set the thermal mug in the console between him and the dog curled up in the passenger seat of his pickup. "Are your muscles getting as stiff as mine?"

Well, *curled up* was a relative term. The moment Trent pulled his attention from the sun rising dimly on the horizon behind Katie's apartment building and spoke to the dog, the former Stinky McPooch leaped to his feet and straddled the center console to rest his neatly trimmed front paws on Trent's thigh. The dog's excited posture and wagging tail diffused the weariness permeating every bone in Trent's body. "You're hungry for some action, aren't you, pal?"

An eager slurp across the scruff of Trent's jaw indicated an affirmative answer. With a laugh, he reached over to attach the new leash to Padre's harness, which peeked through the bright red Kansas City Chiefs sweater he'd gotten to keep the dog warm and to make him an easy target to spot when the mutt dug into the snow he seemed to love so much. "All right, all right, I'm moving."

Padre was in his lap, ready to leap outside into the street, before Trent could turn off the engine he'd been running for the heater and pocket the keys. A slap of cold air and a brisk walk would do him some good, too, after sitting outside Katie's building for most of the night. Olivia Watson and her fiancé, Gabe Knight, had voluntarily ended their date early the evening before to stand watch while Trent went home to shower and try to get some shut-eye. But he'd only lasted a couple hours before coming back to send Liv and Gabe on their way and watch over the Rinaldis himself. There was already more distance than he wanted between him and Katie, and though she was leery of taking any emotional risks and doubtful of her ability to make a relationship work, he had no doubt about what was in his heart. He wasn't going to let any harm come to the woman and child he loved. They were his to protect, even if they never got the chance to become the family he wanted them to be.

"All right, boy." He scratched Padre around the ears and looked into the dog's dark brown eyes, imagining he could talk more sense into him than he'd been able to with Katie last night. "Now mind your manners on the leash. Let's go."

Leading the dog to the sidewalk while he locked up the truck, Trent scanned up and down the block. Although it had been a relatively quiet night, there was plenty of activity this morning, with folks in the neighborhood out shoveling snow or sweeping the blowing flakes off their vehicles and warming up cars as they got ready to head to work or school. He wasn't the only brave soul out walking a pet, either, and there was even one diehard out for a morning jog who'd already worked up enough exertion to mask his face with a cloud of warm breath.

Trent negotiated a silent compromise with Padre by agreeing to walk faster if the dog stopped tugging on the leash. Besides working the kinks from his muscles after sitting in the truck for so long, Trent figured he could kill two birds with one stone, letting the dog manage his business while he scouted the perimeter of Katie's three-story building along with other buildings and patrons of the neighborhood.

While Padre snuffled through the snowdrifts, Trent took note of faces and locations and whether or not anyone was more interested than they should be in anybody else. On the way back, he located the windows to Katie and Tyler's apartment. Behind the curtains and blinds, the lights were on in the rooms he knew to be her bedroom and the kitchen. He slowed his pace when he saw the shadow moving at the kitchen sink and imagined what she might be doing in there. He wondered if she'd gotten any more sleep than he had.

When they'd kissed last night, Katie had given him a little taste of heaven. She'd forgotten the rules, lowered her defenses and clung to him with an abandon that was even hotter and more reality shifting than he'd imagined it would be between them. But then that brain of hers had to kick in. She'd gotten spooked by the possibility of their relationship deepening into something more, and she'd backed off all the way into her violent and unpredictable past. After all this time, Katie still didn't believe in him enough to trust that he'd be there to catch her when she stumbled. He believed in the two of them together enough for the both of them. But she wouldn't let it happen. She blamed herself for screwing up before there was anything between them to destroy.

Okay, so there were a few things about the woman that made him a little crazy—like holding back details after starting a conversation and refusing to explain herself. Like those damn rules, which he supposed were some kind of survival code in her mind. Still, those were just quirks he had to work around; they were challenges he was willing to meet. Trent tried to think of one thing she could do to make him not want her in his life and came up empty. But until she came around to the idea of a relationship, until these threats against her could be stopped, he'd better concentrate on the job at hand. And maybe get back inside the warmth of his truck. "Come on, Padre."

The tan-and-white collie mix trotted along beside him while Trent noted an older woman coming out of Katie's building, trading a friendly nod and a smile with the man who held the door open for her before hurrying in out of the cold. A businessman was backing out of his parking space in the lot while a family was bundling everyone into a minivan. One of the children said something to the mom and she grumbled, fishing her keys out of her pocket and sending him back inside the building to retrieve whatever he'd forgotten. The maintenance super tossed the last of his rock salt on the front steps and pulled the key fob from his retractable key ring to open the door and go in.

Trent glanced up at the kitchen window again. Katie's shadow had moved on to another part of the apartment, leaving him blind to her exact location. Losing track of her for a few seconds shouldn't make him antsy like this. His tired brain needed to tune in to what was off here.

His gaze shot to the front door again. The skin at his nape burned with suspicion. "Ah, hell."

The man who'd held the door for the older woman hadn't used a key fob to enter the building like everyone else. He hadn't needed to.

Trent's breathing deepened, quickened as he glanced around. Everybody else except for the jogger was dressed for the snow-shrouded December morning. But that man…

Brown hair. Long wool coat. *Dress shoes.*

The alarm going off in his head must have traveled down the leash. Padre danced around his legs and woofed.

"Padre, heel." Teaching the dog a new command, he gave a sharp tug on the leash. Padre broke into a run beside him as they made a beeline for the front door. Trent knocked on the window and peered through the glass to see if anyone was inside the lobby. Where had the man gone? "Katie?"

Then he turned to the bank of mailboxes and buzzed her apartment. "Katie? Tyler, you in there?"

When there was no immediate response, he shook the front door handle. He wondered if he could break the lock with a ram of his shoulder, or if he needed to fire a round into it.

"May I help you?" By now he'd gotten someone's attention. The super in the tan coveralls strolled across the lobby, pointing to the no-pets sign on the glass. "I'm sorry, sir. But that dog—"

"KCPD." Trent slapped his badge against the glass and made the startled man read *that* sign. "Open it now. You've got an intruder in there."

"An intruder? But this is a secure—"

"Now!"

"Yes, sir." Jumping at Trent's harsh command, the older man pulled the fob from his belt and swept it over the lock. "Are we in any danger?" he asked, pulling open the door.

"Katie!" Rushing past the super, Trent sprinted up the stairs to the second floor. Padre kept pace, whining with nerves or excitement when Trent skidded to a stop in front of the elevator. Just as he'd feared, the perp had gotten off on the second floor. Katie's floor. A door opened close by and Trent flashed his badge to shoo the curious tenant back into her apartment. "Police, ma'am. Get back inside."

With a quick scan up and down the hallway, Trent saw the rest of the doors were closed or were clicking shut as other curious tenants retreated at the sight of the hulking detective and vocal dog charging down to Katie's door.

"Katie!" His gaze dropped to the nickel-finished doorknob and easily turned it. Ah, hell. He traced his gloved finger over the telltale scratch marks there and on the dead bolt lock higher up, sure signs that both had been tampered with. He glanced up and down that hallway again. One of those closing doors might be hiding a stalker. One instinct said to pursue his suspicion, but another, stronger urge made him flatten his palm and pound on the door. "Katie Lee! Answer me."

"For Pete's sake, Trent, you'll wake the neighbors." The dead bolt turned and she opened the door. Pulling the dog along with him, he pushed her inside and quickly shut the door behind him and locked the dead bolt. "Come in," she muttered sarcastically. "Bring the beast, too. What's a little fine from the tenants' association? Were you the one buzzing to come up?"

"No one came in? No one's here but the two of you? Why didn't you answer?"

"Slow down, Detective."

Her irritation gave way to confusion as he handed the dog's leash off to her and pushed by to make sure everything was as it should be. A blue-eyed woman with damp, freshly shampooed tendrils bouncing against her neck was running around in gray slacks and a flannel pajama top, carrying a blouse she was probably getting ready to change into for work. Breakfast on the table. Lunch being packed. "Where's Tyler?"

"In the tub. Why is the dog here? What is going on?"

He went straight to the bathroom door, pulled off his watch cap and leaned his ear against the wood, relieved to hear the sounds of a little boy playing with ships in the water on the other side. He checked both bedrooms and the hall closet before rejoining Katie in the main room. "Someone tried to break in."

"Inside the building?"

"At your front door. I must have scared him off." Her knuckles turned white around the dog's leash. He should be outside, checking for signs of the intruder's escape route, making sure he wasn't still lurking in the building. But he couldn't leave Katie unprotected, not until he understood what the hell was going on and had a plan to deal with it. "He'd gotten your knob unlocked. Fortunately, you had the dead bolt in place. You didn't hear anything?"

"No. I was running a bath for Tyler."

Speaking of, a barefoot boy in superhero underpants ran out of the bathroom. "Padre!"

"Tyler," Katie cautioned, "where are your clothes?"

"Mom, Padre came to see me." Dropping to his knees, he hugged his arms around the dog's neck. There was licking and giggling and tail wagging and petting before Tyler jumped to his feet and the dog bounded after him. "Come on, boy. Let's eat."

Tyler paused to give Trent a quick hug around his hips, then ran back to follow the dog as Padre sniffed his way around the apartment. The little boy stopped at the table to scoop up a forkful of scrambled eggs and stuff it into his mouth. Then he stabbed another bite and dropped it to the floor, where the skinny dog gobbled it up.

"Tyler," Katie chided. "Not at the table." She hurried to the kitchen window, where Trent was pulling open the blinds to check outside. Where had that guy disappeared to? If he was still inside, Trent would have to do a room-to-room search, and with eighteen apartments in this building, the guy could stay one step ahead of him, sneaking out while he cleared each space. If he'd already made his escape… "Padre can't be in here. Tyler, you need to finish dressing before you catch a cold." She latched on to Trent's sleeve when he brushed past her to get another view from her bedroom window. "This isn't a friendly visit for Tyler's sake, is it? What's going on?" When she peeked out the window behind him, her tone changed from suspiciously annoyed to simply suspicious. "Who are you looking for?"

Trent looked over the top of her head to see a blur of movement. Son of a... The alarm in his blood reengaged. He caught Katie by the shoulders and turned her attention to the man in a long coat stumbling through the snow. "Him, Katie. Do you recognize him?"

Trent was already backing toward the door as she shook her head and faced him. "Who's that? Why is he running?"

"I intend to find out." Trent pulled open the apartment door. "Lock up behind me. No one comes in except me."

"Trent—"

"Lock it, Katie!"

He had to get to that pervert before he reached whatever vehicle he was headed for. Once he heard the secure click of the dead bolt sliding into place, Trent booked it into overtime, running down the stairs, skipping a few with each stride. He shoved open the outside door and rushed straight across the snowy ground. "Police! Stop!"

The man with the dress shoes might have cold feet, but he was fast. He dashed across the street and climbed into a black sports car. He had the engine revving before Trent reached the pavement. What the hell? Who was this guy? What did he want with Katie?

Trent held up his badge and pulled his gun. "Police! Get out of the car!"

But the perp showed no signs of cooperating. He jerked his wheels to the left and floored it.

Trent planted his feet and took aim as the driver swerved out of his parking stall. "Stop! Or I'll shoot!"

He squinted and turned his face from the pelting of slush and ice crystals. The car roared down the street, and by the time Trent could look back and get a bead on the fishtailing back tires, he realized he didn't have a clear shot. There were too many people around, frozen in their morning routines, some ducking behind their vehicles, others standing in open ground, staring at him—including the curvy brunette with her face pressed to the second-story window.

"Son of a…" His breath whooshed out on a frustrated curse as the car veered around the corner and sped away. There wasn't even time to get to his truck and get turned around to pursue the suspect.

But he wasn't about to give up on finding the answers he needed and putting a stop to the danger escalating around Katie and Tyler. With a wave of reassurance to the people around him, Trent holstered his weapon and pulled out his phone.

Max's gruff voice answered. "It's early, junior, and I'm in bed with my wife. This better be good."

"Apologies to Rosie. I need you to run a plate for me."

The tenor of Max's tone changed instantly and Trent imagined his partner rolling out of bed with an urgency belying his burly stature. "You need backup? Everything okay?"

"No. But I'm not sure what I'm dealing with yet." He strode back up the sidewalk "A guy just tried to pick the lock on Katie's apartment. He drove off after I chased him from the building."

"Hell, I'd run, too, if I had a defensive tackle chasing me down," Max teased, writing down the number Trent gave him.

His partner didn't even question that he was at Katie's this early in the morning. "The perp matched the general description of the guy taking pictures at the theater last night. I want to know why he was here."

"I'm on it. You stay with her. I'll call as soon as I know anything." He heard Max exchanging a kiss and muttering some kind of explanation to his wife. "Anything else?"

"Just get me the info, Max."

"Will do."

"Thanks, brother."

Katie was waiting for him when he knocked on her door. Trent pushed inside and locked it behind him. Baggy plaid flannel draping over those generous breasts shouldn't trigger this instant desire in him, but he'd had a lot of practice ignoring those traitorous impulses around Katie. It was harder, though, to ignore the concern in those wide blue eyes, or to turn away from the wary frown that dimpled her forehead. Trent pulled off his glove and brushed her hair away from her worried expression. He'd barely felt a sample of her warm, velvety skin before she pulled away from his touch.

"Did you catch him?" she whispered, darting her eyes toward Tyler and Padre playing on the floor beside the Christmas tree.

Right. The rules. Although Trent wanted nothing more than to take her in his arms and feel with his own two hands that she was safe, she was in touch-me-not mode this morning. He shook his head and unzipped his coat before crossing to check the lock on the kitchen window. "I got the plate number on his car, so hopefully it'll be enough to ID this guy."

He peered outside to see the sun glinting off the snow and the world turning back to normal before heading through the apartment to ensure that all the access points were secure. A parade of mom, dog and boy followed him through the apartment.

"How did he get in?" Katie asked.

"It's not that hard if you bide your time and have a charming smile."

"He conned his way in here?" She snapped her fingers and shooed Tyler and Padre across the hall when they reached her bedroom. "Clothes. Now, young man." Departing on a three-toned sigh, Tyler grabbed Padre's collar and went into his room. Once she was certain her son was changing for school, Katie tugged on the sleeve of Trent's coat and pulled him into her bedroom. "You're going to scare Tyler if you keep this up."

The fresh, flowery scent that was all Katie was stronger in here. But he conquered the urge to draw in a deep, savoring breath and crossed to the curtains to secure the window and fire escape outside. "The dog will distract him."

"Not entirely. He's a sensitive kid." He shivered at the touch of her fingers at the nape of his neck. But what he'd mistaken for a caress was pure practicality. She held up a palmful of road slush that was melting on his collar, then carried it over to the damp towel tossed across the bed from her morning shower to wipe her hand. "My God, you're a cold mess. You were out there all night, weren't you?"

"Most of it."

"I thought I saw your truck. I couldn't sleep, either, after our...discussion." She reached up and used the towel to dab at the moisture still beading on his neck and jaw. Ah, hell. Now, *that* was a caress. Goose bumps prickled across his skin in the wake of her touch, and her soft sigh teased something deeper inside. But she must have realized she'd crossed the very boundary she'd asked him to respect and quickly pulled away to stuff the towel into the hamper in her closet. Her shoulders came back with a forced resolve and she crossed to the desk she used as a home office. She picked up a stack of papers from the printer there.

"So I did some work, too. I compiled a list of Leland Asher's known associates and ran them through my database to see if there were any hits that matched up. I've been doing it backward—lining up the cases and then looking for connections between them to pop. This time I plugged in a bunch of suspect names we've been tossing around and ran them through the cold case data."

Fine. They were safe for now. He couldn't do a damn thing until he heard back from Max. So he let her turn the conversation to work. "Did you find anything?"

Katie nodded and handed him the papers. "Isabel Asher—Leland's sister—was a sorority sister of Beverly Eisenbach's at, get this, Williams College."

He thumbed through the stack. "The place where you and Tyler are doing the play?"

She pointed to the grainy printout from a twenty-five-year-old college annual. "The blonde in the front row is Isabel. Dr. Eisenbach is on the far left."

"Eisenbach's the shrink who counseled Matt Asher and Stephen March as teens?" He recognized the younger images of the two women who'd each held a spot on the person of interest board at the squad's team meeting earlier in the week. "You think that's how Dr. Eisenbach and Leland met? Through Isabel?"

"You'd have to ask Bev Eisenbach to find that out." She pointed to the date at the bottom of the photo. "But there's a reasonable chance that she knew the Asher family years before she counseled Leland's nephew. This is dated before he was even born. Maybe she's more than Leland's latest girlfriend. Having the previous acquaintance could be the reason he selected her to counsel his nephew, Matt. But if they've known each other since they were in their twenties, isn't it possible that their relationship has gone on for a lot longer than we realized? Maybe she counseled Leland for some reason—grief, stress, dealing with his sister's addiction? She might have confidential information on him that we could use in our investigation. Maybe he even confessed to some of his crimes, or the hits we suspect he paid for. Dr. Eisenbach's practice is one of the offices I've sent requests to for information. They confirmed

that Matt Asher and Stephen March were former patients, but any requests for a complete patient list have
been ignored."

"This is good stuff, sunshine. Maybe even enough to
ask the lieutenant for a warrant to get a look at Eisenbach's records." Trent looked at another picture, this
time of a young man with long blond hair or a blond
wig, dressed in a Shakespearean costume. "What's
this?" The actor's dark, beady eyes looked familiar.
"Is this the Grim Reaper?"

Katie hugged her arms in front of her, clearly feeling
a little less comfortable with this piece of information.
"Francis Sergel about twenty-five years ago. I found
him through my facial recognition software."

Trent squinted the name beneath the theater program
picture into focus. "Frank Reinhardt?"

"Sergel must be a stage name he adopted. Looks like
he's playing Hamlet."

Trent couldn't imagine that walking, talking skel-
eton of a man playing anything heroic. "He has ties
to Asher?"

"Lieutenant Rafferty-Taylor didn't ask me to pursue
him as a suspect, so I didn't exactly have permission
to dig through criminal records. But after the last few
nights at the theater, I wanted to know if I should be
worried about him."

Was that what had her squirming inside her own
skin—that she'd broken a procedure rule? "I'll request
it."

She offered up a wan smile. "Thanks."

"Not a problem. I didn't like Sergel or that Doug

Price, either. I want to make sure they check out." He flipped to the next page and skimmed the information. "So Sergel, er, Reinhardt, has a record?"

"Minor stuff. Nothing violent. Possession of narcotics. A DUI. He never went to prison. It was all time served and community service. And court-ordered NA meetings."

"Like Stephen March." And Isabel Asher. And any of a number of pushers and addicts who'd worked for and bought from and crossed paths with Asher's criminal empire.

"A decade earlier, but yes." She sank onto the edge of her bed as if her legs had grown too weak to hold her. She'd made the same realization he had. The team's idea of a *Strangers on a Train* setup behind several of their unsolved crimes could no longer be discounted as a mere theory. "It's a small world, isn't it?"

Trent knelt on the carpet in front of her, relieved to see that she didn't swat away a comforting touch when he rested his hand on her knee. "Cold cases are built on circumstantial evidence more than anything else. There are an awful lot of circumstances that your research has linked together. Now we just have to prove that Leland Asher is behind it all."

Her gaze met his and she tried to smile. "Good luck with that."

"Look, I'm going to take this information and run with it. I'll get Sergel and Price and Dr. Eisenbach and maybe even Leland himself all in for interviews. We'll get the doctor's patient list and see if she counseled Leland. We'll make a case against Asher and put him back in prison where he belongs." He stroked his fingers over the gray wool of her slacks. "But my immediate concern is those threats you've been getting. I've got a call in to Max to see if he can run down the name of that guy who got away. You didn't recognize him, did you?"

"From the back? Running away?"

"He was wearing dress shoes instead of snow boots. Like the photographer you saw at the theater."

The telephone on her bedside table rang and she jumped. Trent squeezed her knee before standing up and giving her the space to move around the bed and answer it. "So that's why he looked at my driver's license."

"If it's the same guy who defaced your laptop, yeah. It'd be easy to find you." Trent caught her by the hand before she left him entirely. "I don't suppose I could talk you into packing a bag for you and Tyler and moving in with me until this all blows over? It's hell sleeping in my truck, and your couch isn't big enough."

He needed her to read between the lines of his teasing tone and understand he was drop-dead serious. *I'm not going anywhere and I'm not leaving you alone.*

Her fingers trembled for a moment inside his grasp before she pulled away and picked up the cordless receiver from its cradle. "Hello? Yes?" Trent watched the color drain from her face. "Who is this? Why are you doing this to me?"

"Katie?"

She punched the button to put the call on speakerphone and held the receiver between them as an electronically altered voice filled the room. "—want to hurt you, Katie Lee. But you've left me no choice. I know what scares you. The dark. A syringe. Your murdering father. Losing your child."

Trent dropped the photos Katie had printed out and grabbed the phone from her hand. "This is the police. Who is this?"

He gritted his teeth at the answering laugh. "You were warned. Even your boyfriend's not going to be able to save you now."

The click of the disconnecting call echoed across the room. Trent hung up her phone and pulled his from his coat. He'd call Max again to find out who'd just dialed her number. Although he'd bet good money this wraith stalking Katie had used an untraceable cell.

Katie sank to her knees, crawling across the carpet to pick up the photos. "He's not going to hurt you, sunshine. I won't let him." His partner picked up. "Max?"

But Katie was more focused on some distant point inside her head than in any kind of shock. She sat back on her heels and crumpled the papers in her fist. "It's these."

"Pictures? Printouts? The mess I made?" After relaying the message to Max, Trent picked up the rest of the papers and tried to understand the wheels turning in her head. "You're not talking to me, woman. What do you mean?"

She blinked and brought those cornflower-blue eyes into focus on him. "It's the research I'm doing on these cold case files." She braced her hand on his shoulder to stand and hurried to her computer. Trent followed, anxious to catch up on her train of thought. "I've opened up the wrong can of worms somewhere—I've breached some piece of information I shouldn't have. That's what he wants me to stop."

Trent looked over her shoulder as she booted up her computer, plugged in her portable hard drive and turned on the hot-spot security device. "The brass isn't about to stop a criminal investigation. Even if the lieutenant takes you off the case and reassigns you, we'll still be going after Asher. Are you sure?"

"Every time I ping another database, every time I send an email request—that's when he contacts me." With the equipment in place, she tucked her hair behind her ears and went to work. "I need to run a full system diagnostic. It may be on my computer at work, too. He's mirroring me."

"What does that mean?"

"Somebody's tapped into my computer. Or maybe the portable hard drive. Even if he's not copying my data, he can see what sites I go to. He's been tracking every movement I make online."

"How can you tell?"

She'd gotten into the belly of the programming now and was scrolling through code. "Every time I get a little more information about Leland Asher, every time I discover another piece of the puzzle that can build our case against him, something happens. That man at the theater. Vandalizing my laptop. He's tracking me somehow. Either visually or online."

Stop what you're doing, the message had said. "They want you to stop investigating Leland Asher?"

She pointed to the gibberish on the screen. "It's all right here. But I've been too distracted to see it. It's a virus, a replicating virus that copies everything I do to another computer. Someone got close enough to my laptop or portable hard drive to plant it."

"At the theater? There's too much security at HQ."

"I don't know. I may be able to track down the source." Her fingers were flying over the keyboard, clicking on icons and typing in commands he didn't understand. "I need to notify tech support at work to sweep the systems, just in case they've found a back door into the KCPD network. But there are enough safe-guards that that might be difficult, even for an experienced hacker. More likely, it's my personal account that's been…"

She picked up the hot-spot device and turned it over. "Do you have your pocketknife?"

Trent reached into the pocket of his jeans to retrieve the knife. He marveled at the woman's intelligence as she pried open the device. "Katie?"

She dropped the pieces onto the desk and sank back in her chair. Trent didn't have to be a genius like her to see that the innards weren't connected, so it hadn't blocked any intrusive signals. She could have been hacked almost anywhere if that wasn't working—at the coffee shop, at the theater, at home.

He pried the open knife from her grip. "Where did you buy that thing? Who would have access to disable it besides you?"

"Anybody. I bought it months ago. I keep it in my bag. If they could get to my laptop, they could get to the hot-spot device. Then I'd be as vulnerable as if I had no security on my computer components at all. I am so going to lose my job over this, aren't I?" She closed her hands into fists. "Such a screwup."

"You're not," he insisted. He dropped down on one knee beside her and captured her jaw between his thumb and fingers to turn her gaze toward his. "This just means there's somebody who thinks he's as smart as you out there. He's a lot more calculating and doesn't give a damn about who he hurts." He tightened his grasp and pulled her forward to meet his kiss. Katie's lips were full and sweet and shyly responsive in a way that shattered the caution around his heart and kindled a fire in his blood. "I believe in you, sunshine. Maybe this is a break in the investigation, an opportunity to trace it back to some hacker with ties to Asher. Now take a deep breath and figure this out."

Her hands came up to cup his face and she smiled. "I don't know why you're so good to me."

"That's easy." He leaned in to kiss that worry dimple on her forehead. "Because I lo—"

"Wait a minute." Trent reeled in the ill-timed confession as a new idea reenergized her. He folded the knife blade and returned it to the safety of his jeans pocket while Katie went back to her keyboard. "I should be able to track back to the date the device was disabled. The time should help us zero in on a location and who could have—"

She drew back with a gasp, her hands raised as row after row of words scrolled across her computer. After the first line, they were the same words, repeating over and over and over until they filled the screen.

Stop, Katie.

Die, Katie.

Die, Katie.

Die, Katie.

Die, Katie.

Die, Katie.

"Trent?"

"Son of a bitch." Trent pulled her to her feet. He wanted to smash the monitor to erase the threats she'd somehow triggered. He would have ripped the whole thing out of the wall and tossed it across the room if some little sane part of his brain hadn't remembered he was a cop, looking at a desk full of key evidence. "Log out of there. Do something. Fast."

Katie quickly shut down her Wi-Fi connection and pulled the cable connecting her router to the internet. He turned off the screen himself before she backed into him. His arms instantly went around her. "Easy, sunshine. You're okay."

She shook her head, the nylon of his coat rustling against her hair. "Why is this happening to me? I'm just one little cog on the team. I'm background. I'm nobody. We're all trying to solve cold cases and connect them to Leland Asher. All I do is the research. Why was that man here? Why is he trying to scare me?"

Probably because they were getting closer to the truth, closer to making a major case against Asher stick. And someone in Asher's camp was targeting Katie because she was the weakest link on the team—she hadn't had police training and she didn't carry a gun, but she was vital to proving that there was nothing alleged about the mob boss and his illegal activities. "Their time to shut us down is running out. Asher gets released from prison today."

She shook within his grasp. He knew the moment she decided she needed him more than she needed the distance between them. Turning in his arms, Katie shoved open the front of his coat and burrowed against his chest. Her fingers clenched in the layers of his shirts and the skin and muscle underneath. Trent threaded his fingers through her damp waves and cradled the back of her head, dropping his lips to the fragrant sunshine of her hair, holding her tightly against his strength.

"Mom? Are you okay?" a soft voice whispered from the open doorway. Despite the grip he had on Padre's collar, Tyler's eyes were wide with concern. Smart kid. He could see his mother was scared.

He just prayed the boy couldn't see that Trent was more than a little frightened for Katie, too.

"I'm okay, sweetie," Katie answered, her voice strong to reassure her son. "I just got some bad news." She tried to push away, but Trent wasn't budging.

Instead, he held his hand out to the little boy. "You're going to come stay at my house for a couple days, buddy. Okay?"

With a nod that didn't quite erase his frown, Tyler left the dog and ran across the room to hug Katie. She lifted her son into her arms and Trent wrapped them both in his shielding embrace.

CHAPTER NINE

TRENT SAT AT his desk, staring at the twelve pictures on his computer. Six victims, six suspects. Plenty of circumstantial evidence to link one to another, but no real proof as to who was ultimately behind either the unsolved murders or the threats against Katie. But the key to solving the crimes attributed to Leland Asher and his criminal network had to be staring him in the face. If only he could get those pictures to talk.

That one of the police department's information technologists was being stalked and receiving threats promising to kill her or harm her son if she didn't stop poking around with her research meant the team had gotten too close to uncovering some long-buried truths. Their cold case investigation was heating up.

Maybe more than Trent wanted.

Not for the first time that day, his gaze wandered across the maze of detectives' desks to the cubicle where Katie sat, surrounded by a desktop computer, a stack of print files and a tall cup of some mocha-latte thing. She wore a pencil in her hair and a hands-free headset to talk on the phone with other tech gurus assigned to the department. The threats that had frightened her at home only seemed to motivate her now. Maybe diving into work was a way to distract herself from the fears for her and Tyler's safety. Or possibly, skipping lunch and never leaving her computer was some kind of atonement for allowing an outsider to breach her computers and gain inside information on the cold case squad's progress on different investigations. Or maybe there was still a little bit of that teenage girl who charged into battle left inside her, and instead of cowing her into submission, the danger that had come to her very doorstep had inspired her to take action—to save the investigation, to find justice for those victims whose murders had yet to be solved, to save her son.

Although Trent didn't understand all the jargon, Katie and the tech team at the lab had scoured all her computers, and, as she suspected, the mirroring had been done through the hot-spot device on her laptop and portable hard drive. The KCPD network was secure and only the public-record files she'd been using in her database had been accessed. Her laptop was back from the lab—unfortunately, with no usable prints but her own and his. And, with a legal warrant and approval from Ginny Rafferty-Taylor, Katie was back at work again, doing a little hacking herself to find out when the virus had been planted so she could determine her location at that time and identify anyone who might have had access to plant the bug in her system.

A paper wad smacked Trent in the forehead, drawing his attention back to the desk across from his. "Really?"

"Hey, I didn't want to be the only one working." Max Krolikowski had plenty of ammunition on his messy desk, but he pointed to the stray missile that had landed on the tidy expanse of Trent's blotter before hanging up his phone. "That's the number that called Katie this morning." Trent unfolded the note and smoothed it open to read the information Max had jotted there. "Just like you suspected. Disposable cell. It's been turned off so there's no way to trace it."

Trent slipped the paper into a folder and glanced down at the license plate number and name of the rental company that had leased the black sports car to a John Smith, aka Mr. Fancy Dress Shoes, aka he still didn't have any freaking ID on the guy who'd gotten far too close to Katie and Tyler that morning. Just a bunch more puzzle pieces and no big picture yet.

"However, it does belong to a type of phone sold exclusively at your favorite big-box discount department store over the past year."

Trent sat back in his chair. Like the anonymous John Smith with the fake license and credit card, that was almost worse than no help. "There are a dozen of those stores in the city. Assuming the perp bought it in KC."

"Yeah, but they all have surveillance cameras in their electronics departments."

"Are you willing to sit through twelve months of surveillance footage from all those stores to see who bought a phone and then try to identify John Smith or anybody else who's come up in one of our cases?"

"It's a long shot."

"It's worse than a long shot."

"But I'd do it for Katie."

Trent agreed. "So would I."

With an answering nod, Max picked up his phone

again. "I'll start calling, see if the stores even keep security footage from that far back."

"I'll find out if this guy used his John Smith ID to buy the phone or anything else."

Trent closed out the pictures on his computer screen but paused before picking up his own phone to help Max with one of the tedious, but necessary, demands of police work. "What's the point of threatening Katie? She's not going to be arresting anybody. This bastard should be coming after me or you or Liv and Jim, or anybody else on the team, if he wanted to misdirect us or slow down our investigation."

His partner hung up the phone without dialing. "You think this Smith dude tried to break in to her apartment to harm her? Not just to steal her computer or something like that?"

"I didn't give him a chance to finish the job. And he wasn't inclined to stop for a chat."

Max scrubbed his fingers over his jaw in a thoughtful sigh. "Are the threats affecting her work?"

Trent glanced over to see Katie riffling through the files on her desk before tapping her headset and answering whatever the party on the other end of the call had asked. "She seems as scatterbrained and brilliant as ever."

"Interesting." If Max meant something by that cryptic response, he didn't elaborate. "But the scaring part's working?"

Trent could still feel the marks on his skin where she'd finally turned to him for solace and held on to him until her trembling had stopped. And he'd never forget the worry stamped on Tyler's sweet, innocent face. "It's even getting to her son. I mean, Jim's at the school shadowing Tyler during the day, so we know he's safe for now. But how do I reassure a nine-year-old that everything's going to be okay if I don't even know what I'm up against?"

"I don't have kids— Hell, that's a scary thought, ain't it—me and kids?" Max propped his elbows on his desk and steepled his fingers together. "But I think you just need to be there for them."

"That's what Katie needs, too." Trent summoned half a grin, appreciating Max's attempt at deep philosophical advice. "But I won't lie. It's hard to be spending that much time with her, given our history."

"It's hard because you're a good guy. You think things through. You wait for an invitation. You don't just haul off and kiss a woman like I did Rosie when we first met and I was toasted out of my…" Max slapped his palm on top of his desk. "Well, hell's bells, junior, you *did* kiss her. And not one of those Dudley Do-Right pecks on the cheek, either, I'll bet."

Groaning, Trent tried to temper Max's stunned excitement. "They were a mistake."

"They? More than once?" Max swore under his breath. "You've been holding out on me. About time it happened between you two."

Trent glared at his partner. "Nothing happened."

"No fireworks?" Max looked disappointed. Oh, yeah, there'd been plenty of spontaneous combustion between them on that kitchen stool. But the *Die, Katie* bombardment on her computer screen had reminded Trent that

Katie needed his protection, not his love. Max leaned forward and whispered, "Wrong kind of fireworks?"

Give his love life a rest, already. "It's Christmas, not Independence Day."

"Huh?"

"Wrong time for fireworks. I was taking advantage of a vulnerable moment." Of several vulnerable moments, it would seem.

Max grumbled a curse and sorted through the scattered papers on his desk. "Junior, you don't know how to take advantage. If Katie wasn't willing, you wouldn't—"

"Tyler's safety is her priority." Trent pulled a phone book from a desk drawer and started looking up numbers, as relieved to be ending the conversation and getting back to work as he'd been to air some of his concerns with his most trusted friend in the first place. "And it should be. It's my priority, too. I want to find out who this jackass is and put him in my interrogation room. I want to get him out of their lives so Tyler can just be a kid again and Katie can…"

What? Go back to being his buddy when he wanted to be her bedmate? Her soul mate? Her everything? Now that she and Tyler were staying with him, his worries about their safety had eased a fraction, but remembering not to push for everything he wanted from her grew harder with every passing minute.

"Earth to big guy." Olivia knocked on the corner of Trent's desk, pulling him from his thoughts. "The lieutenant wants us in her office. The press is covering Leland Asher's release."

Setting aside his troubling thoughts, Trent pushed to his feet, taking a moment to tuck in his corduroy shirt and the thermal Henley he wore underneath before following Liv and Max across the room. Katie ended her call and scooped up her laptop, darting into the office on a waft of flowery scent that reminded Trent of freshly shampooed hair and warm curves pressed against his body. Wisely avoiding broadcasting that woman's physical effect on him, he took a position standing at the back of the room while Katie set up her laptop and sat at the front of the group. When his gaze locked on to a sly glimpse of cornflower blue directed back at him, Trent wondered if Katie was making a point of keeping her distance, too.

"Let's see what our friend has to say." Lieutenant Rafferty-Taylor turned up the sound on the television screen as a twinkling of camera flashes captured the image of Leland Asher walking through the prison exit into the bright, cold sunshine of the wintry afternoon.

Looking like a politician on a campaign stump, Asher waved to the crowd of eager reporters, curiosity seekers and armed guards who were there to make sure nothing got out of hand before the alleged mobster left the premises. Although the once stocky man had lost a lot of weight, probably due to the cancer, there was a sense of entitlement to his carriage. Plus, he wore the impeccably tailored suit and dress coat of a man who still had access to plenty of money. The man with a briefcase beside him led the way to a small podium, where he identified himself as Asher's attorney and made a statement regarding his client's release.

But the words coming from the television were just white noise as Katie began to fidget in her chair. She drummed her fingers over her keyboard without typing anything and kept drawing her hair between her fists in a ponytail before letting it fall back to her shoulders when she realized she had no clip to secure it. What was buzzing through that brain of hers now?

An elbow butted up against his, diverting Trent's attention to his far too observant partner. "You up for this, junior? You want me to take over shadowing Katie?"

"No." He wasn't about to leave Tyler and Katie's security up to anyone else. "I want you to be there to take up the slack in case I can't get the job done."

"You not get a job done? Trust me, junior. That'll never happen."

Olivia sat on the corner of the table. She nodded to the TV. "He's on. Turn it up."

A dark-haired woman wearing a fur coat ran up to the podium to kiss Leland's cheek. The woman had a striking strand of white framing her face when she turned to the camera. And while she looked adoringly up at the gaunt, graying man, he wound his arm around her waist and held her to his side.

Katie pointed to the screen. "That's Beverly Eisenbach, Mr. Asher's significant other. She's the psychologist who counseled Matt Asher and Stephen March as teenagers."

"Any response to your query about whether or not Leland was ever a patient of hers?" the lieutenant asked.

Katie shrugged. "Talk to her attorney and get a warrant?"

Trent tuned out Asher's pontification about learning from his mistakes and how his incarceration hadn't affected his business investments one iota, as well as the updates on his health. Taking Lieutenant Rafferty-Taylor's lead, he turned the gathering into an impromptu staff meeting. "I tracked down the house mother from the sorority Bev Eisenbach and Isabel Asher belonged to. She's retired now, but she remembers the two of them taking classes and hanging out together before Isabel left school. Night and day, she called them. It wasn't just a blonde-brunette thing, either. The house mother said she never understood how two young women with such different personalities got along so well. Dr. Eisenbach was neat, organized, intent on keeping her scholarships and earning her degree, while Isabel was more of a free spirit who was there for the social opportunities."

The petite blonde who led the cold case group folded her arms in front of her and nodded, urging Trent to continue. "Does the house mother remember meeting Leland? Can we prove that Leland and Dr. Eisenbach knew each other twenty-five years ago? And does that information do anything to help our case?"

"The house mother remembers Leland coming on campus to attend events with Isabel. They had no parents, so he was more than a big brother to her."

Olivia chimed in. "We can trace suspected criminal activity to Leland all the way back to that time. He was already starting to amass his fortune, so I'm sure Bev would have been interested in meeting Isabel's big brother."

"Maybe that's what she liked about Isabel," Max interjected. "She could hook her up to a man who was destined to make a lot of money. Clearly, it paid off for her."

Trent thrust his fingers into the back pockets of his jeans. "The house mother remembers the guy Isabel Asher was dating, too. 'A prissy Italian guy' is how she described him."

"Francisco Dona." Katie supplied the name as she typed on her laptop and read the info off the screen. "He was a small-time dealer and user. Looks like they dated each other, or at least used together, on and off for several years until she died. He was questioned as a suspect in Isabel's death, but no charges were ever filed."

Trent picked up on a small detail. "You said *was*. He died in a motorcycle accident. Did anyone ever investigate his death as a possible homicide?"

Katie shook her head. "ME's report said he died of head trauma. He suspected Dona was under the influence. He found a trace amount of drugs in his system."

"But Mr. Dona passed about a month after Isabel's overdose," the lieutenant confirmed.

"There's nothing suspicious about the timing of that," Max groused with sarcasm. "Can anyone say retaliation?"

Trent agreed. "If Leland and Isabel were as close as the house mother claims, then it makes sense that he'd order a hit on Dona. It wouldn't be the first time an accident was staged to cover up a murder."

Katie continued to read the information on her computer. "Even if Francisco Dona didn't provide Isabel with the drugs that killed her, Asher could have still blamed him. According to this, there were no signs of anyone trying to revive Isabel after she collapsed. There wasn't even a 9-1-1 call until her son, Matt, discovered the body."

Even though they were talking about alleged criminals, Katie's voice trailed away in sympathy. She knew firsthand what it was like to deal with the death of a parent, and might even be remembering her own mother's murder. Trent pushed away from the wall where he was leaning, wanting to go to her. But the sharp blue gaze darting his way was a warning to keep his distance. Either she was telling him she could handle this or she was asking him to keep the complications of the relationship growing between them private.

"Great." Liv's sarcasm matched Max's. "Another murder we'd like to attribute to Asher that we can't prove. How does this guy keep getting away with it?" She turned to Katie. "Can we at least talk with the ME who wrote the report?"

"That would be Dr. Carson." Katie turned her focus back to her computer and pulled up the name on the report before shaking her head. "He retired with early-onset Alzheimer's a couple of years ago. Your brother Niall replaced him."

Liv groaned at the latest twist. "Does anybody else think that if we could just shuffle all these players in the right order that we'd solve a half dozen murders and put Asher away for good?"

Trent and Max and Katie all raised their hands and Olivia laughed before Lieutenant Rafferty-Taylor directed their attention back to the television. "He's leaving."

Hand in hand, Leland Asher and Bev Eisenbach walked to a waiting limousine, where another group was waiting for him. Trent recognized Asher's long-time chauffeur and bodyguard and spotted a couple more thugs watching the audience like Secret Service men. A young man with glasses—Leland's nephew, Matt—climbed out of the long black car and extended his arm. The two generations shook hands before Leland pulled his nephew in for a showy hug and whispered something in his ear.

Trent couldn't be certain, but had Matt Asher arched his brows over the rim of his glasses and made eye contact with Bev Eisenbach before the hug ended? Or was he alerting the group to the fans with more questions and accusations surging their way?

Either way, Leland remained coolly unperturbed by the rush of attention and turned at the people calling his name.

"One last question, Mr. Asher." A television reporter with long, dark hair thrust her microphone in his face. "How do you feel?"

"Like a free man." Leland laughed and pulled up his pant leg to show off the parole bracelet on his ankle. "Except for the new jewelry the state has so graciously given me."

He waved aside the follow-up questions and ushered Bev into the limo before he and Matt and the bodyguard climbed in behind her. The network camera panned the crowd, getting shots of protesters and supporters alike, people who thought, like the cold case squad, that Asher had gotten away with murder, and others—

friendly plants, perhaps—who waved signs and shouted about "freeing the innocent."

When the camera scanned back to the limousine driving away, a far too familiar image near the back of the crowd shot adrenaline into Trent's bloodstream. In three strides, he was across the office, tapping at the screen. "Are we recording this? Can we get a recording?"

Katie turned her laptop around and typed. "I can get a feed off the station's website. Wait…"

"What is it, junior?" Max asked.

She pulled up the website as they gathered around her. "I've got it. They're replaying the interview."

"Freeze it. There." Trent rested a hand on her shoulder and pointed to the man in the crowd who'd just snapped a photograph of the group at the limousine. Brown hair, long wool coat. Although he couldn't see the telltale shoes, he recognized the nondescript features and receding hairline. "That's John Smith. That's the guy who tried to break in to Katie's apartment."

"Is he part of Asher's entourage?" the lieutenant asked.

"Is he a reporter?" was Liv's guess.

"Hold on." Katie went for a more definitive answer. Using her mouse, she framed the suspect in the picture and clicked a screen shot of his image. "Now that we've got a face, I can blow it up and run him through recognition protocols. If he's in the system, I can track him down."

She pulled back when a private investigator's license showed up on the screen, along with three different driver's licenses and a state ID card. John Smith apparently had several aliases he used, and not a one of them looked legit lined up like that. But there was at least one thing in common on two of the cards—an address.

Trent pulled his notepad and jotted it down. "That's downtown. Probably an office building."

Katie looked up at Trent. "Go get him."

CHAPTER TEN

KATIE GLANCED OVER for the umpteenth time at her flow-ered bag sitting in the corner of the greenroom back-stage, making sure no one had opened it to mess with the contents inside. Good. Still latched. Still safe.

Her research had indicated that her device had been hacked almost two weeks earlier. That day she'd taken Tyler to school, stopped by the coffee shop, gone to work, and hadn't left until it was time to pick up Tyler at his after-school club and go straight to rehearsal. And since she wouldn't count her son as a suspect, and no one at work had any reason to track her research since they could access the same info themselves, that left someone at the coffee shop or here at the show to have tampered with her hot-spot device.

Her money was on someone involved with the play—or who could hide out at the theater undetected. So her suspicions of everyone here were riding high. But since she was alone for the moment while Doug and the cast were onstage going over last-minute notes before to-morrow's final dress rehearsal, she figured it was safe to let the messenger bag out of her sight for the few seconds it would take her to hang up the costumes she was ironing in the women's dressing room.

She set the iron on its end and gathered up the long dresses she'd prepped for the last run-through before opening night and carried them into the women's dressing room. She could hear Doug Price's voice booming through the auditorium and was glad that Trent was in there with Tyler, maybe trading a wink or a thumbs-up to let her son know that Doug's dramatic speech about "moments" and bringing the audience to tears meant the temperamental director was pleased with the way the show had come together. She was doubly glad that Trent was there to keep an eye on Tyler, to make sure her son had nothing to worry about except remembering his lines and making his entrances.

Because they weren't safe. Not yet. The threat was still out there.

When Trent and Max had gone to John Smith's downtown address that afternoon, they'd found a ransacked office, a few drops of blood that indicated there'd been an altercation of some kind and no sign of Smith. A BOLO on the rental car hadn't turned it up yet, either. That meant Smith, whoever he really was, was still out there, still watching, still looking for a way to get to her. Whether he was a spy for Leland Asher or someone with a more personal interest in her, she felt less and less that keeping Trent at arm's length was a good idea. The only time she'd felt safe since finding that message scribbled in the snow, the only time that Tyler acted like a normal kid, was when Detective Dixon was around.

Katie caught a glimpse of her pale features in the bright lights of the dressing room mirrors and cringed.

No wonder Tyler was scared for her. Sleep had been a rare commodity the past few days. She touched the shadows beneath her eyes and wished she had Trent's arms around her right now, so she could soak up the comfort of his warmth, be reenergized by the thrill of his possessive kiss and feel secure enough to drop her guard for a few moments and simply take a normal breath without looking over her shoulder or second-guessing every move she made and worrying about Tyler.

With the gun and badge on his belt, and the sheer size of those shoulders and chest, Trent didn't exactly fit the role of backstage parent. But he'd made it clear that until he could arrest John Smith and prove that the part-time private investigator/full-time con man was the person who'd threatened her, Trent was going to be spending a whole lot of time with her. His days, at work and here at the theater—and nights, too, sleeping just a few feet away from the guest rooms in his comfortable ranch-style house where he'd put her and Tyler.

Dear, sweet, solid…sexy, distracting, aggravating Trent. He made her feel all prickly inside when he caught her in the crosshairs of those steely gray eyes. And he hadn't been kidding when he'd told her a few nights earlier that a woman would know when she'd been kissed by him. After all these years—seeing him date other women, interacting with him herself—how had she missed discovering the difference between friendship and passion, between a chaste brush of his lips at her temple and that powerful stamp of perfection claiming her mouth?

And how was she was going to fit these deepening feelings for the man, this need for his strength and protection, this desire to hold and be held, back into the rules for emotional survival that had kept her safe and sane since her wild, violent and unpredictable youth? It was impossible to think of Trent as a friend while imagining what it would be like to give in to the temptation of his hard body and potent kisses again. Yet it was equally impossible to imagine how she could have gotten through this week in one piece without the friend she trusted implicitly at her side.

When she focused in on her reflection again, she realized she was stroking her own lips—missing, wishing, hungry for Trent's mouth on hers.

Good grief. Katie's cheeks flushed with emotion and she drew her fingers away from her sensitized lips. She was doing exactly what she'd told herself over and over that she shouldn't. She wasn't just attracted to Trent. She wasn't just turning to him as her cop friend to protect her from a dangerous situation. This wasn't just gratitude for helping her and Tyler time and again. She was falling for Trent Dixon. Falling for the vital, mature man her boy next door had become.

Laughter and the voices of numerous conversations and complaints woke Katie from her bothersome thoughts. Doug must have dismissed the cast and crew for the night, and they were making a mass exodus out the back workroom to the parking lot. Sliding her fingers through her loose hair, she pulled the waves off her face and groaned at the static electricity in the air that left her looking as if she'd just crawled out of bed instead of neatly downplaying the amorous turn of her thoughts. No amount of smoothing could give her a business-as-usual appearance, so she simply turned away from the mirror and hurried into the men's dressing room to pull the costumes that still needed ironing before anyone came in and questioned the embarrassed heat in her cheeks.

She exchanged smiles and a quick good-night with a few of the actors who'd left their coats or purses in the dressing rooms as she carried an armload of shirts and two of the specialty costumes out into the green-room. She draped the shirts over the back of a chair and shook out the long black robe that belonged to the Spirit of Christmas Future.

A shadow fell over her as she spread the drapey material over the ironing board. Katie gasped, startled by the man in black standing between her and the exit door. She put her hand over her racing heart and dredged up a polite smile. "Hey, Francis."

His beady dark eyes didn't smile back. "I don't want any wrinkles in that, understand? I want it to flow as I move, so it looks as though I'm floating across the stage."

She watched the expressive gesture of his hand that demonstrated the undulating movement. "I do my best to make you all look good."

"And I appreciate that. I know I come across as a bit of a demanding actor, but my drive stems from wanting to put on the best production possible." His Adam's apple bobbed up and down as if the next few words were difficult to get out. "Your costumes have helped us achieve that."

Really? A compliment from Francis? "Thank you." He probably expected her to say something nice in return. "And, I must say, you're a very convincing Christmas spirit."

He clasped his hands behind his back, but left little more than the width of the ironing board between them. She didn't know if he was watching to make sure she pressed his costume to his specifications or if he was so socially inept that he was unaware of how his proximity and the musky smell of a long night under stage lights filling the air between them could make her feel so uncomfortable. "It was nice to have you backstage tonight, Katie. Not out in the audience where you distract Douglas."

So much for trying to get along with the man. Her hand fisted around the handle of the iron. "This again? Francis, what did I ever do to you? I'm a volunteer. I love doing theater. My son has made new friends and he's enjoying himself. I'm not looking for a relationship with any man here, and I'm certainly not interested in Doug."

"Protest all you want," he articulated in a disbelieving whine. "I see right through your little helpless-female-with-the-big-blue-eyes-and-perky-boobs act. Douglas doesn't want you for anything other than the thrill of the chase. And maybe to get lucky. If you're looking for a husband, I promise, he'll run as far from you as he can get."

"That's insulting. I am a self-sufficient woman. I have a career. I'm raising my son."

"That's probably why he cast him. Douglas took one look at you in auditions and—"

Katie shoved the iron at him, coming close enough to move him out of her space. "Shut up, Francis, or I will brand you."

"How quaint. Resorting to violence in a meager effort to defend yourself. I was only trying to give you a friendly warning."

"There's nothing friendly about these conversations. You want something from me. You're jealous or insecure or—"

"Heed my words." He leaned toward the ironing board again, perhaps sensing she wouldn't really make contact. "You're not the first pretty woman he's hit on, and you won't be the last. If you're thinking you'll be cast in a show, or your son will get a better part the next time Douglas directs, you're mistaken. I know how power attracts women, and he's using his to entice you."

"He's not a CEO, he's directing a play." Katie plunked the iron down on the collar of his robe, ready to char an ugly hole straight through the heavy cotton if he said one more derogatory thing. She knew all about bullies like Francis. She'd grown up with one. "You need to heed *my* words. I am not the least bit tempted to sleep with Doug or whatever distasteful thing you're insinuating. If he turns you on so much, you can have him. With my blessing."

"You crazy…" Francis grabbed her wrist and the

iron, snatching them away from the smell of singed material. "Stop what you're doing!"

"What?" Anger morphed into fear in a single breath. His particular choice of words surprised her far more than the pinch of his fingers on her skin. Katie tugged at his grip. "What did you say?"

"I said to stop what you're—"

"Mom!" Tyler ran across the greenroom, dropping his book bag at the argument he'd walked in on and dashing around the end of the ironing board to stand beside her and pull on her arm. Oh, Lord. Her little man thought Francis was hurting her. "Are you ready to leave? I am."

"Tyler—"

Francis set the iron down but left his fingers clamped over Katie's wrist. "Back off, Tiny Tim. I'm having a conversation with your mother."

"Not anymore you're not." A deeper voice entered the argument and ended it. Francis's eyes had barely widened with alarm before Trent was prying his grip off Katie's wrist.

Then he went up on his toes as Trent pinned Francis's arm behind his back. "How dare you?" he sputtered through his bushy black beard.

"Don't make me take you in for assault and harassment, Sergel." Trent carried the vile man several steps away before positioning himself between her and Francis. The width and height of his shoulders and back completely blocked Francis from her line of sight. If the no-nonsense authority in his tone wasn't enough, Katie could well imagine the *just try something* challenge in Trent's expression that would keep any smart man at bay. "Whatever your beef with Katie might be, it ends now."

"I'll thank you kindly to keep your hands off me, Detective."

"I will if you keep your distance from Miss Rinaldi."

"Very well." Francis was rubbing his shoulder when he crossed the room to pick up his coat. "But don't say I didn't warn you, Katie." Francis pulled on his long black coat. "Don't trust Douglas. There's been something wrong with this entire production. Strange things happening. People who don't belong hanging around. He hasn't been himself. You and your son are the only thing different about this show and any other play I've done with him."

"Shut up, Sergel. Or Reinhardt or whatever your name is." Trent took a step toward him, and Francis hurriedly grabbed his hat and scarf. "Not one more harsh word to this boy, either. Understand?"

With a dramatic harrumph and flourish of his long dark coat, Francis swept out of the room.

Trent turned. His gaze went straight to the wrist Katie was mindlessly massaging. "Everyone okay in here?"

Katie nodded. Physically, she was fine. But her brain kept flashing with images of messages scratched in the snow or smeared in lipstick. "Francis told me to stop what I'm doing."

"What do you mean?" He reached over the ironing board and scrubbed his palm along the top of Tyler's head, reminding her son that the tension in the room had been neutralized and he could drop his guard and be a kid again.

Katie dropped her arm around Tyler's shoulders and hugged him against her hip, reassuring him with the same message, even though her mind was still racing with suspicion. "He used the exact same words—*Stop what you're doing*. That's just a coincidence, right? Do you think he could really hate or resent me so much that he would want to scare me by hiring that private detective or sending those threats?"

He nodded, giving her misgivings careful consideration. "I don't know. The threats could be some kind of weird jealousy thing—there's certainly something about that prima donna that's not right. But my money's still on Asher and your research." He crossed to the sofa to pick up his coat and shrug into it. "I'll make sure Sergel leaves. You get all your gear packed so we can get out of this place ASAP." After adjusting the hem of his short coat over his holster and badge, he plucked Francis's black robe off the ironing board and tossed it into the men's dressing room. "And forget about ironing that jackass's costume."

Tyler squinched up his face in curious frown. "Mom, what's a jackass?"

Katie squeezed her lips together to stifle her laugh at the innocent question. But a smile erupted anyway, and she walked Tyler around the ironing board to Trent. "You can explain that one, Detective."

"Sorry."

The stricken look on his rugged face stretched her smile farther. Feeling strengthened by his presence and taking pity on his uncharacteristic distress, Katie braced a hand on Trent's shoulder and stretched up on tiptoe. She didn't second-guess the impulse—she simply did what felt like the right thing to do. She slipped her fingers beneath his collar and slanted his head down to seal her lips over his. She might have started the kiss, but his warm, firm lips quickly moved over hers, completing it. The kiss was brief, and the link between the two of them warmed Katie all the way down to her toes. Trent's eyes were smiling above hers when he lifted his head. "So that's what I have to do to get your attention? Get in trouble?"

"You've always had my attention, Trent. I guess it's just taken me a long time to work up the courage to do something about it."

He combed his fingers through her hair and tucked it behind her ear. "I'm willing to take it slow, as long as I know you're on the path with me."

When he leaned in to kiss her again, they both suddenly became aware of the nine-year-old tilting his gaze from one to the other, silently observing the teasing, intimate exchange.

Trent cleared his throat and pulled away, probably worried that he was going to have to explain what was happening between his mother and best friend, too. "Mom, did you mail my letter to Santa?" Tyler asked.

Katie offered a nervous chuckle in lieu of an answer. What was going through that wise little man's mind now? "It's getting late."

Trent nodded. With a hand on her son's shoulder, he scooped up Tyler's book bag and coat and marched him toward the door. "I'll keep Tyler busy so you can finish up faster."

"Sounds like a plan."

He nodded and helped Tyler into his blue coat. "Come on, buddy. Let's bundle up."

"Is *jackass* a naughty word?" Tyler asked, following his big buddy into the backstage area without question.

"Let's talk."

Several minutes later, Katie had unplugged the iron and hung up the shirts, and even Francis's wrinkled costume, when her phone vibrated in the pocket of her jeans. She pulled it out to read a text from Trent.

We're outside. Distracting Ty with snowball fight. Hurry. I'm losing.

Grinning, Katie pulled on her stocking cap and coat and looped her flowered bag over her shoulder before texting a response.

Thanks. On my way. Duck. ;)

She knew a split second of panic when she turned off the light in the greenroom and stepped into the darkness backstage. The work lights were off on the stage and the running lights had been disconnected. She was in utter darkness. Her audible gasp echoed through the storage and work space.

"Is someone there?" a voice asked. Doug Price. As much as she hated to cast him as any kind of rescuer, she couldn't stand to be trapped in the dark again.

"Hello?" she called out. "Please tell me you're near a light switch."

She heard a shuffle of movement, and then a light came on by the exit door. Doug had set his briefcase on a chair and opened it to stuff his director's notebook inside and pull out his cap and gloves. "Over here, Katie. I'm sorry. I thought I was the last one here. I was just locking up."

What had he been doing that he hadn't seen the ambient light from the greenroom on the opposite side of the stage when she'd opened the door? And how had he made his way through the darkness back here? Ultimately, it didn't matter. She just wanted out of this place. "I'm sure I'm the last one now. Thanks for waiting."

Katie wove her way through the prop tables and set pieces that had been such obstacles in the darkness. Not that she completely trusted Doug after the things Francis had said, but she was anxious to get out into the open, eager to get to Trent and her son. But as Doug pulled his keys from the briefcase, they caught on some papers inside, and a thick manila envelope folded in half dropped out. Katie bent down to pick it up. It was heavy, as though there was a stack of large photographs or a couple of magazines inside. "Here. You dropped—"

"I'll take that." Doug snatched it from her hand. He quickly stuffed it into his briefcase and closed it. He took a deep breath, calming the brief outburst. "I'm sorry. Thank you."

Perhaps she was broadcasting her discomfort at being alone with the man, because Doug offered her a courteous nod and pushed open the steel door to a blast of swirling flakes and cold air. "Is it snowing again?" she asked.

"I think it helps set the mood for the play, don't you agree?" Hearing the squeals of a laughing child carried on the wind, Katie quickly slipped out past Doug. She spotted Trent and Tyler down by the footbridge, pelting each other with snowballs. She smiled and headed toward them, considering joining the fun, when Doug turned the key in the lock. "Hold up, dear. I'll walk you to your car."

Trent saw her and waved just before a dollop of snow hit the middle of his chest. He scooped Tyler up off his feet and jogged up the hill as Katie made her excuses. "That's very gallant of you, Doug. But my friend Trent is still here."

"Yes, of course." He switched his briefcase to the opposite hand, away from Trent's approach.

Maybe there was nothing suspicious about his behavior at all, and she was the one being paranoid. "Well, thanks. Only one rehearsal left."

Doug nodded. "We have a great show. Remember the cast party this weekend. I'd love to see you there." Trent arrived and set Tyler on his feet. The two were a pair of snow-dusted clothes and ruddy cheeks, demanding she smile at their boyish behavior. Doug seemed less amused. "You're welcome to come along, too, Detective. If you like that sort of thing."

Trent clapped his gloved hands together, throwing out a cloud of snow. "Oh, I love a good party."

"Yes, well, good night." Doug brushed away the few snowflakes that had fallen onto his shoulders and walked around the corner of the building to his car. She heard his engine start before she would have expected and the cold motor shifting into gear before driving away in a rush.

"It's a good thing he's a director," Trent deadpanned, "because he's not a very good actor. I don't believe he really wants me to come to your cast party."

"I guess he's in a hurry to find another date, then." Katie laughed out loud, feeling the stress of the day and those disturbing encounters with Francis Sergel and Doug Price dissipate. She dropped her arm around Tyler's shoulders, linked her elbow with Trent's and led the way to the parking lot. "Come on, you two. Let's get your truck warmed up before all that snow soaks through to your skin and freezes you."

But she slowed her steps when she saw the other two cars left in the lot. They weren't campus police vehicles, and everyone else from the play had left already. Hadn't they? She eyed the silver sedan with the tinted windows parked near the exit, and the small black car parked beneath the nearest street lamp. Its engine was running, as though someone had parked close to the theater and was waiting to pick up a passenger. Only there was no driver inside.

She didn't have to be a cop to know that something wasn't right. "Trent? Doug and I were the last ones out of the theater."

Trent's hand on her arm stopped her. He pulled out his keys and thrust them into her hand. "Get in my truck and lock yourself inside."

He lifted his coat and pulled out his gun, too. Katie

automatically pulled Tyler away from the weapon. "Trent?"

"Black sports car." He braced his gun between his hands and pointed it toward the car with the running engine. "The license plate matches. Call Max and tell him I located John Smith's car."

The man who'd tried to break into her apartment. "That's him? Why is he—"

"Go." Trent waved her toward his pickup and circled around to approach the car from the rear.

Katie hugged Tyler to her side and backed away. But not before she saw the hand on the steering wheel.

A bloody hand.

"Trent?" She pushed Tyler behind her and inched forward with a ghoulish curiosity. The man was injured. He needed help. No, she just needed answers. She wanted to ask him why he'd been terrorizing her. "Oh, my God."

There'd be no answers tonight. She saw the body slumped over in the front seat. She saw all the blood on his clothes and the car's upholstery.

She clutched Tyler's face against her chest and spun him away from the gruesome sight as Trent opened the car door and checked for a pulse. "Is that John Smith? Is he…?"

Trent nodded and pulled up his coat to holster his weapon. He held up two fingers, indicating the man had been shot twice, and mouthed the word *dead*.

"What's going on?" Tyler's question came from the face muffled against her breast. "Is that guy sleeping?"

With a heart that was heavy with the knowledge that

her son had been anywhere close to this kind of violence, Katie exchanged a silent message with Trent and pulled Tyler toward the heavy-duty pickup with her.

"Katie! Get down!"

Katie heard three little whiffs of sound before Trent came charging around the sports car. By the time she saw the tiny explosions of snow spitting up from the pavement and heard a car door slam, Trent's arms were around her and Tyler, pushing them into a run. "Go, go, go! Run, buddy!"

Someone by the silver car was shooting at them.

When the side mirror shattered, Katie screamed. Trent swept Tyler up into his arms and grabbed Katie's hand, jerking her into a detour from the path of the bullets. "Into the trees!"

Mimicking his crouched posture, Katie pumped her legs as fast as they would go. They zigzagged over the open pavement, taking the shortest path to cover. Katie nearly toppled when they plunged into the snow beyond the curb. It suddenly felt as if she was running in water, pulling her boots out of the sucking, frozen drifts. A bare branch splintered beside them, shooting icy crystals and shards of wood into their faces. Trent muttered a curse and jerked them away from the pelting cascade. She felt the blow of something hard against her hip and stumbled, but Trent's strong arm held her upright and kept her moving. When they reached the fallen trunk of an old oak, he leaped over the mound of rough wood, dead branches and snow and pulled Katie over the trunk with them.

She landed on her bottom, sinking waist-deep into

a drift of snow. Trent shoved Tyler into her arms as another thwap of a bullet hit the far side of the tree trunk. "Stay down! Keep him covered!" he ordered.

Katie was already pulling Tyler beneath her, rolling onto her stomach on top of him and digging down into her bag for her phone. Trent peeked over the top of the tree trunk, drawing two more shots that smacked into the old wood before he ducked back down and drew his gun. Katie punched in 9-1-1 as Trent rose up again and fired off several rounds.

"Mom?" Tyler held his hands over his ears. She felt him jerk against her with every shot Trent fired.

"Stay down, sweetie." Three more shots and the dispatcher picked up. "I'm at Williams College with Detective Trent Dixon. Behind the old auditorium. Someone in a silver car is shooting at us."

Another shot pinged off a metal light by the sidewalk, turning a silver wreath into ribbons floating to the ground. Katie stayed on the line when she heard car tires squealing for traction against the wet, freezing pavement. A car door slammed and Katie's heart squeezed in her chest when Trent pushed to his feet and climbed over the top of the tree trunk. "Stay put!"

"Trent!" Katie shouted her fear as the man who meant so much to her left the shelter of the tree and chased after the car peeling out of the parking lot. She heard pounding boot steps as the ground gave way to asphalt. There were two more shots and the screaming pitch of a car sliding around a sharp turn and speeding away into the night. Katie reported to the 9-1-1 dispatcher that she and her son were okay, but that she couldn't see if Trent or anyone else had been hurt. "There's a dead body here, too. A man who's been shot. Probably by whoever was in the silver car. Send an ambulance," she begged, feeling her extremities shiver with a mix of cold and fear. "Send everybody."

"Max!" She heard Trent's long strides approaching them again and knew he was on the phone to his partner, giving him a sitrep on the shooting.

Although the dispatcher asked Katie to stay on the line, she stuffed her phone into the pocket of her coat, keeping the connection open while she dealt with the more pressing needs of hugging her frightened son and making sure Trent hadn't been hurt. "It's okay, sweetie." She wiped the chapping tears from her baby's cheeks. "Trent?"

"Right here, sunshine." He dropped over the top of the tree trunk and squatted down beside them. He stuck his gun into the back of his jeans before pulling her and Tyler out of the snow and into his arms. "The shooting's stopped. They're gone. There were two men. I think we walked into the middle of a hit."

"What? I wonder if Doug saw it, too. Maybe that's why he drove away so fast."

"Well, he didn't stop to call the police if he did. But Max heard your call on the scanner. He's already on his way. He'll get Liv and Jim moving, too, and notify the lab about our extensive crime scene. Everybody in one piece?"

Katie waited for a nod from Tyler before answering, "Wet, cold and scared out of our minds. But we're fine."

They were all on their feet now, making their way to

the sidewalk and up the easier path to the parking lot. Moving forward and scanning the area for any other unwanted surprises never stopped until they reached Trent's disabled truck. Besides the shattered mirror, he had two flat tires and a cracked window. He opened the passenger door on the side away from most of the damage and reached inside to check a hole in the dashboard. "Good. We'll be able to get ballistics and have some concrete evidence for a change. I got a partial plate on the car, too, but it was moving pretty fast." He turned to pick up Tyler and set him on the seat, facing out, away from the bullet hole. "At least we'll be out of the wind here. I'm guessing campus security will reach us first. Then we can get a door unlocked and go inside."

She could already hear the sirens in the distance. Others had probably reported the sounds of gunfire, too. A chill set in as the adrenaline started to wear off and Katie started to realize the full import of what had just happened. But as Trent straightened in the open triangle of the door and truck frame, she saw the deep rip in the sleeve of his coat and the blood soaking into the layers of insulation and cotton underneath. She grabbed him by the forearm and turned his shoulder toward the street lamp above them, on alert once more. "Trent."

He pulled at the damp material to get a better look. "Oh, man, this was my favorite coat."

Katie smacked the uninjured side of his chest. "Trent Dixon, you've been shot and you're griping about your coat?"

His leather glove was cold against her cheek. But

there was nothing but heat in the quick kiss he gave her before whispering, "I'm okay. We'll fix it at home."

She held on, looking up at him, and whispered back, "You're sure?"

"The shot grazed me when we were running." He winced beneath the white clouds of his breath and glanced down at Tyler. "There's a first-aid kit in the glove compartment. Let's not worry you know who."

"Then it *is* bad." Katie instantly released him and dived inside the truck to retrieve the medical supplies.

"Barely a scratch, I promise."

But she'd raised a smart kid who knew they were talking about him. Tyler swiped at the tears that were still falling, bravely taking control of his fear and confusion. "I can go to the hospital if we have to. I'll watch Mom." He sniffed and rubbed at the red tip of his nose. Katie kissed his cheek and handed him a tissue before tearing open a box of gauze pads. "I'm not scared. But real guns are loud."

Trent squeezed Tyler's knee. "They are, buddy, aren't they? Dangerous, too."

Tyler touched the cuff of Trent's bloody sleeve. "Does it hurt?"

"It stings. It's raw skin and it burns. But like I told your mama, this isn't bad. It could have been a lot worse."

"Like that man in the car?"

Katie's breath locked up in her chest and tears burned her eyes. No sense hiding the truth from him now. She hadn't been able to protect him from violence any more than her mother had been able to protect her. Trent glanced at Katie, then hunched down in front of Tyler for a man-to-man talk.

"Guns can do terrible things, Ty." Trent held out his heavy black Glock where the boy could see it without touching it before sliding it safely back into his holster. "The safety's on now, so it can't hurt you. But when it's not…"

Tyler listened in rapt attention to every word while Katie went to work, cutting away the shreds of Trent's coat sleeve, along with the flannel and thermal cotton underneath. "But guns can save lives, too. Someday I'll teach you how to shoot one safely. Until then, you don't mess with any of them, okay?"

Tyler nodded his understanding.

"But don't worry, buddy. Tonight, they aren't going to hurt you or your mom. I'm glad you're here to back me up. You can help me keep an eye out for that silver car that drove away, in case it comes back, okay? At least until Uncle Max gets here to pick us up."

"Okay."

Before Trent could straighten, Tyler threw his arms around the big man's neck and held on as he stood. Trent wound his good arm around her son and pulled him onto his lap as he perched on the edge of the seat.

Katie let him cradle her son and reassure him that the nightmare had ended, at least for tonight. Seeing her friend being so tender and protective with Tyler allowed her to breathe a little easier, too. Trent was right—the bullet had only grazed him and hadn't ripped through muscle or bone. But it wasn't an injury that was going to stop bleeding on its own anytime soon, so she pulled out a wad of gauze and applied pressure to the wound, willing it to stop, willing this good, wonderful man who clearly meant the world to her son—and to her, she was discovering—to be safe.

By the time she'd tied a longer piece of gauze around his biceps to keep the pressure bandage in place, a campus police car was pulling up. She could see lights flashing off the buildings and trees as KCPD cars and, hopefully, an ambulance arrived on campus.

"You don't think the shooters are coming back, do you?" she asked. "Are we witnesses now?"

"They won't be back tonight," Trent stated in a hushed, sure tone that inspired confidence. "My guess is that they wanted us disabled so they could make a getaway without me following them."

But she saw that he kept his hand on the butt of his weapon, just in case.

CHAPTER ELEVEN

KATIE WAS CLEAN and warm after her hot shower. But even in her flannel pajamas and robe and with a pair of socks she'd borrowed from Trent on her feet, she couldn't shake the chill that permeated her from the inside out.

"They doing okay?" Trent's voice was a deep-pitched whisper in the shadows of the hallway as he stepped out of the master suite and came up behind her to peek into the guest room where Tyler slept with Padre on the long twin bed.

Trent had towel dried his short hair without putting a comb through it and had the damp terry cloth hanging around his bare neck and shoulders above the fresh jeans he'd slipped on. She could feel the heat of his shower radiating off his skin, and breathed in the enticing smells of soap and man. But still, she hugged her arms around her waist and shivered. "They shot at my son."

Trent laid his hand over her shoulder. "The EMT said he was just fine—nothing a good night's sleep and a sense of security can't fix."

She turned her cheek in to the warmth and caring he offered. "You give him that."

"I think that sense of security comes from a mom who's always been there for him."

Katie grunted a small laugh of disagreement, and the tan-and-white collie mix lifted his head at the sound. She was the reason John Smith had become a part of their lives in the first place, although KCPD still wasn't certain who had hired him or why he'd been following Katie. For all she knew, Smith had been executed because he'd failed to break into her apartment and murder her, or retrieve whatever information she'd found that Leland Asher didn't want her to. Some security. More like the magnet for trouble she'd always been.

"Katie?" Perhaps sensing the guilty direction her thoughts had taken, Trent tightened his grip on her shoulder.

But she shushed him and walked into the room to pet the skinny dog that had been a blessing for Tyler to come home to. The two had eaten a snack together and played, and had separated only long enough for Tyler to take a bath and brush his teeth. She scratched the dog around his ears, then pressed a kiss to the soft fur on top of his head. "I'm counting on you to keep an eye on our boy, okay, Padre?" Then she lifted the covers and tucked Tyler's leg beneath the quilt and pulled it up to his chin. She brushed his dark hair off his forehead and kissed his sweet, velvety skin. It was a relief to see the tears had washed away and the frown mark had relaxed with sleep. "I love you, sweetie," she whispered, then winked at the alert dog. "Good boy."

As soon as Katie backed away from the bed, Padre laid his head down over Tyler's legs and she knew her son would be watched over through the night. If only she could let go of the uncertainty of these past few days and sleep so easily.

She looked up to see the big, half-dressed man filling the doorway. The gauze and tape on Trent's shoulder stood out like a beacon in the shadows cast by the lone night-light in Tyler's room, mocking his claim that she didn't screw up relationships, that the people around her didn't get hurt.

But it was too late and she was too raw to have that discussion again. So she grasped at the friendly banter and mutual support system that had always been there between them. "Okay, mister. You're next." She nudged him out into the hallway and pulled the door partly shut behind her. "The doctor said I should replace your bandage after your shower."

She stopped in her bedroom to retrieve her bag, where she'd stowed the extra supplies the doctor in the ER had given them, then followed him through the quiet house into the en suite off the master bedroom. While Trent hung up his towel, she filled a glass with water. "Antibiotics first."

"Yes, ma'am." With a weary grin on his unshaven face, he dutifully took the pill she handed him and swallowed it.

She got the distinct feeling he was humoring her when she closed the toilet lid and had him sit so she could peel the tape off the tanned skin of his upper arm and toss it and the soiled gauze beneath it into the trash. He only winced once and never complained about the pain he must be in as she made quick work of cleansing the open wound and applying a new layer of ointment before covering the injury with a clean gauze pad. But the tape twisted and fought her as she pulled it off the roll and tried to tear the pieces she needed.

"Where are those scissors?" After securing the gauze with one mangled piece of tape, Katie squatted down to open the bag and pull out the contents inside to retrieve the smaller items that had fallen to the bottom. "Just give me a sec." Wallet. Sunglasses. Squashed breakfast bar. Laptop. Mini toy truck. "There they are…"

Katie gasped. She'd been so intent on fixing up Trent and getting back to her own bed, where she prayed a dreamless sleep would claim her, that the damage done to the cover of her laptop almost didn't register. But then she trailed her finger over the small, perfectly round dent in the metal cover. A frightening realization swept through her with such force that it made her light-headed. She wobbled and sank onto her knees. She set the laptop on the tile floor and dug into her purse again. Not for scissors this time. It was… *Oh, my God.* There. Perfectly round and just big enough to slip her finger through. A bullet hole.

"Is something broken?"

Turning, she held up her bag with her finger still sticking through the hole. "I could have been killed. Tyler could have been killed. You could have…" Her voice faded with every sentence until there was barely a breath of sound. "I don't understand why this is happening.'

"Ah, Katie." Trent tossed the bag aside and pulled her onto his lap. "Sunshine, come here."

Dressing the wound was forgotten as she curled up on top of his thighs and leaned into him. His arms came around her and wrapped her up with the heat of his body.

With her ear pressed to the strong beat of his heart, Katie shivered. "I'm so cold."

His big hands moved up and down her back and arms, creating static friction as he rubbed flannel against flannel. But even that electricity couldn't seem to pierce the shroud of despair closing in around her. "You're going into a little bit of shock. Let's get you warmed up."

When he lifted her into the air, she remembered herself. "Your arm. What if it starts bleeding again?"

"Screw that."

"I need to finish dressing it."

He carried her out of the bathroom to the king-size bed where he slept. "Right now, you just need to let me take care of you." Her toes touched the floor only long enough for Trent to pull back the covers. Then he swung her up into his arms again and set her near the middle of the bed. Before she could think to protest, he'd stretched out beside her and pulled the sheet and thick comforter up over them both. He gathered her into his arms and threw one leg over both of hers, aligning them chest to hip, with her head tucked beneath his chin and their legs tangled together. "Think of it as doing me a favor." With her arms caught between them, he pulled her impossibly closer, wrapping her up in the furnace of his body. "I need a break, sunshine. This whole investigation is wearing me out. It'd be nice to not have to worry about you getting into trouble for a little while."

She almost giggled at the teasing remark, but she was too caught up in the drugging effect of his body heat seeping into hers. The tightness in her chest eased, and the shivering abated. The longer Trent held her, the longer he whispered those deeply pitched assurances in her ear, the stronger she felt. The panic lessened. Her jumbled thoughts cleared.

He stroked his fingers through her hair, pressed a kiss to the crown. "You're safe. You're fine. Tyler's fine. And I'm too big to bring down with a piddly-ass shot like this wound."

His wound. It needed to be properly tended. Katie stiffened her arms and pushed against his chest. "Trent—"

"I'm fine, too. You stay right here. This is what *I* need, remember?"

Katie wasn't sure if she'd dozed for a little while or if lying with Trent, bundled beneath the covers to chase away the wintry chill that had derailed her for a few moments, was all the healing she needed to feel more like her normal self again. To believe again that she and her son were safe. To feel as though the mistakes of her past couldn't touch her tonight. Not in Trent's bed. Not in his arms.

It was sometime later, when the wind of a winter storm outside rattled the windowpanes and startled her awake, that Katie realized she'd never returned to her own bed. And now that she was feeling rested and warm—and she couldn't hear any sounds of a boy or dog stirring—she admitted that she didn't want to leave.

"Better?" The drowsy male voice greeted her from the pillow beside her.

Katie smiled. "Much."

"This is nice, Katie Lee Rinaldi." Trent's fingers were stroking lazy circles along her back and hip, and Katie discovered her fingers taking similar liberties across the warm skin and ticklish curls of his chest. "But you know what else I need?"

Her hand stilled and she pushed herself up onto her elbow. Did he want her to finish taping his bandage? Did he need one of the painkillers the doctor had prescribed? "What is it? Anything I can do—"

"I need you to trust me."

"I do." She leaned over him, trying to assess the message in those gunmetal eyes.

"I need you to trust us—even if it's just for tonight."

Oh. Her body tingled in anticipation. "Trent, are you asking me to—"

He silenced her question with a sweetly lingering kiss. His patience with her was as maddening as it was exquisite. His lips ignited a slow burn that seemed to travel from her mouth to every point of her body where his hips and thigh and roaming hand touched her, creating a network of pathways that crisscrossed inside her, filling her with heat and an edgy sort of desire that demanded more than easygoing kisses and tender caresses.

"I know you need me to take things slow." He combed his fingers into the dark waves of her hair that brushed against his chest and tucked them behind her ear, cupping the side of her neck. "I need your brain to help me put Leland Asher away for good, but I need something else from you, too. I need to touch you to believe I didn't almost lose you tonight. I need to feel your confidence and caring to keep me strong. I need to feel your strength, holding me, accepting everything I want to give you and be for you. I'm not just asking for sex, sunshine. I need that closeness we've always shared. I—"

She shushed him with a finger over his mouth. "I think I need that, too. I want all the things I think you can give me. For tonight."

"It'll change everything between us."

Sliding her arms around his neck, Katie fell back onto the pillow, pulling him to her. "I think it already has changed."

And then there was no more conversation. There were only hungry lips and greedy hands and Trent's muscular body moving over hers.

He unwrapped her like a gift, untying her robe, unbuttoning her pajama top. He slipped his hands inside, searing her skin with every sweeping touch, every squeeze of a breast. With his thumb, he teased the sensitive tips to tiny pebbles, generating little frissons of electricity beneath every touch, feeding the current of heat and pressure stirring deep in her womb.

Carefully avoiding his injury, Katie swept her hands over the smooth skin of his back, felt the muscles of his chest quiver and jump beneath her exploring fingers. She sampled the sandpapery line of his chin and jaw, and smiled at the responsive cord of muscle at the side of his neck that made him groan deep in his throat each time she took a nip.

True to his word, he seemed to touch every inch of her body while his wicked mouth worked its magic on hers. He tugged her pajama pants down to claim her hip with the palm of his hand and pull the most feverish part of her body into the bulge thrusting behind his zipper. When he kissed his way down her neck, Katie thrust her fingers into the damp muss of his hair, releasing a spicy scent that filled her nose. She guided his mouth to the straining peak of her breast and whimpered at the bolt of heat that arced through her.

Every kiss was a temptation. Every touch a torment. "Trent," she gasped. "Now. Please."

He threw back the covers to shuck off his jeans and shorts and sheathe himself. The chill of the night had barely cooled her skin before Trent was back, tossing aside the flannel pants she'd kicked off and settling between her legs. "There's no turning back from this," he reminded her, stealing another kiss from her swollen lips.

Katie nodded and pulled at his hips, demanding he complete what he'd started. "I've made some bad choices in my life, Trent. This isn't one of them."

She lifted her knees and he slipped inside, slowly filling her with his length. His dark gray eyes locked on to hers as he began to move. She tried to hold his loving gaze, tried to memorize every second of this stolen time together, but soon the sensation was too much. She could only feel. He slipped his hand beneath her bottom and lifted her into his final thrust. Katie closed her eyes and surrendered to the heat bursting inside her. Seconds later, Trent gasped her name against her hair and followed her over the edge into the fiery inferno.

TRENT AWOKE TO the sound of a phone ringing and an empty bed.

He swung his feet to the floor, trying to orient himself to the long night and the early hour. He scratched his fingers through his hair, instantly remembering how Katie had played with it—and how her fingers had tightened against his scalp, holding his mouth to a sweet, round breast as she gasped for breath and squirmed with delight beneath him. Hell. Even remembering how she'd put her hands all over him with such hungry abandon was enough to make things stir down south this morning.

With a groan of resignation, he scooped up his shorts and jeans, fishing his ringing cell out of the back pocket and checking the number. Olivia Watson. She'd hold for a couple more rings, giving him time to go into the john to splash some cold water on his face and try to get his head on straight before taking a work call.

He'd known Katie had a rockin' body. What fool male wouldn't want to put his hands all over those decadent curves? But he hadn't expected how responsive she'd be to every needy touch. How eager she'd be to explore him, as well. That was the free spirit he'd imagined her to be in his youth. That was the Katie who'd first captured his young heart.

And he sure as hell hadn't expected this gut kick of pain when he realized their time together—a crazy mix of comfort, caring and passion—didn't mean as much to her as it did to him. Hell. She must have left before dawn. The painkiller in his system had knocked him out eventually, and he'd slept longer than usual, oblivious to her efforts to escape and erase any evidence of their time spent together.

The phone was still ringing in his hand when he strolled back into the bedroom and sat on the black-and-gold comforter that had been draped neatly back on the bed—after he distinctly remembered it sliding off onto the floor last night. Katie hadn't left so much as a dent in the pillow beside him this morning. She'd taken every stitch of clothing, even her damaged bag and the contents that had been scattered across his bathroom floor, leaving no trace of *them* behind.

Well, he'd gotten exactly what he'd asked for, hadn't he? One night with Katie Lee in his bed. If only the two of them had been lousy together. If only the hushed conversation and cuddling in between hadn't made him think that it had meant something life changing to her, too. Trent hadn't felt that right inside his own skin for ten years. But expecting Katie to suddenly love him the way he loved her…?

The bedroom door burst open and a nine-year-old and the excited dog chasing him jumped onto the bed. "Aren't you going to answer your phone?" Tyler asked, bouncing up and down on his knees. "It's been ringing forever."

"Tyler." Katie followed a few steps after, hanging back in the doorway. She'd already dressed in a pair of jeans and a sweatshirt and had pulled the sexy waves of her hair back into a tomboyish ponytail. "I told you not to wake Trent."

"But, Mom, he was already awake." Tyler threw himself on the bed, which bounced like a trampoline with his light weight. "Padre and I peeked."

Katie shook her head at the bouncy boy and whining dog and frowned an apology at Trent. "I didn't know if I needed to answer the phone for you."

Was this entourage the reason she'd left him this morning? Letting Tyler see the two of them share a kiss was one thing, but explaining what it meant when Mommy and Trent slept in bed together was something else. Or was that just the excuse she was using for pretending as though last night had never happened?

"Nope. I got it." He punched the button on the phone and put it to his ear. "Olivia. What's up?"

"Sorry to wake you, Sleeping Beauty, but I'm at the ME's office at the crime lab. My brother Niall just completed the autopsy on your private detective. We got an ID on John Smith."

"Hold on a sec, Liv. Katie's here with me. I'm going to put you on speakerphone." Katie hustled Tyler out of the room with orders to finish his bowl of cereal and get dressed for school. Then she nodded and came back to stand beside Trent and listen in on the call. "Tell us about John Smith. Which one of those aliases was real?"

"None of them. None of those identities existed until about ten years ago. John Smith is the most recent incarnation. The man had a knack for reinventing himself."

Normally, all the details were important. But he was

only in the mood for straight answers this morning. "You said you had a match."

"We do. His fingerprints are in the system."

Katie pulled the phone down to her level and asked, "Then why didn't this guy's real identity pop when I ran the search on him?"

"Because Niall found the prints in the archives." Katie tilted her confused frown up to meet his. The KCPD archives were the files where cases that had been solved were stored. Or where crimes that had passed their statute of limitations—meaning the police could no longer pursue them—had been filed away. "Does the name Francisco Dona ring a bell?"

Katie's encyclopedic memory came up with the connection first. "Isabel Asher's boyfriend? The guy Leland blamed for her death?" She shook her head. "There was a motorcycle accident. Francisco Dona is dead."

"He is now." Olivia's sarcasm wasn't entirely for humor's sake. "The fingerprints don't lie. This guy has been able to fly under the radar for ten years. Somehow, he got his prints in a DB file and a John Doe was cremated in his place. He was reborn as a new man several times over, most recently as John Smith, private eye."

Trent tried to have some respect for a man who could change his identity as readily and completely as the WITSEC division of the US Marshals' office could. But all he could see was a criminal who'd gotten far too close to Katie and Tyler. "So if he knew we were tracking Leland Asher and putting together a case against him, Francisco Dona—Mr. Smith—would have a personal stake in finding out what we know."

Olivia agreed. "If Asher found out the man he blamed for his sister's death was still alive, he'd make fixing that mistake his number-one priority once he got out of prison. He'd certainly want to make sure the man paid before the cancer got him."

That dimpled frown had reappeared between Katie's eyebrows. "I get why Francisco Dona would come after me. I'm the information guru—I'd be his best source for finding out where we are in the Asher investigation and what the team's chances are of putting him back in prison for life."

"But?" Trent prompted, wondering what wheels were turning in that clever mind of hers.

"But if he had access to my laptop, which he did when he or someone else planted the mirroring program, then why threaten me? Why warn me to stop? He should want every piece of information he could steal from me."

"Are we dealing with two different cases here?" Trent suggested. "Smith might have been after Katie, but somebody else was after Smith."

Olivia had her own idea. "Or maybe trailing Katie was Smith's effort to try to escape from Asher's retribution one more time, but he failed. Still, how did Smith get access to Katie's computer in the first place?"

Katie spoke up this time. "I have a theory on that." She glanced up at Trent, perhaps offering an explanation for her hasty retreat this morning. "A couple of weird things happened at the theater last night."

"Besides finding a dead body and getting shot at?"

What else had he missed besides Francis Sergel putting his hands on Katie?

"I did some research this morning. The bullet just dented my laptop—it still works." When she gestured for him to follow, Trent went into the spare bedroom with her. He tried to ignore that all her things had been moved in here and focus on the restraining-order record she pulled up on the screen. "There have been sexual harassment complaints filed against Doug Price. I found a record of a college student who went to a judge after she discovered Doug hiding a camera in a women's dressing room and taking pictures without her consent."

Trent borrowed one of Max's choice curses. "How does this guy get to work in community theater?"

"Because it's a volunteer position with a volunteer board, and sometimes it's hard to find people with the skills to organize and run a show who are willing to give up that much of their time." Katie shrugged. "And probably because people don't talk about it enough. I've found three different theater companies where Doug has volunteered in Missouri and Kansas."

"And you think he planted the device to sabotage your computer?" Olivia asked.

"He could have been blackmailed into doing it. It fits our *Strangers on a Train* theory about someone manipulating others to commit crimes for them." Trent was less than thrilled to hear about Katie's encounter with Doug Price last night. "He was eager that I not touch or see whatever was in that envelope. I wonder if they were photographs, or copies of them. And the price to keep them from going to the police or going public was tampering with my computer."

Olivia seemed to agree it was a strong possibility. "Do you think he killed John Smith? Or Francisco? Or whatever we're calling him now?"

"I don't think he'd have the guts to pull a trigger. But maybe he saw something and that's why he was in such a hurry to leave—especially if Smith was his blackmailer."

"You want me to bring Doug Price in for questioning?" Olivia offered.

"Yeah. Put Max to work, too." Trent had a feeling that after months of hard work and dangerous setbacks, a lot of cold cases were about to break wide open. "I want to know if John Smith was tracking Katie for his own survival or if someone else hired him. If so, who? And why?"

Katie nodded. "And if last night was a hit ordered by Asher, how did he find out John Smith's real identity?"

Trent headed back to his own room. "I want Leland Asher in my interrogation room. Today."

"I'll clear it with the lieutenant and have Max pick him up."

"Katie and I will stop by Smith's office to see what we can find there before coming in."

Trent hung up and went to work, unlocking his gun from the strongbox in his closet and sliding the weapon onto his belt. He started to pull on a thermal undershirt but realized the dressing on his wound needed changing. Unfortunately, it was a two-handed project. He pulled off the twisted tape and soiled gauze and dangled it at Katie's door. "A little help?"

"Come on in." She set down the blouse and sweater she'd been getting ready to change into and picked up her bag with the first-aid supplies. He sat on the edge of the double-size bed while she doctored him. "Jim's coming by to take Tyler to school again and watch him until we pick him up. And then I'll start pulling everything KCPD has on Francisco Dona and John Smith. I'll get a brief together on Asher and his minions before you run your interviews this afternoon, so you know who all the players are."

After the first piece of tape was secured on his shoulder, Trent caught Katie by the wrist. Even if she was going to pretend it hadn't happened, he needed to say something about last night. "Damn, you smell good in the morning." He watched the blush of heat creep into her cheeks as he lightly massaged the warm beat of her pulse. "You were amazing last night. But I missed you when I woke up. I gather you don't want Tyler to know what happened."

Katie twisted her wrist from his touch and cut another length of tape. "If he doesn't know how close we got, maybe he won't get his hopes up and think—"

"That you and I could be a real couple."

She positioned the tape over the gauze and gently smoothed it into place. "Trent. Last night was like a fairy tale. Tyler had a dad and a dog, and you were completely wonderful to me."

"But?" He was wary of where this explanation was going.

"Obviously, this isn't over yet. Between a mob boss and a dead private detective, there are still so many things that could go wrong. You've already been hurt. Tyler was frightened out of his mind. And, let's face it, I wigged out on you." She picked up his thermal shirt and helped him slide his arm into the sleeve without disturbing the bandage. "I've never been part of the story where they all live happily ever after. I'm afraid a few moments like last night, that idyllic perfection, aren't real."

He pulled his shirt on over his head and slipped the rest of it into place before standing beside her. He dropped his head to whisper against her ear, "It is for me, sunshine. As far as I'm concerned, the fairy tale is real." He inched in a little farther and pressed a kiss to her hair. "I just need you to decide when or if you're going to accept that I'm in love with you and that you're in love with me. I want to be a father to your son and a husband to you. And you know damn well that I'd be good at both."

He couldn't lay it on the line any plainer than that. With his heart and future in her hands now, Trent left her standing there in pale silence and returned to his own room to put on his badge and go to work.

CHAPTER TWELVE

WHAT JOHN SMITH'S office lacked in decor, it more than made up for in messiness.

Katie helped Trent sort through the rows of file cabinets, looking for anything useful. Folders had been stuffed into drawers without regard to labels or alphabetizing. Whoever had gone through the office before them hadn't been there to rob Smith because they'd left behind a bottle of scotch and bag of marijuana that had been stashed in the back of one drawer.

She'd at least been able to make more sense out of his desktop computer. It appeared he'd used it mainly for word processing and internet research, so she'd easily tracked several of the searches he'd recently made—including a floor plan for the units in her apartment complex, news updates on Leland Asher's release from prison and several searches of medical sites to find the prognosis and life expectancy for a sixty-year-old man diagnosed with lung cancer.

"Looks like he's been tracking Asher for years," Katie reported.

Trent nodded, looking over her shoulder to read the monitor. "That clued him in on when he needed to change his identity again. If Asher got too close to finding out he was still alive, Francisco would go underground for a few months and reinvent himself as someone else."

"The medical searches probably meant he was hoping Leland would die soon. Maybe that was why he was at the press conference, to see with his own eyes whether the man who wanted him dead had long to live."

Trent went back to the file cabinets to continue his search. "Unfortunately for him, he miscalculated. Leland's men got to him first."

Katie rolled the chair away from the desk to help Trent dig through the remaining mess for other useful clues. There was one more piece of information she could get off Smith's computer—who had hired him to spy on her—but they needed a different warrant to breach the confidential agreement between investigator and client. While Lieutenant Rafferty-Taylor pleaded their case to a warrant judge, she and Trent were spending their morning in dusty cabinets, sharing terse, business-only conversation.

"Katie." His sharp voice pulled her from her thoughts. He set a bent folder on top of the cabinet and opened it. "Is this who I think it is?"

Katie joined him, reading the name scrawled across the top of the first page. "Stephen March." She flipped through the pages to see copies of March's time spent in drug courts and rehab, along with a criminal complaint Stephen March had filed against his sister's fiancé, Richard Bratcher, which had been thrown out of court. "This shows March's motive for wanting Bratcher dead, as well as blackmailable offenses that could be used to get him to kill Dani Reese." She dug farther into the drawer in front of her. "These are all people Smith investigated?"

"Looks like it." He peeled a tiny slip of masking tape off the inside of the drawer. "I wonder."

"What is it?"

He showed her the hyphenated list of numbers before crossing over to the safe behind Smith's desk. He knelt down and twisted the numbers on the dial. "This guy was resourceful, but I don't know that he knew much about security precautions." Trent opened the door and pulled out three thick manila envelopes and stacked them on top of the safe. He pulled a fourth one out and dumped the contents out beside the stack. Out tumbled bundles of money. Twenties, fifties, hundreds. "I'm guessing this was a cash business. Probably a smart idea for a man who had to change identities and bank accounts every couple of years."

"Trent." She pulled another folder from the file drawers. "This says Hillary Wells." There were other files in this cabinet that matched names in her own research. "That creep piggybacked off all my work. In some of these, he's gone to websites I checked and printed off the exact same information." She didn't know whether to feel angry that he'd stolen her months of dedicated research to use for some nefarious purpose or violated to think John Smith, aka Francisco Dona, had followed every thought, every move, she'd made on her computer—and she hadn't even known he'd been lurking, watching.

"I think we're onto something here, sunshine."

Katie snapped out of the emotional debate. Trent hadn't used her nickname since that conversation about fairy tales earlier that morning. In fact, he'd barely looked at her. And he certainly hadn't kissed her or held her or touched her in any way since dropping that bomb of an admission this morning.

I just need you to decide when or if you're going to accept that I'm in love with you and that you're in love with me. I want to be a father to your son and a husband to you.

That promise was everything she'd wanted growing up. But a life's worth of mistakes and tragedies made it difficult to believe in that promise. How was she supposed to do the right thing when she wasn't sure what that was anymore? How could Trent love her enough to risk a relationship with a woman with all her phobias and eccentricities and emotional baggage that came with the package? And was it worth the risk of her and Tyler losing him from their lives if the relationship didn't work? Then again, maybe she'd lost him already by not giving him the answer he'd wanted this morning.

And the idea of not having Trent's strong arms and stalwart presence and beautiful soul in her life anymore already felt like a very big mistake.

But Trent was talking work now, not their personal lives, where she got him shot and broke his heart. She circled around the desk to join him. "What did you find?"

He pulled another manila envelope from the safe and

handed it to her. "Check inside. I'm guessing that envelope you saw with Doug Price held something similar."

Katie pulled out a stack of photographs. "Oh, my." These were images of scantily clad women, obviously taken by a hidden camera. She even recognized an image of the college student who'd sued Doug for harassment. "Oh. My."

"You blackmail a man into doing a job for you, then you keep an extra copy of the evidence for insurance purposes."

Katie stuffed the pictures back inside the envelope. "This man was horrible."

"Which one?" The phone in Trent's pocket rang before she could answer. Katie waited in anticipation until he nodded. "Yes, ma'am." She sat at the desk again and booted up the private detective's computer, waiting for the order. "We've got the warrant. Do it."

One keystroke and she'd know who'd hired Smith to spy on her. She leaned back in the chair, surprised by the answer on the screen. "There's only one name here. One person who hired Smith to watch over all these people."

"Please tell me it's Leland Asher."

"No. Dr. Beverly Eisenbach."

TRENT GLANCED AROUND Ginny Rafferty-Taylor's office, as anxious to get this show underway as the drumming of Katie's fingers or Max's pacing would indicate.

Four suspects. Four different strategies. Four different plans of attack.

And if the team was as good as the lieutenant seemed

to think, then Leland Asher would be on his way back
to prison by the end of the night.

The petite lieutenant picked up the stack of folders
Katie had prepared and handed them to Trent. "Are you
ready to do this?"

"Yes, ma'am."

"How do you want to handle it?"

Trent glanced over to Katie's big blue eyes staring
up at him. He couldn't, wouldn't put his heart out there
again for her to torment until she decided whether she
was going to live her life taking risks or holed up in
the security of lonely nobility. But whether he got his
fairy-tale ending or not, he'd be damned if anyone was
going to hurt her or Tyler again.

He nodded to her, making that silent vow, and headed
out to Interview Room 1. "I'm going to pick off the little fish first."

In the grand scheme of things, Doug Price was an
easy interrogation. Trent was twice the older man's size,
and all he had to do was stand and dominate the room
to get the play director to talk.

He tossed the stack of lewd photos he'd gotten from
John Smith's safe and fanned them across the table in
front of Doug and his attorney. "Anything look familiar to you, Mr. Price?"

His lawyer tried to keep Doug from saying anything,
but the man already had some of that oversprayed hair
falling out of place. He sat forward in his chair. "Where
did you get these?"

Trent tossed a crime-scene photo of John Smith's

bloody face on top of the other pictures. "From this guy."

Doug cringed and pushed the photos away. But he cracked like an egg. "John Smith. He's a private investigator. He told me he'd given me the last copies of those pictures when I saw him last night. I had no reason to kill him. I was doing him a favor." A favor in the sense that Smith hadn't given Doug any choice. "Smith said if I kept an eye on Katie and helped him get access to your team's investigations that he wouldn't turn any of those photos over to the police."

"So you sabotaged Katie's laptop and left those threats for her? You assaulted her in the women's dressing room?"

"It wasn't assault. I was removing a camera. I wasn't expecting her to be there. I just wanted to get away."

"I think we can safely say that your career in community theater is over." Trent pulled out a chair on the opposite side of the gray metal table. Doug started to relax, but Trent decided to stay on his feet and catch him off guard. He pulled three more photographs from the file Katie had prepared. Three more links in the chain of related crimes she'd dug up in her extensive research. He set the pictures down in front of Doug, one by one. "Do you know any of these people?"

"No. No." He pointed to the last one. "Her. I don't understand what she has to do with any of this."

Interesting. "Who is she to you, Doug?"

"My therapist. I saw Dr. Eisenbach for a few months years back. Court-ordered sessions. The judge said I had an addiction to pornography."

Bev Eisenbach and Matt Asher clammed up behind their attorneys when they were separated into two interview rooms. But as Olivia slyly observed when she and Max *accidentally* allowed the two suspects' paths to cross in the hallway across from the restrooms, the twenty-two-year-old and the woman old enough to be his mother clearly knew each other. They'd called each other by their first names in a quick, hushed conversation, and their fingers had met in a quick squeeze.

Now, there was an odd couple.

They each truthfully claimed to have shared nothing with Trent, then whispered something about promising to remain silent.

So the two had a plan that they'd clearly been working on together for some time…while their uncle/boyfriend had been locked away in prison. Instead of kowtowing to the boss, they'd been plotting behind his back. Setting Leland up for murder? Or taking over the criminal empire from a dying man?

The information Olivia had fed Trent between interviews made him grin. Bev and Matt's conversation had given Trent some key intel to use as he moved on to his final interview with Leland. He grinned because while they acted as though Leland was on his way out of the business, and they were setting themselves up to take his place, someone had forgotten to tell Leland.

Trent's approach to a man of Leland Asher's self-appointed stature was different than the intimidation he'd used with Doug Price or the friendly charm he'd turned on his nephew and Bev Eisenbach. "How long do you have to live, Mr. Asher? Years? Months? Weeks?"

Leland smiled. "I like a man who's direct, Detective. I can talk to a man like that."

Trent leaned forward in his chair, matching Leland's confident posture. "Did you have any dealings with Craig Fairfax at the penitentiary infirmary?"

"Fairfax?" Leland scratched at his gaunt cheeks. "Poor bloke. Terrible cough. I always thought he was going to hack up a lung. Very difficult to have a conversation with him."

"So you did interact with him. Did you ever talk about Katie Lee Rinaldi?"

"Who?"

Trent steeled his gazed on Asher, knowing Katie was watching in Lieutenant Rafferty-Taylor's office through the closed-circuit camera overhead. This would be a tough line of questioning for her to hear, but since she was part of the team, she'd insisted on listening in. "A girl Fairfax kidnapped ten years ago."

"Oh, that Katie. Tragic upbringing from what I hear. Yes, I believe she's the district attorney's daughter now." Close enough. Apparently, Fairfax had been filling Asher in on Katie's family history. "Goodness knows, Mr. Fairfax has a vendetta against that man. If he could get out of prison, I'm sure his first stop would be the DA's house, or perhaps his wife's school—or at the home of this Katie you mentioned. Yes, I remember he definitely has a score he wants to settle...*if* he were ever to be released from prison."

Trent's hand fisted beneath the table at the indirect but abhorrent threats, although he betrayed nothing to

Asher. "Do you have a score to settle, Mr. Asher? With Francisco Dona, perhaps?"

"I have no comment."

"What about John Smith? Do you know anyone by that name?"

"Not very original, is it?" Trent waited until Leland answered the question. "No, I don't believe I do."

"But you know Dona."

"Knew, Detective. Past tense. Dona died in a motorcycle accident several years ago."

"Did he?" Trent wasn't intimidated by the man's condescending tone. "If you discovered Mr. Dona was alive after all these years, you'd want to do something about it, wouldn't you?"

Leland checked his brittle nails before leaning forward and resting the elbows of his tailored suit on the table. "I liked you better when you were straightforward, Detective. You know as well as I do that Francisco is a sensitive subject for me. He turned my sister on to drugs and then killed her with them. At the very least, he was a coward and let her die without raising a finger to help. Isabel was the light of my life. Francisco snuffed that light out."

He wanted straightforward? "Did you murder Francisco Dona last night in retaliation for your sister's death? Or hire someone to murder him?"

"So he is dead." Asher leaned back in his chair and smiled. "I'm a dying man. Whether it was ten years ago or yesterday, knowing he died before me makes me very happy."

Leland checked his watch and glanced at his attorney. "Will there be anything else, Detective Dixon? I have a dinner engagement I don't want to miss."

"Just one last question and then I can let you go."

"What's that?"

"Did you know that your girlfriend, Beverly Eisenbach, and your nephew, Matt, have been having an affair while you've been incarcerated in Jefferson City?"

Leland leaned over to whisper something with his attorney before answering.

"Yes."

KATIE KNEW SOMETHING was terribly wrong when the cast came out for curtain call at the final dress rehearsal. There were only five Cratchit children crossing to center stage. Where was Tiny Tim? "Where's Tyler?"

She ran down to the stage and straight up the stairs, pushing aside actors while the music was playing and they were still taking their bows. She wasn't going to lose him again.

"Wyatt? Kayla? Have you seen Tyler?"

The other children seemed startled to realize one of them was missing.

"No, ma'am."

"We were playing cards backstage at intermission. He said his last line, didn't he?"

Yes, her son had the last line of the entire show. Then the actors had all exited backstage to line up for bows, and now… "Francis." She caught the tall actor by the sleeve of his robe before he went back onstage. "Have you seen my son?"

She heard him snorting beneath his mask. "No director. Missing actors. Crazy costume ladies dashing across the stage. You know what they say—a bad dress rehearsal means we'll have a stellar opening night."

"Stuff it, Francis. Have you seen Tyler?" He tugged his robe from her grasp and ignored her question. "Then is Trent here yet?"

Francis snickered from behind his mask. "It's not my job to keep track of your child or that bruiser boyfriend of yours."

"Francis, please."

"That's my cue."

Trent had promised to be here by the end of the rehearsal. Maybe Trent had arrived early and he and Tyler had gotten to talking backstage and her son had simply missed his cue. Katie hurried back to the greenroom.

He'd had to stay late at the precinct office, walking Doug Price through booking, writing up reports on his interviews with Leland and Matt Asher and Beverly Eisenbach, and sitting down with the rest of the team to determine whether they had enough circumstantial evidence for arrest warrants yet. Normally, Katie would have been part of such a meeting, but Lieutenant Rafferty-Taylor had excused her for Tyler's benefit. With the threat of John Smith no longer in the picture, Katie had figured she could go to the final dress rehearsal without the benefit of a 24/7 bodyguard. Even so, Trent had insisted a uniformed officer accompany them, and he'd promised to join them at the theater as soon as he could get away from work. After all, Tyler still wanted him to be a part of his life, even if Katie needed time to decide how to respond to Trent's ultimatum.

But maybe that need for an evening of independence to figure out her future had been a mistake.

She hurried past Ebenezer Scrooge himself, knowing there would be no other actors behind him. The crew members thought Tyler was onstage or had made an emergency run to the bathroom and forgotten he had to go back out.

She found Tyler's street clothes still on the hanger in the men's dressing room, although his coat was gone.

Katie quickly slipped into her own coat and pulled out her phone. He wouldn't have been so foolish as to go out and play in the snow, would he? Just in case, she hurried across the backstage area and stepped outside. "Tyler?"

Not trusting her son's safety to anyone else, Katie punched in Trent's number and lifted the phone to her ear. It rang once before she saw the silver car, just like the night before, waiting in the crowded parking lot. She saw Leland Asher nod to her before climbing into the backseat. "Oh, no. Tyler!"

She started to run. But strong arms locked around her from behind, knocking her phone into the snow and lifting her off the ground. A rough hand and a pungent cloth muffled her scream, and within seconds, her knees grew weak and the world faded into black.

THE NIGHTMARE DIDN'T go away when Katie awoke.

It had just taken on warmer temps and a posher backdrop.

She was still a prisoner, like she'd been at seventeen. And her beloved little boy was once again in harm's way.

Instead of being handcuffed to a bed in a makeshift hospital ward, waiting to deliver a baby, she was seated at Leland Asher's ornate walnut desk in the study of his mansion, hacking into a computer system for him. She didn't need to be drugged or kept in chains in order to cooperate. The two thugs who'd kidnapped her and Tyler had already shown her Matt Asher's dead body and promised to do the same to her nine-year-old son if she didn't do their boss's bidding.

There was something seriously twisted inside Leland Asher's head to make him order his bodyguards to lure Tyler outside the theater with a story about her getting hurt in the parking lot. Now he had them tie Beverly Eisenbach to a brocaded Queen Anne chair before thanking them for their years of service and dismissing them, promising each a healthy bonus in their bank accounts. Then he'd kissed his longtime girlfriend and stuffed his wadded-up handkerchief into her mouth to muffle her protests and pleas for mercy. With Matt Asher dead, Leland weakened by his illness and the hired help dismissed for the night, Katie even briefly considered standing up to Leland herself, maybe shoving the desk chair at him and making a run for it with Tyler, or whacking him over the head with this computer.

But as if sensing her tendency to tempt fate, he used the one thing she cared about most to force her to unlock code and break through firewalls and search through servers to access the information he wanted—he stood in the center of the room framed by windows and floor-to-ceiling curtains and simply rested one hand over the shoulder of her son and held a gun in the other.

Her sinuses reeled with a headache from the knock-out chemical they'd used on her, but her synapses were firing on all cylinders. She'd been at the computer for about an hour since getting her instructions, but in reality, she'd gained access to Beverly's medical files within the first fifteen minutes. She'd spent the rest of the time fighting for survival in the best way she knew how. She prayed her desperate plan had worked and that it had worked quickly enough for her and Tyler to have a chance to escape.

She rested her fingers for a moment before looking up at the gray-haired man. "I'm in."

"I want you to access her private files."

Beverly screamed through her gag, rocking back and forth in her chair, pulling at the ropes that bound her.

"I need a warrant to do that," Katie explained.

Leland put the gun to Tyler's head and Katie bit her lip to stop from crying out. "Here's your warrant. Now do it."

Katie's fingers sailed over the keyboard again. "You keep looking at me, Tyler. Think about Padre. He's going to need you to give him some extra exercise to-night because we'll be getting home so late." She locked her gaze on to Tyler's red-rimmed eyes and smiled. "You focus right here, sweetie. I love you. Don't ever forget that, not for one second." He wiped his nose on the sleeve of his costume and nodded, trying so hard to be brave and remain calm for her.

She glanced down at her work, wanting to do everything she could to maintain Tyler's focus on her and keep him from witnessing a gruesome crime or becoming a victim himself.

Don't make a mistake. Don't make a mistake.

Since Leland hadn't questioned anything she'd done so far, Katie pretended the extra commands she typed in were necessary to retrieve the sensitive information that the law and a stubborn girlfriend wouldn't give him. The counseling office's patient list was already on her screen. But with her fingers flying over the keyboard, she embedded a message and sent it to Trent's phone. The message was sent and gone by the time she'd reached Bev Eisenbach's confidential files.

"Have you finished yet?" Leland was growing impatient.

She couldn't push her luck too much further. "Just about."

Leland kept his grip on Tyler but switched the gun back to Beverly as tears smeared her mascara and she whimpered for forgiveness. "Miss Rinaldi, I remind you that I'm a dying man."

"I'm in the system." *Find us, Trent. Find us.* "I'm pulling up the patient files now. What do you want me to look for?"

Leland smiled, pleased with her success. Keeping a grip on Tyler's arm, he walked over to Beverly and pulled the gag from her mouth. "It was quite a clever plan all those years ago that you came up with, darling. Care to explain yourself?"

Bev coughed for a few seconds before she could speak. "Leland, dearest, you know I've always had your best interests at heart. Look at all I've done for you. I convinced that tweaking drug addict to kill that reporter who was going to expose your connections to the senator. I did the world a service by having your men kill Lloyd Endicott so that Dr. Wells would murder that horrible Richard Bratcher. I found out Francisco Dona was still alive. I found out he was working as a private detective."

"No. No, dear. You kept that from me." He drew the gun across Beverly's forehead, and Katie nearly screamed at the horrible images he was exposing her son to. "All these years I thought I'd avenged Isabel's death, only to find out that my nephew—her own son—knew he still breathed air, and you two hadn't done a damn thing about it. I had to have my men take care of it."

Katie was a bit of a brilliant geek herself. She'd already tapped into her KCPD account and was mirroring everything that she was doing here on the department server. She'd pinged Trent's phone—Max's, Olivia's and Jim's, as well. Lieutenant Rafferty-Taylor received a notification of the new files uploading. Katie had even copied a notice to her surrogate father, the DA.

Look at Miss Katie Lee Rinaldi—taking a huge risk, bending the rules, doing whatever was necessary to protect the people she loved. She was charging into battle, taking on a known criminal to save her son and her own life one more time.

Read between the lines, Trent. Find us.

She'd always been able to get herself into trouble, but Trent would always be there to help her get out of it—to catch her when she fell, when she was frightened, when she was terrified her next mistake might cost her everything she held dear.

Be patient with me a little longer, babe. I love you. I need you. I'm in love with you.

A loud crash at the front door shook through the house. "KCPD! We're coming in!"

Tyler cried out with a startled yelp.

"It's okay, Ty," she reassured him. "They're using a battering ram to break down the door."

"At last." Leland smiled from ear to ear. "I wondered how long it would take the police to find you."

"Asher!" A deep, familiar voice echoed through the house.

"Mom!" Tyler recognized Trent's voice, too. She saw him pull from Leland Asher's grasp.

She put up her hand, cautioning him to obey. "Shh, sweetie. Remember you're playing a part. You're the good little boy who does whatever Mr. Asher says, right?"

Tyler's frightened eyes locked on to hers again and he nodded.

The next voice Katie heard was Ginny Rafferty-Taylor's. "Leland Asher. Your house is surrounded. Your chauffeur and bodyguards have been neutralized. It's just you and me and a lot of very angry cops."

"I'd be happy to talk with you, Lieutenant."

The team must be working its way through the mansion while the lieutenant stalled Asher. "I need to talk to the hostages first. I need to know they're okay."

"Are you?" Leland tightened his grip on Tyler's collar and Katie nodded. "Answer her."

"It's Katie, Lieutenant. Tyler and I are both fine. But Mr. Asher has a gun."

Leland laughed. "Of course I have a gun. All your police friends have guns—it's only fair. Please. Welcome to my home, Lieutenant."

Oh, God. Now his bizarre actions made sense. "He wants you to come in. He wants... Oh, God, please don't hurt my son."

"Did you find the evidence I requested, Miss Rinaldi?" Tears stung her eyes and she reached out for Tyler. "Miss Rinaldi."

She forced her attention back to the computer. "Yes. Dr. Eisenbach has notations in her patient files. Those with secrets she can use to blackmail them, those who need a favor and will do something in exchange for that favor." What more did the man want from her? "Could I please have my son?"

The lieutenant's voice sounded closer when she spoke again. "Are you sure everyone is okay? Your nephew is here. He's been shot, Mr. Asher. He's dead."

"Yes, I did that."

He was confessing to murder with dozens of cops swarming the estate? With three witnesses who could testify against him right here?

Katie was more certain than ever that this monster intended to commit suicide by cop. He was a dying man, determined to set his affairs in order—to eliminate those who'd betrayed him and then die instantly himself, avoiding a lingering death.

But with her innocent boy smack-dab in the middle of all those guns? She couldn't let that happen.

"Don't shoot! Please don't shoot! There's an innocent child here." Katie reached out again. "Please, Mr. Asher. May I have my son?"

"Soon, Miss Rinaldi." He turned his attention to Tyler. "Would you like to go over and sit with your mother?"

"Yes, please."

"When she's done working. She's proven more loyal to her loved ones than my family has been to me." Leland looked around the room, perhaps seeing the movement of SWAT cops taking position outside the windows. "Did you find the information I was looking for, Miss Rinaldi? Has my beloved Beverly betrayed me?"

Katie looked at the incriminating evidence she'd pulled off Dr. Eisenbach's computer records. The notations Leland Asher had asked her to find were right there.

Francisco Dona, aka John Smith, is alive. Can use him to eliminate threats and provide surveillance to ensure jobs are completed as ordered in exchange for keeping his identity from Leland.

Matt Asher's hatred for his uncle can be used to my advantage. String him along with promise of helping him take over the business. He can do the dirty work and I can reap the profit. (I've earned it.)

Stephen March, Hillary Wells, Doug Price and many more—their names were all there. The psychologist had counseled all of them, forced them to do her bidding, first to please Leland—to become an indispensable ally with hopes of eventually becoming his wife or business partner—and later to eliminate Leland himself when his promises of power and position turned out to be lies.

But once Katie gave Leland the information he wanted, the bullets would start to fly. And Tyler—her son, her angel—would be caught in the crossfire.

"Miss Rinaldi. My time is running short. I'm sure your compatriots are closing in on my position and lining up kill shots even as we speak. Is the information there? Did my love betray me?"

Beverly wept in her bonds, begging to make amends. "Leland, please."

"Miss Rinaldi?"

Katie pointed to her face, silently telling Tyler not to look anywhere else, to hold fast to the love in his mother's eyes.

"Miss Rinaldi?"

"Yes. It's all here. Beverly and Matt have betrayed you."

"Thank you."

Without missing a beat, Leland shoved Tyler toward Katie. Beverly screamed as he turned and fired a bullet right into the middle of her forehead.

Katie lunged for her son and wrapped him in her arms, dragging him beneath the sturdy walnut desk as a pair of smoke grenades crashed through the side windows, filling the room with a stinging gas.

"Close your eyes, Tyler. Hold tight to me." Oh, thank

God, thank God. But Leland still had a gun. A lot of people still had guns.

"No!" Leland shouted in a rage. "Shoot me! Shoot me!"

"Drop your weapon, Asher!" That was Trent. His voice was muffled by the mask he wore, but there was no mistaking the deadly authority in his tone.

"Drop it!" Max was in the room, too.

"This one's dead," Olivia announced, moving away from Dr. Eisenbach's slumped body.

Jim Parker was there. Even Lieutenant Rafferty-Taylor had a bead on the man her team had finally brought down. "Drop it, Mr. Asher. You're surrounded. We have oxygen masks. You do not."

"No! You have to shoot me!"

Katie hugged her body around Tyler's as tightly as she could when she felt the barrel of Asher's recently fired gun singe the nape of her neck. "Don't hurt my son!"

Leland yanked on the collar of her blouse to pull her from beneath the desk. But six feet five inches of defensive tackle slammed into the older man and flattened him on the floor.

"It's over, Asher. You're done." She could hear him kicking Leland's gun away and pulling the handcuffs from his belt. "Sunshine, you all right?"

"Yes." The lieutenant helped her crawl out from under the desk and stand.

"Tyler?"

"I'm okay." Katie hugged her son tightly to her chest, assuring her boss with a nod as Max, Olivia and Jim circled around the imported rug where Trent was hand-cuffing a winded Leland Asher. "Mom, my eyes hurt."

"Keep them closed, sweetie. It's the cloud in the air. It's making Mr. Asher cry, too."

Lieutenant Rafferty-Taylor radioed backup that it was clear to enter and that they'd need two extra oxygen masks.

"Is Trent okay, too?" Tyler asked, hugging his arms tightly around her waist.

Trent Dixon, Katie Rinaldi's best friend, the man she loved—the man who didn't yet know how much she loved him—hauled Leland Asher to his feet and handed him off to Max and Jim. He peeled off his gas mask as the smoke in the air began to dissipate. "Read him his rights and arrest him for everything in the book."

Leland sneered at the much bigger man. "You're wasting your time, Detective. I told you I was dying. I was simply setting my affairs in order."

Trent leaned in. "You don't get to take the easy way out, Asher. You just confessed to two murders, and I bet we can close out a dozen more because of the evidence Katie sent us. More important, you threatened the lives of the two most important people in the world to me. Now, whether you have a year or a month or they find a cure for cancer and you live to a ripe old age, you are spending the rest of your days in prison."

CHAPTER THIRTEEN

THE COLD CASE squad and their loved ones filled up an entire row of the theater. Ginny Rafferty-Taylor and her husband, Brett, flanked the son and daughter who sat between them. Katie suspected they had a young starlet in the making with their daughter sitting on the edge of her seat for the entire show.

Uncle Dwight slipped his handkerchief behind Tyler's cousin Jack and poked Aunt Maddie, who wept silent tears at every poignant moment of the show.

Jim Parker and his very pregnant wife, Natalie, sat on the aisle so she could sneak out to use the restroom at several private intermissions. He wore a red tie and she had on a green maternity dress, adding a festive color to the group who'd all come to see Tyler in his debut role onstage.

Reporter Gabe Knight nodded sagely at several of the show's classic scenes, all the while holding hands with his fiancée. Olivia Watson might be a tough chick on the outside, but she was all smiles and thumbs-up to Katie as Tyler uttered the last line of the play.

Even Max Krolikowski, as gruff and Scrooge-ish as they came, draped his arm around the shoulders of his wife, Rosie. He nodded at something she whispered in his ear and pressed a kiss to her curly red hair.

They'd all been focused so long on closing KCPD's unsolvable crimes that it seemed odd to see this group of friends coming together to celebrate the holiday and show their support for a brave little boy who'd nailed every line and entrance, and whose very life was the best present a mother could ever have. Katie was grateful for her family and friends. They'd had each other's backs and saved each other's lives.

And when Tyler came out with the other children to take his bow, they all rose as one and joined the applause with the rest of the audience.

But it was in the quiet moments backstage, after the others had gone home and Katie was stuck in the greenroom ironing costumes and ignoring Francis's blow-by-blow critique of their opening night performance, that she got the best present of all.

"Low clearance, buddy."

Trent ducked through the greenroom door, carrying Tyler on his broad shoulders with the same joy and love that Ebenezer Scrooge had carried Tiny Tim through the streets of London on Christmas Day. Trent even shook Francis's hand and congratulated him on his performance, rendering the temperamental actor speechless for a few moments before he beat a hasty escape.

"You ready to go, sunshine?" Trent set Tyler on his feet and hurried him into the dressing room to retrieve his coat. "I promised this hot young actor that I'd take him out for ice cream if he stayed in character for the whole show."

"And I did, Mom," Tyler bragged, galloping back out to join them. "I'm getting a root-beer float."

"Sounds a little chilly for a December night. Do you mind if I tag along with you for some hot chocolate?"

Trent leaned over the ironing board to steal a kiss. "Maybe it's me who should be asking if I can tag along and be part of the family celebration."

Katie cupped the side of his jaw in her hand when he would have pulled away. She lost her heart in the depths of those dark gray eyes. "You will always be a part of this family, Trent. You saved our lives. You made my son feel safe and you helped me learn to not just trust, but to embrace what I feel."

"And what do you feel, Katie Lee Rinaldi?"

"That I love you. That I've always loved you. I'm just sorry it took me so long to realize I'm *in* love with you, too."

Trent took her hand and led her around the ironing board to pull her into his arms and claim her mouth with a kiss. "I'm in love with you, too, sunshine."

Several seconds passed before Katie remembered they had an audience and pulled away—but only to welcome Tyler into the circle of this loving man's arms.

"Mom, you don't have to mail my letter to Santa. I already got what I wanted for Christmas."

Trent agreed. "I think we all did."

"I haven't said yes to your proposal yet." She felt glaring eyes from above and below and laughed. "Yes. Of course, the answer is yes."

* * * * *

YOU HAVE
JUST READ A
HARLEQUIN®
INTRIGUE®
BOOK

If you were **captivated** by the **gripping, page-turning romantic suspense,** be sure to look for all six Harlequin® Intrigue® books every month.

It all began with a kiss. At least that was the way Chloe
Clementine remembered it. A winter kiss, which is nothing like
a summer one. The cold, icy air around you. Puffs of white
breaths intermingling. Warm lips touching, tingling as they
meet for the very first time.

Chloe thought that kiss would be the last thing she
remembered before she died of old age. It was the kiss—and
the cowboy who'd kissed her—that she'd been dreaming about
when her phone rang. Being in Whitehorse had brought it all
back after all these years.

She groaned, wanting to keep sleeping so she could stay
in that cherished memory longer. Her phone rang again. She
swore that if it was one of her sisters calling this early…

"What?" she demanded into the phone without bothering
to see who was calling. She was so sure that it would be her
youngest sister, Annabelle, the morning person.

"Hello?" The voice was male and familiar. For just a
moment she thought she'd conjured up the cowboy from the
kiss. "It's Justin."

Justin? She sat straight up in bed. Thoughts zipped past at
a hundred miles an hour. How had he gotten her cell phone
number? Why was he calling? Was he in Whitehorse?

"Justin," she said, her voice sounding croaky from sleep. She cleared her throat. "I thought it was Annabelle calling. What's up?" She glanced at the clock. *What's up at seven forty-five in the morning?*

"I know it's early but I got your message."

Now she really was confused. "My message?" She had danced with his best friend at the Christmas dance recently, but she hadn't sent Justin a message.

"That you needed to see me? That it was urgent?"

She had no idea what he was talking about. Had her sister Annabelle done this? She couldn't imagine her sister Tessa Jane doing such a thing. But since her sisters had fallen in love they hadn't been themselves.

"I'm sorry, but I didn't send you a message. You're sure it was from me?"

"The person calling just told me that you were in trouble and needed my help. There was loud music in the background as if whoever it was might have called me from a bar."

He didn't think she'd drunk-dialed him, did he? "Sorry, but it wasn't me." She was more sorry than he knew. "And I can't imagine who would have called you on my behalf." Like the devil, she couldn't. It had to be her sister Annabelle.

"Well, I'm glad to hear that you aren't in trouble and urgently need my help," he said, not sounding like that at all.

She closed her eyes, now wishing she'd made something up. What was she thinking? She didn't need to improvise. She was in trouble, though nothing urgent exactly. At least for the moment.

Don't miss
Rugged Defender *by B.J. Daniels,*
available November 2018 wherever
Harlequin® *Intrigue books and ebooks are sold.*

Love Harlequin romance?

DISCOVER.

Be the first to find out about promotions, news and exclusive content!

Facebook.com/HarlequinBooks

Twitter.com/HarlequinBooks

Instagram.com/HarlequinBooks

Pinterest.com/HarlequinBooks

ReaderService.com

EXPLORE.

Sign up for the Harlequin e-newsletter and download a free book from any series at **TryHarlequin.com.**

CONNECT.

Join our Harlequin community to share your thoughts and connect with other romance readers!
Facebook.com/groups/HarlequinConnection

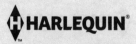

HARLEQUIN®

ROMANCE WHEN YOU NEED IT

HSOCIAL2018